D0950053

THE
SISTERS
OF THE
WINTER
WOOD

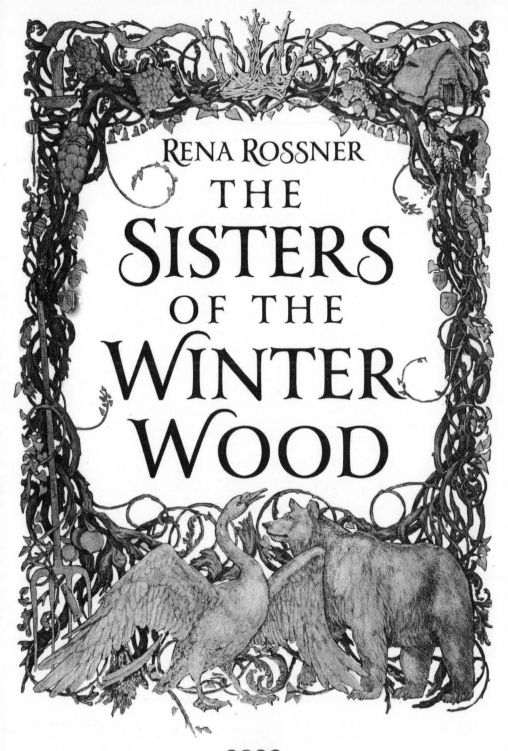

RENA ROSSNER

THE
SISTERS
OF THE
WINTER
WOOD

REDHOOK

www.redhookbooks.com

This book is a work of fiction. Names, characters, places, and incidents are the product of the author's imagination or are used fictitiously. Any resemblance to actual events, locales, or persons, living or dead, is coincidental.

Copyright © 2018 by Rena Rossner

Author photograph by Tomer Rottenberg
Cover design by Lauren Panepinto
Cover art by Rebecca Yanovskaya
Cover copyright © 2018 by Hachette Book Group, Inc.

Hachette Book Group supports the right to free expression and the value of copyright. The purpose of copyright is to encourage writers and artists to produce the creative works that enrich our culture.

The scanning, uploading, and distribution of this book without permission is a theft of the author's intellectual property. If you would like permission to use material from the book (other than for review purposes), please contact permissions@hbgusa.com. Thank you for your support of the author's rights.

Redhook Books/Orbit
Hachette Book Group
1290 Avenue of the Americas
New York, NY 10104
hachettebookgroup.com

Simultaneously published in Great Britain and in the U.S. by Orbit in 2018
First Edition: September 2018

Redhook is an imprint of Orbit, a division of Hachette Book Group.
The Redhook name and logo are trademarks of Hachette Book Group, Inc.

The publisher is not responsible for websites (or their content)
that are not owned by the publisher.

The Hachette Speakers Bureau provides a wide range of authors for speaking events. To find out more, go to www.hachettespeakersbureau.com or call (866) 376-6591.

Library of Congress Control Number: 2018947892

ISBNs: 978-0-316-48325-4 (hardcover), 978-0-316-48329-2 (ebook)

Printed in the United States of America

LSC-C

10 9 8 7 6 5 4 3 2 1

In memory of Nettie Bunder ז״l
(1921–2017)
who taught me all the Yiddish I know

Oif a meisseh fregt men kain kasheh nit.
(Don't ask questions about fairy tales.)

—Yiddish saying

For there is no friend like a sister
In calm or stormy weather;
To cheer one on the tedious way,
To fetch one if one goes astray,
To lift one if one totters down,
To strengthen whilst one stands.

—Christina Rossetti, *Goblin Market*

1

Liba

If you want to know the history of a town, read the gravestones in its cemetery. That's what my Tati always says. Instead of praying in the synagogue like all the other men of our town, my father goes to the cemetery to pray. I like to go there with him every morning.

The oldest gravestone in our cemetery dates back to 1666. It's the grave I like to visit most. The names on the stone have long since been eroded by time. It is said in our *shtetl* that it marks the final resting place of a bride and a groom who died together on their wedding day. We don't know anything else about them, but we know that they were buried, arms embracing, in one grave. I like to put a stone on their grave when I go there, to make sure their souls stay down where they belong, and when I do, I say a prayer that I too will someday find a love like that.

That grave is the reason we know that there were Jews in Dubossary as far back as 1666. Mami always said that this town was founded in love and that's why my parents chose to live here. I think it means something else—that our town was founded in tragedy. The death of those young lovers has been a pall hanging over Dubossary since its inception. Death lives here. Death will always live here.

2

Laya

I see Liba going
to the cemetery with Tati.
I don't know
what she sees
in all those cold stones.
But I watch,
and wonder,
why he never takes me.

When we were little,
Liba and I went to
the Talmud Torah.
For Liba, the black letters
were like something
only she could decipher.
I never understood
what she searched for,
in those black
scratches of ink.

I would watch
the window,
study the forest
and the sky.

When we walked home,
Liba would watch the boys
come out of the *cheder*
down the road.
I know that when she looked
at Dovid, Lazer and Nachman,
she wondered
what was taught
behind the walls
the girls were not
allowed to enter.

After her Bat Mitzvah,
Tati taught her Torah.
He tried to teach me too,
when my turn came,
but all I felt was
distraction,
disinterest.
Chanoch l'naar al pi darko,
Tati would say,
*teach every child
in his own way,*
and sigh,
and get up
and open the door.
Gey, gezinte heit—

I accept that you're different, go.
And while I was grateful,
I always wondered
why he gave up
without a fight.

3

Liba

As I follow the large steps my father's boots make in the snow, I revel in the solitude. This is why I cherish our morning walks. They give me time to talk to Tati, but also time to think. "In silence you can hear God," Tati says to me as we walk. But I don't hear God in the silence—I hear myself. I come here to get away from the noises of the town and the chatter of the townsfolk. It's where I can be fully me.

"What does God sound like?" I ask him. When I walk with Tati, I feel like I'm supposed to think about important things, like prayer and faith.

"Sometimes the voice of God is referred to as a *bat kol*," he says.

I translate the Hebrew out loud: "The daughter of a voice? That doesn't make any sense."

He chuckles. "Some say that *bat kol* means an echo, but others say it means a hum or a reverberation, something you sense in the air that's caused by the motion of the universe—part of the human voice, but also part of every other sound in the world, even the sounds that our ears can't hear. It means that sometimes even the smallest voice can have a big opinion." He grins, and I know that he means me, his daughter; that my opinion matters. I wish it were true. Not everybody in our town sees things the way my father does. Most women and girls do not study Torah; they don't learn or ask questions like I do. For the most part, our voices don't matter. I know I'm lucky that Tati is my father.

Although I love Tati's stories and his answers, I wonder why a small voice is a daughter's voice. Sometimes I wish my voice could be loud—like a roar. But that is not a modest way to think. The older I get, the more immodest my thoughts become.

I feel my cheeks flush as my mind wanders to all the things I shouldn't be thinking about—what it would feel like to hold the hand of a man, what it might feel like to kiss someone, what it's like when you finally find the man you're meant to marry and you get to be alone together, in bed…I swallow and shake my head to clear my thoughts.

If I shared the fact that this is all I think about lately, Mami and Tati would say it means it's time for me to get married. But I'm not sure I want to get married yet. I want to marry for love, not convenience. These thoughts feel like sacrilege. I know that I will marry a man my father chooses. That's the way it's done in our town and among Tati's people. Mami and Tati married for love, and it has not been an easy path for them.

I take a deep breath and shake my head from all my thoughts. This morning, everything looks clean from the snow that fell last night and I imagine the icy frost coating the insides of my lungs and mind, making my thoughts white and pure. I love being outside in our forest more than anything at times like these, because the white feels like it hides all our flaws.

Perhaps that's why I often see Tati in the dark forest that surrounds our home praying to God or—as he would say—the *Ribbono Shel Oylam*, the Master of the Universe, by himself, eyes shut, arms outstretched to the sky. Maybe he comes out here to feel new again too.

Tati comes from the town of Kupel, a few days' walk from here. He came here and joined a small group of Chassidim in the town—the followers of the late Reb Mendele, who was a disciple of the great and holy Ba'al Shem Tov. There is a small *shtiebl* where the men pray, in what used to be the home of Urka the Coachman. It is said that the Ba'al Shem Tov himself used to sit under the tree in Urka's courtyard. The Chassidim here accepted my father with open arms, but nobody accepted my mother.

Sometimes I wonder if Reb Mendele and the Ba'al Shem Tov (*zichrono livracha*) were still with us, would the community treat Mami differently? Would they see how hard she tries to be a good Jew, and how wrong the other Jews in town are for not treating her with love and respect. It makes me angry how quickly rumors spread, that Mami's kitchen isn't kosher (it is!) just because she doesn't cover her hair like the other married Jewish women in our town.

That's why Tati built our home, sturdy and warm like he is, outside our town in the forest. It's what Mami wanted: not to be under constant scrutiny, and to have plenty of room to plant fruit trees and make honey and keep chickens and goats. We have a small barn with a cow and a goat, and a bee glade out back and an orchard that leads all the way down to the river. Tati works in town as a builder and a laborer in the fields. But he is also a scholar, worthy of the title Rebbe, though none of the men in town call him that.

Sometimes I think my father knows more than the other Chassidim in our town, even more than Rabbi Borowitz who leads our tiny *kehilla*, and the bare bones prayer *minyan* of ten men that Tati sometimes helps complete. There are many things my father likes to keep secret, like his morning dips in the Dniester River that I never see, but know about, his prayer at the graveside of Reb Mendele, and our library. Our walls are covered in holy books—his *sforim*, and I often fall asleep to the sound of him reading from the Talmud, the Midrash, and the many mystical books of the Chassidim. The stories he reads sound like fairy tales to me, about magical places like Babel and Jerusalem.

In these places, there are scholarly men. Father would be respected there, a king among men. And there are learned boys of marriageable age—the kind of boys Tati would like me to marry someday. In my daydreams, they line up at the door, waiting to get a glimpse of me—the learned, pious daughter of the Rebbe. And my Tati would only pick the wisest and kindest for me.

I shake my head. In my heart of hearts, that's not really what I want. When Laya and I sleep in our loft, I look out the skylight above our heads and pretend that someone will someday find his way to our cabin, climb up onto the roof, and look in from above. He will see me and fall instantly in love.

Because lately I feel like time is running out. The older I get, the harder it will be to find someone. And when I think about that, I wonder why Tati insists that Laya and I wait until we are at least eighteen.

I would ask Mami, but she isn't a scholar like Tati, and she doesn't like to talk about these things. She worries about what people say and how they see us. It makes her angry, but she wrings dough instead of her hands. Tati says her hands are baker's hands, that she makes magic with dough. Mami can make something out of nothing. She makes cheese and gathers honey; she mixes bits of bark and roots and leaves for tea. She bakes the tastiest *challahs* and cakes, *rugelach* and *mandelbrot*, but it's her *babka* she's famous for. She sells her baked goods in town.

When she's not in the kitchen, Mami likes to go out through the skylight above our bed and onto the little deck on our roof to soak up the sun. Laya likes to sit up there with her. From the roof, you can see down to the village and the forest all around. I wonder if it's not just the sun that Mami seeks up there. While Tati's head is always in a book, Mami's eyes are always looking at the sky. Laya says she dreams of somewhere other than here. Somewhere far away, like America.

4

Laya

I always thought
that if I worshipped God,
dressed modestly,
and walked in His path,
that nothing bad
would happen
to my family.
We would find
our path to Zion,
our own piece of heaven
on the banks
of the Dniester River.

But now that I'm fifteen
I see what a life
of pious devotion
has brought Mami,
who converted
to our faith—
disapproval.
The life we lead

out here is a life apart.
I wish I could go to Onyshkivtsi.
Mami always tells me stories
about her town
and Saint Anna of the Swans
who lived there.

Saint Anna
didn't walk with God—
she knew she wasn't made
for perfection;
she never tried
to fit a pattern
that didn't fit her.
She didn't waste her time
trying to smooth herself
into something
she wasn't.
She was powerful
because she forged
her own path.

The Christians
in Onyshkivtsi
built a shrine
to honor her.
The shrine marks a spring
whose temperature
is forty-three degrees
all year,
rain or shine.
Even in the snow.

It is said
that it was once home
to hundreds of swans.
Righteous Anna used to
feed and care for them.
But Mami says the swans
don't go there anymore.

There is rot
in the old growth—
the Kodari forest
senses these things.
I sense things too.
The rot in our community.
Sometimes it's not enough
to be good,
if you treat others
with disdain.
Sometimes there's nothing
you can do
but fly away,
like Anna did.

5

Liba

When we get back from our morning walk, Mami is in the kitchen making breakfast and starting the doughs for the day. Tati shakes the snow off his boots as he walks in. "*Gut morgen*," he says gruffly as he pecks a kiss on Mami's cheek. She pins her white-gold hair up and says, "*Dubroho ranku*. Liba, close the door quickly—you're letting all the cold in."

I let the hood of my coat drop down. "Where's Laya?"

"Getting some eggs from the coop," Mami sings. She and Laya love mornings, not like me, but I'd wake up early every morning if it meant I got time alone with Tati.

I shrug my coat off and hang it on a hook by the door as Mami pours tea at the table. "*Nu?* Come in, warm up," she says to me.

I shake the chill off and start braiding my hair, which is the color of river rocks. Long and thick. I can't pin it up at all. "Your hair is beautiful like moonstone, *dochka*," Mami says. "Leave it down."

"More like oil on fur," I say, because it's sleek and shiny and I never feel like I can tame it. It will never be white and light like hers and Laya's.

"Do you want me to braid it for you?" Mami asks.

I shake my head.

"Come here, my *zaftig* one," Tati says. "Your hair is fine; leave it be."

I cringe: I don't like it when he calls me plump, even though it's a term of endearment, and anyway, I know what comes next. Laya walks in and he says, "Oh, the *shayna meidel* has decided to join us." The pretty one. I concentrate on braiding my hair.

Laya grins. "*Gut morgen.* How was your walk?" She looks at me.

I shrug my shoulders and finish braiding my hair, then sit at the table and lift a cup of tea to my mouth. "*Baruch atah Adonai eloheinu melech haolam, shehakol nih'ye bidvaro—Blessed are you, Lord our God, king of the universe, by whose word all things came to be.*" I make sure to say every word of the blessing with meaning.

"*Oymen!*" Tati says with a smile.

Instead of trying to be something I will never be, I do everything I can to be a good Jew.

6

Laya

When I was outside
gathering eggs,
I searched the sky,
hoping to see something—
anything.
One night I heard
feathers rustling
and turned around
and looked up—
a swan had landed
on our rooftop.
It was watching me.
I didn't breathe
the whole time
it was there.
Until it spread
its wings
and took off
into the sky.

Every night I pray
that it will happen again
because if I ever see
another swan,
I won't hold my breath—
I will open the window
and go outside.

That's why I rake my gaze
over every flake of bark
and every teardrop leaf,
hoping. I see that
every finger-branch
is reaching for something.
I am reaching too.
Up up up.

At night I feel
the weight
of the house
upon my chest.
It's warm
and safe inside,
but the wooden planks
above my head
are nothing like
the dark boughs
of the forest.
Sometimes I wish
I could sleep outside.
The Kodari is
the only place
I feel truly at home.

But this morning
I'm restless
and that usually means
something is about to change.
That's what the forest
teaches you—
change can come
in the blink of an eye—
the fall of one spark
can mean total destruction.

There is a fever
that burns in me.
It prickles every pore.
I'm not happy with
the simple life we lead.
A life ruled
by prayer and holy days,
times for dusk and dawn,
the sacred and the profane.
A life of devotion,
Tati would say.
*The glory
of a king's daughter
is within.*

But I long for what is
just outside my window.
Far beyond
the reaches of the Dniester,
and the boundaries
of our small *shtetl*.

It hurts,
this thing I feel,
how unsettled
I've become.
I want to fit
in this home,
in this town.
To be the daughter
that Tati wants me to be.
To be more
like Liba.
Prayer comes
so easily to her.

Mami understands
what I feel
but I also think
it scares her.
She is always sending me
outside, and I'm grateful
but I also wonder
why she doesn't
teach me how to bake,
or how to pray.
It's almost like she knows
that one day
I will leave her.

Sometimes I wish
she'd teach me
how to stay.

I close my eyes
and take deep breaths.
It helps me
resist the urge
to scratch my back.
I want to crawl out
of this skin I wear
when these thoughts come
and threaten to overwhelm
the little peace I have,
staring at the sky,
praying in my own way
for something else.

Something is definitely
inside me.
It is not glory,
or devotion.
It is something
that wants to burst free.

7

Liba

Night falls and Tati comes home from work. It's well past eleven. Laya is already asleep beside me. She was restless all day, I could sense that—and I wanted to ask her what was wrong, but I never got the chance. Suddenly, there's a knock at the door.

And another.

The knocks are so loud, they feel as if they could wake the dead. I can't imagine how Laya sleeps through it. I creep to the top rung of the ladder to our loft, where I can just barely see the door. Tati goes to open it. Mami baked all day and into the night—*babka* for matters of the heart—and I wonder if she knew that this was coming.

Is it the Tsar's army? Have they come for Tati? So many men from our town have been conscripted recently. Their absence in the village is felt—lights in windows have gone out all over town.

I know, we all know, that something as small as a knock—the rap of knuckles on wood—could change our lives forever. If the Tsar's army comes for you, they take you for twenty-five years. And we know it means some people might never return.

I wait for the world I've known to crumble, with the scent of chocolate in the air.

"Who is it?"

There's a muffled answer and Tati unbars the door.

A man I've never seen before steps inside. He bows before my father and I see Tati put a hand over his mouth and cry out.

"Yankl?"

But the man doesn't rise until Tati places his hands upon his head and blesses him.

"*Ye'varech'echa Adonai ve'yish'merecha*—May God bless you and keep you..." I don't understand why my father says the priestly blessing. He normally only says it on Friday nights with his hands on Laya's head and mine—just after we sing "*Shalom Aleichem*" inviting the angels into our home and before he blesses the wine.

The man lifts up his head and kisses my father's knuckles.

"Yankl!" my father says again. The men embrace. "What brings you here?" Tati asks. "How did you...?"

"It wasn't easy to find you, Rebbe, I'll tell you that much."

Mami takes a step forward and bows her head in his direction. "Can I offer you something hot to drink? I just made *babka*."

"This is Adel, my wife," Tati says to the strange man. And to my surprise, the man looks at her and says, "I remember."

He wears a large cloak that looks like a bearskin, and underneath it, a satin overcoat with white stockings that end in large black boots.

"Please—take a seat." Mami beckons the men to the table as she goes to the kitchen. I can hear her fill the kettle and put it on the fire.

The man sits down at the table and stares at Tati. "It's good to see you, Berman."

Tati grunts. "What brings you all this way, my brother?"

Tati has a brother?

The man starts to sway back and forth at the table as if in prayer. "*Oh-yoy oh-yo-yoy, oh-yoy*," he chants. "The Rebbe is sick, Reb Berman. He doesn't have long to live."

I see Tati's face go slack, white almost, like he's seen a ghost.

"Here, have a tipple of something." Mami takes out the schnapps and offers both men a glassful.

The man—my uncle?—takes a healthy gulp, shudders, and continues. "We need you to come home. The Rebbe needs you, Berman...we all need you. Please come back before it's too late." He takes another gulp of schnapps, then picks up the mug of tea.

Tati shakes his head. "I have to speak to my wife."

"There isn't much time," Yankl pleads. "It may be too late already."

"Then what are you doing here? Leave," Tati growls, and slams his glass on the table.

"Berman..." Mami goes to put her arms on Tati's shoulders.

"I said I'd never go back, Adel. You know that."

"You can't send Yankl back out into the cold."

Tati grunts and says, "Will you stay the night?"

Yankl stands up. "No. You're right. I should head back right away. I gave you the message." He shrugs. "What you do with it is on your conscience."

"Get out of my house!" Tati yells.

"Berman!" Mami scolds.

I hear Laya turn over in bed.

Tati grumbles, "*Es tut mir bahng*—sorry," and looks up at his brother. "I'll think about it, okay?"

Yankl walks to the door.

"Yankl, I didn't mean it. You can stay the night. You are always welcome in our home," Tati says.

"It's all right," Yankl says. "I'd best be going back."

"I'll pack you up some food," Mami says, "and a thermos of tea."

He hesitates, then nods.

Mami busies herself in the kitchen, but otherwise there is silence in the room. The brothers seem to look everywhere but at each other.

"*A bi gezunt*," Mami finally says, bringing him a packed basket. She adds in a low voice, "I'll talk to him. He'll come. Don't worry."

And just as quickly as he'd come, the man is gone.

"Why did you tell him that?" Tati growls when she closes the door.

Mami sits down at the table and takes Tati's hands in hers. "Calm yourself, Berman. You have no choice, and you know that. You must go back to Kupel. You have to pay your respects."

"No choice is also a choice," Tati grumbles. "They never had respect for you, or for me and my choices."

"Maybe he wants to make amends…"

"We haven't had word in over a dozen years. They cast us out! I swore to you. I swore to myself that I would never go back. And now they want me back? Me, they said, not you. I won't go."

"Yankl didn't say that," Mami sighs. "You know how I feel about your family…but if your father goes to his *oylam, chas v'shalom*—God forbid—and you don't make it back there, you'll never forgive yourself."

"And then they'll never let me leave. I'm next in line. You know that. And if they won't accept you, I want no part of it. What—I should leave my wife and daughters to go see a father who never approved of me?"

Mami's long thin hands grip Tati's large ones tightly, her knuckles white. "Yankl wouldn't have come unless the situation was dire. I think you should leave now. Tonight. I'll stay here with the girls." She looks into his eyes and says, "I trust you. I know that you'll come back for us."

"It's not about trust, Adel," Tati says ruefully. "What would happen if you went back to your family?"

Mami shakes her head. "I could never."

"So why is this any different?"

"Because the Rebbe is on his deathbed! Really, Berman?"

"And if Dmitry was dying?"

Who is Dmitry? I wish I understood half of what they are discussing. Everything feels both foreign and familiar all at once, as if these are someone else's parents—but also, as if these are things I've heard them discuss in my dreams.

"It's not the same and you know it. I'm sick of this life we lead," Mami says. "A hovel at the edge of the forest? A *shtetl* full of *nebbishers* who talk behind our backs every chance they get. This town is a dead end. We are on the brink. Maybe this is your chance at salvation. To reclaim all you lost."

"Maybe we should go to your family, then, eh? Reclaim them."

"You know we can't do that."

Tati raises his voice. "So why is this any different?"

Mami starts to cry.

Tati gets up and goes to put his arms around her. "You chose this life. You chose me. Are you saying you regret that choice?"

"No, never!" Mami looks up. "But maybe you can have both. Them *and* me. You have a chance now. You know I never will."

"Adel." He hugs her tightly and sighs. "I will only go if you come with me."

"What? And leave the girls?" Mami's voice is shrill and I hear Laya turn over in bed again.

"If we get there and the Rebbe, my Tati, is willing to finally accept you," he says in a voice that sounds cracked, "*publicly*, then we can come back here, get the girls, and move back to Kupel. But I won't expose them to that kind of spectacle unless I know what my father's answer will be. They must accept you first. That's my condition."

"We can't leave the girls."

"The *kehilla* will take care of them. And anyway, they don't have travel permits. None of us do. I won't take the girls on the road and expose them to that kind of danger. If we are caught, it will mean certain death." Tati rubs his hand across his forehead. "For now, they're safer here in Dubossary."

"Are you *meshugge*? They'll be prey to any man!"

"Liba won't let that happen. She's stronger than she knows."

"Maybe we should tell them…"

Tell us what?

"No! We said we'd wait until they got engaged and we'll keep to that. No need to worry them before that. The townsfolk are *mensches*. They'll take care of our girls and keep them safe."

"No girls should be without parents," Mami says.

"Liba will keep house until we return. She's nearly eighteen."

"Which is even more of a reason for us all to go back. What kind of future does she have here? You always say that no one from this town will marry our girls. Well, here's your chance. Liba is almost of age. You can't wait forever. It's time, Berman."

"When the time comes, I will find them worthy husbands. Don't you worry about that."

"When? How old does Liba have to be? You'll wait until she's too old for anyone to want her and then see what's left? Let them come with us. Please?"

My skin suddenly feels cold, coated with pinpricks of ice.

"No!" Tati says. "My girls are more precious to me than rubies and pearls. I won't risk their lives on the roads."

I can tell that Mami's crying in earnest now.

"Adel…" Tati's voice is instantly soft.

"No!" Mami cries. "I gave up everything I was—everything I had—for you. I did everything right, and it still wasn't enough.

Not here, not there, maybe not anywhere. There's no love lost between me and your family. But it's not like things are all that much better here. I hear what people say. I know how they talk. Please go alone. Do it for me. For us. Get his blessing. Then come back safe and sound and we'll either stay here, or we'll go."

"And what if they don't let me leave? What if I can't come back? What if my father is on his deathbed for months? I can't take that chance. I'll be lost without you. You know how they get into my head. You are my life, *gelibteh*, I can't go without you by my side." He lowers his voice and suddenly sounds nothing like my father. "I don't trust myself when I'm with them."

Mami shakes her head and makes a fist. "And if someone murders the girls in the night, or ravages them, you could live? You're a beast to think to leave them."

"I am a beast," he chuckles, "but I haven't acted like one in many years, and you know that better than anyone." Then he looks at her solemnly. "In times like these, people change. Maybe everything will be different. And if not..." I can see my father swallow hard, his jaw working. "You're right. I have a responsibility to my parents. At least to mourn, to say *kaddish* at my father's grave if it comes to that."

"You know...if things don't work out...there are other places we could go. People speak of America."

"America is a fairy tale."

Mami throws her hands up in defeat. "You're impossible." She shakes her head and sighs. "Fine. I'll come with you."

Tati takes a deep breath and softens his tone. "The girls will be okay. We *will* come back for them, I promise. Adel...I know you think that I'm against you in this, but I'm not. It is honestly safer for Liba and Laya to stay here."

Mami seems to make a decision. She gets up and walks across the room. She takes something out from the trunk beneath their bed.

"Adel…" Tati whispers.

"Don't stop me, Berman. I need to think. I have to get out of this cabin."

Mami holds up something white that looks like a cloak, and drapes it over her shoulders. She rubs her arms as if goose pimples dot her skin. She begins to shiver and shake, then hunches down on the ground as if she's in pain. Her arms arc up, graceful, yet contorted at odd angles. The air shimmers. I don't understand what I'm seeing, only that I can't look away. Little wisps of white start to coat her face, then her arms, and feathers, long and white, burst out of every pore. The dress she's wearing falls to the floor in a pool of cloth, leaving her naked, except it's not skin I see anymore, but soft white down that shines in the light. She curls into herself, like a white ball of cloud, except for her arms—they reach for the sky. I blink, and in that instant, her arms become ivory wings, feathered and majestic in the moonlight that streams down from the skylight above our heads. My mother is a swan.

My hand is over my mouth. I'm doing everything I can not to shout, not to make a sound. I'm so busy watching the swan in our kitchen that I don't see my father reach into the trunk. When I notice, he's taking out a brown fur cloak, one I thought I'd seen him wear before, but maybe not. This one looks different—the fur more lush and lifelike. Like the bear cloaks the townsfolk wear to celebrate the new year. Then I hear a noise that doesn't sound very manlike and my heart skips a beat in my chest.

I look over, and in the space where my father had been, there's a bear. This time I nearly do cry out—in fear! I've never seen a bear so large. It's twice his size, like a mountain of rich dark earth. Its eyes are dark and shining, like orbs of obsidian stone, and its teeth, sharp and yellowish, terrifying, poke out of a long snout. The nose at the end of the snout is double the size of a human nose. The bear takes a step forward. His fur is so brown it looks black, like the bark of a birch tree, rippling in a sheen with every move he makes to reveal powerful muscles and paws with claws that look sharp as daggers and dig into the wooden floor. *It's a dream*, I keep telling myself, *it must be a dream. A fairy tale coming to life in my head, nothing more.* I look over at Laya and see that she's still sleeping. *Maybe I'm sleeping too?*

I'm trembling so hard I feel as if I might tumble down the ladder.

The bear nudges the front door latch open with his snout and looks back at the swan. The swan leaps onto his back as he lumbers out of the house, careful to close the door behind him. I let myself breathe hard once the door closes. I clasp and flex my fingers, trying to wake myself up, but my fingernails feel sharper and when I look down at them, they've grown black and dark, with fine points that almost look like claws. I cry out and reach for Laya, but when my hand hovers over her sleeping form, I see that the hair on my arm has nearly doubled in volume and thickness. I bring my arm back, afraid of what my own hands might do. I hold myself instead, trembling in fear. I close my eyes and let the tears that have gathered fall onto my nightgown, afraid to rub my own eyes and do them damage, and too scared to move lest Laya wake and see what's happening to me. *It's a dream, Liba, just a dream*, I keep telling myself. *When you open your eyes everything will go back to normal.*

I lie down in bed and try to steady my breathing. I wait, my heart thundering in my chest, until I hear the rustling of bedcovers and the sound of my father's snores. I open my eyes and look at my still-shaking hands—they look completely normal. I take a deep breath and creep down the ladder, determined to see my parents as I've always seen them—human and whole.

Mami is awake, drinking tea at the table. I sit by her feet and put my head in her lap.

"I had a bad dream," I say in a shaky voice.

"What did you dream?"

"I heard you and Tati speaking," I confess.

"Oh, *dochka*. You heard?" She takes a deep breath. "And saw?"

I nod. "Everything," I say, and my voice shakes.

It's in that moment that all I've ever known changes. Mami always says that fairy tales are real. With my head in my swan-mother's lap, I start to believe—and I wonder which tale is ours.

Mami leans down and embraces me.

"It wasn't supposed to happen like this," she says. "But it's not everything." She shakes her silky white-blonde hair and her tears fall on my cheeks. "There are things I need to tell you."

But Mami doesn't say anything more, and soon I get up and silently make my way up the ladder back to bed. All night I watch the windows and the doors. I can't sleep. Yankl's words about the Rebbe dying scare me because I don't know what it will mean for our future. But the truth of what I've seen my parents become scares me even more.

Tati always says that every heart has its secrets, and it is not our role in life to try and uncover them. I've uncovered my parents' secrets, and more terrifying than anything, I think that means I have a secret too.

As I watch Laya sleep, I see her scratch in places where only wings grow, and then I know. My body is thick and large-boned while my sister's is lithe. We both eat fish, but I hunger for meat. We both love the Dniester River, but I'm drawn to its dark places, while she loves the tall trees that line its banks and the open air above. My hair is coarse and black-brown, but hers is blonde like Mami's…nearly white. Everything makes sense suddenly, and yet nothing makes sense at all.

There have always been rumors about the Kodari forest and the hidden things within it.

Now I know we are a part of that unseen world.

8

Laya

When I wake in the
  morning,
something is different
but I don't know what.
Liba's still sleeping;
her eyes look puffy and red.
Mami's not in her bed.
Tati still snores.
Something is wrong.

I want to ask the air, the sky.
I go outside to the forest
and make mute offerings:
bits of string, twig and bark
collections I leave on trees
like I am claiming them—
this one: mine mine mine—
now tell me a secret.

I ask the leaves
Where's Mami?

Why was Liba crying?
But there are no answers.
I cross and re-cross
imaginary lines
and mark lichen-green rocks
so I can find my way home.

The elegant stems that sway
with the contours
of the river
nod and drop like feathers
and I feel recognition
in the half-light.
Is this for me?
An answer?
A bare moment
like finding sanctuary
from a storm.
Where is she?

I see a swan
swimming in the river
and hear the happy syllables
of birds, the whistling
of wings, the coos and calls
that answer.
Coo coo coo.

I want to add my voice
but these are dialects
that I don't understand.
Not Yiddish—
the *mamaloshen*—

or Mami's Ukrainian;
something else,
something other.

There is light out here
and air and voices
in the trees:
wind
birds
insects
and sometimes other things,
creatures that have no names,
and music that calls to me—
bells, I hear bells.

At first I think
it's the river—
skaters on the ice
wear bells
on their ankles—
but these are not the sounds
of bells I know.
Bells bells bells
late in the night.

Many rivers flow
into the Dniester.
I have followed
the ways they change
and lead to villages
huddled along shores.
People talk
on the banks of rivers.

They think
that no one hears them.
I do.

I watch ice skaters
and fishmongers
and I listen
to their idle talk.
I see young people
from our town,
skating down the river
as if they don't have a care
in the world.

I watch the couples
holding hands as they skate.
They take breaks
and find copses of trees
where they think
no one can see them
and they kiss.
The air fogs around them.

Will I ever feel as free
as they look
on those skates?

I am always looking
for someone,
or something,
hiding just beyond the forest,
past the river,
above the trees.

A place.
A story.
A person.
A different kind of life.
Someone who understands me.
Who sees
what I see,
feels what I feel,
who knows,
the way I do,
that there must be
a different way to live.
What would happen
if I found it?

9

Liba

The next day, Mami and I are at the stream behind our house doing laundry. Laya is…off, like she always is. Mami lets her go. She always does. I am the one who stays.

We dip the clothes and linen into the freezing stream and rub the cloth raw with large rocks. I lean over the bulge my stomach makes and suck it in, even though it hurts to do so. I hate the way I look, like a boulder at the edge of the river, while Mami folds herself down and up. There is always space between her and the river, always air surrounding her. Laya is just like her—thin and full of light and air. *How did I not see it before? How did I not know?*

Mami is distracted. She looks around us constantly, waiting for something.

I don't know how to bring up what I saw last night. Part of me still hopes it was a dream, but I know in my heart of hearts that last night held truths I've always half known. The way I know which path to take in the forest because the earth and the trees just look right. The way that sometimes, a trail even *smells* right. And before last night, none of that made sense, and now it does somehow, and that is more confusing than anything.

"What are you doing?" I ask Mami.

"Making sure that we're alone."

"I don't see anyone."

"In the woods you are never alone, *malyshka*. Come closer."

I gather my skirts and sit beside her. Her legs are doubled beneath her, but my legs cannot move the way hers do. I sigh and try to get comfortable.

She cups her hands around my ear.

"There are things you need to know before we go to Kupel. Things your sister will need to know someday. I know you saw us last night, but there are things you don't understand. Things you haven't seen." She takes a deep breath and closes her eyes. "Tati is not Laya's father. Laya's father was a swan, like me."

"What...?" I feel as though a rock tumbles out from under me and I'm falling. My stomach is in my mouth; my mouth is full of fur. I can't breathe. *How?*

"There isn't time." Mami takes my face in her hands and fixes her gray eyes on mine. "I'm a swan, as you saw. I come from a family of swans."

I try to wriggle out of her grasp. Seeing them that night was one thing—but hearing her story now, I'm not sure I want to know.

"Liba, *bud'laska*." She grabs my arms. "Please—there isn't time."

I swallow and shiver as though there is a sudden gust of wind.

"I wasn't meant for life as a swan. As my family flew high above the trees each winter, my eyes would scan the ground and the paths between the trees. When we flew again in summer, I would watch the rivers and the hilltops. Sometimes you know when you don't belong, but you don't know how to leave. We spent our summers at Onyshkivtsi, but at times we would land close to here and spend time on the Dniester. I always wandered far away from my flock. One day I came across your father. I heard a noise and saw dark fur on the ground, struggling. I hid behind a tree. He was caught in a trap. He had fallen into a pit. I was fascinated—he was so large, so clearly of the earth and forest.

"Soon after, I saw a man lead him by a chain out of the pit and to a clearing. They played a song—"*Hupp Kazak, dada dada dada*"—"Hupp Kazak, get up if you can." It was a party of sorts, out in the woods, held for the local landowner. They made the bear dance in a duel with a man. Whoever danced better would be set free. But when your father (in bear form) out-danced the man beside him, the villagers attacked him and threw him back into the pit. And I knew then that I had to do something. No creature should be caged like that. Nobody should treat an animal with such cruelty. I didn't yet know he was a man.

"I waited until the middle of the night and then flew down into the pit. He bared his claws and gnashed his teeth, and at first I thought that was the end of me, that he thought I was supper. But then he felt me tug on the chain with my beak, and slowly, inch by inch, I unfurled my wings and beat at the air and pulled him up out of the pit. I used my beak to pick the lock. Swans are stronger than they look, *malyshka*, never forget that. He looked into my eyes and I saw a tear there, and then I knew—he was not as he seemed. It was the first time I realized that my family of swans was not the only one that could change what they were. I was enchanted. I'd found the possibility of a different kind of life.

"As soon as the lock sprang open, he transformed before my eyes. A man, with dark intense bear eyes, whose fur became dark hair and muscles. He took me—still in swan form—into his arms and thanked me. It was my turn to watch his eyes grow as the air shimmered around us in the copse of trees and he found a naked woman in his arms—not a swan."

"Mami..." My stomach feels like it's on fire.

She smiles as she smooths my hair. "We spoke all night. He told me about his people, *Chassidei Berre*, his *shtetl*, Kupel, and how he'd been captured—he too had wandered from his flock with a desire to see how others lived. But he fell into a trap. The landowner there trapped bears and then used them to force his tenants to pay rent. The custom was widespread—just like when people dance in bearskins to chase away bad spirits in honor of the new year. Except in this case, if you didn't pay your rent and taxes on time, the only way to win your freedom was to best one of his bears. Most men didn't survive the duel, as his bears were well trained.

"Your Tati's great-grandfather, the *Shpoler Zeiyde*, would often offer to take the place of other Jews in this dance. He was a man who bested the bear of his local landowner so many times, earning his freedom and the freedom of other Jews, that he became a bear himself. *Sometimes you become what you need to be in a time of great need*, that's what your father always says. And there is always a need to protect the Jewish people from those that seek to harm them. Everyone who descended from the Shpoler Zeiyde took on his form. Your father's people are Chassidim, *Berre* Chassidim, but they are also bear-men.

"I wanted to know everything about him. I wanted to know if I too could find a way to be something other than what I was. He brought me home to his family and told them how I saved him, but they only called me names, like *shikseh*, *tsatskeh*, *nafkeh*, and *goy*. He was outraged. He'd brought home an outsider who'd saved his life, and still it meant nothing to his insular family. The more time we spent together, the more we admired the strengths we saw in one another. We were falling in love, and the way his family treated me only pushed us closer together. We decided to run away. There was no other way for us to be together. He left everything he knew, everything he was.

"But when we went to my family, they didn't accept us either. *A bear marrying a swan?* It was unheard of. They wouldn't offer him a place in the flock. And my parents told me that if I stayed with him, I would be cast out.

"We wandered the forest alone, sleeping in caves, bathing in rivers, foraging the forest for sustenance. Your father had one last idea. He said that his family would accept me if I converted. I studied and prayed; I did everything right. I took on your father's faith and dunked into a river seven times to purify myself and become a Jew. But his family still wouldn't accept me. I wasn't a bear. I would never be a bear. They cursed us and told us never to return. Swans are fierce, *dochka*—we do not easily take on another form.

"But your father loved me, and I loved him. What we felt between us was warm and alive and free in a way that neither of us had ever known that love could be. So we started over in a bigger town, a place where both Jews and non-Jews lived side by side, here in Dubossary. A place where nobody would know who and what I was, and what your father was, the dynasty he came from—a place where perhaps a bear and a swan could be free.

"Your father built us this house and you were born, Liba. The baby of our love. You were the most beautiful thing I'd ever seen. You come from two proud houses. And I wouldn't have it any other way."

She's still talking, but I break out in a sheen of sweat and fear. I've always known that I was not like my sister, but this is too much. Everything I've ever known has been turned upside down. While Mami's story should feel like coming home, like swimming in an icy-cold river for the first time in spring, all I can think is, *What else is there that I don't know? What else lives deep in the Kodari—and beyond? What other sorts of creatures?*

"Liba," Mami continues, "pay attention—there's more. One night I was alone in the cabin and a swan came to the window. He was my intended. Swans mate for life and he had never mated with anyone else. Sometimes you become the person you want to be, you give up everything that you are…but family and faith have a way of calling you back…

"He came to me in human form: he was naked, long and lean, his skin glowed in the moonlight like mother-of-pearl, and I couldn't help but be mesmerized at the sight of him. Something deep inside me recognized him, and then he touched me…"

"Mami…" I close my eyes.

"No, this you must hear. I startled and made to run away, but in an instant he was white, dressed in feathers and glory, with a crown of gold upon his head, his beak black, his eyes like obsidian stone, but soft and wise and kind. I stared at him and he bent his head beneath my palm. He left one feather and I knew he meant for me to take it. It was as if he wanted me just to see him, to recognize him, to know that he still lived, and that he had never forgotten me.

"For years I would hear the sound of wings when I slept, and sometimes in the forest I would look up, thinking I'd heard something, but there was nothing there. Yet still I knew that he was around, somewhere. He followed me. I'd see the shadow of a wing in a tree and my hair would stand on end.

"One night, your father and I fought and he stormed out. We can't fight our natures, even though we try. A bear will always be a bear, and a swan a swan. Everyone fights, *malyshka*; everyone questions their choices. Even people who love each other. As I cried myself to sleep that night, I took out the feather and held it to my chest. My tears fell onto its downy softness and before I knew it he was there. I heard the singing of his wings like an echo of the wind, and saw him, silhouetted in the moonlight. I let him into the cabin and he cradled my head like I was something precious. Like he'd been waiting for me all his life. I was sad, missing my family and that way of life. I felt caged by our cabin and the life I'd chosen. He kissed the tears from my eyes…"

She pauses, her eyes wet and shimmering. She looks off into the distance.

"He kissed me and said, 'I will always come for you.' I was

angry with your father. And I'd been promised to this swan-man first...something in his blood sang to mine. He was soft and beautiful and graceful. I was young and it was like coming home after not flying for years. I'd never felt anything like it. Until this day I still haven't. He kissed me again, and I couldn't help it. I kissed him back. Soon your father came home and caught us together. He thought that Aleksei was taking me by force...Your father went into a rage—he shifted into a bear—he attacked Aleksei..." Her voice cracks. "There was so much blood," she breathes out, hand clasped over her mouth.

"No! Mami...no..."

"Aleksei tried to fight back. We were covered in his feather cloak; he shifted, but he was no match for your father. I screamed and screamed but I was paralyzed with fear. I was scared that in his rage your Tati would kill me too. I couldn't save Aleksei. I wasn't brave enough.

"I trembled and cried, draped in Aleksei's cloak; the cabin was covered in feathers and blood. I felt arms around me. It was your father. He was shaking too. He said he would never forgive himself for not being there to protect me, thinking I was crying and shivering because I'd been taken advantage of. He was terrified by his own rage. He swore that he would never be a bear again. I didn't know what to say. I didn't know what to do. I was terrified of what would come out if I opened my mouth, so I said nothing.

"When Aleksei never made it back to his family, they followed the trail of his scent. They wanted to kill Tati in retribution. But by then I knew I was with child again—your sister—the only daughter of Aleksei Danilovich. When the swans came, your father offered himself to them. He was horrified at what he'd done and was willing to accept judgment—even if it meant his death. A life for a life. But I would have been left with nothing, bereft of both the men I loved. I begged my family to spare your father's life and they agreed, but only if I allowed them to take

Laya from me when she was born. I agreed—I had no choice. But since then, every year when they've come, your father has protected us—even in human form he never let them take her. As long as he was with me, I never feared for Laya.

"Now there are things in these woods that are more dangerous than bears and swans, *malyshka*." Mami strokes my cheek, tears in her eyes. "There are creatures stalking the woods, just waiting for a chance to strike at the hearts of men. I hear rumors when I walk in the forest, echoes in the woods, from birds and other creatures." She shakes her head. "Your Tati and I must go to Kupel. His father, the Rebbe, has taken ill. He may pass away. Your father must make amends, and try to see if they'll accept him back into the fold. He's next in line to take over from his father, to run the rabbinical court, but he won't assume the reins unless his father accepts me, and both of you. I don't want to leave you, but your father gives me no choice." Mami takes a deep breath, looking like she is trying hard to hold back tears. "I need you to protect Laya. I fear that the swans will come for her without your father here to protect her. Know this, Liba—you are stronger than you believe. You too can become what you need to be in a time of need."

"Mami, the other night..." I look down, not sure if I want to tell her what happened to my hands and my arms. I take a deep breath, "I think I know what you mean," I say instead.

"Tati should be the one to explain what you are and what to expect, but we don't have time. Dubossary is safe. Don't be afraid, and should danger come, trust your instincts. Laya is young and searching for something. She is not strong in her faith, like you. Already I see the longing in her eyes when she looks at the sky. This may not be the life for her, but I want her to be free to make that choice. I don't want anyone to make it for her.

"I took your Tati's faith on as my own, I believe in *Eloykim*.

I want that life for your sister because I believe it is a good life, a just life. But she must choose it herself. It won't be real to her until she does.

"I never spoke to my family again, but I see them every fall when they fly over Dubossary on their way south. They circle the cottage, looking for Laya, and sometimes I hear their feet on the roof and the rustling of feathers…there is always one swan…" Mami wipes a tear that's trailing down her soft white cheek.

"Whatever choice she makes, Liba, just make sure it's her own. If they come…" She looks away, along the river, as though she can see its end. "She should have a chance to get to know her people. Laya is younger than you are; she doesn't know her mind the way you do. But I still won't make the choice for her, and neither should you. One day you will wonder too… When that day comes and you get the chance to meet Tati's family, you'll understand, and I trust you to make the right decision. There are many young men in Kupel who would be eager to marry the daughter of the next Rebbe…"

My stomach twists.

"But first we must see how they receive us, if they've changed."

She holds her arms out and embraces me. "We only want what's best for you, Liba. For both of you. Open your hand," she whispers.

It's only then that I realize that my hands are clasped tight into fists. I open my hands and gasp. My nails are long and almost black. My stomach rumbles. "Mami!" I cry.

"Oh, Liba!" Her eyes are wide. "I must tell Tati." She shakes her head and sighs. "We should not be leaving you, not now, not like this…If the Rebbe wasn't on his deathbed…" She closes her eyes. "*Dochka*, you may be all that stands between your sister and the swans. Do you understand? If they come, you will know what to do. Help her make the right choice. Do you hear me? It is not for nothing that you have claws."

I nod, trembling.

"I'm giving you this."

She puts a feather in my palm. It's stained with rusty spots that look like blood.

"Should Laya ever need anything, should either one of you ever really be in danger, all you need to do is say his name, Aleksei Danilovich, as you hold this. We will also speak to some families in town before we go and ask them to look out for you. But if you need the swans...if there is no other choice...they will come if you call them. They owe me that because no matter what, we are still family. But they won't want to leave without Laya. I leave her life in your hands, Liba, do you understand? Make sure it's a life she wants. That's all I ask."

I swallow hard and nod once more. "Does Laya know?"

"I hope to tell her before we go, but I've told you now. You know everything you need to know. We love you. Both of you. *One light, one dark*, your father always says with pride. He loves you both the same.

"If all goes well, Tati will find a match for you there, in Kupel. Somone just like you. We'll all go back for your wedding, please God. You will be the most beautiful bride." Her eyes glisten with tears.

But what if I don't want to leave Dubossary? I think but don't say because it's all too much. I'm not sure I know what I want anymore. *What if I don't want a Chassid? Or a bear?* I shudder and rub my arms, suddenly feeling a chill. *What if the man Tati chooses has other customs and ways? What if he doesn't let me learn Torah and study with him like I study with Tati—always asking questions?* I open my mouth to say something, but Mami keeps talking.

"We won't be gone long, a few weeks at most. And hopefully we'll come back with good news. Listen to me. Know this—anything is possible, Liba, anything. There are lots of different kinds of beasts in the world, and the Kodari holds many secrets. People are not always what they seem. And you are more powerful than you've ever dreamed. If you're ever in danger, you can draw on that power to save your sister, and yourself."

10

Laya

I open the skylight
above our bed
and go out onto the roof.
I search the sky
for feathers.

Mami comes back
from the woods with Liba.
Laya, come down,
she says, *I need your help*
in the orchard.

I help her pick berries
until they stain my fingers
and my lips.

Mami looks
up at the trees;
she sniffs the air
and waits,

watching silently.
She looks up again.

What are you doing? I ask her.
Making sure that we're alone,
she says.

She enfolds me
in her soft embrace,
and whispers in my ear.
There are things
you need to know.

What things?
I ask her.
Hush, just listen, she says.
Your father is a bear.

I flinch and make
to move away.
I stare at Mami
like she's lost her mind,
but she grabs my wrists
and draws me closer.
There isn't much time
and I must tell you everything.
Listen. Your father
is not your real father;
he is only Liba's father.

I fight my mother's arms.
Why are you telling me this?

Mami holds me even tighter.
Please. I will explain.
I bite my lip and swallow hard.
I close my eyes
and let myself be
still still still.

Mami tells me
a story
about a bear
and a swan.

We lived in a cave,
she tells me,
and I would sit
and stroke his fur
and watch the stars
above, dreaming
of a different kind of life.

I loved him like I loved
the sky, the air and sun,
the rain and moon and stars,
she says, as she strokes
my hair.
He was beautiful and dark,
funny and wise.
I thought I would never
find anyone like him
as long as I lived.

Soon I became pregnant with Liba.
She was born, a tiny cub

brown and white and fierce.
And I thought she was
the most beautiful thing
in all the world
but I was wrong.
Because when you were born
I learned that I am blessed
beyond measure
because both of you
are the stars
in my sky. Laya,
I am a swan.
And you are a swan
like me.

I start to shake
in my mother's arms,
Stop! You're making this up.
Why are you telling me this?
I struggle to break away
but her hands are firm.

No, Laya.
She looks into my eyes
and I see myself
reflected in the gray
that stares back at me.
Eyes like mine
and skin that's white,
hair that's fine
and golden.
I don't understand
but I want to hear more.

My arms go slack
as she kisses
the top of my head.

My great-grandmother
was the third daughter of a Tsar;
she married the Emperor
of Russia. One day
he went away
and in his absence,
she gave birth
to a beautiful baby boy.
Her sisters were jealous of her;
they sent a message
to the Emperor
that she'd given birth
to a beast,
a creature so hideous
that none could bear
to look at it.
The Emperor sent word to wait
until he got back
but the sisters forged a note
that said: cast my wife off
in a barrel, with her son,
and send them out to sea.

While out at sea
they came upon a swan
who saved them both
from drowning.
The swan fell in love
with the Tsar's daughter

and together
they started a family.
The Emperor mourned
and worshipped her
all his life.
People still do.
She is Anna of the Swans.
She became a saint
and people pray to her now.
She became
what she needed to be
to save herself.

One day, before you were born,
Berman and I fought.
He stormed out.

Your real father, Aleksei,
heard my cries
and came to me.
I was wrong.
It was the wrong thing to do
but Laya, you must know
he did not force me.

What? I shake my head,
struggling again.
Silence! Mami says.
She speaks faster now,
more urgently,
but in a voice so low
I struggle to hear
what she says.

Tati caught me with your father;
he turned into a bear in rage;
Aleksei was killed,
and with his dying breath
he shifted into a swan
one last time.
Tati looked at me,
jaws full of blood and flesh,
and realized what he'd done.
He killed a man.
But not just any man.
A swan, like me.
My mate.

I fainted from shock,
and pain, and fear,
and when I woke
Tati was a man again.
He offered to leave,
to go away
in shame for what he'd done.
He shed his cloak that night.
He said he would not shift again.
That he'd never
go back to his family.
He left it all behind.
For me.
For us.

But soon I found out
I was pregnant again.
I didn't know
until I saw you

that you were
Aleksei's daughter.
There was no mistaking
the color of your hair,
your eyes, dark
like mine, and your skin
lily-white and soft,
like down, swan-skin.
Laya, until you were born,
I'd never known true grace.
You completed our family
and I regret nothing.
You were worth
all the blood and pain.
I'm only sorry—
I will be forever sorry—
that you will never know
Aleksei Danilovich.
Your father.

You are a swan, dochka,
just like Saint Anna,
and you too can become
what you need to be
when the time comes.

But one day, Tati's people
will come for Liba.
He may have forsworn
his family,
but she is his heir:
he is next in line
to be the Rebbe

to replace his father,
and she is his daughter,
like royalty for his kind.
She will be sought after
by men and boys
who wish to claim
your Tati's throne.

When the Rebbe dies,
they will need a successor
and I don't know
what Tati will choose.
If they come for her,
make sure Liba knows
that she can choose.
She doesn't have to live
a life she doesn't want.

The changes are upon her.
Soon they will be
upon you.
You can fly, dochka,
don't ever let anyone
tell you that you can't.

But always be wary
of what, and who,
you leave behind.

You must stay here
and stay safe.
This may not be
the warmest town——

people do not understand
our ways—but it is safe here.
The people in these shtetlach
fear the things
that they don't understand.
But they are good people.
They will protect you.

Mami stops and looks
around the forest.
My world tilts on its axis.
The forest is suddenly silent.

So Tati knows that I'm not his?
I ask.
Mami ruffles my hair.
One light, one dark,
he always says with pride,
you know that.
He loves you both the same.

Will the swans
come for me? I ask.
Sometimes, I dream
of this one swan...
Shhh! Mami says
and puts her finger
on her lips,
I hear something.
We race back home.
When we get
to our front door
she puts her hands

on my cheeks
and looks into my eyes.
People become swans
because they need to fly away.
One day you will fly.
When the time is right.

I want to tell her
that I always look for swans,
that I see them
in the woods sometimes
and even on our roof.
That there is always one
that comes to me
in my dreams.
He has dark eyes,
and he is white.
So white.

But Mami opens the door,
and walks through.

11

Liba

Laya is putting on a white dress with wide sleeves that almost look like wings. We are getting dressed in our finest clothes for Sara Bayla Kassin and Aryeh Lev Melnik's wedding. I almost say something to her, but the words won't come. *Do you know what you are? Did Mami talk to you too?*

We are all going: Mami, Tati, Laya and me. Everyone in the village has been preparing for the wedding for nearly a month now, but the last few days in the *shtetl* were especially busy. Nissel the Baker closed his shop because he had to make so many onion rolls for the feast, and people ordered *challah* from Mami instead. We knew we'd be busy, filling all the orders, but nobody in the *shtetl* ever misses a wedding, not even Mami and Tati.

I'm comforted by the fact that they haven't left yet, that at least we get this one last night together. As we leave to make our way to Weissman's Hall where the wedding will take place, Tati stops to kiss the *mezuzah* on our front doorpost and he says the wayfarer's prayer. We are only walking from our home to the town so I want to ask him why he says it, but the way he looks at the woods around us makes me keep my mouth shut. My heart beats fast and I squeeze Laya's hand. She doesn't seem to notice my apprehension. Her cheeks are pink and her eyes are bright and

I know that she is only thinking about the party, the dancing, the *klezmer* music and the cheery night ahead of us. I admit that I look forward to the food and the general atmosphere, though I am not much of a dancer. My stomach has been rumbling for days, and nothing I eat seems to stop the hunger. All I can think about as we walk are Mrs. Weissman's *varenikes*. They are soft and plump and the onions and *gribenes* she serves them with are always so crispy. Her *borsht* is thick and creamy and she never skimps on the marrow bones that flavor it. There will be sweet wine too, and Mami already brought over some of her flakiest *rugelach*. I lick my lips in anticipation.

When we get closer to town, we are greeted by children who light the way to the hall with the lanterns they normally carry home from *cheder*. There's always something that's chilled me to the bone about those long lines of wavering lanterns. Our town is safe, I know that—there's nothing to fear. But still, when Tati sees the children he tsks his tongue, and I know exactly what he's thinking, because I think it too. Children shouldn't be out like this so late at night. Anything could happen.

I'm grateful that I never had to go to school so late, even though I remember there were days when all I wanted was to know what happened behind the walls of the *cheder*. Just once I would have liked to climb onto the roof of the Talmud Torah or the Grand Yeshiva in Kishinev, like Rabbi Akiva did in one of the stories Tati told me, and listen to the sounds of their Torah. Would I have more friends if I were a boy? Would I be invited to more parties? If only Tati would let me go to the Hebrew school that Pinny Galonitzer opened, but girls and boys study there together in Hebrew—*lashon hakodesh*, the holy tongue. Tati would never approve. These are silly dreams, I know. I am not a boy. I will never be a boy. *But I may be a bear*, I laugh to myself.

Dovid Meisels, the butcher's son, has invited me so many times to the *Chovevei Zion* youth meetings that take place in the Hebrew school at night. But Tati won't let me go: he's strict about our socializing with boys. He says that we have the rest of our married lives to talk to a boy—the one we marry—and that spending time with boys now, at our age, will only lead to things that are forbidden. Like touching, or kissing. But I think that perhaps if I went to these meetings, I would feel less like I am always on the outside of the *shtetl* looking in.

Laya has always run with a gang of kids from the town—Jews and non-Jews. She doesn't need to go to any meetings—she makes friends everywhere she goes. I see her with Jennike Belenko and Alla Navolska, and with boys like Mikhail Sirko and Ivan Tsipkin, thick as thieves the four of them, Laya sometimes tagging along even though she knows that Tati would never approve. She's also friends with Jewish girls her age—Tziporah Beltser and Miriam Groysman, even with Sara Bayla, who is getting married tonight. Laya gets along with everyone. I wish it were that easy for me. I never know what to say or how to act. I prefer the pages of my books—they don't talk back and ask questions that I don't know how to answer.

As we near the hall I can already hear the sounds of the music being played by Iser Klezmeke and his *kapelye*. I see Aaron Kartoffle, the matchmaker, guarding the door, welcoming all the Jews of Dubossary to the wedding. He's not letting anyone inside the hall yet. I'm sure his wife Yiska is already inside, just tasting a *bissl* of everything in the kitchen. It's not uncommon for girls in our town to marry as young as twelve. At eighteen I must be the oldest unmarried girl in Dubossary, with Laya coming in a close second. I hope Aaron doesn't say anything to me tonight, especially now that I know what I am and who I must marry. I should be happy, excited even, because I know what the future holds, but somehow the thought makes me sad. I don't know if I want to marry someone I've never met before.

Aaron's eyes don't meet mine. He doesn't greet us, or even

look our way. I'm a bit relieved. But still, it stings. Maybe I'm not pretty enough. Or maybe Mami's conversion is a stain that we can never wash away.

The *chuppah* ceremony takes place outside, under the stars. The white canopy is already set up. Its four corners flap in the evening breeze, almost like wings. Mami looks happy. And even I agree: this night feels like a little bit of light in our darkness. Mami and Tati are going soon, but not yet, not tonight. For one last night, we can be a family.

As Sara Bayla starts to circle Aryeh Lev seven times, her mother Rivka Kassin and her soon to be mother-in-law Gittel Melnik each hold candles in their hands. Laya puts her arm around me and rests her head on my shoulder. She sighs audibly, and I can't help but grin.

"Soon it will be your turn," she whispers.

I shake my head. "No. Not yet." But somehow saying that turns my stomach, because it might be sooner than I think. I want to say more to Laya, but I don't want any of the *yentas* like Elkie Zelfer to hear. Her husband is called Reb Motel the Silent for a reason—he can't get a word in edgewise.

"Don't you have eyes for anyone here?" Laya asks.

I let my gaze drift from the scene of Sara Bayla's slow circles around Aryeh Lev to the faces on the men's side. I see Tati standing there with them, watching the bride and groom as though they are everything that is holy and good in the world. I see too that there are many wandering eyes that are not watching what is happening under the *chuppah*, but instead are searching the women's side in the same way that we look at them.

Laya sighs again. "I'd be interested in Pinny Galonitzer if he wasn't so set on moving to *Eretz Yisroel* next year."

"Really?"

"He's handsome," she whispers, "and I do wish to travel,

just not to there…" My eyes follow hers, and we both see Pinny looking at Fayge Tennenbaum who stands almost near the door of the hall.

"Looks like he might be taken…" I whisper.

Laya shrugs. "You never know…*Nu?* What about you? Nobody here catches your eye?"

I shake my head. "You know Tati doesn't want me to marry someone from the *shtetl*." I almost add, *He wants me to marry a bear*, but I shudder and rub my arms to make it look as if it's from the chill in the air. Sara Bayla stops her circles and Rabbi Borowitz recites the blessing over the wine. Laya and I both say, "Amen!"

Then she elbows me. Hard.

"Ouch! What?" I hiss at her. People are now looking at us. Laya cups her hands around my ear. "Don't look now, but I think that Dovid Meisels is looking at you."

"Where?"

"Two men behind Moishe Fishel."

I make a face because Moishe Fishel is the last man on earth who I want to think I might be looking at him. He works at Tomakin's tobacco factory, his teeth are a horrid shade of yellow, he always smells like smoke, and he is most definitely still looking for a bride.

When Aryeh Lev places the ring on Sara Bayla's finger and says the words that bind her to him—"*Harei at mekudeshet li*—Behold, you are betrothed to me—*kadat Moshe ve'Yisroel*—in accordance with the laws of Moses and Israel"—everyone exclaims, "*Mazal tov!*" and I take the opportunity to flit my eyes up. As I do, two brown eyes meet mine across the room and I blush. My first instinct is to look away, but Dovid holds my gaze with his and something in me decides not to look away for once. *We're at a wedding. What harm could come of it? Maybe if I drink*

*and dance enough tonight, I can forget who and what I am and what
the future has in store. What harm could come from trying to be more
like Laya—free and open to possibility—just for one night?*

Dovid smiles at me and I see that he has a dimple. *Maybe if
you looked at people more, they would look back.* I swallow hard,
silencing the voice in my head. I quickly look away, only to see
Laya grinning from ear to ear. She saw. Of course she saw. And
now my face is most certainly flushed as pink as the roses that
Mami embroidered on my blue dress.

When the Rabbi finishes with the seventh blessing and Aryeh
Leib breaks the glass, everyone breaks out in jubilant song: *Od
yishama b'arei Yehuda...Soon there will be heard in the cities of
Judah, and in the streets of Jerusalem. The voice of joy and gladness,
the voice of the bridegroom and the voice of the bride.* I think about
that lone gravestone in the cemetery and of the names that no
longer can be seen on it and the song gives me chills. I shake
my head. *Enough morbid thoughts for one evening, Liba, tonight
you will have fun!* I brave another look up, just to see if Dovid is
still there, but he isn't, and part of me is relieved. I take a deep
breath. Weddings bring out strange emotions in us all. It was just
a glance across the square, nothing more.

We follow the bride and groom into the hall with Yankl the
Violinist accompanying them. Inside, Velvel the Crier, Yankl Kol
Mikdash Kretenko, Motti the Flautist, and Sender the Trumpet
are already starting to play, with Herschel Everything Holy on
the tuba, Big Isser on the drums and Gutnik on the trombone.
Shevchenko the Goy is also there, and Boiko the Fiddler. Nobody
misses a Dubossary wedding.

I smell the fried onions and the raisins from the sweet *kugels*,
the roasted chickens and the heady scent of the *borsht*, and I grin.
Laya is already jumping with the beat, as are many of the others
that surround us. We crowd into the hall and everyone starts to
take their places at the very long narrow tables that line the room.

"We need to get a corner seat so that I can get up and dance," Laya says as she pulls me after her and winds herself through the wedding guests. We take a seat and I see that already there are small portions of gefilte fish at each table setting. My mouth waters. Laya sees where I'm looking and she laughs. "Careful with the horseradish—I hear it's Mrs. Tennenbaum's and that it's strong enough to wake the dead."

I cover my mouth with my hand. "Who told you that?"

Laya waggles her eyebrows at me. "I think she's trying to kill anyone who might try to talk to Fayge."

"Either that or give them bad breath."

We snicker.

"You brave enough to try it?" Laya challenges.

My eyes meet hers. "Watch me," I say.

The music starts up in earnest and Laya bounces out of her seat and is swept up by the tide of dancers. She doesn't let anyone or anything stand in the way of her having a good time.

I pick up a fork, about to taste the sweet fish and its spicy beet-red sauce, but when I look up I see Dovid looking at me. He tilts his head at the dance floor and raises his brows in question.

I look back at him, imagining for a moment that I could be brave like Laya. I feel something reach across the expanse of the room as my eyes meet his again, and my body flushes from head to toe. I break the connection. My stomach twists. *Look away, Liba. Look away. He's not for you.*

I turn my attention back to the gefilte fish, but suddenly I'm not as interested in it as I was before. I think about Tati, what he looked like the other night when he turned into a bear, and I know that I will never be normal. Dovid Meisels, the butcher's son, is most definitely not meant for me.

I get up and go outside to get some fresh air. I waited my whole life for Tati to say that he was going to find me a scholar, someone worthy of me—I just never thought that it would be a bear.

I see my father standing just outside the door to the hall.

"Tati?"

"Hi, *maydele*. What are you doing out here?"

"I could ask you the same thing."

He shakes his head. "I offered to guard the doors, just to make sure no hooligans find their way inside, looking for a free meal. The members of the *kahal* are all taking turns. I said I'd give them a break. Shmulik the Knife just took a stroll around the back—I asked him to. Something's not right tonight. I can feel it in the air. But I hope I'm wrong."

I narrow my eyes at him. "What does it feel like?"

Maybe this is where he tells me more about himself—and me. I wonder if I should tell him what happened to my fingernails and my arms? Unless he already knows...

He grins. "*Bubbemeisses*, this *schnozzle* of mine—it's too big for its own good. Not like yours, *maydele*," he chuckles. "I wouldn't wish this nose on anyone. Go back inside, *zeiskeit*. Enjoy the festivities. Only the *Aybishter* knows when we'll have another wedding in Dubossary."

I want to ask him what he means, if that means I won't get married here, but I know that tonight is not the time and this is not the place. Suddenly being outside is not the relief I thought it would be. I take a deep breath and go back inside. I see that the *borsht* is being served and I hurry back to my place. There isn't much in the world that'll keep me from a hot bowl of Mrs. Weissman's *borsht*.

12

Laya

I hear them talking
as I spin and skip
across the dance floor.
Dvora Averbacher,
the tailor's wife, says,
Just look at her hair,
unbound like that—
who does she think she is.
She's talking
about Mami.

And Haimke Schlessinger,
the watchmaker,
says to Velvel the Druggist,
Oh, his royal highness is outside
guarding the door
like he owns the place.
What a fantazyor,
thinks he's better
than all of us.
He's talking about Tati.

I dance and smile
and pretend
that I don't hear
everything they say.
Liba looks sad,
and introspective,
and I wonder what she knows,
what Mami told her,
but I won't let her mood
ruin my good time.
Who knows when
we'll get another chance
to dance like this.

I bat my eyes
at Haimke
and take a silver
cup of wine
from his hand.
He is too *farschnickered*
to do anything more
than just smile,
eyes glazed.

I drink half the cup,
then stop,
Liba looks like
she's about to cry.
I dance my way
over to her
and give her the cup.
Drink up, I say

as I twirl back
to the dance floor.

The wine
makes my head spin
my feet
make my dress spin
and then Pinny Galonitzer
asks me to dance.

He takes my hand
and I gasp.
Men and women
are not supposed to touch
before marriage.
Not that I haven't
held the hand
of a boy before.
But here, people can see.
Here, people will talk.
I should glance around
and see where Mami is,
where Tati is,
but he slides his arm
around my waist
and I don't care
what anyone thinks
anymore.

First I see people
watching us,
as we sway
and spin

across the floor.
But then
another couple joins us.
And another.
And another.
And soon there are dozens
of couples, arm in arm,
dancing.
Men and women, touching.
And for the first time
I feel like maybe
I do fit in here.

Pinny whispers, *You look*
beautiful tonight.
My smile is wider
than I ever thought possible.
What about Fayge? I tease.

Fayge would never
dance with me like this.
He cocks an eyebrow
and I laugh.
You're different,
Pinny Galonitzer, I say.
I like that.

You're different too...
he says, and looks
into my eyes,
and for a moment
I think he wants to kiss me—
my heart speeds up.

Yes, I want to say,
yes, please.
He laughs,
Sometimes you're too different,
and the moment is gone.
I see the joke
dance in his eyes.
Like maybe it wasn't
the compliment
he meant it to be.

I shake my head
and look away,
picking up the tempo;
I won't let
negative thoughts
ruin this.
We are giving the *shtetl*
a far more precious gift tonight—
the gift of joy,
light and laughter.

He's breathing hard,
but he keeps up with me.
*I didn't mean that
in a bad way*, he says.
It doesn't matter, I say.
Let's just have fun.

The music changes,
but we keep dancing.
*You need to learn
to take a compliment*, he says.

I think you take yourself
too seriously.
Come to our meetings...
A whole group of us
are planning to move
to Eretz Yisroel *next year.*
I shake my head.
You don't know my father.
He must be outside
or he'd never let me
dance like this.
Pinny spins me
fast, and hard.
But I know you,
Laya , he says,
and I know that
you will find a way.
He lets me go
and I twirl
in a spin
that sends me half
across the room.

When I look back,
I see he's dancing
with someone else.

13

Liba

The town is quiet the next morning. Everyone is nursing a hangover of one form or another. But Tati comes back from his morning prayers and looks as if he's seen a ghost. He doesn't say anything, but he spends the afternoon writing a letter at his desk, and finally, as we sit down to Mami's chicken soup and *mandlen*, after Tati makes *kiddush* over wine and *motzi* over *challah*, he tells us.

"I heard in the marketplace today that in Gomel a Jewish woman refused to sell a barrel of herring to a watchman because he wanted to pay only a kopeck for it. The Jewish merchants in the marketplace fought the watchman to help protect the woman, who was only trying to earn an honest living, but the non-Jews in the town came to that watchman's aid, and one of them was killed. They're now saying they will attack the Jews in retaliation."

We sit in stunned silence.

Mami clears her throat. "Well. That could never happen in Dubossary. The Jews and non-Jews get along so well here."

Tati shakes his head. "Of course it won't happen here."

Mami nods her head.

Shabbes comes and goes and Tati doesn't mention it again. I stay awake all Friday night wondering if I should tell Laya what I

saw, what I know, what I heard. I wait. Hoping that she'll bring it
up, that she'll tell me that Mami spoke to her too. Maybe Tati will
say something tomorrow at lunch, I think, after he comes home
from synagogue when we eat our second *shabbes* meal.

But the whole next day goes by and Mami and Tati don't say
anything. I bury my nose in Tati's books and read my favorite stories, ignoring Laya as much as possible so that nothing
slips out.

On Saturday night, after the *havdallah* ceremony that separates light from dark, the sacred from the profane, we sit down
for *melaveh malka*—the meal that ushers out the sabbath bride.
Mami makes *fluden* and brews a pot of rose-petal tea and I realize
what is coming—*rose to ease the nervous spirit*—and I'm angry at
the china teapot, because what is about to happen is something
that no tea or pastry in the world can heal.

"*Ze seudas Dovid malka meshicha*—this is the feast of David,
our anointed king!" Tati says.

"*Oymen*," we all answer.

He booms out the blessing over baked goods, eyes closed,
face seeking the sky, blessing God and holding a piece of *fluden*
in his hand.

"*Oymen*," we all answer again, but none of us move to take
tea or cake.

"Your father and I have decided," Mami says in a hushed tone,
"that we must go away for a while. Tati's father, the Rebbe, has
taken ill, and he may not have long left to live. This is something
we've been discussing ever since Tati's brother Yankl came to our
door a few nights ago, but last night we made a decision. We are
both going to Kupel."

Laya looks at me, then at our parents, and I know that she's
wondering how much I know.

"Will we be coming with you?" she asks.

"No," Mami says. "You will stay here and take care of each

other. I've asked Zusha and Hinda Glazer to keep an eye out for you. They've an extra bedroom in case you need a place to stay for *shabbes* or just a home-cooked meal. And they'll come by every few days to make sure you don't need help with anything. We will return, hopefully soon. Perhaps the Rebbe will get better, and if not..." She looks at Tati. "Well, then we'll come back when things have been taken care of. And perhaps when we come back, we will have—*be'ezras Hashem*, please God—good news."

"How could the Rebbe's death be good news?" Laya asks, stealing another glance at me.

I feel like a sword hangs over my head. As if one way or the other, this trip of theirs is going to decide my future, my fate. And even though it's something I've been waiting for all my life, I'm not sure I want that future anymore, so I stay silent.

"We want to meet your parents, Tati, don't we, Liba? Our Bubba and Zeiyde!" She looks at me again and I nod. "What if it's too late? What if we never get a chance to?"

"No," Tati says. "It's too dangerous for Jews on the roads right now—we have no travel permits, and it's certainly not safe for young women. The Rebbe is not a well man. This isn't a simple visit home."

"Which is all the more reason why we should come with you!" Laya says.

I know I should be backing up my sister, agreeing with her. But if there's one thing I know for sure—I don't want to go to Kupel. Not now, maybe not ever. If fate finds me, so be it, but I'm not willfully bringing myself any closer to becoming a beast. I've known all my life that I was different—overweight, not graceful like Laya, not beautiful—but I don't want to be a bear, and I certainly don't want to marry one.

"So it's better that we never meet the Rebbe?" Laya says. "That we never see the town you came from? We're doomed to spend the rest of our lives here and never leave?"

"If things go well, we may move back there," Mami says. The way she says it makes me feel like it's a wish she's not sure she wants to make.

In two days my whole world has shifted. What I thought I knew is now wrong; what I thought I wanted has completely changed. I don't know who I am anymore.

"So we're just supposed to stay here, alone, and take care of everything until you come back? What if you never come back? What if something happens to you?" Laya's eyes are wide and angry. "Liba, I don't understand why you have nothing to say."

"What am I supposed to say?" I try.

Laya looks from Mami to Tati, then back to me, and I feel like something shifts inside her too. Like maybe she's seeing me, all of us, in a different way.

She launches herself at them, crying and clinging tight, begging them to take us with them.

I can't take it anymore. I get up from the table, knowing that the sound my chair makes scraping across the floor is the loudest act of disobedience I've ever made. But I don't care. I don't want them to see me cry. I climb the ladder up to the loft and curl up in bed.

I hear Laya talking to Mami and Tati for a while, their voices soft and steady. But I don't want to listen anymore. I've heard enough.

"Laya, it's late," I hear Mami say after a while. "Liba is already sleeping; go join her. I think your sister needs you right now."

I can imagine Laya looking up at the loft, trying to decide if she even cares. But she must agree, because I hear Mami kiss her and say, "The Glazers have promised to take good care of you. Go to sleep, *malyshka*. Say the *Shema* before bed—tomorrow is a new day."

Laya slowly climbs the ladder. She lies beside me. "You knew," she whispers. An accusation.

There is nothing I can say.

Mami and Tati climb the ladder to kiss us both goodnight. We are awake, but neither of us stirs. Laya is shivering, and I stare out the window at the forest. I squeeze my hands so tight that I feel my fingertips tingle. When I look, my nails are dark and long and sharp, like they were that day in the woods with Mami. My heart beats fast and I hide them under my pillow. I turn over in bed. And that's when I see that Laya's watching too.

14

Laya

They pack to go
and make their way
out in the cold.
I see their huddled shapes
out of the window,
only wanting distance,
and feel near-empty.
The truth of what I am
of what Liba is
feels like a sudden wall
between us.

She hides her hands
under her pillow.
I don't know what to say.

Tomorrow, Liba says,
I'll make some babka.
She doesn't say tea.
I miss them already, I say.
The light is blue

and the grains of wood
on the rooftop beams above us
look like feathers.

So do I, Laya,
Liba says,
but we have things to do.
The cow to milk,
the goat to tend,
and clothes to wash,
the cheese to make,
and dust to sweep.
She says it sadly,
and I feel like
there is something else
that she's not telling me.

I know that I will
never smell a rose again
without remembering tonight,
and I want to tell her this
but I don't think
she'll understand.

I open my mouth to ask,
Did Mami tell you things too?
But Liba says,
It'll be like playing house.
You'll see.
It will all work out.

I close my mouth
and say nothing.

I don't want to play.
And I think
the first chance I get
I'm going to see
if I can fly.

In the silence,
I hear music
in the distance.
Like the cooing
of a thousand doves.
A symphony
of bells and peals,
and whistles in the trees.

We lie like cygnets
in a bed of fur,
still and awake
with our thoughts.
But I feel utterly alone.

15

Liba

The next morning, Laya wakes up first, then she wakes me. The world is quiet and just beginning to stir.

Perhaps it was all just a dream. I slept late, and downstairs Mami and Tati are stirring and soon I will smell mandelbrot *and dandelion tea.*

I turn over in bed, feeling larger and clumsier and more bear-like than ever. I lift my hand up—my fingernails look normal. *If Tati was here I'd be gone already, following him to the cemetery. But I don't want to go there anymore.* I stay in bed and hear Laya outside, milking the cow and checking for eggs. I hear her take in logs for the fire and bring in herbs for tea—and that's when it hits me. They're gone.

There's no one to take care of us. No more soft voices downstairs; no more arms to hug me and hold me and make me feel safe and warm. No one to bar the door at night; no one to open the curtains come morning. I won't hear Tati getting up extra early to go down to the river; I can't ask him any more questions.

I won't hear Mami's lips murmuring softly as she prays. No one will put on the tea; no one will make supper, stoke the fire, or chop the wood. Only Laya and me. A silence of absence fills the house. It is hollow. It echoes with loss. I know in my bones that nothing will ever be the same again.

16

Laya

Liba didn't wake up
early this morning
like she usually does.
I'm worried about her.
I've never seen her
like this.
Sad, quiet, thoughtful.
So I get up
and do the chores,
and let her sleep.

When I was outside
I heard doves.
An army of them.
They weren't soaring
through the trees—
they sounded like they
were coming for me.
Me me me
I wanted to say,
Yes!

Take me away
from here.

I follow the sound
to the river.
And instead I see
a dozen white swans,
flying above
the frozen Dniester.
I reach my arms up
to the sky,
thinking, maybe if I try
hard enough
I'll feel something.
But my arms
start to hurt
from being up so long,
and nothing tingles
or burns.
I don't know
what wings are
supposed to feel like.

When I open my eyes
the swans are gone,
and I see boys
there instead,
skating. Mikhail and Ivan
are racing down the river.
Why are they out
so early in the morning?
I see Jennike and Alla
racing after them,

laughing, with bells
at their ankles.
I pause to watch them,
wishing I had skates,
wishing I could race
down the river with them
and feel the wind
biting my cheeks.

Then I hear a shout,
from down the banks.
Mikhail's uncle, Bohdan,
is huffing after them.
Come back here,
you rascal! he shouts.

I duck behind a hedge.
But Mikhail bolts,
Jennike on his tail.
She catches
her foot on the ice.
and falls.
She hits her head.
My hand is
over my mouth.
She is splayed out
on the river.
I want to help,
but I don't have skates,
or wings.
I turn to run back home,
to go for help,
I see blood on the ice.

But Mikhail is there,
helping her sit up.

She moves,
tries to get up;
they help her.
She'll be okay, I breathe.

I follow them
as they carry her
off the ice.
Bohdan is arguing
with Mikhail.
I tiptoe
through the trees
and follow them
to Bohdan Sirko's house.
*Maybe they'll
go for help?*
I think.
Should I go?
Then I see Mikhail run
out of the house
and I feel better.
I shouldn't get involved
anyway.
Tati would want me
to stay away.

I wander
through the woods
some more
until I reach the old oak tree,

then I decide it's time
to go back home
and check on Liba.
I feel a bit shaky,
not quite as enamored
by the river anymore.
Ice skating looked so free—
like flying—but nothing
is free around here.

I hear something
in the woods.
I stop and listen.
It's the same sound
I heard last night.
Peals and bells.
I hide behind
the garden shed.
And see them
through the trees.
A troupe of men.

They march
through the glen
beside the river.
My river.
They don't stop.
Stop stop stop
I want to say,
Where are you from?

I dart out,
from tree to tree.

There are seven of them.
Men and nearly men,
one honey-blond,
one russet-haired,
one almost silver-white,
one chocolate-brown,
one black as a coal,
one copper
and one sable.
They sing and call out
through the trees,
a soft and mournful melody.
Come buy, come buy,
I hear them cry.
They whistle as they walk.
They carry golden trays,
push wheelbarrows
of copper bowls and
baskets, burlap sacks.
There are no *kuppels*
on their heads;
no *tzitzes* sway.
Who are they?

They laugh and jostle,
leer and joke,
looking very much
like brothers.
I know the language
of siblings.

One stops
just where the glen

meets the stone circle
past the river.
He listens to the trees.
I hold my breath
and stand stock still
still still.
His eyes meet mine,
just for an instant.

I run.

17

Liba

The door to the cabin opens in a rush of air and light.

"Liba, Liba, Liba, wake up, wake up!"

I groan and turn over in bed. *Did I fall back asleep?* "What time is it?" *What's wrong with me?*

"Who knows? Time to get up, up up." Laya shakes my arm. "You're like a hibernating bear."

I shoot up in bed, heart pounding. "What did you say?"

Her eyes meet mine and I see fear in them. She opens her mouth, then closes it, as if she realizes what she just said.

"Laya," I say, "what—?"

"You have to come," she says, interrupting me. "You have to see—there are strange men in the glen." She tugs at my arm.

I rub my eyes and start pulling on clothes as fast as I can. "Men? What kind of men?" *Swans?*

"Come on!"

"I'm coming."

I mumble my prayers as I follow her down the ladder.

"I got up early, milked the cow, checked for eggs, and brought in the wood, then I heard singing and the sound of wings. Birds, I thought..."

I swallow hard. *Birds?* Tears well in my eyes. I'm not ready for this. *Could they have come for her already?* I wish Tati was still here. I wish Mami had told me more...

"I heard a melody last night in bed, and this morning, it sounded closer. First I went to the river, and I saw a flock of swans..."

"What?" My heart takes off inside my chest.

"They flew off so I came back home. But the sound just kept getting closer and closer. So I went back out into the woods. I hid. I waited and watched." Laya's hands flit, fast as humming-bird wings. *It's not something I can un-see now. Not something I can un-know.* "Come...! Follow me."

My feet drag, but Laya's steps are light.

She pulls me outside after her into the woods; we crouch behind a bush. And I see them. *Swan-men? Could it be? I sniff the air. No. Something other.* And I shiver because I don't know how I know. My heart beats even faster, because sniffing the air is something Tati would have done, and suddenly I feel more bear-like than ever.

"Laya, let's go back inside," I whisper.

The tallest among them, coal-haired, cocks his head at the trees, listening. He takes out a tiny flute and begins to play, almost as if he can tell he has an audience. His face is pointed from his nose down to his chin; he has small eyes and his teeth are narrow. There is something almost rat-like about him. He plays and the music makes the forest come alive. I wouldn't have believed it if Laya had told me, but I see it with my own eyes. The leaves and branches sway to his tune, and we watch as winding twigs and offshoots make their way to him, brown snakes of vines, green-crowned. *A tree charmer? Is there even such a thing?*

We cannot look away.

The tendrils weave themselves into a circlet of leaves and nuts and stems. A crown. The coal-haired one places it on a rock and looks straight at us, at Laya. He winks.

She gasps and makes to turn away, but his voice is honey-sweet and kind. He whispers, uncovering a tray of red and orange fruit, "Come buy, come buy." And before I can pull Laya away, before I can tell her that we should run, that we should hide, that I don't like the look and feel of this, Laya is up and walking towards him.

She empties her pockets; she has no coin. But still she walks towards him, entranced. "Laya!" I whisper. "Laya!"

He shrugs and bows in the direction of the crown as if to say, *This is a gift.*

He blows a kiss and just as I feel like I'm about to bound out of the bushes on all fours and scare him away from my sister, he sets off again, accompanied by the same bells and whistles.

Laya runs over to the rock. She gazes at the crown from all angles. She pokes it. Nothing moves.

I walk towards her. *"Chap nit!* Don't touch it," I say.

"Why not? It was a gift. He meant it for me. I like it."

"Haven't you read any fairy tales? This doesn't end well."

"And you read too many books. Fairy tales are *narishkeit.*"

You're wrong. I close my eyes and rub my face. *They're real.* And I think, *Maybe she doesn't know?*

We hear the flute again off in the distance, and Laya looks like she wishes to follow it. I put my hand on her arm. "Laya... *shoyn.*" I shake my head, "let's go home."

She picks up the crown and lovingly caresses every curve of its branches. "It's the most beautiful thing I've ever seen."

"What if it's enchanted?"

"Oh shush. There's no such thing."

"Right. Just like there's no such thing as a man playing a flute and trees dancing and turning themselves into a crown. Cast that thing off."

Could they have been swan-men? I still wonder. Somehow I know they're not, but something doesn't sit right. *Who are they? Or better yet, what are they? And why are they here?*

Before I can stop her, Laya places the crown upon her white-gold head and laughs and twirls.

"Laya, take that thing off right now."

"Never!" she laughs.

"Then I'll take it from you," I say, and make to grab it.

"No!"

Laya runs back in the direction we came from, and I barrel after her.

I chase her through the forest, the yard, then to the river, but Laya is faster.

"You can't have it. It's mine." She squeals and climbs a nearby tree and hides it at the very top. When she climbs down she says, "See if you can get it now," sticking out her tongue at me.

"No good will come of this," I tell her.

"No good comes of anything anymore," Laya says sadly.

"Just don't bring it in the house."

"Yes, Mami," she mocks in a sing-song voice.

I scowl and lumber back to the cottage.

We hear the sound of birds, a call and answer. We stop and look up at the sky. Laya turns her head from one side to the other, as if to trace the sound. A blur of white rushes through the trees, and then takes off.

18

Laya

Later that afternoon
I go back out
to the forest.
I tell Liba
that I'll be in the orchard
looking for winter
berries and nuts.
But really, I'm looking
to get lost.

When I'm alone in the forest
I watch the shadows
and the sounds of all the birds,
the water rushing, always
rushing rushing rushing
on its way to somewhere.
I am rushing too.
I just don't know where.

When I was little
I used to ask Tati questions.

How do birds fly?
(Because God wills it.)
Does God live in the sky?
(God is everywhere.)
Why do we pray?
(Because God likes
the sound of our voices.)
I never liked his answers;
I don't think
he liked my questions.
After a while I stopped asking,
and started looking
for my own answers.

Birds fly because they have wings.
God doesn't live anywhere—
I'm not sure he exists.
We pray because it makes us feel
like someone's listening...
even if they're not.

If I go back down
to the river,
maybe Jennike will be there.
And I can watch her skates fly
across the ice
and pretend she's me.

Sometimes when I'm at the river
the spaces between
my fingers tingle,
and my toes.
It's an itch I cannot scratch.

My back aches
when I look at the sky.
I feel my neck
stretch, like my whole body
yearns for something more,
and I'm sore for days.

I never knew before
what any of it meant—
the rushing
I always felt
in my veins.
But now I know
what it is
what I am.
And I wonder
if that swan
that I saw
on our roof
was looking for me.
I still don't know
what any of it means.
Only, that when I see
birds fly
it feels
like hunger.

19

Liba

I feel the crown of leaves and branches outside like a *vechter*—a sentinel up in the tree, watching over us. I don't like it there.

I don't sleep well that night. I hear the fingers of the trees tap-tap-tapping against our windows and I imagine crowns of twigs come to life, growing tendrils of vines that wind their way in through the cracks in the logs of our cabin and twist their way around Laya's neck and my wrists and ankles, binding us here.

Something in the woods feels off to me, like Tati said he felt that night at the wedding. I hear whispers in the trees that sound like more than wind. My eyes pop open and I think I hear the patter of bird feet above our heads, like the stories Mami told me. I don't know what I fear more—the woods or the sky. But surely I'm being silly. There is nothing to fear in these woods, in this small town. Nothing ever happens here.

Yet, I check my fingernails ten times today at least. I feel my teeth with my tongue for sharpness. I feel the hair on my arms, constantly trying to tell if it's grown. I've never been beautiful. I will never be beautiful. But I never wanted to be a bear.

Except today I want to protect my sister. For the first time ever, in the woods, I think maybe I wouldn't mind some claws after all.

I try to keep busy with chores all day. I take the milk that Laya brought in and make it into cheese and butter, like Mami taught me. Laya feeds and cares for the chickens, and takes their eggs. The birds have never liked me, and now I know why.

I go to the bee glade behind the copse of trees to the side of the house and jar some honey. Laya goes to forage for herbs and nuts and berries in our orchard and further afield, while I tend to our small garden. I try to keep Laya from going out, in fear of those men we saw, but she is gone before I even get a chance to bring it up. Should I keep her inside? Jail her? Is that what Mami would have wanted? I'm not sure I could if I tried.

And worse, for the first time I wonder if she's even safe with me. What if I shift suddenly. What if I become the bear that she should fear? Maybe what happened to Tati with Aleksei can happen to me too?

I bake all day. It is the only thing that keeps my hands busy. I try to remember Mami's recipes. I put ingredients into a bowl and judge by scent alone. A little flour, butter, cinnamon, too much, no, just enough, and honey, yes, a bit more. For Mami it is effortless. She'd stick her hands into a bowl, and suddenly there'd be cake and dough and bread. Is it magic or skill? I don't know, but whether I like it or not, it seems I have only my nose to guide me.

I bake *lekach* cakes—for happiness—trying to force myself to smile. If I smile enough, will it make me feel happy?

"Let's go to town tomorrow," Laya says at dinner. "Maybe we can find out who those men were and where they came from..."

I furrow my brow at her.

"And we can visit the Glazers," she continues, "and check in with them and tell them we're okay. Maybe we can even get a tipple of something..."

"Laya!" I shout, but then feel bad. I shouldn't be shouting at my sister.

"I'm joking...sort of," she grins. "Something to warm us up on cold winter nights...it couldn't hurt..."

"Tati would never approve!" I say.

"Oh hush. Mr. Glazer always poured me a *bissl* when no one was looking. We're nearly adults, you and I. If I were married at fifteen like Sara Bayla, nobody would say boo to whatever I wanted to drink."

"You plan to get married now? Good luck with that. To whom?"

"I'm just saying."

"And anyway, that's not a reason to visit the Glazers."

Laya rolls her eyes at me. "Well, they certainly haven't visited us yet."

"It's only been a day!"

"Come on, Liba...let's go to town tomorrow. Maybe we'll see Dovid..." She waggles her eyebrows. "The wine is just a bonus!"

She's right: a trip to town won't hurt. Though spring is on its way, it's still winter and there are no fruits or vegetables to eat. Zusha's vineyards may not be full of crimson clusters of grapes, but he has other fruit trees in his orchards, and who knows what else he secreted away for winter? And I wouldn't mind talking to Hinda. She has a soft-spoken way about her.

It was terrible when the army came to take Isaac, their only son, away. He's serving in the Tsar's army now, like all the others that have been taken, and he will do so for years...some say as many as twenty. I shudder and say a silent prayer that they will never come for Tati.

"Liba..." Laya reaches over and touches my cheek. "Are you okay?"

"I'm fine!" I shake her hand off.

"Let's go visit the Glazers, and after, we can go sell some honey in the market."

"I suppose so." *It's better than staying here, where I feel like a sitting duck, listening for the ominous sound of wings above our heads and dreaming of renegade tree crowns and strange men in the woods.*

"We could sell cheese too, and your *lekach* cakes! Oh, why didn't we think of this before?" Laya claps her hands.

"Because Mami and Tati don't want us to peddle anything. You heard the story about the herring barrel."

"Well, Mami and Tati are gone, in case you didn't notice. And we have to find a way to live."

"I know," I say.

"Liba?"

"Hmm?" I start another bowl of batter for the honeycakes.

"Did Mami…umm…talk to you before she left?"

I look up and her dark eyes meet my blue ones. *This is it. This is when I'm supposed to tell her everything…but what if she thinks I'm a beast, a monster? I'm not sure I'm ready to share the way I feel just yet.*

I sigh. "I was up when Yankl came that night. I heard everything they said. Mami spoke to me a bit after that, telling me more about why Tati has to go…why we've never met his family…"

"Why didn't you tell me?" Laya interrupts.

I shrug my shoulders. "There wasn't time," I say as I mix the batter in the bowl. But my mind races. *I'm scared, Laya,* I want to tell her. *There are changes happening to my body and there's nobody here to explain them to me—I'm becoming a bear, not a beautiful swan like you. I'm afraid that I'll lose control, that soon I'll hurt everyone around me.* I want to tell her everything—all my fears. But the words don't come.

Silence feels like a tangible thing between us.

"I think it will do us both good to get out," Laya says, breaking the silence.

I look back up at her and see a spark in her eyes and I smile.

"We could be taken advantage of…" Laya taunts.

"I think I can protect myself," I snort.

"Hey!" Laya cries. "And you think that I can't?"

I shoot her a look.

"Right. Of course. Sensible Liba. Liba always does everything right. Liba doesn't dance with boys at weddings, or talk to strange men in the woods," Laya sings.

"Oh shush...wait...how many strange men have you talked to?"

"You're ridiculous," Laya shakes her head.

I sigh. "Let's see how many more cakes I can make."

The next morning, we pack up a basket and set out on our way.

"Liba, do you ever wonder what life is like for other people in other places?" Laya asks me as we walk.

"Of course I do—everyone does," I say.

"But do you ever wish you could live somewhere else?"

I pause to think. "Like in Kupel?"

"No, I mean, someplace completely different. Far away from here."

"Like *Eretz Yisroel?*"

"I don't know. Or another country."

"Well, actually...Dovid's family sent his oldest brother Avrom to America."

"Really?"

"They want him to check it out and if things are good, they may join him there."

"Would you ever think about going to America?"

"I mean, I like to read about other places, but I'm not sure I'd want to live somewhere that foreign. The more I think about it, the more I want to stay here. I'm not even sure I want to go to Kupel."

"But...don't you want to get married? Haven't you always said that you were waiting for Tati to find you the perfect match—a Chassid from his town? Someone as learned as you are?"

I shrug my shoulders. "I'm not sure that's what I want

anymore. I don't know if I want to marry someone I've never met. Life is good here—the Jews and non-Jews get along and work side by side in the tobacco factory, and the dried fruit plant. We have everything we need right here."

Laya snorts. "Except eligible bachelors. And Jews who don't hate us because we're different…"

"That's not true. The Glazers and all the men from Tati's *shtieble* like us—and the others—they just don't understand. It's human nature not to understand someone who's different from you."

"I don't believe that. I think all people are the same—Jew, non-Jew—we're all human, God created us all."

"Yes, but we are the chosen people, *Am Yisroel*."

"Do you really believe that? If we're so special, so chosen, why do bad things happen to us?"

"Because God seeks to test the ones he loves." But even as I say the words, they don't feel quite as true as they've always felt before. *Is God testing me? Why am I questioning everything I thought I once knew? Why can't I just be normal, like all the other girls in our town?*

"That doesn't make any sense to me. Wouldn't God protect the ones he loves and make sure nothing bad ever happens to them?"

"We are an *am segula*—a treasured people—that's what Tati says. What other nation has lasted so many years in so many different places, and no matter what happens to us, we still remain strong and connected to each other—a community?"

"A community that judges us, and talks about us behind our backs."

"That's not true, Laya. Not everyone. Just the *yentas*. But they would still lay down their lives for us, you know that, right?"

She shrugs. "Sometimes I wonder."

"Maybe things would be different for you in another Jewish community," I offer.

"Oh, but not for you?"

It's my turn to shrug. "I kind of like it here."

"Maybe things would be different in a non-Jewish community," Laya says.

"*Chas v'shalom*, Laya, *umbeshrein*."

"Oh, stop it—do you really think that God is listening?"

"*Hashem* is everywhere. Of course he's listening."

"I don't know. Sometimes I think he isn't."

"Layooshka, I know it's hard. But we'll get through this. You'll see. Mami and Tati will be back soon. Let's find a place to go for *shabbes* meals, to the Glazers—or somewhere else. I'll ask around. I think what you need is a good meal and some *shabbes zmiros*. Songs always cheer you up."

She shakes her head as if to say, *That is not what will make me feel better at all.*

20

Laya

We get to town
with baskets full
and stomachs empty.
The trees shine platinum
in the morning light
and the forest sings.
When we reach
Zusha and Hinda's
sturdy home
there's no one
inside.

*Perhaps they went
to market*, Liba says.
We walk down the alleyway
that leads past the fountain
and into the town square.

We circle the square
looking for Hinda
and Zusha.

Past Meisels' butcher's shop
and Mottke the Blacksmith,
past Nissel the Baker's
and Krakover's pharmacy.
Nobody has seen them.
Nobody knows
where they are.

A peddler came
to town yesterday.
He said that people
are disappearing
all the time
and not from conscription.
He said there's something
in the woods,
Elkie Zelfer says.
First your parents—
where did they go,
by the way?
And now this…
He says there are bears,
wild and hungry.
Liba's eyes grow wide.
I take her arm
and pull her way.
My heart beats fast.

Rivka Kassin repeats it.
Yudel says that Zusha
didn't go to shul
this morning, and Heshke says
he didn't pick up

the barrels he ordered.
There was a man
who came through town
this morning, and he says
there's something
in the woods.

I want to go find Pinny
and ask him what
the *kahal* knows,
but I must get away
from Liba to do so.

Lately she doesn't approve
of anything.
But she looks haunted,
and I'm worried about her.
What am I going to do
if the bears come?
Could they
have gotten here
so soon?

Let's see if we can
find out more
by selling some of
what we brought,
I say.

We walk around the square,
calling:
Honey and cheese,
come buy, come buy,

home-baked lekach *cakes,*
come feast your eyes.

Nobody wants to buy.
Everyone asks nosy questions.
I heard your father
didn't show up for work.
Did he go to the woods
to pray?
Bluma Kiner asks.
I shake my head.
Where did they go then?
Meh. No, matter.
Less competition for us now
with your parents gone.
She sniffs at the baskets we carry.

I shoot her a glare
and steer Liba away.

We pass a fruit stand.
Come buy, come buy,
we hear the voices cry.
I know those voices.
I stop in place.

Laya, don't! We can't afford
anything, Liba cries.

I just want to look, I say.
Did you see the apricots?
And the figs?
Liba shakes her head. *We can't.*

Sometimes I feel
like my sister and I
don't speak the same language—
like we really do come from
different species entirely.

Why don't you go see
what the Meisels have to say?
I offer, hoping
that Dovid will
distract her.
She craves more details
about those bears
like I crave that fruit.

Liba hesitates,
then she nods.
Just for an hour.
She looks distracted.
But don't go near
those boys that sell the fruit,
she says, then shivers
and rubs her arms.

An hour, I say,
and cross my fingers
behind my back.
I'm going to get
to the bottom of this.
Nobody is taking
my sister from me.
The day is a plum—
mine for the plucking.

21

Liba

Secretly I'm glad to leave Laya's side. The talk in the market-place makes my skin crawl, along with something else I can't name. Something *is* in the air, and if there are bears in the woods, that scares me more than anything. What kinds of bears? Wild bears? Or bears like me?

I'm even starting to understand how Laya feels, wishing we could live somewhere other than here. But as I walk, I shake my head of all those thoughts. Dubossary is a good town, and these are all good people. I know they are. They are nosy because they care. It's just this sense of unease I feel, and the fact that Zusha and Hinda have disappeared without a trace...

My stomach rumbles again. I've had a fierce craving for meat ever since Mami and Tati left, which I've folded up inside me like a secret. I store the hunger away, not daring to peek in and see what's really there, what it might mean. But I'm scared to go to the butcher's. Part of me wants to see Dovid again—my stomach pinches with something like excitement every time I think about him—but I'm also scared to see him. What if he asks questions about the bears too? What if he says something about Tati and Mami...and then I don't feel the same way about him anymore? Could he ever see beyond what I am? Is it pointless for me to hope for a normal life when my future will clearly be anything but?

Dovid used to be a runt of a kid, making faces at me as he walked to and from *cheder*. But he no longer spends his time burying bugs and playing with marbles, hiding while playing *bahalterlekh*. I can still hear the silly way he used to count in my head, *eyn, tsvei, drei, lozer lokser-lay*. He's grown up now, and I like the way I feel when I think about him. Maybe I don't want Tati to find me a *shidduch* after all. Maybe everything I've ever wanted is right here.

Still, there is only one butcher in town; Rabbi Borowitz made sure of that last year when someone came to our *shtetl* with a forged de-veining certificate. I have no other choice. Tati always brought home meat that he slaughtered. He *shekhted* and salted it himself. "We have different standards," he'd always say. "Never give up on your standards, Liba."

But Tati isn't here right now and I don't know what my standards should be anymore. Our pantry supplies have dwindled. Mami and Tati didn't have time to restock because they left in such a rush. Maybe it's time for me to start making my own decisions.

My stomach rumbled all night last night, and as the wind howled outside and the branches scratched at our windows, I felt as if the trees were saying, *Let us in*. As if they wanted to reclaim our house, curling their branches around everything we hold dear.

I feel the truth of what I really am—what I might be—churning deep inside me. But more than anything, it feels like something vital—a deep and primal urge. I've seen creatures in the forest, but lately I smell them too, and that smell travels from my nose down to my tongue and I feel like I can sometimes taste them, succulent and wild. It scares me, because we don't eat that kind of meat.

I know what might be happening to me; I just don't know if I want it to happen, and I have a feeling that there's nothing I can do to stop it once it starts.

I clench my fists and dig my nails into my palms to stop the tingling that's always there now, just beneath the surface. My mouth waters as if on cue. I need to stop these things I feel. Maybe I'll be able to think clearly if I satisfy the cravings. That's why I need to visit the butcher. Not because of Dovid. I'll see if I can barter something. Anything. Maybe the taste of some fresh meat will keep the urges at bay.

I walk past the non-Jewish candle and hat shops, the dry goods and furniture stores, past the Jewish and non-Jewish merchants with their wandering eyes and wagging tongues, past the Great Synagogue and the church, straight to the Meisels' butcher's shop.

The closer I get to the shop, the more my stomach hurts. I say a silent prayer that Dovid won't be there and I can get in and out without embarrassing myself. Even if he's there, maybe he won't say anything. I didn't dance with him at the wedding; I showed no interest. He was looking at me—nothing more. I'm building a fantasy in my head that has no basis in reality.

When I see the door, I hesitate. I feel as if I'm crossing some kind of line, which is ridiculous. *It's just a butcher's shop, a kosher one*, I tell myself. But somehow this is different. *Tati wouldn't eat here—it isn't kosher enough for him.* I feel guilty. *How quickly I've lowered his standards to half-mast...*

Just as I nearly turn and run, the door to the shop opens and Dovid Meisels steps out. My eyes catch his and my heart feels like it's spinning in my chest.

He furrows his brow when he sees me standing still. *Breathe, Liba, breathe.* I step forward, one step, then another, until I'm sure that my crossing the street almost looks natural, like it's what I intended to do all along.

"Liba?"

I swallow and look up into his eyes—as brown and warm as I remember them—and suddenly I feel a new kind of hunger. I force a smile and clear my throat. "Good morning, Dovid."

He closes the shop door behind him. "Are you all right?"

"Yes, of course. Why wouldn't I be?"

"We thought you were gone, all of you. They say your father didn't show up for work. He hasn't been seen in the village. And the Glazers…there were rumors that…but…" He shakes his head. "But never mind. You're here!"

This was a bad idea.

He runs a hand through his hair. "So you didn't leave?"

"Just my parents—we stayed here," I say.

"Where did they go?"

"My Tati's Rebbe took ill. They fear he has very little time left. So my parents went and Laya and I stayed. Anyway, I should go. I…I have somewhere I need to be." I turn to cross the street. *Dovid is no different than all the* yentas *in the market. I don't know why I even thought about him in any way at all.* So many things are buzzing in my head. *People say there are bears in the woods, the Glazers were supposed to be watching out for us but now they're gone…I'm scared and I wish I could tell Dovid how I feel, but I can't.*

"Don't go. Talk to me, Liba. Can I help you?"

I shake my head, no. Tears bite at the sides of my eyes and suddenly I realize how much I miss my parents. I finally get a minute alone and everything feels like it's about to fall apart. When I was with Laya, I somehow managed to hold it together. But now my chest hurts and all I can think is, *Why did Mami and Tati have to go?* I'm frightened by the changes in my body, by what I feel around me—like a constant hum that's coming from the forest, from the air. Maybe this is the *bat kol* that Tati was talking about, but I have no idea what it's trying to say. And I can't explain any of that to Dovid.

Suddenly I hate everything about myself, the way my large and hungry body betrayed me and led me here when I shouldn't have left Laya's side. *Where is she? I should be with her. What if the swans come?*

"Come inside. Please," Dovid says. "I'm worried about you."

I turn around and follow him. I don't know why. I see his hand on the handle of the door; he opens it slightly, and the scent that wafts out is the end of me. I bend over in pain, my stomach rocked with a cramp that only comes from hunger, and everything unfolds inside me.

22

Laya

I wanted to find Pinny,
but I can't resist their voices.
Come buy, come buy,
I hear them cry.
I'm drawn to them
like I was in the clearing
in the woods.

Their stand is overflowing
with haggling folk
and wide-eyed girls.
I hear snippets of discussions:
everyone talks
about the Glazers,
my parents, stories
from other towns.
Men come to buy
and then march on,
but women linger,
maids and wives.
They caress fruit

and ogle men.
I loiter at the back
of the crowd.
The Jews, I hear,
their foreign influence,
it's causing unrest
in the cities—
first they compete
with our businesses,
then there are deaths
and assassinations,
it's all their fault
we live in poverty
and fear of what
tomorrow brings.
I shake my head.
Who said that?

But then I spot
sun-ripened pears and apricots,
peaches, plums, and quinces,
grapes and pomegranates,
oranges, lemons, and cherries.
Cherries cherries cherries.
There are melons and berries,
apples and dates, more fruit
than I have ever seen. My mouth
is dry with thirst. I long to feel
the burst of ripened flesh, of summer
fruit in winter, and berries
though the ground is full of snow,
fall fruit when leaves have fallen
from the trees trees trees.

He sees me,
the tall black one.
Crown-maker,
I think, and he smiles
and takes a bow.

I blush and turn to go,
hearing Liba's warnings
in my head,
but he holds
a fruit out in his hand
and my mouth waters.
I think about the questions
I want to ask.
The answers
I want to hear.

Come buy, come buy, he says,
his voice like honey.
My stomach clenches.
I have no coin, I say,
but thank you
for the crown.

Another brother steps beside him;
he is fair, with ginger hair
and eyes of green and gold.
Now who is this? he asks
with a glint in his eye.
A changeling from the woods?
A swan-like nymph?
His brother shrugs.
She has no coin.

No coin? the fair one sings.
She must not be a Jew—
all Jews have coins,
he laughs.
My face is red.
I swallow hard
and shake my head.
I walk away as
a tear falls.
There are
no answers here.

What now? No tears.
Suddenly he is
beside me.
Come here with me,
the green-eyed man says softly.

I have honey and cheese
and cakes my
sister made, perhaps
you'll trade? I ask,
hope-full full full.

You have a sister? he asks.

I do. She was here
with me, she wandered off, I say
and look behind me.

Is she as lovely as you
are beautiful? he asks.

He doesn't think
I'm Jewish
but something about that
makes me feel good
and a little bit daring.
Maybe I can pretend
to be something other
than what I am
just for today...

His hand is on my arm;
his fingers are long
and elegant; I like the way
his skin looks
against mine.
Different. Other.

You are a free spirit. Like me,
he says. *Nothing can
contain you.
Where are you from?*

The woods, I say,
I think I saw you there.

I'm Fedir Hovlin, he says,
and takes my hand in his.

I swallow.
Laya Leib, I say,
as he raises my hand
to his mouth.
His kiss sends tingles

up my arm and
down my spine.
My heart
beats faster.
Nice to meet you.
I lick my lips.
Would you like
to buy some honey?

He grins and winks.
I'm after honey
of a different kind.
Come by tonight, he says.
We light a fire in the woods,
just past the giant oak,
through the pine glade.
Come by. He puts
his hands together
as if in prayer.
It's a good party:
we serve wine and mead
and fruit, succulent
and sweet, like you.

My eyes are wide
and I can see a glint
of fire in his.

Is this what I've been missing
all this time? There is a world
out there, people I've never met,
and light and life and fire.

Fedir reaches out
to touch my hair.
Startled, I pull back.
But he has a lock
of my hair, wrapped
around his fingers.

*You look nothing
like a Jew*, he says,
carefully considering
the strands he holds.

I swallow hard.
I need to go, I say.

What's your favorite fruit?
he calls out after me.
I open my mouth
and a word tumbles out.
Apricots.

Come by, he calls out
after me,
*come by, come by.
When moonlight
sets itself high in the sky.*

I flee. And it's only when I stop
that I see it in my hand:
an apricot, golden and warm
and bursting with juice.

23

Liba

Arms hold me and I'm being helped into a chair.

"*Ribbono Shel Oylam!* What is this?"

"She was outside the shop."

Where am I? Did I faint? I've never fainted. "I'm fine, I'm fine." I find my voice.

"*Narishkeit.* Sit down and I'll get you something hot to drink."

No no no, my stomach says. *That is not what will solve this.* I shake my head because I'm worried that if I open my mouth I will vomit.

"Maybe she's hungry?" Dovid says.

I hear a voice in my head that says, *Yes…give me one of those raw shanks hanging over there—I want to gnaw on that…*I shiver. *What's happening to me?*

"Of course. I'll be right back." I hear her mutter to herself, "*A ritch in kop,* those parents. What were they thinking? At a time like this? First Jennike Belenko, now the Glazers…"

"Mama!" Dovid says. "She says the Rebbe's ill, her father's father, that's why they left."

"*Oy.* I'm bringing some barley soup, *deigeh nisht!*"

What happened to Jennike? But my stomach cramps again and I bend over in pain. I moan.

"Hold on, Liba. Mother is bringing you something."

I open my mouth because I want to tell him how beautiful his cheeks look when they're flushed like that, so beautiful I want to lick them, but I realize what I'm thinking and I shut my mouth in horror and close my eyes so as not to look at him anymore. *Am I attracted to him? Or do I just want to eat him?* Tears start to fall. *Why am I even in here? I should never have left Laya's side.*

Mrs. Meisels comes over with a bowl of stew. "Hold this," she says to Dovid. She puts her hands on my arms. "Liba, love. Try to sit up."

I sit up slowly and open my eyes. "I'm okay. I'm okay." My mouth waters.

"You are most certainly not okay, *maydele.*"

Dovid holds out the bowl and my eyes meet his for a brief second, but I force them down to look at the bowl. *This is food*, I tell my stomach. *Look at it. He is not food.*

"*Ess gezunt,*" Mrs. Meisels says. "Go on, eat up."

My hands shake as I reach for the spoon, and somehow I make it to the bowl and then to my mouth. I start groaning at the taste, the texture of the meat, the flesh between my teeth. I shovel everything in as fast I can, as though I can't possibly get it inside me fast enough. I am drowning and this is air, this is life, this is food, real food.

I look up as I scrape the last spoonful from the sides of the bowl—Dovid and Mrs. Meisels are watching me wide-eyed.

Dovid has a wry smile on his lips.

Oh dear God, what have I done now?

Mrs. Meisels pats me on the shoulder. "You were just hungry. Nothing shameful in that." She takes the bowl and comes back with a cloth. She whispers in my ear, "That's to wipe your mouth, love."

My eyes meet Dovid's. He's still grinning.

I realize why he must be staring at me, and I feel my face go full-out red. I take the cloth and wipe my face.

Good on you, Liba. Embarrass yourself in front of the first boy who's ever looked your way, even if he was only looking at the stew all over your face.

I hand the dirty cloth back to Mrs. Meisels.

"Thank you. I…" I look down at the ground. "I'm sorry."

"*Shtuss!* Don't be ridiculous." There is pity in her eyes. "Why didn't they take you with them, *maydele?*"

I swallow, still tasting meat at the back of my throat, unsure what to say, but I decide to trust her. "My father's brother came—he said that the Berrer Rebbe, my father's father, took ill and is on his deathbed. My father wouldn't go without my mother. They have no travel permits. The Glazers were supposed to be looking out for us. We came to the market today and we heard… that they're gone."

"No travel permits? He was a smart man not to take you with him." She shakes her head. "Such *tsuris,* crazy times we live in. Did you hear what happened in Gomel? And the roads are not safe. *Be'ezras Hashem,* these things will pass right over Dubossary, *tfu tfu tfu.* Nobody knows what happened to the Glazers. I don't believe the rumors. They must have had their own reasons for going." She stops to think. "But it is curious that they didn't think to come tell you. Why didn't your father let people know he was leaving either? We would have stepped in."

"My father only trusts his *kehilla*—the Chassidim. And he did tell someone—he told the Glazers." I frown. "What happened to Jennike?"

"Nobody knows. She's been gone for a few days now. Her mother is beside herself with worry. I think she took up with those no-goodnik fruit sellers–those boys are too handsome for their own good, if you ask me. But who knows? Maybe she ran away."

"It doesn't seem likely that the Glazers would have left if they promised Tati to take care of us, does it?"

Mrs. Meisels shakes her head.

"But it's okay, really. I'm nearly eighteen. I can take care of things. It's just me and my sister. "

"Eighteen is nothing," she tsks. "You're all alone in those woods! Anything could happen to you and nobody would know. Come here for *shabbes*, *maydele*? You and your sister?"

I nod enthusiastically before I even realize what I'm doing. Dovid laughs.

I blush again. *Clearly this boy just likes to laugh at me…maybe I won't come back here after all.*

"I mean…I'll have to ask Laya," I say, "and only if it's not too much trouble…I…I can bring *babka*."

"We'd be delighted, wouldn't we, Dovid? Your mother's *babka* is the best in town, even if…"

"Mama!" Dovid warns.

They look at each other and something passes between them.

"I should go," I say.

I'm not sure I want to know what they're going to say about me or Mami when I leave. There's a reason my mother never fit in here—nobody gave her the chance. You're not supposed to make a convert feel that they're different; you're never supposed to remind them of their past. Tati taught me that. But nobody around here seems to know those laws.

Still, part of me doesn't care. I want to spend the first weekend away from my parents with a big family, siblings around a table, candles lit and a table full of *shabbes* food, not alone with Laya in our cabin. My mouth waters just thinking about it. Especially the meat.

*Right, Liba, time to go before you make an even bigger fool
of yourself.*

"Thank you," I say.

Mr. Meisels comes out from the back room, which makes me
realize that he must have been listening. He hands me a package
wrapped in paper and string.

My eyes grow wide. "Oh no, I couldn't possibly. Tati wouldn't
want us to take charity."

"*Narishkeit*, take it," Mrs. Meisels says. "We don't give hand-
outs. Trade me for some honey. I saw fine-looking jars in your
basket there."

I nod and hand one over. "Thank you. Thank you so much,"
I say, and wrap my arms around her.

She laughs and hugs me back. "You're welcome, dear. It's nice
to have a *maydele* over here, eh, Dovid?"

"Mama!"

"*Oy.* Best be on your way. We'll see you soon?"

I nod my head again, not trusting my mouth anymore. As I
walk to the door of the shop, Dovid follows me.

"I need to go find my sister," I say.

"I'll walk with you," he offers as I open the door.

"No. No, that's not necessary," I say, not sure I want to be seen
walking alone with a boy in town. People will talk.

"My mother will smack me if I don't at least walk you out,"
he whispers. "Like Abraham escorted the guests out of his tent,
at least *daled amos.*"

I can't help but smile. He recites Torah law like my father
would. "Well, in that case…"

He offers to take the basket from me. I put it down so he can
take it without touching me. "Shall we?" he says.

As we walk out of the butcher shop and towards the market
stalls, I feel this distance between us like something I want to
bridge. I've never felt this way before.

"The *kahal* already has *shomrim* taking turns walking the town at night," Dovid says, "like they always do on *shabbes*, but I'm going to talk to Father about sending out some patrols in your direction too until the threat of the bears is gone. Pinny is organizing things with Shmulik the Knife and some others. We've been meeting at Donniel Heimovitz's place. I can…I can volunteer for first shift tonight," he says and I think I can see him blushing out of the corner of my eye.

This boy isn't for you, my mind tries to reason.

"Oh. That's really not necessary," I say, though my heart beats fast at the idea of seeing him again.

"Of course it is! Liba, wild bears are dangerous."

I shake my head, "I don't think there are bears…I mean…I've never seen anything like that out by where we live." I don't know what else to say. *The only bear in the woods is me?*

"I have to go," I say. "I think you've walked me far enough." I reach out my hand for the basket, but he doesn't put it down. Part of me suddenly wants to feel the forbidden tingle of his hand against mine, but I'm careful to take it from him in a way that our fingers don't touch. *Can this day possibly get any more strange?* "Thanks for everything."

"You're welcome, Liba. I hope to see you again soon—maybe tonight. I'll stop by?"

"Oh…okay," I say, because I really have no idea what else to say. "Bye!" I quickly turn and run as fast as I can back to the village square. I don't give myself the chance to take back what I just agreed to, even though I know I should.

24

Laya

When I get back
to our meeting point
Liba is not there.
I wait wait wait.

The apricot in my pocket
pulses and burns.
I'm thirsty and hungry
and it begs to be eaten.
*It's kosher, what could
possibly be wrong?*
It's just a fruit.

Liba arrives, breathless.
*I lost track of time,
sorry,* she says.

*What is that package
in your basket?* I ask.
She hesitates.

*It's okay. We both have
different hungers*, I say.
She swallows. *It's meat;
I traded it for honey.*

*I talked to them,
the fruit sellers,*
I tell her quickly,
before I lose my nerve.
*They're handsome, Liba,
and kind. They must be
from far away
to have such fruit.
They offered me some…*

You didn't…? she says.
I took just one, I say.
Laya!
But meat's okay, right?
I spit back.

Liba's eyes go wide,
*That's totally different!
It's kosher—the Meisels are Jewish!*

*Tati never trusted
the Meisels'* kashrus, I say.
*You know that.
This isn't just about meat.*
I hold the apricot
in my hand.
There's nothing *trayf*
about fruit. I take a bite.

They are after one thing
and one thing only, Liba says.

And all Dovid wants
is to make sure
you're well fed, right?
I hear Fedir's voice in my head:
It is honey of a different sort I seek,
and I smile.
I seek something too,
I want to know
where he's from,
where he's traveled.
And what Fedir knows
about the bears
in the woods.
And I will find out tonight.
It's cold outside,
but his voice makes me feel
warm all over.

25

Liba

I see the way Laya looks at the door and the window. She can't go out tonight. Not with the Glazers and Jennike missing, not with the strange men in the marketplace and the rumors of wild bears. Those fruit sellers may not be the swans that Mami told me to look out for, but they aren't Jewish, and nothing good will come of this. It's too dangerous out there. If she goes, I must go too. I made a promise to Mami that I would protect her. And I will. Wherever she goes, I will follow.

When I think Laya is asleep, I go downstairs and sneak pieces of raw meat from the white-wrapped parcel I put in the icebox. My stomach doesn't hurt so much anymore.

I lie down on Mami and Tati's bed downstairs to wait for Dovid, and think about his eyes, and the way I wanted to feel the touch of his fingers. I start to imagine a different future than I've ever dared to dream about before.

26

Laya

I pretend to sleep
waiting for Liba
to drift off.
I'm going tonight
no matter what.
It's just a walk
in the woods.
The forest will
protect me.
I know its ways.
Nothing bad
will happen.

I take an apricot
out of the bag
while I wait,
and bite into its flesh.
The juice drips
down my chin.
I suck on the fruit

until my lips are red,
until I'm satisfied.

When I stop
hearing noises
from down below,
I open the window
above our bed.
As I climb
out onto the roof
the air churns
and in a burst of white
a swan lands beside me.
I nearly cry out in fear
and lose my footing.
Is it the same swan as before?
My heart beats fast.
I'm scared to move.
I see its dark eyes
watching me.
I reach my hand out,
slowly, so as not to startle it,
I want to feel the touch
of feathers.
The swan doesn't move,
and when my fingers graze
its feathers—my whole body
trembles, ice-cold but hot
at the same time.
The swan takes a step back
then launches itself
off the roof
and takes off.

I want to follow it,
but I don't know how.
I take a deep breath,
close my eyes, and jump.
For a second,
it feels like I'm flying.
My shoulders ache
and the hairs on my arms tingle;
it feels good.
I shiver from something
that feels like more
than just a chill,
a hum in the air,
as though the sap
in all the trees around me
is buzzing
and I am as much a part
of this forest
as the leaves
on all the trees.
I land hard,
on my feet,
and nearly tumble
to the snow,
but I manage to
stay upright.
I grin in triumph.
I didn't fly,
but it's a start.

I walk through the woods
to the glen
that Fedir described.

But the hair
at the back of my neck
stands on end.
I know someone
is watching me.
Is it the swan?

I stop and wait
for the sound
of a branch cracking,
for movement in the sky,
or the shine of fur
in moonlight.
I shriek
and nearly leap
in the air
as someone grabs
my arms
from behind.
Stop! Let me go!
I cry out.

The arms
spin me around
and one hand
hovers over
my mouth.

Shhhh...Fedir grins.
It's just me.

My heart
is beating so fast

I don't know
if I can speak.
You scared me,
I say in a shaky voice.

I didn't mean to.
I was on my way to see
if I could get you
to come out tonight…
and then I found you!
His grin is wide.

I take a deep breath.
Well, I'm glad
you didn't make it
all the way to my house.
I was coming
to find you.

Good girl, he purrs
and something about
the sound of it
spreads warmth
from my stomach
down to my toes.

He fingers my hair
like he did
in the market
and brings it
to his nose.
You smell divine, he says,
like a lily

of the valley.
Did you know
they grow in Japan?

I gaze into
his green-glass eyes
and shake my head.
Have you been there?

Of course.
We travel everywhere.
Did you know
the lily of the valley
has a berry,
red as your cheeks
and just as sweet?
He drops the lock
of hair and trails
his fingers softly
down my cheek.

Is that where
you get all your fruit?
From your travels? I ask.

We travel far and wide
and buy the seeds,
but we grow
all the fruits
in our orchards.
I'll show you.

You have orchards here?
With fruit in winter?

We have all that
and much much more.
He rubs his thumb
across my lips.
I am transfixed.
I cannot look away.
My body thrums
with heat.
How can anything
that feels this good
be bad?

We water the roots
of the trees
and keep them warm,
like your hands,
like your lips.
He takes
my hands in his.

Where his hands
touch mine
my skin tingles,
something runs
through my veins;
it's intoxicating.
I stare at his eyes
and glance down
at his lips;
I feel daring
and free.

He dips
his head down.

I think
he will kiss me,
but this is crazy,
I barely know him—
yet I can't deny
the way I feel.

Can I kiss
your berry lips?
he whispers.

I know it's forbidden.
This.
Him.
Touch.
But I nod and feel
his lips touch mine.

27

Liba

The next day we are both up before dawn. Laya offers to milk the cow and churn the butter. I don't question it. I collect honey and make *mandelbrot* just like Mami would have, crisp on the outside and soft at the center. We drink cherry jam tea and pick at the ends of the *mandelbrot*. Laya's lips look sore. Red and ripe. And her eyes look tired. But I think I must be imagining things. They must be red from the tea. Maybe she didn't sleep well.

"Should we…?" Laya starts.

Just as I say, "Why don't we go…?"

We laugh and set off together for town, baskets in tow. Like Tati always says, better caution than tears, and we are safest when we are together, yet somehow I don't think this is how Tati meant it.

I don't leave Laya's side. We wander the square, selling honey, cheese and *mandelbrot*. This time people buy. Esther Feldman takes a jar of honey, God knows she has coin enough: they are the wealthiest people in our town, with money from their dried fruit packing plant, and a large home with acres of orchards on the river. Heshke the Cooper buys some cheese. I suspect he does it out of pity, but I can't think too much on that now. We use the coin we earn to buy more flour and dry goods.

I see how Laya's eyes drift across the marketplace every chance she gets. "Don't even think about it," I say. "Those boys are nothing but trouble. If you want to see someone, go to one of the meetings that Pinny runs."

Laya makes a face. "Why don't you come with me to one of the meetings? Dovid goes…"

"Because…"

"I know, I know. Tati doesn't approve. Honestly I don't know why you have such a problem with me talking to the fruit sellers—are you convinced they'll cheat me because they're not Jewish? They're human beings too, just like we—"

"Don't be so sure," I cut her off.

"Now you're acting *meshugge*. What is there, a fly in your brain? It's just fruit."

"I heard that every time people go there they buy more than they intend to, and that women in town crave their cherries so badly they cry for them and won't be consoled."

"Who did you hear this from?"

"Elkie Zelfer, but that's not the point! Esther Feldman said it too."

Laya makes a face. "Well, obviously Esther said it. They're taking business away from her orchards and from their factory. Clearly those are just vicious rumors."

"They're true. I heard Jennike Belenko's father caught her with one of them behind the stand. He kicked her out. Nobody's heard from her since."

"What?" Laya whispers.

"I heard about it yesterday from Mrs. Meisels. You didn't know?"

"No. Since when did you become a *yenta*?"

"It's not a rumor if it's true."

"Wait, when was this?"

"I don't know. A few days ago?"

"I saw her on the river a few days ago. Ice skating with Mikhail...and she..." Laya trails off. "That's strange."

I shrug. "I don't really pay attention to what the *goyim* in this town do."

"I wonder..."

"What?"

"I can ask Fedir when he last saw her..."

"Who?"

"Jennike."

"Fedir? Is he...? Laya! I told you not to go near them!"

"Well, I treat all human beings equally—unlike you!"

"That's not true!"

"It is true! You don't care about the non-Jews in this town. You only care about other Jews. If you were really so holy and devout, you'd care about everyone—all of God's creatures. Sometimes I just don't understand you. You don't even have eyes for someone who is handsome and clearly has taken interest in you. How can you wait and wait forever for the promise of some stranger that Tati is going to set you up with? Don't you want to fall in love and make your own choices? Not everything that Tati says is true..." Laya sighs and shrugs. "But what should I expect? You're just like him," she says in a huff and walks off.

Sometimes there are things about what it means to be a Jew that I feel like Laya doesn't understand. There's a reason we only marry within our faith; there's a reason we keep to ourselves—it's the non-Jews who don't understand our ways, not the other way around. But Laya has a way of turning everything on its head even to the point of making me question my own beliefs. Being around her is dizzying.

I sigh and go after her. As I walk, I decide to ignore her accusations and think about Dovid instead. I feel my face flush. *Did I miss him last night? Did he come by and knock, but I didn't answer? Maybe he didn't come by...*and I'm not sure if I'm disappointed, or relieved. *Anyway, he spent the entire time I was in his house just laughing at me.*

"Ha! I see it in your face!" Laya says suddenly.

When did I catch up with her?

"What?" *My face? His eyes…* "No…it's…I was thinking of something else."

"I knew it! There's life in you yet!"

I shake my head.

Laya looks at me skeptically.

"Look," I say, "it doesn't matter. Jews or non-Jews, there's something odd about that fruit. I'm glad we don't have money for such things."

"Oh, come on! I saw you downstairs. Were you waiting for someone? Dovid, maybe?"

"What? No!"

"Liba, I tell you everything."

I tilt my head at her now and raise my brows. "Everything?"

"Okay, *almost* everything."

"Hmmm…now I just have to figure out what else you haven't told me—"

We're so lost in our banter that we don't notice a man approaching us from across the square. I look up, laughter still plain on my face, and I stop in place. He's handsome, young, and well dressed. He wears a long black *bekishe* coat and a black hat just like Tati, but his looks stylish, clean, and new. I've never seen one like it before. *Who is he?*

"*Shalom aleichem,*" he says.

"*Aleichem shalom.*" I nod my head modestly and look down, as I'm supposed to do. Still, I can tell that he's staring at me.

"Would you like to buy something?" Laya asks. She's not afraid to look him in the eyes.

He holds out four coppers in his hand and gestures to our baskets. "Some honey."

Laya looks from me to him.

I hold my basket out and glance up. The look in his eyes is haunting, familiar, but I'm not sure why.

He takes two jars of honey, but his eyes don't leave mine as he drops coins in the basket without touching my hand. He doesn't stop watching me. I don't know what he's looking for, or what he seeks in my face, but it makes my skin crawl. Suddenly I'm cold, chilled to the bone. *He's not supposed to look at me this way—it's not modest.* I pull my scarf more tightly around my neck.

"*A dank*," he says.

"*Tze gezunt*," I answer automatically.

Laya asks, "Where are you from?"

"We're just passing through. I'm Ruven. What's your name?" he asks me, but Laya answers.

"Laya. And this is Liba."

"No last name?" he says gruffly.

I don't like the way he's looking at me. I swallow.

Laya shakes her head and tugs on my arm. "We should go," she says. "*A shaynem dank!*"

He bows his head at both of us, but looks back up at me one last time before he turns around and walks away.

We watch him retreat, and when I look down into the basket, I realize he left too much money there. I look up. "Wait, your change!" I yell after him. There was something about his eyes, the cut of his jaw…

He doesn't stop.

I see Laya watching him too.

"Four coppers, Liba!" Laya elbows me. "We've never made so much!"

I'm still watching him. He walks until he reaches the edge of the forest, then disappears into the trees.

Who is he? Where is he staying? I shiver and rub the bumps that appear on my skin.

"Let's go home. I don't feel well," I say.

Laya puts her hand on my brow. "Perhaps you've caught a chill."

I shove her hand away. "Don't be silly. He just…something feels off."

"The only thing that's off is how much money we have! I'm going to buy some fruit!"

I shake myself out of my stupor. "Don't you dare!"

"Ha! I knew that would get you! Come on, Liba…you can take two and go buy some meat and I'll take two and go buy some fruit. Just a *bissl*. Deal?"

"No, Laya. You shouldn't."

Laya scowls.

I start walking, the heavy old ivy-wood basket tucked tightly under my arm. The basket feels heavier somehow, despite the lack of honey in it now, as though the coppers weigh much more than they should.

"So, what do you want to get started on when we get back home?" I ask Laya. "Maybe we should get ready for *shabbes*," I say, thinking this is a good time to bring up the invitation we have from the Meisels for Friday night dinner.

Silence.

"Laya?" I look around and stop. Laya's gone. "Laya?" My heart picks up. I look down at the basket—two coins are gone. *How did I not notice? How did she move so fast?* I put the basket down and frantically search the market for her with my eyes.

She wouldn't… I think to myself. But something in my heart tells me that I know exactly where she's gone.

I sigh and start to cross the marketplace in the direction of the fruit stand.

I do admit I feel the draw of the stand too. There's something about it. But it's not the cornucopia of fruits that pulls me in. It's something in the eyes of the boys there. One of them has

the greenest eyes I've ever seen. They look like forest leaves in
dappled sunlight, and something about them makes me want to
gaze into them and lose myself. Which is why I avoid looking.
But it's something else too. They draw people to them with the
way they talk. They appeared in town and it's as if no one has
anywhere else to be. They appeared in town just as Jennike and
the Glazers disappeared...

I walk faster, and sure enough I find Laya at the fruit stand,
salivating over a golden tray of apricots, and speaking to the
green-eyed man who stands behind the market stall.

"Laya!" I tug at her pale green sleeve.

"...in the forest?" I hear the tail end of her question.

The green-eyed man shakes his head.

Laya looks at me. "Fedir," she says, "this is my sister, Liba."

He reaches out his hand and takes mine before I can pull it
away. "The pleasure is mine," he purrs. My hand tingles where
his flesh touches mine, but not in a way that I like.

I yank my hand back. "Laya, let's go home."

"Would you just let me look at them for once?" she says.

"The men, or the fruit?"

"Liba!"

"We need to go."

"Have you ever seen anything more luscious?" She licks
her lips.

Yes, yes, I have, I think, *on the face of a boy who apparently only
likes to laugh at me.* But I don't say it. Instead I deliberately avert
my eyes from the fruit and the handsome boys that sell them, and
grab Laya's arm, staring down at her worn leather boots and the
ground beneath her feet, tugging her away.

"I heard that some men were giving you trouble in the square
today." Fedir's voice is high-pitched and a bit shrill, like it has yet
to turn into the voice of a man.

No stranger than you are, I think. "It's none of your business," I say. "Laya, we need to go."

"Can I tempt you with a pomegranate? Red and ripe and full of juice. Red as your lips. Come taste, come buy, give it a try!"

"Come buy, come buy," the brothers echo in a chorus that sends shivers down my spine.

"Oh come on, Liba, just a *bissl*," Laya begs.

"Sweets for the sweet, just one try, the meat of a pomegranate seed to eat," Fedir croons.

"We're going now. Thank you, but we have no money for such indulgences. *Zay gezunt!*"

"Yes, we do, Liba! Now we do!"

"Hush, Laya!"

"The name is Viktor." Another brother holds out his hand and something in me wants to touch it, but I don't. "It would be my pleasure to make your acquaintance."

Laya takes my hand and puts it in his. "Don't be rude!" she hisses.

I swallow, alarmed at this sudden change in my sister's behavior. Laya would never have forced me to touch a stranger before. *What is happening?* I quickly pull my hand back.

I look up and see his blue eyes boring into mine. His hair is blond and sleek, but the way he moves unnerves me; he slinks around the stand like a weasel.

Fedir's eyes look only at Laya.

"*Tonight?*" he mouths at her.

My heart stops.

"*I'll try*," she mouths back.

I take her arm and try to drag her away, but not before I see that her coins are gone and a big brown bag tied with string sits in her basket.

"Farewell, lovely ladies with skin so white and hair so fair,"

Viktor sings. "Like maidens in a fairy tale. Noses small, and eyes so blue, you look nothing like a Jew. Come back tomorrow, both of you…"

I pull Laya away as fast as I can across the square.

My heart beats fast. I'm deeply unsettled by the things I hear them say. *I don't remember hearing anyone in our town say something negative about us before. They'll quote anything at you to sell those fruits, and even toss in a few anti-Semitic slurs. I don't like this at all.*

"Don't be mad at me, Liba," Laya says. "I wanted to know if they knew anything about Jennike, if they'd seen any bears out in the woods. Anyway, aren't you human? Don't you want to taste some of that fruit? Just once in your life? We're so lucky to have them here. In winter of all seasons! Do you know that they grow all the fruits themselves? In their orchards? Imagine that! They collect the seeds and the saplings on their travels, and bring them all back here. They have a special method of watering the roots of the trees so they stay warm in winter. I'd love to be married to someone who has orchards like those and to travel the world with him finding new fruits and bringing back saplings…"

"Who's filling your head with all this nonsense? And why in the world are you talking of marriage—with a *goy* no less?"

"You sound like Tati." She rolls her eyes at me. "Not everyone wants to live and die alone like you with your nose stuffed in a book."

"*Shtuss.* I don't want to live alone. I'm just not tempted by stupidity. I will marry someone…" I almost say, *that Tati chooses for me,* but I don't. "Just not some *goy* fruit merchant from who knows where. What could you possibly have in common with someone like that? Anything that circumvents the laws of nature like that must be enchanted."

"Maybe they're just really *talented* gardeners, did that occur to you? Why are you so quick to judge?"

"*Pfft.* Yeah. I'm sure they're talented in lots of ways."

"Liba!"

I stop walking. "Laya, there's something off about them. Do you know what I felt when you put his hand in mine?"

Laya sighs. "Yeah…isn't it dreamy?"

"No! It's not dreamy. It's unnatural. Nobody should make you feel that way the moment you meet them, the instant you touch them!" *But that's how Dovid made me feel—and we didn't even touch.* I swallow hard, not knowing what to think anymore. I say the words I know I'm supposed to say. "That's why we're not supposed to touch before marriage. And did you hear what they said about us? About Jews? Why would you want to have anything to do with someone like that?"

"Just because that was the first time in your life that you ever felt anything…"

"Laya! That's not true."

"Oh, really?" She waggles her eyebrows. "It's Dovid, isn't it? What happened? Did you hold hands? Did my saintly sister kiss a boy? Oh, now I simply must know."

"No! Stop. Enough. I promised Mami and Tati that I would keep you out of trouble, and that's what I intend to do. Would you be gallivanting around with *shaygetzim* if Tati was still here? You wouldn't dream of it."

"But he's not here, Liba. And everything's changing," she says soberly. She takes a deep breath. "I'm changing."

I swallow hard and stop and look at her. *Could things be happening to her too? I'm older and I only just started feeling the changes in my body, the echo of fur under my skin, the pinch of sharper teeth, the razor's edge of claws…*

"I don't know what I want anymore, Liba," Laya says in a way that feels like it could be me speaking, and suddenly I think, *Maybe she's just as scared and confused as I am.*

"Laya, I…sometimes I feel the same way."

"It's just that maybe now that Mami and Tati are away, I finally have a chance to figure stuff out. They can't keep us cooped up in that cottage forever. I'm older now, and I want things I didn't want before. Mami told me that as you get older you start to feel things you never felt before. Especially..."

"Especially people like you and me?" I say.

Laya looks up at me, shrugs, and looks at the ground. "What I feel when I look at Fedir is exactly what Mami told me she felt the first time she saw Tati. And he didn't 'enchant' her. She wasn't even Jewish and he married her. Why should things be any different for me?"

"It was different with Mami," I say.

"How would you know?" Laya looks at me, eyes blazing. "You're just like those river rocks you love so much. Cold and stoic. Maybe your *beshert* will be just as cold as you are—a match made in heaven. God save me from that kind of future!"

I shake my head and feel tears in my eyes. *I'm a beast, Laya*, I want to say. *I'm not like you. It's so easy for you and Mami to love and be loved—you are light and beautiful and I am cumbersome and plain*...but I don't. I can't. I don't say anything at all.

Our parents have barely been gone a week and already Laya and I are fighting. She's all I have in this world. I can't lose her. Then I truly will have nothing.

"When?" My voice scratches my throat.

"When what?"

"When did you see him?"

"What? Just now. In the marketplace."

"And he managed to spin all those fanciful tales about orchards and marriage? Just now?"

Laya blushes. "I met him in the glen," she whispers. "Last night."

"By chance?"

"Sort of."

I raise my eyebrows at her.

"I wanted to ask what he knew, if he'd seen anything…any bears," she says.

"Why?"

"You know, to see if the rumors were true."

"Oh."

"Look. We talked. Fedir snuck up on me. He gave me a fright. He's so graceful, I didn't see him coming. Isn't that strange? I mean, you know me: I hear every movement in the forest, but he snuck up on me."

Of course it's strange! Why doesn't she see that? Then I think, *Maybe she doesn't want to see it.* That thought chills me to the bone. *I really am going to lose her, to a swan or to a fruit seller—does it really matter? I know what choice she is going to make, and it's not going to be me. I'm not going to tell her everything. I want to hold on to my sister for as long as I can.*

"Liba?"

"What?"

"Did you even hear me?"

"Of course I did."

"Why aren't you yelling at me?"

"Because you know better. You don't need me to tell you to stay away from those boys."

"Oh come on, what could they possibly do?"

"Do I really need to answer that? Don't be naive."

"Well, I'm going tonight. And you can't stop me."

"Going where?"

"See! You weren't listening. I'm not going to repeat myself." Laya crosses her hands over her chest and turns her back to me.

"Laya, wait! It's *shabbes* tonight. Friday night…"

"So?"

"So? Mami and Tati leave and now you don't keep *shabbes*? We were invited—"

"I'm not going to do anything wrong. Just go for a walk before *shul*..."

"So maybe I'll come with you."

"No, you won't! You'll just ruin everything. You're not my mother or my father, and I'm going to do what I like. I'll fly to get there if I have to, even if it's on *shabbes*! You can't control me." Laya turns and runs into the woods.

Fly? Did I hear her say fly?

My heart cracks into a million pieces.

As I walk back to the house, my heart hurts. *I should be swooning with her over those boys. I would give anything to be normal. But my dreams have teeth and claws and bloody feathers and birds that fall from trees and rip my sister from my arms.* And suddenly I'm filled with rage at Mami and Tati for leaving us and burdening me with secrets that don't feel like mine to tell. My fingernails tingle.

Why aren't I the swan? The shayna meidel—*beautiful and lovely and free? Instead I'm large, and awkward, and afraid of what I feel.*

I look at my hands and see that my nails are getting sharper. *Why? I don't want to be this thing that I'm becoming.* I slump down to the forest floor and dig my fingers into the soft loam until I can't feel them anymore. Everything hurts. My hands, my feet, every pore of my body. I feel faint and jittery.

I focus on the feel of the earth between my fingers. The sounds of the forest all around me. The ground beneath me hums with the sap of all the trees. We are connected to this land. Laya and I belong in the Kodari and in the orchards and vineyards that line the banks of the river. We are creatures of the wood. It's hard to imagine living anywhere else but here.

But I know from Tati's books that the Jews were uprooted from land like this in Jerusalem and Babylon. *By the rivers of Babylon there we sat and also wept when we remembered Zion...*Tati used to sing that every Saturday afternoon at *shalos seudos*—the third meal. It's hard to breathe. Will we one day weep over Dubossary, over the quiet life we had here, like we weep over Babylon and Jerusalem? One day soon, my sister and I will both go our separate ways. I feel like we are on the cusp of that change. My tears wet the earth.

But then I feel the fine brown hairs on my back prickle. Someone is watching me.

I crouch down, look around, and scent the air. There. I smell it. I turn and see a swatch of fur in the trees. I run after it, but it disappears from view. I search the woods all around me, but it's gone. I'm alone in the woods. My whole body seizes up in fear.

28

Laya

Back home,
the air stirs
outside my window.
Something is brewing.
If there are bears
in the woods,
I must find them
before they find
my sister.

I brew chamomile tea
to quiet my mind
and make extra,
a concentrate
we can use
on *shabbes*.
It's a habit
I can't break.

But really
I want ginger

for the fire
that runs
through my veins
when I think of Fedir.

For the way
my lips tingle
and burn
at the thought
of his lips
on mine.

My tongue aches
as if it were dry.
Will he taste
like apricots
tonight?
Or something else
entirely?

My hands
only want
to touch his
again.

I want answers
that only he
can give.

29

Liba

My fingers are black with soil, but my fingertips are white and whole again. I wait and listen some more, heart pounding in my ears, then turn and run all the way back home.

Who was that man we saw in the marketplace? Should I let the kahal *members know? Maybe Laya's not the only one who needs protection. Maybe we all do.*

I wipe my dirty hands on my skirt and open the front door. Laya yelps as she sees me.

"You're here!" I say.

"Where else would I be?"

"I thought that maybe...you'd gone already."

Laya smiles. "I made tea, and extra for *shabbes.*"

My heart softens. *Everything is okay. Everything is going to be okay.* "I love you, Laya-bell. I'm sorry. I just feel so responsible all the time. I don't want anything bad to happen to you. You're all I have left in this world."

"I love you too." She comes over and hugs me.

"I miss Mami and Tati," I admit. "I'm worried about them. And I'm tired of trying to be strong."

"I know," she whispers as she strokes my hair. "And I know

you're just looking out for me. But I can't stay cooped up like this. I need to be out and about. I want to find out what people know."

"I know. I'm sorry. But...Laya, what exactly did Mami tell you before she went away?"

"I know what you are, Liba."

My heart thuds. "You do?"

"I feel like maybe I've known it all along. When Mami told me—it just made sense. So many things make sense now."

I don't know what to say. "Do you ever feel...I mean, have you started to...?" I close my eyes and decide to just say it: "Sometimes my nails grow long, and I feel my teeth sharpen. I'm hungry all the time," I admit.

"My shoulders itch and my arms ache, and sometimes I feel I could jump off a tree and the air would catch me."

I stare at Laya and she stares back at me—we're seeing each other with new eyes. But I don't know how to tell Laya that the swans might come for her. I don't want to tell her. I'm scared of losing her. Instead I say, "Laya, if you ever see swans in the forest—will you tell me?"

"I see swans all the time."

I swallow. "You do?"

"Yeah. On the river, in the sky. And there's one that I've seen land on our roof...Will you tell me if you see bears?"

"Yes, but...stay away from them, okay? Don't go out on the roof when you see a swan. Can you promise me that?"

Laya nods, but I can see in her eyes that she doesn't mean it.

"Do you really think there are wild bears in the woods?" I ask her.

"I don't know, but I'm going to find out."

"Well, I felt like something was watching me this afternoon when I was walking back here. I tried to follow whatever it was, but I wasn't fast enough. The only thing I saw was fur.

Watch out tonight, Layoosh. I used to think the only bear in our woods was me."

"I'll be careful, but you should be too! Don't go running after strange bears in the woods."

I roll my eyes. "I'll try not to. But can you promise me something else?"

"What?"

"If you ever see me...change...run as far away from me as you can."

"What? Why?"

"Because I don't trust myself. I'm scared. What if I can't control what happens? What if I hurt you?"

"I trust you," she says.

I sigh. "Well, at least one of us does."

"What does this mean for you and Dovid?"

I shake my head. "There is no me and Dovid." Saying those words makes my belly ache.

"Don't think that way, Liba. You can find a way to make it work."

I shake my head. "I wish these things came as easy to me as they do to you. Just be careful, okay? I don't trust Fedir...What if there's someone else who's meant to be in your future?"

"He'd better hurry and show himself." Laya crosses her arms over her chest.

"I think you should give someone else a chance before you decide."

"Right, and you should definitely give a couple guys from town a chance too, eh?"

"It's different."

"No, it isn't."

Laya holds my gaze. I see the reflection of my ice-blue eyes in her brown-black ones, and I know that nothing between us will ever be the same again. But maybe that's okay. Maybe it's the way that things are meant to be. We are always changing, like the moon.

"Perhaps it's safer in town?" Laya says.

I shiver, thinking of what I saw in the woods. "I've been wondering the same thing." *Suddenly I don't feel so alone anymore.*

"I know you've spoken to the Meisels—do you think they'd take you in?" Laya asks.

"Me? What about you?"

"I don't know if I can leave the forest."

"What are you, *meshugge?* I'm not leaving you here alone. I don't know what's out there, and Mami and Tati would have wanted us to stick together."

"Mami and Tati are gone. They may never come back."

"They will come back," I whisper, but my voice cracks.

"They abandoned us."

"Laya, that's not true...Tati went to visit the Rebbe, who is on his deathbed. What was he supposed to do? Not go?"

"We need Tati here. Things are happening here."

I want to argue with her, but she's right. I do wish they had stayed. I don't tell Laya about the humming I felt beneath the ground because I don't know how to explain it, and I don't know if she'd understand. Maybe it was just a figment of my imagination. But then I realize that it's not just that I think we should stick together—I don't want Laya to go walking in the woods tonight alone because it means that I'll be walking in the woods alone too.

"Sometimes at night I hear all kinds of sounds," Laya says, "and even though I'm scared, I want to know what's out there. Do you hear the noises too? The scratching on the roof?"

I swallow. "Yes."

"Our house feels like a cage," she says.

"Of course it does...but that's because you're a bird," I laugh.

"It's not funny." Laya scowls.

I put my hand over my mouth, sigh, and tuck one of Laya's white-gold locks behind her ear.

"*Ich hob dir lieb!* Forever and ever," I tell her. It's what Mami would say.

"I love you too. Forever and ever," Laya replies. She cocks an eyebrow at me. "Even if I move away and marry someone smolderingly handsome?"

I think of Dovid and his warm hands and eyes and even his laughter at me. I think about what it would be like to see him again. To sit around the Meisels' table and feel like I belonged.

"Even if," I say. "But not if it's Fedir Hovlin!"

"Why, you…" Laya lunges for me and smacks me with a kitchen rag. I shriek and run out the door into the meadow. We chase each other until we hear the kettle's shrill whistle.

"The tea!" Laya yelps and runs inside to take the kettle off the fire.

I follow her back in and my heart is less heavy. Whatever comes, we will face it together.

30

Laya

I wait until Liba
is taking
a pre-*shabbes* nap.
Then I slowly,
silently creep
creep
creep
down the ladder.

I take my cloak off its hook,
careful not to make it rustle.
Then I open a window
and climb out.

31

Liba

I wait until Laya climbs out the window. I pretended to nap. It's something I do well: pretending. It's all I do lately. Now that I know what I am—a bear, a beast—I can pretend to be a normal girl. It feels good to pretend, because I can't face the alternative.

I wait until she's gone. I'm already dressed in my *shabbes* clothes. I climb out of bed, step down the ladder, put on my cloak, and follow her.

32

Laya

I hear Fedir's voice
in my head
like a song:
Come by! Come by!
I hum as I creep
through the trees.

I feel the sap
of the trees
beneath my feet
and all around me.
The branches
and the leaves
sing with me,
zmiros and *niggunim*.
My own kind of
shabbes songs.
They point me
in the right direction.

I dance over roots
and under boughs.
Past the old giant oak,
and through
the pine glade.
My head is full
of night and air.

As the branches
start to thin
I see the dance
of orange flames
poking through
the woods ahead,
like gems on trees.

I stop and let the leaves
cover me, peeking
at the clearing ahead.
The brothers sit
around a bonfire,
and with them
many girls,
nearly a dozen.

The fire rages,
orange and angry,
and everyone holds
wooden goblets
filled to the brim
with dark and rosy liquid.

The goblets pass
from hand to hand,
and lip to lip.

My mouth opens,
nearly tasting
what they sip.
I walked so far.
I'm tired
and thirsty.
All I want
is a drink.

It is honey
of a different sort
I seek.

33

Liba

I slip through the trees and the branches. I try to follow her. At first she walks slowly, humming to herself, then she dances faster and faster until I lose sight of her completely.

I try to scent her in the air, but I've lost my way. I don't know where she went.

I wander left, then right, then left again, past a giant oak and into a pine glade. I watch and wait and listen, but the forest is silent. I don't know which way to turn, and suddenly I'm scared. I feel a buzzing in the air, my fingertips tingle. It's as if the forest doesn't want me to continue. I hear a branch crack and all my hairs stand on end. I am all alone in a large, dark forest. This was a bad idea.

I pull the hood of my cloak up. The sensation of the fur on my cheeks sends a chill down my spine. I feel the hair that lurks just beneath my skin. It wants release. I grit my teeth and shut my eyes and will everything to stay as is.

I start to tremble. I hear another branch crack, sounding closer this time, and even though I don't know where I'm going, I start to run. My body wants me to get down on all fours, to feel the forest loam between my fingers again, but I don't give in to the impulse. I just run as fast as I can.

The woods have never scared me before—they have always been my haven—but my heart thumps with a beat so fast I feel as though there are drums thrumming in my ears.

I run until I see something familiar through the trees. The village! I'm so relieved I start to cry.

I run to the Meisels' door and knock.

34

Laya

Some of the girls
are sitting on laps,
others lurk in shadows
but I can see them kissing,
sucking at the lips
of girls and boys
looking as if madness
were upon them.
I see someone
that looks like Jennike.
My heart beats fast.
Perhaps she isn't missing?
Was she hiding out here
the whole time?
I linger in the woods
with only the shadows
of the trees to hide me.
Watching, waiting.
I can't tell if it's her.
I'm cold, it's dark
and the flames look so inviting.

I see Fedir across the fire.
His eyes flit around the glen
as though he can sense
something in the wind.
Me.

This is everything
that Liba warned me about,
everything she tried
to protect me from.
Goyishe boys
with wine and cheer
and groping hands
and tongues.
On *shabbes*,
no less...

He sees me.
My eyes meet his
across the flames.
I blink and in an instant
he's beside me.
How did he move so fast?

35

Liba

I can see the fire burning inside. The windows are lit up and woodsmoke rises from the chimney. I smell chicken soup and *schmaltz*. *Challahs* fresh from the oven. Our home used to smell like that...Tears continue to wet my eyes. I miss my parents so badly it hurts. I wouldn't be scared of strange sounds in the woods if Tati were still here. I wouldn't be wandering alone in the woods on a Friday night if Mami were home and these smells were coming from her oven. I linger just outside the door, gathering courage from the air and waiting for the tears to subside.

I hear laughter from inside. More than one voice. And I smell *kugel* and brisket wafting from the chimney with the smoke. I'm about to knock again when the door opens.

"*Gut shabbes!*" Mrs. Meisels says. She is dressed in a green velvet dress and her hair is covered in a lace *tichel*. Her cheeks are red and shining.

I swallow. My hands are trembling. My mouth struggles to find words.

"Is everything okay, *maydele*?" Mrs. Meisels asks.

I shake my head, no. And realize I forgot the *babka*.

"Come in, come in. Take off your coat." She coaxes me inside. She hangs my coat on a hook by the side of the door. There is the smell of iron in the entryway, a good smell. And lavender hangs above our heads.

My heartbeat slows. *This is a home*, I think. *Our house doesn't feel like a home anymore.*

"Shhh. Dry your tears. Where's your sister?" she asks.

I shake my head.

Then I see Dovid. His eyes grow wide and he's beside me in an instant.

"Is everything okay? Where's Laya?"

Of course he asks about Laya. What must I look like? My cheeks tear-streaked, my hair wild.

I don't know what to say. *My sister's in the woods with* goyim? "I'm sorry I'm late," I say instead. "I was following Laya, but I lost my way in the woods. I heard something and I got scared. I ran as fast as I could, but I forgot the *babka* at home."

"Where was Laya going?" Dovid asks. "Should I go look for her?"

I don't want to tell him. I don't want him to think I'm like her, that I would ever desecrate the sanctity of *shabbes*. My father is a learned man, and though my mother is a convert, she is devout. For the first time in my life I'm embarrassed by my sister. Something I've never felt before. And I realize that maybe I don't want to be like her after all.

"No. She's fine," I say. "She went to meet some friends."

Mrs. Meisels saves me. "Now's not the time for questions. The men just got home from *shul*. We were about to sing 'Shalom Aleichem.' Come, sit down. Join us."

My stomach rumbles and I swallow. "I would love that."

I follow Mrs. Meisels and Dovid into the dining room. His three brothers are seated with his father. *Shabbes* candles illuminate the center of the table and the *challahs* are tucked under an embroidered cover like two babies in their beds.

The heady scent of pine is in the air above the odor of chicken soup and meat, and something else, something green and wild. Cedar smoke dances in the hearth and I feel safe and warm and welcome. I forget about the woods and the dangers lurking there. I forget about who Laya's with, and why. I forget about the Glazers going missing, and Mami and Tati being gone. I smile and listen to the sound of singing and let myself enjoy a home-cooked meal and company as if it's the most natural thing in the world.

36

Laya

*Y*ou came, he purrs.
  I did, I smile, *but*
I should go.

Why? His eyes grow wide.
You've only just arrived!
We're just getting started.
Kliment plays a mean fiddle,
and Miron, as you know,
is magic on the flute.
You must stay for a bit
and feast upon the music...

Music? On *shabbes?*
I shrug my shoulders.
Thank you, but I really
must be going. My sister
is waiting for me...

He looks
into my eyes
and sighs.

What? I say.

*You are like
a moon-lit
poplar branch,*
he whispers.
*So strong and wild.
I've longed to see
the way the fire
dances in your eyes…*
I shake my head
and turn away.
*From the moment
I first saw you
in the woods,* he says,
*like a lily growing
in the forest, all alone,
my heart and mind
have thought of
nothing else
but you.*

Stop, I say.
You're scaring me.
He tucks a strand
of hair behind my ear
and whispers,
I wasn't done…
I shiver.

*Is Jennike here?
I thought I saw her before,*
I ask before I lose my nerve.

Girls come and go,
he says. *I don't keep track*
of anyone but you…

Have you seen
strange men
in the woods?
I say.

Nobody is out here
but us, me and you,
he says.
I look around
and see that we
are suddenly alone.
Where did everybody go?
I'm confused
and a little scared.

The moon wanes
and the night
grows late,
he answers.

I should go,
I say.
Go go go.
My sister
is waiting
for me.

Stay? he begs.
Just for a spell,

one song.
He takes my hand.
Come to the fire
for a bit,
warm yourself
before you go,
and drink some wine,
at least.
I feel his pulse
beating against mine.
Vein to vein.
His hand so large
and soft.
Just one song, I say.

He whoops in victory
and picks me up
as though I am
a feather in the wind.
He carries me over
to a wooden chair
that looks like a throne.
He puts a wooden goblet
in my hand. It's carved
with trees and fruit
and little men.
A gust of wind
blows smoke
into my eyes
and everything
goes soft and blurry.
I shouldn't drink, I say,
though I am thirsty,

and in my head I think:
It isn't kosher.

But Fedir presses
the goblet to my lips,
and I smell apricot,
and plum plum plum.

I touch my lips
to the liquid,
cherry and lemon,
honeyed dates
and red ripe grapes
and baking apples.
I sip, and sip again,
and drink in lusty gulps
until it's gone,
and lick my lips.
Fedir, I say,
but what about
the bears?

What bears?
he asks.

The wild ones,
I say.

I think you may
have had
too much
to drink.
He grins.

And all the time
he watches me.
The way
my mouth moves
and my throat,
the way I lick my lips
with my tongue,
the way it darts
out of my mouth,
tiny and pink.
He's like a cat
watching a mouse,
I think. But then
his lips touch mine
and everything around us
disappears. I drink him in,
ravenous, I can't get enough
of his lips, I nip at them
and tug at his tongue
with my teeth,
sucking on his lips
like they are life
and air,
like I am thirsty
and his lips
are an oasis
in the desert.
I feast on them.
On him. As
everything around me spins.
He breaks the kiss,
both of us breathless, eyes wild,
lips swollen

and red.
I shake my head
and rub my eyes
trying to clear
the glare, the fog.
I lean in again
so close, my lips
almost at his,
and beg for more.

37

Liba

After he sings *"Ayshes Chayil"* Mr. Meisels makes *kiddush*. His family passes one silver cup around the table, from lip to lip. We sip the sweet red wine.

Then we go to the kitchen to wash our hands before the bread.

"You still didn't say where your sister went..." Dovid asks as we line up behind his brothers at the sink.

I sigh. I might as well tell the truth. "To the Hovlins...I tried to stop her. I thought I should go with her, to keep her out of trouble, even though it's not very *shabbesdik*."

"What happened?" he asks.

"I lost sight of her. And then I heard a noise and got scared," I say. I find myself blushing again and I don't know why. "But I really didn't want to go there anyway. I wanted to come here."

"I'm glad. I wish I'd thought to offer to come get you. Nobody should be walking in those woods alone."

"I'm worried about her," I admit.

"The *kahal*'s sent out extra patrols. Perhaps that's what you heard," Dovid says.

"Has something else happened?"

"Nothing you don't already know about," Dovid says.

"I really should go find her." My eyes dart to the door.

"Liba, don't go," he says. "Please?" The look in his eyes is so tender, it sends shoots of warmth through my whole body.

"Come, eat with us," he says. "There are men out there patrolling the woods. She'll be safe tonight. Let's wash our hands."

I let out a breath.

I watch him pour water three times over one hand, then three times over the other. He says the blessing out loud, his voice bright and clear, and my stomach clenches—but not from hunger this time.

He waits for me as I rinse my hands after him and say the blessing quietly. Then we go back to the table and sit down.

Mr. Meisels says the *brocha* over the *challahs*, his voice loud and sonorous.

Then he passes out a tray of sliced bread for us to take. Tati always ripped pieces from the *challah* and threw the bread to each of us. A Chassidic custom. This seems more civilized. I like it.

"For you, *maydele*," Mrs. Meisels says, and gives me the first bowl of chicken soup.

I sit down and place a napkin on my lap. I bring a spoonful of soup to my lips. It's hearty and delicious. Fluffy *kneidlach* and *lokshen* float in the golden broth. I eat slowly and carefully, trying to savor every mouthful. I think that perhaps it's okay for once to want something for myself—a home, a family. Someone else can look out for Laya tonight. The swans won't come if she's with Fedir, and there are men patrolling the woods.

The table is quiet. I look up and see that they're all watching me. I finish chewing the bite that's in my mouth and quickly wipe my fingers and my chin. *What did I do wrong this time?*

I look down and see that my bowl is clean. Have I embarrassed myself again?

"It's okay, *shayna meidel*," Mrs. Meisels says. "My boys just aren't used to girls with such a hearty appetite."

My heart skips a beat. Nobody ever calls me a *shayna meidel*. Those are words reserved for Laya, not for me.

Mr. Meisels slaps the table and the plates jump. "Nothing like a woman with a little flesh on her," he says, a gleam in his eye, and he motions for Mrs. Meisels. He smacks his thigh and she blushes and sits on his lap. He puts his arms around her. "I like it when there's more of a woman to love. Especially this *zaftige* woman."

I am mortified. Tati would never speak to Mami that way, or have her sit on his lap in public.

"It was delicious," I whisper. I don't know what else to say.

"Nothing like Mama's cooking," Dovid's brother Joseph says.

"To Mama, our *ayshes chayil*!" his youngest brother Benji toasts, and raises his glass.

The men and boys all clink their glasses and drink the wine. I haven't touched mine; I was too busy trying not to make a fool of myself at the table. *So much for that*. I pick up my glass and clink it around and when my cup hits Dovid's he grins at me and winks. When I drink I'm very warm inside, from my head down to the tips of my toes, and though it likely has something to do with the wine, the look in Dovid's eyes makes me feel like it might be something more.

I put my hands down in my lap and grip my napkin so as not to do anything else embarrassing. Dovid's brothers and even Mr. Meisels all get up to help clear the table. Dovid watches them and when their backs are turned I feel the brush of his fingers against mine under the table—tentative and soft.

My heart beats so fast I'm sure they can hear it in the kitchen. But my hand responds to his before I can overthink anything, and he laces his fingers with mine. His hand is warm, his grip comforting and strong; I don't pull mine away.

38

Laya

My head clears
and my lips pulse
and throb in time
with the beats I hear.
The fog clears
and suddenly we're
not alone anymore.
Miron plays his flute,
and Kliment's on the fiddle,
and the music
is like rain.
Nothing like *klezmer*.
I feel the moonlight sway,
the heavens open up,
every sound is in my ears,
every taste is on my lips,
and I get up and start to dance,
twirling, spinning to the music.
More, I cry, breathless,
eyes wild and lit by flame.

I don't even know
what I'm asking for.
More music?
More kisses?
More wine?
More dancing?
More moonlight?
I suck down another glass
of wine, and then another,
licking at the rims of goblets,
catching every drop
with my tongue.
I can't get enough
of all the flavors,
the taste of fruit
and moonlight.
Blueberries, blackberries,
strawberries, damsons,
currants and gooseberries,
figs and cranberries,
pomegranates, mulberries,
melon and raspberries,
every taste but one…
Where did he go?
I need his lips
on mine.
I turn
and see Fedir
at my side,
his green-gold eyes
and his lips,
exactly where

they should be.
Waiting for me.
And I know
what I want
to taste next.

39

Liba

I feel as if I'm made of flame. I let go of his hand and get up out of my chair. "I should go look for my sister," I say.

"I'll go with you," Dovid says and also gets up.

"Nobody is going anywhere until they have brisket and *kugel*," Mrs. Meisels announces as she comes in bearing trays overflowing with meat and potatoes. "Let a goose loose in the oats and she will starve to death," she clucks, looking at me.

I blush and sit back down again. I put my hands in my lap. *I guess I can wait just a bit longer.*

Dovid piles my plate high with brisket.

"They are gathering men to go out tomorrow night and hunt the bears," his father says.

"What?" My stomach clenches.

"I'm going to walk you home—" Dovid says.

"After we finish eating!" Mrs. Meisels sings.

"After we finish eating." Dovid clears his throat. "We can look for Laya on the way."

I take a bite of meat and I have to close my eyes because it's heaven. I groan and take another bite. This time, I know that when I open my eyes, Dovid will be laughing at me. But I don't care. Something about his laugh, and his hand—everything about him—makes me feel good and warm and happy. And I think that maybe I want to feel this way for as long as I possibly can. Maybe it's my turn to choose.

Besides, something tells me that Laya might not want to be found.

40

Laya

His lips leave mine
and I reach for him
again, but he takes
my hand in his
and kisses it instead.
My body flushes
the same color
as the wine.
He spins me round;
we dance and twirl
and twist as fire burns
and moonlight smolders
high above the trees.
We kiss. Again.
And again.

His lips taste like a missing flavor.
A fruit I never knew existed.
Laya…he purrs again, and I like
the sound of his voice in my ear,
his lips on my lips, his tongue

meeting my tongue.
The tastiest fruit,
I think. *I wonder*
what it's called?
His hands are on my chest,
feeling the roundness
of my breasts;
my arms are up
around his neck
stroking the back
of his head;
my hands,
tangled in his hair,
then up and down
his back, and lower still.
How could I have thought
that this was wrong?
It feels so good.
He feels so strong.
I am hungry,
and he has fruits galore.
I would never be hungry again
if I was with him...

Fedir looks into my eyes.
I arch my neck back up
and nibble at his neck, his jaw.
More, I giggle.

The moon wanes, he says.
The fire dims and dawn
stretches her wings above us.

What? I pull my lips
away from his ear.
But I said… I wrinkle my brow.
I thought I'd only stay a while…
And you did, he grins,
but minutes become hours
in the blink of an eye.

He gives me a basket
full of fruit.
I can't take this, I say.
For your sister and you
to share. He puts it in my hands.
I have no coin, I say.
You have gold aplenty,
he answers.
I squint my eyes.
Nothing makes sense.
The most precious of metals,
he says, fingering my hair.
Pay me in gold.
One lock of your hair.
But why? I ask.
So that I'll never forget you.
His eyes are sad.
It's just hair. I shrug.

His eyes glow with firelight.
He takes a dagger
from his belt
and cuts a piece.
Then takes out
a small pouch

and places
my hair inside.
He hangs the pouch
around his neck.
Now you will always
be close to my heart,
he says and picks me up.
I squeal, but he is strong
and I am tired.
I will take you home, he says.
Home home home, I think.
I hug him and peck
a kiss on his cheek.
Okay, I say, not even wondering
how he knows where I live.
But what about
the bears?
I mumble.
I will keep you safe tonight,
he says.
The wine clouds
my good sense.
I put my arms
around his neck,
and nestle my head
against his chest.
And fall asleep.

41

Liba

After dinner, Dovid and I walk back to the cottage. First there is distance between us; the space between our bodies is like a hum—charged with possibility. But once we get deeper into the woods, he lightly brushes his hand against mine, and I don't hesitate. I twine my fingers with his. I'm worried about Laya, wondering where she is, and his hand in mine feels like comfort. "Don't worry," Dovid says. "We'll find her—I'm sure she's fine." It's as if he knows exactly what I'm thinking.

I go back and forth between looking around the forest for her, and reveling in the feel of his hand in mine. Who knows what the future has in store for me? His hand feels like a chance. And I want to take it.

Halfway there I stop.

"Are you okay?" he says.

"Yes, wait," I whisper.

"Why did you stop?"

"Shhh…I just want to listen for a minute," I say softly.

"Did you hear something?" he says into my ear.

And now I'm aware of his breath in my hair, his lips so close to my ear. He puts his hand on my back, as if to steady me, or to protect me. And I can't deny that it feels so good I want to cry.

I'm the bear! I want to say. *I'm supposed to be the one who protects everyone*, but I'm scared and the warmth of his hand on my back feels so good that I close my eyes at the sensation. *This is wrong, Liba.*

I turn around and his hand falls away. I look at him. I want to drown in his eyes. They are kind and warm and brown. There is something in the air—a different kind of hum. This one bounces between us, echoing off our bodies, twined with the light puffs of steam that our breathing makes in the cold air. My eyes skim his face and fall down to look at his lips. My pulse beats and it feels like the forest around us responds with a thrum of its own. The branches seem to creep closer, and the moon shines more brightly, illuminating Dovid's face with silver light.

We hear the crack of branches and I startle. *We need to find Laya.*

"What was that?" I whisper.

Dovid puts his arm around me and pulls me close as he looks around.

"I think it was just the rustle of the wind in the trees," he says.

I nod. "Sorry. I'm just a little jumpy." I lick my lips and swallow, willing my breath to still. "I'm worried about Laya. I'll feel better when I know she's home, safe and sound." I start to walk again, but Dovid pulls me back.

"What did you see in the woods on your way to our house?" he asks, searching the trees around us with his eyes.

I swallow and take a deep breath. "I thought I heard someone following me."

"I really don't like you being out here alone…"

"Which is why I'm worried about my sister. We should keep walking. It's not the first time I've heard something strange in the woods. Yesterday I could've sworn someone was watching me too. At first I thought it was this man who approached me in the marketplace. He said his name was Ruven, he looked like a Chassid, but there was something strange about the way he looked at me. How often do strange men come to Dubossary?"

"Not very often, but recently more and more."

"Exactly."

"But it couldn't have been him tonight. It's Friday night—he would have been in *shul*, right?"

I nod.

"Except...I didn't see a man like that in *shul*," Dovid says.

"There's more than one *shul* in our town. Maybe he went to pray where Tati prays sometimes—at the *Chassidishe shtieble*."

"True."

"Something's been off for a while, Dovid. My Tati said it to me on the night of the wedding. He kept saying there was something in the air. I don't want people to think I'm crazy—but I think he's right. I feel it too. And it all started when the Hovlins came to town."

"I don't think anyone is going to think you're crazy, Liba. People are missing...I really think you should tell the *kahal*. Come to our next meeting, it's *motzei shabbes*."

I shake my head. "I'm not sure how much it will help. It's not like I understand what I feel. And I don't really have a description of anyone—just a stranger named Ruven, and all he did was buy honey from me in the marketplace. That's not really enough to make anyone guilty."

"It is in times like these."

I narrow my eyes at him. "Why?"

"Because I don't want anyone looking strangely at you..." Dovid leans forward. I think he's going to whisper something in my ear, but instead, his lips touch mine. I'm so shocked I freeze. I pull back to say, *"Dovid, no, it's* asur," but he leans forward again as if asking for permission. I move a tiny bit closer to him. I can't seem to stop myself. His lips start moving against mine before I get a chance to say anything. It feels as if he's saying, *Have you been waiting for this too?*

His lips are so soft, and my body pounds with the heat that races from our mouths down through every part of me. I feel as if I'm on fire, as if the two of us here in this copse could ignite the forest and raze it to the ground. But then I feel pain in my mouth: my teeth hurt. In response, my lips grow more insistent, pressing harder; my tongue meets his and my teeth nip at his lips. I taste blood and pull away. Panting.

I turn from him. I'm trembling. My first kiss and I drew blood. I managed to muck this up too. My face is red and flushed and my teeth ache. What's wrong with me? I tasted his blood on my tongue and every pore of my body felt like it was going to explode. *Was I going to eat him?*

"Liba?" He bends his head down and takes my chin in his hand. "Are you okay?" His eyes search mine.

"I'm sorry. I'm so sorry."

"For what?"

I'm shaking too hard to answer. I turn and run. All I want to do is get back home and find Laya. I'm terrified of nails that turn black, long teeth that grow, fur that could sprout in all the wrong places. *This was a bad idea. There's a reason these things are forbidden. To protect us. To protect him from me.* Tears stream down my face. I only want to get home and find my sister and lock the door to our cabin and never come out. *Why did Mami and Tati leave us? Why?*

Dovid catches up with me and grabs my arms.

"No! Let me go!" I cry out.

"Shh…Liba…stop…don't be afraid." He lets go. "Why are you running from me?"

I shake my head as the tears keep falling.

"I need to find my sister."

"Okay, I'm coming with you. You don't have to run."

"Did I hurt you? Please! Just tell me…" I ask him.

"Hurt me?" he says.

Everything stops around me: time, trees, leaves, air. "I did. I can tell. I'm so sorry," I say. *I am a beast, not a girl*, I want to say.

"No! No…" He looks into my eyes. "Liba, you didn't hurt me!"

"I didn't?"

He shakes his head. "I liked it," he says. "You're a fierce kisser." He waggles his eyebrows.

I shake my head and blush, trying not to laugh even though I want to. I press my hands to my eyes to stop the tears.

"Why did you run from me?" he says.

"Because I thought I bit you…I've never kissed anyone ever in my life. I thought I did it wrong…"

"You didn't do anything wrong. That was…the most amazing kiss I've ever had…"

I open my eyes, "You've had others?"

He blushes. "No."

"Oh," I say.

"Liba…you're as pretty as the moon, bright and shining. Your hair is like the night, and your lips…I've never tasted anything like them. Please don't run from me."

I can't believe his words. These are not words that have ever been meant for me. I shake my head. "Why are you saying these things?"

"What do you mean?"

"People don't say these things to me." I look down at my feet.

"Hey…" He puts his fingers on my chin and I look up at him. "You light up every room you're in, Liba. You have since you were a little girl. There's an intensity to you. You take things seriously; you watch the world and think critically about it. There's something beneath the surface of your skin that I want to learn all about. I always have."

I can't believe his words.

"Can I confess something?" he asks.

I nod.

"I've always been jealous of you and your father. The long walks you take together, the way he always seems to share his wisdom with you—I've watched the way you drink in everything he says. The way you look at him with admiration—as though he is the sun and you just want to soak in all the light he can give you."

"You were jealous of me?" I laugh. "Dovid, I've spent my life longing for the way that you and your friends can study Torah and Talmud. Wishing I was a boy so I could learn too. My Tati only started studying with me because he saw the way I looked at the yeshiva, the way I would stand outside its doors, hoping to hear what was happening inside."

"Well, *I'm* glad you're not a boy," Dovid says.

"Me too," I whisper. And for the first time, I think I might mean it.

"Touching your hand under the table set my body on fire," he says, "and kissing you just now…"

"But it's *asur*, Dovid." I swallow hard, saying the right words but not wanting to hear them.

His eyes are wide and warm and honest. "I know. But I couldn't help myself," he says. "I've been trying to get your attention for years, and that night at the wedding—it was the first time you ever even looked my way."

"What? No." I shake my head. "You're making this up." *How could he have been watching me all this time and I never noticed?*

"I'm not," he says, and his eyes are clear with the truth of his words.

"I'm sorry..." I say. "I didn't mean to be so rough. I felt this rush of feelings and my heart was racing—my blood felt like it was boiling, and I felt..." I swallow. "...like I wanted to devour you whole..."

He laughs and his whole face lights up.

My face turns red. I wrap my arms around myself. "Why are you laughing?"

"Liba..." He puts his hand on my cheek and my body starts to rage and burn again, but I don't pull away. "It's what I felt when I was kissing you too. Like I couldn't get enough. I want to get to know everything about you—inside and out. Can you give me the chance?"

"You don't understand. I don't normally break the rules like my sister does. I don't dance with boys at weddings, I'm not fun and full of life and beautiful like she is," I say in a rush.

"You are to me," he says as he strokes the side of my face with his thumb. "And I don't like dancing at weddings either—I was just hoping you'd look my way."

"Oh good, so we can not dance at weddings together," I laugh.

His eyes turn serious. "I'd like that a lot."

My eyes meet his and we stare at each other in silence.

"It's normal to feel this way about someone?" I whisper.

"Completely." He brushes a lock of hair behind my ear. "And I'm so happy right now."

"Why?"

"Because it means you feel the same way I do." He leans forward and I think he's going to kiss me again, but he doesn't. He presses his lips to my forehead and puts his arms around me.

It's the first time I've felt warm and safe since Tati left.

"Come," he says, and he reaches for my hand. "Let's go find your sister."

We walk until we reach the cottage. He kisses me again at the door, a chaste kiss this time, but still it lights my face on fire.

He waits at the door as I unlock it and go inside. Instantly, I see Laya. She's asleep in Mami and Tati's bed.

I breathe out a huge sigh of relief. "She's here," I say. "Thank God." I turn to him. "Thank you."

He grins. "The pleasure was mine." He waggles his eyebrows and I blush again. I don't think I've ever blushed so many times in one night. I didn't know my body was capable.

"So...I guess I'll see you tomorrow?" he says.

"Maybe. Be careful going home."

He takes my hand and kisses it. "I will," he says. "Goodnight, Liba of the Moon."

I close the door and collapse, my back against the wall. Too many emotions swirl inside me.

But Laya's home and safe. And that's what matters most of all.

42

Laya

My lips hurt
and my stomach aches.
I can't sleep.
I hear Liba come in.
I pretend to be asleep
until she climbs into bed
beside me.
As she sleeps,
my eyes caress the fruit
he gave me.
The basket is beside me,
but I don't think
I could eat a thing.
I've had too much wine.
Too much fruit.
And no answers.
But I just want
to kiss him again
and again
and again.

43

Liba

I startle awake and realize it's late morning. I sit up in bed, but when I see Laya sleeping beside me I'm relieved. My stomach rumbles, I'm feeling lightheaded. I watch Laya's chest rise and fall. *Poor little bird, she must be so tired.*

I don't dare wake her. It's *shabbes*. She can sleep in. I get up and make tea from water we left on the *blech* overnight. I'm about to slice myself some *babka* when I remember the meat in the icebox. I open the package of meat and moan as I chew. I feel better almost immediately. And I know in my heart it has more to do with meat than tea.

Laya is still deep in slumber. Mami always says, *When you sleep you grow.* I'll let her sleep. As long as I know where she is, my heart is calm.

I go outside to check on the cow and gather the eggs. The hens peck at me, but not Laya, never Laya; she has a way with birds…I think about the night before. Despite what Dovid said, when I tasted his blood it felt like something else. It terrifies me. Perhaps he thought it was normal, but what if the next time I kiss him I do something more? What if hair grows on my arms? What if my nails grow into claws? I don't know if I can risk it. I wish Tati was here. But even if he was, would I dare to ask him such questions? No. I would never tell him that I kissed a boy, and certainly not one he would never approve of. I must not kiss Dovid again. It's the only way to keep everyone safe.

Still Laya sleeps.

"Rise and shine, sleepyhead," I sing.

Laya's eyes twitch but she doesn't respond.

"*Gut morgen!* The day awaits! It's *shabbes*—let's go to *shul*. Sleepy *shlofkepele*, wake up, wake up!"

Laya smiles and stretches her arms up over her head.

"*Mmmore...*" she mumbles. "*...Mm...mm...more...yes... mmmm...*"

"You're dreaming, silly girl," I say. I caress her cheek, and with her eyes still closed, she sits up in bed. In an instant she's upon me. She presses her lips against mine.

"Laya! Stop!" I struggle against her. "What are you doing?!"

She opens her eyes, looks at me and in an instant, she breaks the kiss.

I laugh uncomfortably and ruffle her hair. "Must have been some dream."

She rubs her eyes and touches her lips, which look red and swollen.

Did she kiss Fedir last night? She must have. I should be angry and worried—this is my little sister whom I'm supposed to be protecting, but who am I to judge when I made the same choice last night? Neither one of us is following in Tati and Mami's path right now, and with them not here, I don't know if it's my role to police who she spends her time with. The swans haven't come—that's what I promised Mami I would protect her from. Maybe that's enough.

"*Shul* will be over soon!" I say cheerily.

"Oh," Laya says. "*Shul*. Right." She looks around as if she can't remember where she is.

"Dovid invited me to the *kahal* meeting tonight. Pinny will be there…I thought maybe you'd come with me?" I ask as she gets up and gets dressed in her *shabbes* clothes.

"Okay," she says listlessly as she sits down to sip tea. When the tea touches her lips, she winces. I swallow hard. Something is wrong. I kissed Dovid fiercely last night, but my lips don't look like hers do. But if I ask about her night she may ask about mine, and I'm not ready for anyone to know what happened between me and Dovid, so I say nothing.

We set out arm in arm for the village. But instead of chattering endlessly, Laya is silent. She gazes at the forest absently, searching all around her.

"Do you see it, Liba?" she whispers at one point.

"What?"

"All the fruit. The orchards. They're filled with light."

"What are you talking about? There are no fruit trees here," I say.

Laya rubs her eyes and looks around again. "Oh, you're right," she says.

We keep walking.

I don't know what to make of it or what to say.

I start to pay closer attention. There is a mist in the trees that the light shines through, and the branches of the trees rise around us like a crown, their arms reaching for the sky. It's a fine winter day and the snow is melting. But I don't see any fruit. There is a buzzing under everything, what I've been hearing all along, but it's quieter today, like the rushing of a distant stream. I scent the air, searching for something amiss, and that's when I smell it—something earthy, an animal scent. Musky and wild. I whip my head around, from side to side, behind me and in front again, but I don't see anything. I only feel it. I sense a pair of dark eyes, waiting and watching.

I shiver and rub my arms under my coat.

"Let's go to *shul*," I say, and pick up our pace through the woods. I want to go straight to the Great Synagogue in the center of town. It's not where Tati *davens*, but it's where the Meisels pray. I need to find Dovid. But as we reach town I feel Laya drifting in the direction of the *goyishe* marketplace—the one open on *shabbes*. Her eyes look only in one direction. I'm rushing off to find Dovid, so who am I to judge?

My heart breaks. I don't want to say the words I'm about to say—my chest feels heavy—but what can I do? I'm not Laya's mother or father...she must make her own choices. Anyway we're safe now, in town and not in the woods, not in our house where I listen endlessly for the sound of wings in the wind and bears on the prowl.

"Go there, Laya," I sigh. "I know it's *shabbes* but...go. I know you want to. Just be careful. And don't eat anything, okay? We'll meet up back here and walk home together."

Laya's eyes perk up. She smiles for the first time all morning. "Okay," she says, as if in a dream.

Which puzzles me even more. She should fight me, or smile and run in his direction. Something is wrong with my sister—I know it like I know the truth of what I am deep in my gut. I watch her walk away, listing left and right as she goes, stopping to twirl herself in a lazy circle and stumbling on.

I want to keep watching her...but I also want to talk to Dovid. I must thank his mother for last night, and give her the *babka*, and I want to tell him about Laya and what I felt this morning again in the woods. I sigh. I should also make it clear to him that he and I can never be. *It's for the best*. But somehow I know that if I try, the words won't come. Because deep inside, I don't really want to say anything at all.

44

Laya

My feet fly as if they have
wings.
Yet I wonder
why I move
so slowly.
I don't care
if it's *shabbes*—
I only want
to see Fedir again.

Did you sleep well?
he says when he sees me.
Mmmhmmm, I nod.
It is the only sound
I can make.
My lips are sore.
I feel my cheeks flush.

I clear my throat,
Did you? I ask.
Like a baby, he says,

I smile, picturing
him curled up.
Picturing me
curled up beside him.
Come by tonight? he asks.
*I can't…*I say.

Liba wants me
to go with her
to the *kahal* meeting.
But I don't tell him that.

But you must, he says,
You're all I think about.

Me too, I say.
I think of nothing else.

So come! he says.

*My sister says
it's dangerous
to be out in the woods.
People are missing.*

We heard, he says.

I wrinkle my brows
Do you know anything?
His eyes go wide.
*You haven't heard
about the murder?* he says.
What murder?

He tsks. *You're too pretty*
to worry about such things.

I don't understand.
I want to ask more
but he grabs my wrist
and tugs me back
behind the stand.
He presses me
against the stall and puts
his arms around me.
You taste like berries
and sunshine,
he whispers into my hair.
He nuzzles his head
into my neck
and I squeal.
He kisses my ear,
my neck, my collarbone,
up and up,
a trail
towards my lips.
You taste like apricots…
and wine,
he says.
I whisper back
against his neck,
You taste like fire.
I lick his neck. *And salt.*

Why do I feel this way?
Is it the wine? I ask.
He laughs. *I hope*

it's more than that.
You sure tasted like wine
last night, he says.
His lips meet mine
and I groan.
I'm sure people
can see us,
but I don't care.
I feel intoxicated,
I can't stop.

I want to ask more questions—
the word *murder* spins
around in my head—
but I can't
make out the shape
of what I want to say.

I open my mouth
to ask, but he answers
with his tongue,
and I can't get enough
of the sensation of
his lips on mine.
His tongue,
searching for mine.
His hands in my hair,
on my arms,
and lower, still lower.

45

Liba

I walk as fast as I can to the *shul*. I don't want to leave Laya for long. What if Mami and Tati come home and hear that their daughter was in the marketplace on *shabbes* morning talking to those *shkotzim*—or worse?

I wait outside the men's section of the *shul*. Soon they start to stream out. I see Dovid—I want to go to him, but I don't want to make a scene. I wait, hoping he'll see me first.

He looks up and his eyes find mine. His face lights up with a smile so wide that it breaks my heart. I feel my chest clench and I look down.

"*Gut shabbes!*" he says. "I didn't expect to see you here."

"*Gut shabbes,*" I whisper.

His father walks by. "*Gut shabbes!*" he says.

"Father, we'll just be a minute?" Dovid asks.

He grunts, "Not too long."

Dovid turns back to me. I can't stop looking at him, remembering everything. The way his lips felt, his arms holding me tight, his eyes searching mine, clear and true. My body on fire at his touch.

I shake my head. *Focus, Liba: remember what you came for.* But

I see him blush and somehow I know that he's thinking the same things about me.

"Let's walk," he says.

I follow him until we duck into a quiet little courtyard, and then into an alleyway between two buildings. He looks around, making sure that we're alone, then takes both of my hands in his. His hands are so warm and soft. I know I should end things now. There is no future for him and me. Just heartbreak. But I can't bring myself to say the words.

I open my mouth to say something, anything, but he says, "Listen, did you hear? They found Jennike's body."

"What?" My heart stops, and I feel like I can't breathe.

"In the Feldmans' orchard, down by the river. They're certain it's a bear. I'm going out with the search party tonight. I'll bring you to the *kahal* meeting and take you home afterwards. I'll come back later, when I can."

"Jennike was killed by a bear? Here? In Dubossary?"

"I know—it's crazy. Nothing ever happens here. Don't worry—I'll make sure that we search around your cabin too. I'm going to make sure that we find what it is out there before it gets anywhere near you."

"I can't believe it." *Could there be another bear in these woods? A real bear—or a bear like me?*

Dovid tugs his hand through his hair. His *kuppel* falls off. He bends down to pick it up, kisses it, and puts it back on his head. "Listen, I'm worried about you. I don't want anything to happen to you. I know that all of this is very recent, I mean, since last night—" He blushes. "—but really, it's been longer, right?"

I force a laugh. "Yes."

"Please be careful," he says. "I mean, I've known you all my life but last night I felt like I'd met you for the first time. I can't stop thinking about you. I know we barely know each other— but we sort of do. I mean…"

"I know what you mean." His stumbling words echo the things that my heart says.

Everything about being with him feels so right. He makes me laugh. I love how he's so strong and sure of himself all the time, except now when he's flustered, and I feel like it's a moment that's mine—one that only I get to see, and I like that. I don't have many secrets—only one very big one—but being here with Dovid makes me feel like I have another secret, and it's one I don't want to share with anyone else in the world. Mine. My heart says. Mine.

Dovid makes me reckless. I never could have imagined touching a boy before marriage. Not until Mami and Tati left and dropped something into my lap that changed everything. Nothing feels the same anymore, and I like the person that I am when I'm with Dovid—the way he looks at me, the way he challenges me to be brave and a little foolish. I feel like I deserve a chance to try to be a little more free—certainly before Tati comes back and my life changes yet again, maybe forever.

I see Dovid watching my eyes and it feels like he's reading in them everything I'm not saying.

And before either one of us can say anything else, he leans forward and presses his lips against mine.

This time I don't bite—well, maybe only a little.

46

Laya

I wander back
to the cottage alone.
Was I supposed to
meet my sister?
I don't remember
anymore.
All I can feel
are his lips lips lips.
I'm so thirsty.
I pick thistles
and dandelions
and weave them
into a crown.
I laugh. It looks
a little like
the crown that
Miron made for me
that day, except it's green
and white and a little
red with blood.
No matter.

I put it on my head
and hum one of the tunes
that Miron played
on the flute
last night.
I walk into the house.
Strange that
the door was open.
I close it behind me.
Soon I will
get out
of this small town.
Fedir promised.
Nothing really
matters anymore.
Except his lips
on mine.
I turn around
and then I see
a bear.
There's a bear
in the cabin
with me.
"Liba?" I say
but the bear doesn't answer.
My heart beats so fast
I feel as if it will leap
out of my chest.
My shoulders ache
and my arms buzz
all over. I back away
and reach for the door
and when I look

at my arm
I see wisps
of white feathers
starting to bloom.
I scream
and open the door
and run out.
I hear a noise
like a honk
and look up—
there's a swan
in a nearby tree.
I climb
up the tree,
but when I reach it,
the swan
takes off
and flies away.

47

Liba

"Come join us for lunch," Dovid says, his breath hot against my cheek.

This is all moving too fast, I know it, yet I can't seem to stop.

"I can't. Your mother didn't invite me," I say.

The closeness of him awakens everything inside me. I feel wild and free for the first time ever. I don't want these feelings to end.

"Don't be ridiculous." He puts his fingers on my chin and tilts my face up so that my eyes meet his. "Of course you're invited." There is so much sincerity in his eyes, so much truth and simple goodness. "Mother's *cholent* is the best in town," he grins, and his dimple appears.

I reach up my hand and touch the place where his cheek becomes indented, then pull my hand away and shake my head. *Now, Liba, tell him now. Stop this madness. You know better.* "I have to go home and eat with my sister. I need to talk to her about last night. Dovid, I…"

"I love that about you…"

"What?"

"How much you care about your sister. I know it means that that's how you'll care for your own family someday. It means a lot to me. I'm so close to my brothers."

"Dovid, stop!" My head suddenly hurts and my heart races. I'm scared, but I don't know why. "I have to go."

"Okay," he sighs, and tucks a lock of hair behind my ear. "I'll pick you up tonight? Before the meeting?"

I nod, even though I shouldn't.

"I have to go," I say.

He nods. "Be careful." He leans over and pecks me on the lips.

My lips part and I kiss him back. Being with Dovid makes me feel more. Brave. Like I could stand up to my parents someday and tell them how I feel, what I want.

I pull away from him and turn to go before I make an even bigger fool out of myself.

"*Gut shabbes*, Liba!" I hear him call out as I walk away.

I can't help but smile as I walk as fast as I can to the place I said I'd meet Laya. But when I get there, she isn't there. I wait for an hour, watching the townsfolk go about their business. I watch couples walking arm in arm—it almost looks natural, like we Jews are the only ones who do things differently. *Why shouldn't a man and woman hold hands if they choose to?* I see mostly people walking home from synagogue, and non-Jews making Saturday purchases. It's obvious that everyone knows about Jennike: people are walking a bit faster, looking right and left and nearly sprinting home, relief clear on their faces when they open the door to their homes.

I wait for Laya for what seems like forever, but she doesn't show. I put the hood of my coat up over my face and walk quickly over to the fruit stand, hoping that no one sees me. I can't believe I'm going to the marketplace on *shabbes*. *I'm adding sin upon sin in my father's absence. What has become of my good sense?* But when I get there, I don't see Laya.

I look for Fedir through the crowd—all non-Jewish neighbors of ours, people I know, people I've seen in town. Already I hear the whispers. *Murdered? Can you believe it?* The crowds are abuzz with the terrible news. "They say it was a bear, but I heard it was a Jew," I hear someone say and I turn my head. *Who said that?* I keep walking, turning this way and that in the crowd. I pick up the voice again—or is it a different voice? "The Jews think they're better than we are. They avoid our shops. Did you hear what I heard? It must have been a ritual. Last night was Friday night. Who knows what they do in those synagogues. I bet they use blood." I can't believe my ears. I turn and see that it's Vasyl Tsulenko, the greengrocer.

"I heard they're training a militia—I see them on patrol," I hear Anton Gutzo, the clockmaker say. "Perhaps this is just the beginning. Next they'll need more blood."

Why are people saying these things? I don't understand. I nudge my way through them, looking for Fedir. "The Jews have all the jobs," I hear Sophia Katyuk, the milliner's wife, say. "That's why my son Denis is unemployed. He came back from the army, and there's nothing left for him here. And as if that isn't enough, now they're murdering us. If the Jews left Dubossary, we would all be better off."

My eyes well up with tears. These people are our friends, our neighbors. Why would they say such things?

I finally get to the front of the stand and I see Fedir. His eyes find mine. "Where is my sister?" I whisper.

He shrugs. "She was here earlier. She must have wandered off."

"Don't lie to me." I raise my voice, not caring if I make a scene. "Where did she go?"

His eyes suddenly change. They pin me where I stand. "I said she was here earlier, and she isn't here now. Do not accuse me of lying. You Jews are all the same," he spits.

I'm shocked. I don't know what to say. I swallow hard. "Okay," I say, scared by the look I see in his eyes. "Okay."

I run all the way home. The branches of the trees feel like

they are all in my way—separating me from my sister, grab-
bing at my arms and legs, trying to stop me, to prevent me from
getting to her. I feel them lashing at my face and arms, trying to
trip me. A vine tangles itself around my wrist and I have to rip
free. *Something is wrong; something happened to her—I feel it in
my heart, in the air. Just let her be home and safe,* I pray. *And if she
is, I'll never sin again.* Shema Yisroel, I say. *Please God, open my
lips so my words will declare your praise. Hear my prayer and listen
to me, Lord—I will not sin again with these lips and with my hands.
Just let Laya be safe.*

When I burst through the front door, I see Laya sleeping in
the rocking chair.

"*Danken Got!*" I say, breathless. But there is a scent in the air
that I can't shake. *Someone was here. Something was inside. I know
that smell.* My heart struggles to catch up with my mind. My skin
grows cold and I slump down onto the floor. *It's the scent of a bear.
It was here, in this house, and I wasn't here to protect her.*

She opens her eyes and blinks and looks around the room, as
if she isn't quite sure where she is.

"Laya! Are you okay?" I get up and rush over to her, taking
her in my arms.

"There was a bear, Liba. I came home and the door was open."
She's trembling.

"Shhh…"

"I ran out, and then there was a swan. It saved me. I followed
it up a tree and waited for the bear to go. But I was so scared and
my skin…my back…it's starting, Liba…I felt it. There were
feathers…"

*A bear? Did it come for me? But why? And a swan? Are these
the swans that Mami said would come for her? Things are happening too fast.*

"You disappeared. We said we'd walk home together."

She starts rocking again. She starts to hum and twirl a crown of thistles between her fingers. I look down and see that her fingers are covered in blood.

"Your fingers! What happened?"

She looks down and sees the blood. She shrugs. "I didn't notice." She tosses the thistle crown to the floor. "Let's make tea."

"First let's dress your fingers." I take hot water from the kitchen and strips of white cloth. "Did you hear about Jennike?"

She nods.

I don't know what to say.

"I went to the market to find you. They're saying horrible things about the Jews. Fedir…he wasn't nice to me." I want to find the words to tell her what he said to me, but I don't even know how to begin.

"You've never liked him," Laya says coldly, and I feel her pull away from me.

"Laya-bell, that's not true," I say, even though it is. *She's right: I don't trust Fedir at all.* "I'm just…worried about you."

"They won't find her," Laya says.

"What? Who?" I stop what I'm doing and look at her.

"Jennike."

"What do you mean? They found her in the Feldmans' orchard. What do you know?"

She shakes her head.

I take her fingers in mine and clean them. "Laya, look at me. What do you know about Jennike?"

She stares past my head at something I can't see. "I don't know what you're talking about."

"But you just said…" I wrap her fingers in mine. "If you know anything, you should tell the *kahal*."

She's still looking past my shoulder. I turn to look at what she sees, but there's nothing there. Just a cat at the window.

I stomp my foot and hiss at it, but it doesn't move.

"One day I will grow wings and leave you," Laya whispers.

"What?" My heart plummets.

She shakes her head from side to side.

"Laya, you're scaring me," I say.

She doesn't stop.

"Laya!" I take her head in my hands. Her head stops, but her body is shaking. I help her to our parents' bed, cover her in a blanket and lie down beside her, cradling her trembling body in my arms.

What now? I think. *What sort of sickness is this? Should I fetch a doctor?* I get up and pace around the cottage, not knowing what to do.

I pile more blankets on top of Laya, and she seems to stop shaking. Maybe she just has a fever. I'll wait it out. No need to get someone on *shabbes*.

I tie bundles of lavender to the windowsills to rid the house of the smell of the bear, and spend the rest of the day reading one of Tati's books of Talmud, losing myself in the arguments about the waxing and waning of the moon. I watch Laya sleep, drifting in and out of a dream, whispering nonsensical things. The ancient arguments help me understand what is happening around me. They remind me that in every generation Jews have struggled with an enemy, and they have always found a way to prevail because they kept the commandments and followed the laws and let the Torah be their guide. People are scared by what happened to Jennike and the disappearance of the Glazers, that's all. The Talmud reminds me that just like we wait each month for the sliver of the crescent moon, and it comes without fail, the sky going from darkness to light, so too will we see the end of this. The *kahal* will work with the police to get to the bottom of things and everything will go back to normal. What I don't find in the pages of the book is what to do when you know there was a bear in your house, or when your sister follows a swan up a tree, or what to do when you're scared because you are a bear, when as much as you want to protect your sister and everyone around you, you really have no idea where to even begin.

When the sun sets, there's a knock at the door.

I walk on tiptoe and peek out the window. "Dovid!" I say, as I open the door.

"I came as soon as my father said *havdallah*."

Before he can say any more I launch myself at him and his arms are suddenly around me. I can't help myself. I spent the day alone, and I don't know what's wrong with Laya. I'm scared about the bear, and the things I heard in the marketplace. I'm worried about Laya, and with his arms holding me close I feel less alone. As he holds me, I start to cry.

He lets go and takes my face in his hands, wiping away my tears with his thumbs. "Liba, what's wrong?"

"It's Laya. She's not well. And she says…she came back here and there was a bear in the house."

"A bear? Liba, you have to move in with us. I don't care what people say—I won't let you stay out here anymore like this. It's *sakanas nefashos*; your lives are in danger!"

He looks over at Laya and sees her as I see her, asleep but not asleep.

"How long has she been like this?"

"Since I got back. We were in town. After I saw you I went to meet her, but she never showed up. I…went to the marketplace to look for her…Dovid, they're saying horrible things. You won't believe what I heard. They think we had something to do with Jennike's murder because she was found in the Feldmans' orchard. The *kahal* has to do something! I ran all the way home and when I got here she was in that chair just rocking and rocking. She said she ran from the bear and climbed a tree until it left the house. When she came back in and locked the door, she couldn't stop shaking."

"Has she eaten?" Dovid crosses the room to Laya's side.

"I've tried everything, tea, *babka*, nuts…"

"Fruit?"

My eyes meet his.

"The *kahal* cancelled the meeting tonight. They're redoubling their search, together with the police and the non-Jewish men from the village. I'm supposed to be out with them now; I took two shifts. We will get to the bottom of this, Liba. We will find that bear and rid our forest of the threat. I'll be around all night so I'll check back in with you when I can, but I must go tell the others what happened here. If you think she needs to see the doctor, I can go get him too."

"She said something strange about Jennike," I say.

His eyes go wide. "What?"

"She said they'd never find her. But I told her that the police found her body. I tried to get her to tell me what she knows, but she won't say anything more."

"What do you think she knows?"

"I don't know." I frown.

"Should I ask my mother to come here? I can go get her now. I hate the thought of the two of you alone out here."

"It's okay. We take care of ourselves."

He raises one eyebrow.

"What? We do! This is just…" I wave my hands in the direction of the bed. "People get sick. It happens all the time."

"And bears wander the woods and enter people's homes? These are not normal times."

"I don't know what to do."

"Maybe I should get my father. What she knows might be important."

"I know, but if she won't say anything to me, I doubt she'll talk to your father."

"I should go get my mother. Maybe she'll talk to her."

"Are you sure?"

"You take care of Laya and I'll take care of you. And I think you should have some company. Bar the door behind me and try to get her to tell you what she knows, okay? I still think that you two should move in with us for now."

"I don't know. But thank you, Dovid," I say.

"I don't like this, Liba. I don't like it at all."

"I know."

"I'll be back soon," he says, and runs out.

I feel ashamed. He doesn't know what I am. I'm a bear, just like the one in the woods.

A few seconds after Dovid leaves, I change my mind. I rush to the front door and open it. I want to call after him to tell him not to bother, not to bring his mother, that I don't need their help. I'm a bear, what could I possibly have to fear? Another bear? But the words refuse to come. The cold air swallows them.

I look back at Laya. Maybe I'll draw her a bath. I lock the door behind me and walk down to the river to get some water. *I have nothing to fear.* I tell myself. *I'm a bear.* Maybe if I repeat it enough, it will feel true.

I walk through the orchard between our house and the river. The trees are not yet in bloom, but they will be. I see the ripening of shoots, the little buds on branches breaking through and searching for the light of the sun. It's the most beautiful place when all the fruits are heavy on the trees. A magical glen.

I think about the fruit that Laya thought she saw when we were walking. Clearly she imagined that. Maybe she imagined what she saw happen to Jennike too? The forest has never betrayed us before. As I wash my hands and fill a bucket, a fish swims by. Before I know what I'm doing, my hand is in the river, swiping at it. The river is ice-cold and my hand feels frozen, but I still catch it on the first try. I've never done anything like this before, but it seems natural, like I've been fishing this way my whole life. When I lift my hand I see that I've speared the fish with five long and ugly claws. I scream and drop it back in the river. I run all the way home, cradling my hand. When I arrive, I see that the front door is wide open. I run inside, heart racing. I see the empty bed. Laya is gone.

48

Laya

I see her leave.
She goes outside,
busy with some chore
or another.
She won't notice
if I'm gone.
I'm here
but not here.
I slip the key
from my pocket
and unlock the door.

I walk until I reach
the old oak tree.
The pine leaves part for me
like curtains.
They steer me
to the clearing.
The needles feel good
against my skin.
I see the orchard ahead,

full of heavy fruit
that glistens with dew.
I feel the pulse
of the land;
it pumps life-blood
into the trees,
the sap of the trees
rushing to fill
the fruit
full to bursting.
I touch my wrist
to a tree, wanting
to feel the throb
against my skin,
wanting it
to fill me up too.
Tendrils of green vine
reach for my wrist
and strap themselves
around my fingers,
I gasp and pull
my hand away.

I turn and see
Fedir, waiting for me.
I run into his arms.
My sister said
terrible things, I tell him.
She said that Jennike
is dead, murdered,
but I saw her here last night.

Sometimes, he says,
our siblings can betray us.
Come, there's something
I want to show you.

Where are we going? I ask.
He grins. *I made us a picnic.*
I love picnics, I say.
Fedir kisses me on the nose
and takes my hand.
You are not meant
for life here
in this village, he says.
When we leave this town
you will come with us.
It's a wonderful way
to live. Never grounded,
never obligated
to anyone
or anything.

I like the sound of that, I say.
He leads me a short way
into the forest
to a blanket.
Golden trays of fruit
and wine are waiting.
Come, sit, he says,
All this for me? I ask.
The world for you, he says.
I blink my eyes
and see the sun
shining down on us,

but then a flap of wings
obscures the light—
a large white bird.
I look down and see
the forest floor,
a threadbare blanket,
a rotten apple,
and a moldy cup.
I look back up
to the sky
but the bird is gone
and everything is
as it was.

Fedir is there
beside me.
He touches
his lips
to the back
of my neck
and brings his arms
around me.
He holds
a wooden goblet
full of wine
in front of me.
I drink.
I close my eyes
and savor it,
feeling alive again.

This may be a sin,
but if so, then

I'm a sinner.
I turn around
and face Fedir.
His lips
meet mine mine mine.

I drink him in.
Sucking at his lips
like I can never
get enough
of the sensation.
More! I say.
He laughs. *Is that
your favorite word?*
With you it is, I say.
my voice is hoarse.
I feel my body flush
from head to toe.
I lean in for another kiss.

But his finger
is on my lips.
Wait, he whispers.
Let me feed you.
I wish to treat you
like a queen.

I open my mouth.
He places an apricot
between my teeth.
This apricot is sweet
and tart like you, he says.
Juice drips down my chin.

He leans forward
and licks his way up
from my chin
to my lips.

Apricots are my favorite,
I say between kisses.
I take another bite,
and suck the juice
from my fingers.
Fedir stops me.
He takes my hand in his
and licks my fingers.

He feeds me more fruit
and we kiss until our faces
and fingers are sticky
and wet wet wet.

49

Liba

I climb the ladder. I check under the blankets. I go back outside, circle the house three times; I even go down to the stream. I can't find her.

Where could she have gone? I wonder with rising panic, thinking about the state that she was in—not fit to walk, or run, or fly...

Who took her?

I grab my cloak and tear off into the woods, running. Maybe I can still save her before it's too late.

I run straight into something large and strong, but it's not a tree. It's a man. I open my mouth to scream, but his hand covers half my face.

My blood runs cold. *This is it,* I think. *This is how I meet my end.*

"Shhh..." he says. "Don't be afraid."

My heart beats so fast I feel like it will burst out of my chest.

I recognize him. The man from the village. Ruven. *Is he the one that took Laya? And Jennike?* Another man comes up beside him. He's broader and older, with a gray and white beard. He's also dressed like Ruven, and he grins when he sees me.

Maybe the townsfolk were right to blame the Jews, I think, and that scares me most of all.

"Who are you?" I say against his hand, my teeth suddenly feeling sharper, wanting to bite him.

"We knew your father," the older man says. His voice is gruff. "I'm Alter, and this here is Ruven, but I think you met him already."

I swallow. *Should I yell? Can I scream and alert the men patrolling the woods? But I want to know if they took Laya. Where they took her.*

"What do you want?" I say against his hand. *He's a Chassid. He shouldn't be touching me. This is wrong. So wrong.*

"Where is he?" Ruven asks. "I'm going to remove my hand. Please don't scream."

"Who?" I say, still muffled.

"Your father," he says.

I spit at him when he removes his hand. "I should scream," I say. "The *kahal* is out. It's only a matter of time before they find you. Tell me what you've done with my sister. And Jennike."

"Your sister?" Ruven huffs. "I didn't take your sister. But there was a girl with white-blonde hair I saw a little while ago. She was with a *goy* in the woods. If that's your sister, you should tell her to watch the company she keeps."

Nothing makes sense. Are they telling the truth? "Who are you and what do you want?"

"I'll say it again: we're looking for your father," Alter says.

"Is he in trouble?"

"Trouble?" Alter grunts. "I hope not. We just wanted to speak to him. We're from Kupel."

"Kupel!" My heart lurches.

"Yes." Ruven nods. "It's where he's from."

"I know..." I say, and I hear my voice trembling. "My Tati went to Kupel..." I tell them, not sure if I'm saying the right thing. Not sure if I should tell these men anything at all, or admit that Laya and I are alone in the woods, without our parents to protect us...

"Interesting..." Alter says.

"Where are you off to?" Ruven asks. "The woods aren't safe."

"Have you been watching me?" I don't answer his question.

"Like we said, we've been looking for Berman," Alter grunts.

I shrug. "Well, he's not here right now, so you can stop following me."

"You didn't answer my question," Ruven says. "Where are you off to?"

"*Es iz nit dayn gesheft,*" I say. *Nowhere that concerns you.* I look away as if I'm ashamed. "To town. To see…my boyfriend." *I'll deflect their attention.*

"Your boyfriend?" Ruven replies.

"Yes," I say to him. "Actually, he's supposed to come back here any minute." I don't like the way they look at me.

Is Tati in trouble?

"I must be going," I say.

Alter nudges Ruven, "*Der emess iz der bester lign*—she must be telling the truth. I can't imagine her father would approve of a boyfriend—from here no less."

Ruven narrows his eyes. "You're not worried about your sister?"

"Have you been following her too?" I bark at him. "Maybe I should just go straight to town and find the leader of the *kahal.*"

Alter laughs. "The *kahal* isn't going to do anything about us, child."

"Fine. I told you the truth. My father's not here. Now leave me alone." I put up my hood. From deep inside my chest I feel a rumbling. There are icy prickles all over my skin. I don't like these men, and I will definitely say something to a member of the *kahal.* I walk away from them and take deep breaths as I go. I force the prickles down under my skin. I swallow again and again until my chest feels better. I pull my cloak tight and snug around me and set back off at a brisk pace. *Better not run for now,* I tell myself. I don't want them to be suspicious, even though everything inside me feels like I should flee.

50

Laya

I lie back on the blanket, still
sucking on my sticky fingers.
Fedir drops a grape into my
mouth. I gulp it down
but stop the next one.
*I don't think I can eat
another bite*, I say.

Fedir pouts. There is
mischief in his eyes.
He lies down beside me
and we kiss some more.
He stares into my eyes
and picks a leaf out of my hair
that looks golden.
I look up and see
a canopy of trees above us
and all the leaves
are silver
and gold.

Come live with me
and be my wife, he says.

I sit up. *What?*
You heard me, he says.
Be mine forever.
I wrinkle my nose.
But I just met you.

I'll build us a house,
next to our lodge
a little ways away,
in the forest, he says.
His eyes are crystal
clear and green
and I want so badly
to believe him
but I don't know
what I want.

You're meant
for me, he says.

How can you know
for sure? I ask.
He takes my hands in his.
I love you, Laya.
I've never felt this way
about anyone before.
You're as pretty as a swan
and fierce, but kind.

A swan? I think.
How does he know?

I remember
my sister, Liba,
my mother,
and Saint Anna
of the Swans.
I blink my eyes
and up above
the leaves are
brown and green
not gold.

You don't belong here,
Fedir says, and trails
a finger
down my neck.
You belong with others
like yourself.

He's right,
I think,
then shake my head.
What does he mean by that?

He places
my hand
on his heart.
Look at me, he says.
I look. And all
is gold again.

I swear it.
Upon my blood.
He bites his thumb

with teeth that suddenly
look sharper
than they should.
Blood pools.

I shudder.
Then think,
That's how much
he loves me,
so much
that he bites
his own thumb.

Give me yours,
he says.
I stretch out
my hand.
You are pricked
already! How?

I was playing
with a thistle, I say.
Making a crown.
Teach me
the magic
of the trees.

I will, he says,
All that and so much more.
He kisses my thumb
and nips it gently,
pressing my thumb to his

and as our blood mingles.
I feel a rush that goes
straight to my head.
I fall into his arms
and everything goes
black black black.

51

Liba

I run straight to the Heimovitz house, where Dovid said the *kahal* usually meets, but nobody's there. Of course. I knew that. Still, I was hoping someone would be home. I go next to Rabbi Borowitz's house. His wife, Rebbetzin Faygie, answers, but the Rabbi's not home either. "They're all off looking for the bear," she says, wringing her hands.

I find myself in front of the Meisels' house. I know that Dovid isn't there and neither is his father. But maybe Mrs. Meisels will know who's around, who I can tell. I knock on the door.

I hear a voice. The door opens. "Liba? *Vos iz mit dir?* What happened? Come inside, *maydele*. Quick. *Arein.*"

"I'm so sorry, Mrs. Meisels. I didn't know where else to go…"

"Come sit by the fire, dear."

I follow her inside and the smell of meat overwhelms me. My stomach rumbles and I feel the cut of sharper teeth in my mouth. I stop in my tracks. Suddenly I don't trust myself. "I should go… I'm sorry to have bothered you."

"*Narishkeit.* Tell me what's wrong."

It all tumbles out of me. "My sister came home earlier and found a bear in our house."

"*Oy vey iz mir,*" Mrs. Meisels says.

"She's okay—she climbed a tree, and the bear left, but now she's shaking and trembling with fever. I ran down to the river to get water to draw her a bath, and when I got back she was gone. I tried to run and follow her trail, but…these men in the woods stopped me—" My voice cracks. "I don't know who they are. They said they're looking for my Tati, but they scared me. Maybe they took Laya? They said they saw her walk off into the woods with someone else. Maybe they were lying to me? What if they killed Jennike? I ran straight here to find Donniel Heimovitz or Rabbi Borowitz or someone from the *kahal* to tell them. But nobody's around."

"*Hashem yishmor*, what kind of men were they?"

"They looked like Chassidim, like my father. But when my sister was shivering with fever, she mumbled something about Jennike. I don't know what Laya knows. I could be wrong— maybe Laya is out with one of the Hovlin boys—but she was in no state to go out. I know the *kahal* is out there hunting for a bear. What if they shoot Laya by mistake? What if…?"

"Slow down, slow down. You're making no sense. Just sit and eat a bit. *Essen*. Food always makes me feel better. There's no use going back out there. You're safe here. The men are out, yes, but they'll be back, and they can handle some strange men in the woods, *nishtgedeiget*. They can tell the difference between a girl and a bear, *maydele*. And perhaps they'll even find your sister. There's no better searching you could hope for than all those men out there, combing the woods. *Husht* now. There's nothing more you can do."

"No, but I must!" I stand up. "She's my sister! My responsibility! I've already failed my parents in so many ways…she's seeing that *goy*…I've done everything wrong, and she's all I have left."

"Liba!" Mrs. Meisels grabs my arm like she means business. "I forbid it. *Gott in himmel!* How old are you?"

"Nearly eighteen."

"Seventeen and living all alone in that big forest? And your sister? Just sixteen, isn't she?"

"Nearly sixteen…"

"I don't know what your parents thought, leaving you girls, Rebbe or no, but I will tell you something: no seventeen-year-old should ever bear that kind of burden, and they should not have left you alone in the woods, not in times like these."

I shake my head. "They didn't know."

"I know that your parents like to keep themselves apart, and I know that they have their reasons, this town hasn't been particularly welcoming to them, especially your mother, but that doesn't mean that we don't take care of our own. It's a *shunda.* What if something happened to you, *chas v'shalom!* What if one of those men had harmed you?"

I shake my head. "The Glazers were supposed to be…"

She shakes her head. "*Gott in himmel,* maybe these men are responsible for the Glazers' disappearance too? Who knows? Desperate times make for all kinds of criminals. I forbid you to go out there again. We are going to lock all the doors and windows right now and huddle down on the sofa in front of the fire with a cup of tea and wait for the men to come back."

I feel helpless. I can't believe that Laya's gone. Why did I leave the house? Why did I go to the river for water? I never should have left her side. I can't help the tears that come. Nothing feels like it will ever be the same again.

"Sit, *maydele.* Let me get us something hot to drink, a bowl of soup to eat, and you can tell me everything again, from the beginning. I don't have a daughter, only sons, and I'm in need of female company tonight."

She serves me and I can't help but dig in. I don't remember the last time I ate. I eat until the hunger fades, but this time, the ache in my gut doesn't go away.

"I don't like those Hovlin boys any more than you do," Mrs. Meisels says, "but I don't think they're at fault here. They're just young men, full of beans and mischief. I don't know who those strange men from Kupel were, but your sister has her head on right. Sleep here tonight. Let me take care of you. When Dovid comes home, I'll bed him up with one of his brothers."

"But what if Laya goes back home and I'm not there? What if the bear comes back?"

"I'm not letting you go back out there, do you understand me?" She raises her voice. "Your parents may be gone but some-one needs to tell you what's what."

We sit in silence by the fire waiting for the men to come home, but everything catches up with me and soon I find myself nod-ding off. I lie down on the sofa and try so hard to keep my eyes open, but my body won't let me. Mrs. Meisels ushers me up the stairs and to Dovid's bed. It smells like cedar and wood smoke and falling leaves. "I'll wake you when they get back home," she promises, and kisses my forehead.

As I fall back asleep, my mind races. *I still don't understand why they're looking for Tati.* I'm worried about Laya, but I'm grateful for company, for the safety of a home. Mrs. Meisels is right: there's nothing I can do about it now. Not with those men out there. Not with a bear in our house. It's better if I stay put. I'll just close my eyes for a bit, until Dovid gets back. He can go with me to find Laya.

I dream that I'm fishing in a stream for wild salmon. I wade in up to my knees and feel the cool stones beneath my feet, the rush of water, and as a fish swims near and slips between my ankles, it's as if every muscle of my body knows what to do. I reach one hand down and—lightning fast—I swipe at the fish and catch it. Just like I did in the woods. It's only when I bring the still-writhing fish up out of the water that I see I've mauled the fish straight through.

I wake up with a gasp and look down at my hands. My fingers are claws again. I quickly hide them under the blankets. *I must leave this house. I am a danger to everyone. What if I hurt Mrs. Meisels?*

I wait until my big bear heart stops thundering in my chest and I get up, careful to keep my hands in my pockets. I tiptoe down the stairs and see Mrs. Meisels snoring by the fire. I put on my coat, unlock the door and step out of the house. I take off at a run, hoping that if I'm fast enough, no one will stop me. My hands want to touch the earth; my toes want to feel the forest floor beneath my feet; I feel like I can smell and taste every aspect of the forest. As air cycles through my nose and into my lungs, I suddenly know every tree and plant; I can sense every creature around me. Something is wrong in the forest. I can smell rot, something coppery, almost like blood. My body churns with raw energy, my fingernails are full-out claws, and the fur on my coat matches the brown pelt that has partially sprouted on my arms and legs. My teeth are long and sharp, my nose perhaps a bit more snout-like, my eyes so wide that I take in elements around me I never noticed before—places where I know creatures have burrowed for the winter, scratches against tree bark marking territory, and trees that part the way for me, their branches like a curtain pulling back, revealing endless wilderness. I feel like I could just keep running, so dark and deep and wide is the Kodari. But I must focus on the scent of home. I'm no longer scared of myself—all thoughts of *I don't want to be a bear* are gone and replaced by a feeling of power. A feeling of rightness. A knowledge that nothing will get in my way because tonight I have claws and teeth.

But when I finally find myself on the threshold of home I stand up and see that my skin is white and whole again, and I stop and look up at the moon, tears streaming down my face. I'm not sure if I'm crying because of the relief I felt to just let myself go—to let myself be free—or because I finally became the thing I never wanted to be—a beast. I wrap my coat around me for warmth and open the door.

I'm surprised to find Laya fast asleep in our parents' bed, as if it had all been a dream. I swallow hard and rub my eyes. *Did I imagine everything? Was she here all along? What is happening to me?*

I crawl into bed beside her and wrap my thick limbs around my sister's thin ones. Something changed in me tonight, and somehow I know I won't hurt Laya. She means everything to me. I burrow my coal-black hair into the pillow beside my sister's golden locks. I don't think of anything but the fact that she's here and safe and whole and in my arms. I fall asleep.

52

Laya

I wake up, throat parched.
Liba is asleep beside me.
I detangle myself from her arms
and pour myself some water.
I drink a full glass
but I'm still thirsty.
My fingers are
sore sore sore,
and my lips
and other parts
of my body
that I didn't know
could feel sore.

I drink again,
and again,
but nothing quenches
my thirst.
My throat burns,
and my stomach
churns from hunger.

There is only one thing
I crave.

I scratch my back
in the same two places
that always itch,
and watch my sister sleep.
Tears fall from my eyes.

53

Liba

The door to our cottage bursts open and I wake with a start. "Who's there?"

"You're here!" Dovid says.

"Dovid! It's…it's morning…are you all right?"

His eyes are red-rimmed; his lips are faintly pink—they look cold and parched. He licks them and clears his throat.

"I see you found your sister."

"Just now. I mean, I came back last night and she was here, so yes."

"Mother said you came to visit. She said you fell asleep in my bed, but she woke up and you were gone. We thought…" His voice cracks. "Liba…I thought you were gone too…" His eyes glisten with tears. "You worried her. You worried me," he says.

"I'm so sorry…"

"I was scared that something happened…" He rubs his sleeve across his eyes.

My heart clenches. "I didn't mean…" I shake my head. "I didn't think."

He licks his lips again and nods, but then he looks away. *I was so worried about Laya, about myself, that I forgot there are other people who care for me now too…*

"Come in—please sit down…" I don't know what to say.

Laya is already up on her feet. "I'll make tea."

His curly hair looks tossed from wind and weather. *Like brown sheep's wool I'd like to run my fingers through…*

"What's wrong?" he says.

"Nothing. I was…just looking at you. Sorry. It seems as though I've lost my head. It was a strange night."

"Indeed."

I cringe. His mother must have been out of her mind with worry.

"Did you find anything out there?" I ask.

"Nothing. More of a feeling in the trees, like something was watching us. We all felt it. Like a prickly sensation in our bones, especially out past the old oak tree. Mother told me that you bumped into some men?"

Laya freezes in place. "What men?"

"They said they were looking for Tati," I explain. "One of them was that man, Ruven, who bought honey from us in the market square."

My eyes meet Laya's across the room.

"What were their names again?" Dovid asks.

"Ruven and Alter," I answer.

"No last names?" he asks.

I shake my head.

Laya brings over the pot and two mugs. "Will you have some tea?" she says.

Dovid nods and quips, "It'll save me the trouble of having to go back home and explain to my mother that I came all this way to check on you and you didn't even offer me something to drink." He grins and looks at me, but I see that the smile doesn't reach his eyes. "You never know, my mother might be on her way here now to scold you and ask why you didn't even offer her son a hot drink after he was up all night searching the forest for you two."

I can't help but smile a bit. "She wouldn't…" I say.

"My mother's a formidable woman," he says.

"It was a terrible thing I did last night, leaving like that. I don't know what I was thinking." *If he cares so much about me, what will happen when he finds out what I am? When I tell him that there's no way that he and I can be together?* I fold my hands down in my lap and look at them. "She was perfectly lovely to me last night."

"You must still be on her good side." Dovid winks and takes a sip of tea.

"Your bed was very comfortable last night."

My sister's eyebrows rise. "And where were you going to sleep when you got home, Dovid?"

He shrugs his shoulders and says, "With my younger brother, Benji. I don't mind."

The words hang in the air.

"So—tea?" Laya's voice rings out.

"Yes, please," I say, and laugh nervously.

"Maybe I should go outside for a walk?" Laya says.

"No!" Dovid and I both counter simultaneously.

"It's cold out there," I say.

"I should be going anyway," he says.

"But you just got here!" I say, and I put my hand on his. Laya looks at my hand; Dovid looks at my hand. I put it back in my lap.

"Why don't the two of you go for a little walk while I clean up here?" Laya offers. "You can accompany him part of the way back to the village."

"No, I won't go that far. I'll just walk you out," I say. "Laya, we'll just be right in front of the door." *There's no way I'm leaving Laya alone again.*

"Okay," Dovid says.

As soon as we're outside, I take his hand in mine. He brings it to his lips and kisses it.

"Are you okay?" He brings me close to his chest.

"Yes…" I take a deep breath. "Follow me," I say. *We'll just go behind the house, not far…*

I feel like I need to see the river. My inner compass takes me there. When I can see it, everything makes sense. The water pulses through the forest like blood through a vein and the sound clears my head.

"Mother said you ate like a bear." Dovid grins, this time with more feeling.

"That's an embarrassing thing for a mother to say."

"Heh. I guess it is. I don't think she meant it that way. I think she meant to say that you were hungry—both of you must be—living out here all on your own."

I shrug my shoulders.

"It's nothing to be ashamed of."

I rub my arms nervously. *This is where I tell him. Right now, Liba.*

"Hey…" Dovid stops and turns my face to his. He put his hands on my arms to warm them. "Liba. Hunger is nothing to be ashamed of. Your parents shouldn't have left you like they did."

"They did what they had to do."

"But you're only…how old are you?"

I turn away from him. "I'm old enough."

"Well, I'm eighteen and I still rely on my parents for all sorts of things. I can't imagine living alone yet."

"I'm not alone. I have my sister. And my parents are coming back."

"Mother said that Laya was gone. That you feared her missing."

"I did."

"Was she with Fedir again?"

I sigh. "It's not like the whole town doesn't know."

"Those boys are good fun and I know all the girls like them, but there's something off about them."

"I know."

"The whole town searched for bears in the woods last night too, and not one of them made an appearance to help. Strange, isn't it?"

"I didn't know that." I shiver. "That's very strange."

"Do you find them attractive? Do you desire that fruit?"

"Dovid! I would never! How could you think that of me?"

"Just curious." He shrugs. "All the other women in our town seem to be enamored with them."

"They're not my type. And my father would never approve of me behaving like that with a *goy*." I blush. "Well, with any-one really."

"He won't approve of me, you mean."

I close my eyes. "I didn't say that."

"But it's what you meant."

"Dovid, my father…he's very particular. He…well, to be honest, I think he plans to look for someone for me in Kupel."

I see Dovid's face fall. "Is that what you want?" he says, his voice soft.

I shake my head. "No. I thought…my whole life I thought that I did. But…things are different now."

"What's changed?"

I look up at him. "I found you." I can't believe the words I'm saying, but as they leave my mouth, I know they're true. And I don't want to take them back.

Dovid pulls me into a hug and holds me tight against his chest. "If I was a father, I would want my daughter to be happy," he says into my hair.

I laugh and look up at him. "That only works if your daughter isn't Laya," I say.

"What about those men you saw?"

I shake my head. "I honestly don't know who they are. They said they came here looking for my father. They're from Kupel—but that's where he went. It doesn't make any sense."

"I don't like it at all."

"Neither do I. Listen, I have to go back inside and take care of Laya."

"Looks to me like Laya takes care of herself."

I shake my head. "I know she seemed better just now, but she could barely lift her head yesterday. I'm not letting her out of my sight. If she goes missing again, you don't know what it's like to feel that way about someone you love…"

"Actually, I kind of do…"

I blush and look down at my feet. "I'm so sorry I scared you. I promise I'll never do that again."

Dovid puts his arms around me again. He nudges my neck with his nose. Each time he touches me it's as though a thousand tiny pricks of flame ignite themselves inside me. I know he wants to kiss me, but I'm worried that we've been out here too long.

"I should go back inside."

He clears his throat. "Go check on her and come back out."

I shake my head.

"Five more minutes?"

I nod.

"You know, it's really beautiful here," he says.

"You never come here?"

"Nobody in the village willingly goes into these woods. Everyone says that they're enchanted or haunted—depends on who you ask."

I laugh. "The only thing haunting these woods is me." I blush and quickly add, "And my sister."

"Formidable ghosts."

"This is Kodari, ancient forest. These trees have lived longer than any of us, and they will live long after we are all gone from Dubossary."

"We're never going to leave Dubossary...The Jews have been here for nearly three hundred years!"

I shake my head. "I don't know. Your brother went to America. Maybe he'll send for all of you. Maybe things will get worse for us. You know our history...Wherever the Jews go, the land prospers, but somehow the land finds a way to spit us out."

"It's not the land," he says. "It's the people."

"I've been hearing horrible things in the marketplace." I rub my arms.

Dovid nods. "It will all work out, you'll see. We'll find the bears and prove Jennike's death had nothing to do with us, and they'll forget all about it."

"I hope so."

54

Laya

As I clear the teacups
and saucers,
I think about Dovid and Liba.
He looks at her like she
is light and air, like she
is fresh, like sweet grass
and river water, like a storm
at the start of summer,
like he could wrap himself
in her smell forever.
Fedir doesn't look at me
like that.

Suddenly my stomach cramps.
I bend over in pain.
I feel a thirst so strong
it threatens to rend me
in two.

I limp over to the table,
still hunched over,

and pick up the pot of tea.
I put the spout in my mouth
and down its contents in one go.
But it doesn't quench my thirst.

I sink down
on the packed-earth floor
clutching my stomach.
I hear the sounds
of bells and whistles,
of the flute,
and the violin,
melodies I'd heard
by the campfire.

I feel like my brain
is on fire.
I clutch
at my head;
my stomach hurts—
what is happening to me?
I lie down
on the floor
holding everything
and nothing
nothing
nothing.

My back itches
like it always does,
my fingers and toes feel like
they've been pricked by

a thousand tiny shards
of glass.

There are stars in my eyes.
I try to breathe
but there are
swirling planets
beneath my eyelids,
and a face,
soft and kind
with black eyes
and white wings.

Mother?
But then the woman
is a man,
a young man.
He sits beside my head
and caresses my brow
and kisses my forehead,
and begins to rub
my back.
The pain
dulls to an ache.

You can fly,
he says.
*You will soon
grow your wings.
Your time is coming.
Dream of the tops of trees,
air on your face,
sun on your back*

and clouds.
You are different, Laya,
you are special,
you are hope...

I dream that I soar
high above
this small town.
I fly above our dense,
dark woods.
I have wings and webbed feet
and I circle the village
until I come to a clearing
and see the Hovlin glen
and the lodge.
I try to land,
to go to Fedir
who is waiting
for me,
but I start to
fall
fall
fall.

There are tears on my face
and feathers everywhere.

55

Liba

When we get back to the cottage, cheeks flushed from the nip of cold in the air, and I open the door, my eyes are still on Dovid. It's only through seeing his eyes widen that I know something is horribly wrong.

I turn my head and see Laya on the floor, pale, unmoving, and covered in feathers.

"Laya! No! *Oy* no!" I run to her and cradle her head in my lap. "Laya! Laya, wake up this instant! *Oyfvakn!*"

The swans! Everything my mother feared would happen has come true and I missed all the signs. What happened? How did they get in? And where did they go?

"Shall I go get the doctor?" Only when he speaks do I notice Dovid kneeling beside me.

"Yes. Just help me get her up onto the bed."

"This is all my fault. I shouldn't have kept you out there with me for so long."

"It's okay—it's my fault too."

"Are you sure we should move her?" he asks.

"I don't want her to lie on the cold floor."

We lift her as though she weighs nothing.

"I don't know…" I feel as though all sensation has left my body. "I don't know what to do."

"I'll go get help and bring the wagon back. We can transport her that way in comfort."

"Okay," I say. "Okay." But nothing is okay at all.

As Dovid runs out the door, I sit on the bed with Laya's head in my lap. I watch her frail form take slow shuddering breaths. I examine the feathers on the floor. *Did the swans come just now when I was outside? But I was watching the house, wasn't I?* No, I wasn't. I was distracted by Dovid. *Still, how did I not notice the flap of their wings?* At some point Laya opens her eyes, just a small slight fluttering. Had I not been watching so closely I would have missed the movement entirely. Laya's lips mouth the words, "Fedir…need Fedir…"

"You need that boy like you need a hole in your head," I tell her. "I'm here, and I'm going to nurse you back to health." I get up to fetch her a cup of water, but by the time I make it back with the drink, her eyes are closed again. I put the cup to her lips, but she doesn't open them. I dip my fingers in the water and wet them, but Laya shuts them even tighter.

"Come on, Laya." I try to get her to sit up to drink, but everything I tip into her mouth just dribbles down her chin and onto her dress. She starts to shiver. I lay her down and cover her with blankets.

Tea, I think. *I'll make tea.* That's what Mother would do. *What herbs for chills and dehydration?* I putter around the kitchen shoving odds and ends of herbs into a teapot. *Maybe it's love-sickness? Heartsickness? Or something else entirely?* Rosehips and peppermint, birch leaves and blueberry, ginger and elderflower… *What else, what else?* I don't understand the language of herbs. My fingers want to knead dough—it's the one thing that I do understand.

You can't save someone who doesn't want to be saved, a voice says in my head, but I know it's not my mother's voice. It sounds like Mrs. Meisels...

And just as I set the tea up to boil, Dovid comes back with his mother.

"*Oy*, Liba! You poor dear!" She runs over to the kitchen to hug me.

"No, no! Mrs. Meisels, please. I'm fine. I'm so sorry I worried you last night. You must have been terrified. I was just so worried about my sister..."

"Of course, my dear, of course. I've grown quite fond of you, you know. I think that a few people would be heart-broken if anything were to happen to you." She motions with her eyes to Dovid.

"Please help my sister..." I rasp out. "I don't know what's wrong..."

Mrs. Meisels bends over Laya's fragile form. Feathers still swirl around the room in the breeze; they seem to have a life of their own. I let out a sob and sink into a chair.

In an instant, Dovid is beside me. "Liba? Are you okay?" He looks over at his mother.

He takes his jacket off and wraps me in it. "What's the matter?" he says.

"The feather. I need to find it," I say.

"What? There are feathers everywhere," he says.

"I don't know where I put it."

"She's talking gibberish." Dovid looks at his mother.

Mrs. Meisels shakes her head. "Crazy times we live in, Dovid, crazy times..."

"What should I do?" he asks her.

"I think Liba suffers more from shock than anything. We'll take them home with us. I can care for them there and we can call the doctor."

The kettle howls and Dovid goes over to take it off the fire.

"I made tea," I say.

Dovid takes a whiff and wrinkles his nose. "You sure you want to drink this?"

"I made it for Laya. She has to drink," I say, rubbing my forehead with my hands and pressing my fingers to my temple. *I'm supposed to hold one of the feathers in my hand if I want the swans to come. Where is it? Where did I put it?*

"Okay then, we'll try some." He pours two mugs and brings one over to his mother.

"A spoon, *ketzele*. Bring me a spoon," she says.

But try as she might, she can't get Laya to drink any more than I could. Dovid brings me some too. I let the steam coat my face, but my hands shake and I can barely hold the mug. Dovid takes it from me.

"Let's go—there's more that I can do for them in my own house," Mrs. Meisels says.

Dovid picks Laya up off the bed. He wraps her in my mother's quilt.

I squint at him. "What are you doing?"

"We're going back to our house, *maydele*," Mrs. Meisels answers. "The doctor will come there to see you both. The woods are no place for two young girls alone and it's about time someone made the right decision."

"No. We can't leave. Maybe we should...I need to..." I shake my head. I can't find a way to explain. Fedir, the Hovlins, the bear, the men in the woods, the swans, the chickens out back, the cow, the goat, the garden, our parents, and a thousand other reasons come to mind. But I'm overwhelmed, and the fight goes out of me. Maybe it would be nice to have someone else worry about these things. Just for a day...or two.

Dovid takes Laya outside and comes back inside to help me. I stand up and pause to peck Mrs. Meisels on the cheek, but as

I make my way to the door, Dovid picks me up and carries me outside. I'm surprised that in his hands I feel as though I weigh as much as a feather. As though I'm no burden at all.

I drape my arms around his broad shoulders and press my lips to his scruffy cheek. "Thank you," I whisper in his ear. I feel his cheeks flush. And I see Mrs. Meisels look over and smile.

As the wagon makes its way back to town I rest my head on Dovid's shoulder. He holds me to him with one hand, while his other hand grasps the reins. I watch the trees around us, and the sky. *This is the right decision. If the swans came in my absence, maybe taking Laya away from the cottage is the best thing to do. If I hide her at the Meisels', they won't find her.*

We will be in town, just paces away from a doctor, but also from the fruit stand. I can go give Fedir and his brothers a piece of my mind. Tomorrow morning I have every intention of interrogating every one of those Hovlin boys. This plan seems to make more sense the longer I think about it. In town, I can investigate.

I snuggle closer to Dovid and let the sway of the wagon and the clop of the horses lull me to sleep.

I wake to the smell of cedar wood, smoke, and fur. At first I think I'm dreaming—that I'm warm and comfortable in Dovid's arms...*In Dovid's arms!* I sit up in bed, only to find that I've been joined by the Meisels' dog, Heldzl. *Where's Laya?*

I bolt up, eyes wild, my hair a dark tangle of sleep. "Laya!" I burst into the kitchen, only to find the entire Meisels family sitting at the table, eating. "Where's my sister?" I say, knowing full well that I look unkempt and that I'm dressed in only a night-shift. I shiver, feeling the blast of winter air that comes from the opening front door.

Dr. Polnikovsky walks in, shuffling his feet at the entrance of the house to rid his shoes of debris. "How fares our patient this morning?"

"You mean the sleeping one, or the *meshuggene* one that's decided to join our breakfast table in her nightshift?" Dovid grins.

My face reddens. "All you have to do is tell me where she is…" I whisper.

Dovid nods his head in the direction of the front room. "It's warmest in there—we built the fire up high all night."

I rush through the kitchen to the living room and see Laya fast asleep on the sofa they made up as a daybed. She looks a bit less pale, but still she barely moves. I want to go to her, to hold her hand, to embrace her, but seeing that she's okay and still sleeping, I remember my manners and make my way back to the kitchen.

"My apologies. I just…I didn't know where she was," I say, pointedly staring at my bare toes.

"You can thank me well enough when you've gotten some clothes on, dear. Now run along and make yourself decent," Mrs. Meisels says.

I blush and walk over to the doctor. "It's a pleasure to make your acquaintance. If you'd be so kind as to wait for me, I'll be right back. I'd like to hear all about my sister's condition."

Dr. Polnikovsky smiles. "Well, I suppose one of Mrs. Meisels' *schnecken* and a cup of strong hot coffee might persuade me to linger a bit longer. Just as soon as I've checked on the patient, that is. As long as there isn't a need for a second consultation?"

"Oh no, sir," I whisper, chastened. "I'm quite sane, I promise."

At that the entire Meisels family chuckles, causing my cheeks to burn even brighter. I bow slightly in a gesture that is almost a curtsey, turn, and flee the kitchen back to the safety of Dovid's room.

When I've made myself presentable, I go back out to the common room, where I find Dr. Polnikovsky conferring with Mrs. Meisels.

"Liba, so nice of you to join us," he says as I enter the room.

"How is my sister?" I ask.

"I would keep a close eye on her if I were you," he says. "Watch that she doesn't sleepwalk or decide to go a-wandering. The fever that's come upon her might make her delusional. Do everything you can to get her to consume something, anything, broth or tea, some biscuits, or I fear she will waste away before your very eyes. Keep her warm at all times."

"Is there nothing else we can do?" Mrs. Meisels asks.

"I'm afraid not, Rukhie. Either the fever breaks and she starts to eat and drink again, or..."

"No. Don't say it," I interrupt. "She will get better. I know she will. She has to. I will nurse her back to health."

Mrs. Meisels embraces me. "You don't have to do this alone, *maydele*, I'm here to help you."

"I know. And I thank you. But...perhaps it was a mistake to move her."

"I do not think that relocating the patient caused any further illness," Dr. Polnikovsky says.

I nod.

"We will work all of this out." Mrs. Meisels rubs my back.

"I don't deserve your kindness..." I gesture at the room, the doctor who is packing up his bag to take his leave. "How much do I owe you, Dr. Polnikovsky?"

"Now, don't be silly," Mrs. Meisels says. "I've already taken care of that. I've never had a daughter. Always wanted one. I think you'll do nicely...if you'll have me. I mean... us..." She gestures at the door, just as Dovid makes his way into the room.

I think of my own mother, and part of me wants to say, *But I already have a mother*, then I think about how different the two of them are, and how nice it would be to be included in their loud and boisterous family. Mami has always shared a special bond with Laya—something I could never be a part of. And here, I always feel so warm, so accepted. I can picture it—a life with Dovid. *Shabbes* meals around this table...

As long as they don't find out what I really am.

Then it's Mrs. Meisels' turn to blush. "I didn't mean that the way it sounds..."

"Ah, yes she did," Dovid says. "She always means what she says—don't let her fool you!"

Mrs. Meisels and I burst into a fit of giggles.

"What?" Dovid says. "What'd I say?"

56

Laya

The black-white ghost of sleep
flits in and out
of this strange room.
The shuffle of a sheet and blanket
folding and enfolding
spills like sand over me,
the air is a reprieve.

My breath changes; it rises
and falls like leaves in the wind.
My limbs feel lighter,
my arms more graceful.

There were feathers in the air
wrapped around me.
Now there is the weight
of a blanket on me
and thirst thirst thirst.

In my dreams
the swan-man visits.

He turns me around
and around, and I become
a creature of night and air;
black and white
and black again.
Who is he?

Dawn crests
but it brings with it
only more pain.

57

Liba

I get up early the next morning, and after Mr. Meisels and the boys go to synagogue, I step out of the house and walk to the marketplace. But when I get there, it's too early; the Hovlins have not yet arrived at the square. I pace up and down the plaza, awaiting their arrival.

I hear them before I see them. Miron plays the flute and the brothers follow with their constant refrain: "Come buy! Come buy!"

Today their song gives me goose bumps, and I rub my arms to shed the way the music chills my bones.

They lazily wind into the square, walking in a form of dance, a stroll. I see Fedir; he doesn't sing. Something in his face looks sad, as if he has lost something.

I wait until they get to the stand, then I corner him. I jab him fiercely in the chest. "What did you do to her?" I say, eyes cold as steel.

"To who?" he says, feigning a lazy smile. But I see his eyes shift.

"You know exactly who I'm talking about. My sister."

"What's wrong with your sister?" His lip curls down, and I know that he is hiding something.

"If you don't tell me what you did to her right now, I'll…"

"You'll what?" Miron says, striding over towards Fedir and putting one of his lanky arms on his shoulder.

"I'll tell everyone in town that you are the ones responsible for Jennike's disappearance." I look at Miron's eyes to try and see what is hidden there. I cross my arms over my chest.

Miron sneers. "As if anyone would believe a Jew. Don't be ridiculous. You're nothing more than a trickster *zhydovka* like all the other *zhyds* in this town. Jennike was a lost soul. Just like your sister. We had nothing to do with it. Perhaps you should ask your own kind what they did to her. From what I've heard, there are many…creative ways you Jews use blood."

"You *mamzer!*" I lunge for him.

Fedir grabs me by my cloak and I feel like he's about to throw me down onto the floor. "Dirty Jew," he says, spitting in my face. My eyes well with tears. He brings his mouth up to my ear and whispers, "Find me later. I will help you." Out loud he says, "You *zhyds* and your conspiracies. Your sister is worth ten of you in beauty and in wits. She doesn't stick her nose where it doesn't belong." He pushes me away and turns his back to his brothers.

I stumble away, breathing hard. I don't understand. My eyes meet his again. I'm about to walk away, but I see him mouth, "Find me." He licks his lips lasciviously and lunges towards me, tongue out, as though he is going to lick me. All the brothers watch and laugh. Miron crosses his arms, puffs out his chest and smirks.

I run all the way back to the Meisels' house, face burning in shame, but with a tiny bird of hope in my chest. I'll meet him, even though he's repugnant. If he knows anything about Laya's illness or Jennike's murder, I'll take the risk.

I burst into the kitchen. Mrs. Meisels takes one look at me and opens her arms. I fall right into them, sobbing onto her broad shoulder.

"What happened, Liba?"

I try to put words together, but I can't manage to get anything out.

"Shhh...after a good cry, your heart is lighter. Go on, *maydele*, let it all out."

"I hate them!" I burst out. "Those Hovlin boys—they are horrible people. Anti-Semites, all of them. They need to leave, to go back where they came from. They've infected this town with their poison. I don't want Laya to go near them ever again!"

"Well, you'd best discuss that with her."

"If she ever even wakes up again..." I sniffle.

"Why don't you go see for yourself?"

"What?"

"Laya is up, and feeling better..."

"She is?"

"She is." Mrs. Meisels smiles.

I wipe the tears off of my face with my sleeve and run into the living room. "Laya!"

"Liba..." Laya replies in a tired voice. "What's wrong?"

"It's nothing." I shake my head.

"Why are we here?"

"When Dovid left yesterday, I went outside with him for a bit. I didn't think that we were out for that long." I take her hand in mine. "When I came back inside you had collapsed and there were feathers all around you. Do you remember anything?"

Laya purses her lips. "No. I was thirsty, and my throat hurt. The last thing I remember was feeling dizzy." Laya shrugs. "I feel better now."

"I'm glad you're feeling better," I say. "I think that we should stay here for a bit. There are things I need to tell you." *I sound like my mother. If only she were here right now...she'd know what to do...* "The Meisels have offered us hospitality until you feel back to yourself."

"No!" Laya squeaks. "I can't. I mean, we can't. I mean... what about...?"

"Dovid says he'll take care of the animals and check on the house. And anyway, I think it's better that we're far away from there right now."

"No! Liba, I have to go back to the woods. I simply have to." Laya sits up suddenly and is the most animated I've seen her for a long time.

"Why? To meet Fedir again? I forbid it. You should hear the things his brothers said to me this morning."

"You can't forbid me anything. You're not my mother."

"You are not seeing that boy anymore. He's a *goy*, Laya. A *goy*! What would Mami and Tati say?"

"It's not your place to approve." Laya starts coughing, and I suddenly feel remorse for speaking harshly.

I put my arm around her and kiss her forehead. "I'll get you something to drink," I say, and go back to the kitchen.

I sit with Laya after that, trying to get her to drink tea, but she lies on the couch listlessly, staring out the front window at the falling snow. I don't bring up Fedir again. I stroke her hair and stay beside her.

Soon it's time to eat lunch. Laya sits at the table with us, propped up with pillows and covered in blankets. Lunch is hot *borsht* with meat. I savor the thick, tender chunks of meat, the tangy beets, the smooth broth. *I could get used to this*, I think, and glance over at Dovid. I like the idea of a warm cozy home like this, in a town. As much as I love our woods, maybe it's not so good to be so isolated. The people in town that I thought were gossipy *yentas* are mostly nice people. They mistrust what they don't understand, just like I do...

I glance over at Laya. Sun slants on to warm her face, illuminating just how pale she looks. And I see that she eats nothing. I shake my head because it's clear to me in the light of the afternoon sun that this house, this family is just another thing in our lives that's too good to last.

After lunch, Laya goes back to the living room and lies down. I get her settled on the sofa.

"I want to go home," she whispers, twisting her hair and looking down at the hand-stitched quilts that cover her lap and shoulders.

"I know you do, and I promise we will. Soon," I say, stroking the fine hairs on her arm absently.

Laya gets more agitated. "I don't like to be caged, Liba. I don't like to be inside so much. I need fresh air."

"But you're not well, Layoosh. You have to rest and get better. I don't think it's good for you to be out there in the cold."

She shakes her head back and forth, and twists her hair again, faster now. "Everything hurts," she whispers. "And what if... what if I try to fly, Liba? What if my wings grow?"

I swallow hard. "I'm here, Laya. I'll make sure that doesn't happen. You can control it, I promise. I didn't think I could... but I can, more and more now."

"Have you...changed? Have you really turned all the way?"

"No, not yet, but I've come close. And I was scared before, but when it happened—it felt good actually. Kind of freeing."

"That's what I want to feel," she says under her breath.

"I know. And you will. But you have to get better first. Laya-bell, I need to tell you something important."

"You've finally found someone? I know that already," she says lazily.

"Listen to me!" I'm suddenly angry at her and I don't know why. Why does everything come so easy to her but I take ages to even know my own heart? "I'm supposed to go meet Fedir now."

"You're what?"

"Fedir. I'm supposed to meet him."

"Why are you meeting my Fedir?"

"Because you need to get better."

"Fedir can make me better."

"Yes, well, I know that's what you think, but frankly, I don't want that boy anywhere near you. I will suffer his presence if it means I can figure out how to help you feel better."

"Why is Fedir any different than Dovid?"

"What do you mean?" I wrinkle my brow.

"You know that Tati won't approve of Dovid. Well, he won't approve of Fedir either. What's the difference?"

"The difference is that Fedir is a *goy* who says nasty things about Jews! How could you like someone like that?"

She shrugs. "Some of the things he says are true."

"Laya, how could you say that?" I put my hand on her forehead. "You're not well. Do you hear yourself? You're a Jew!"

I remember Mami's words…*Laya's father was a swan, like me.* But Mami converted, and Laya was raised Jewish. It shouldn't matter…should it?

"Tati won't approve of anyone," Laya says. "I might as well choose who I want."

For a moment, I envy her clarity, but I say, "It doesn't work like that."

"Why not?"

"Because there's a chance that Tati will approve of Dovid… maybe he'll come around…"

"Mami was a *goy*. She converted."

"You think Fedir will convert for you?"

She shrugs her shoulders. "I don't see why it matters."

I think about the way that Fedir spat at me. The hate I saw in Miron's eyes. "I love you, Laya. I want you to be happy…but this…it's not the way. It's not our way."

"Maybe I want a different way…"

My eyes fill with tears.

Laya puts her head on a pillow and languidly stretches out her limbs on the sofa. "All Fedir has to do is kiss me. Then I'll feel better."

"You cannot be healed by a kiss, and you cannot live on love or infatuation or whatever this thing is—a sick obsession. That is certainly something you've read about in fairy tales."

"No, not in a book. Mami told me."

I snap to attention. "Mami told you what?"

"Stories."

"What kind of stories?"

"Oh…this and that…things."

"She told you that you can be healed by a kiss? She read you stories, you mean."

"Same thing. Fairy tale, shmairy tale. It's all true, you know."

I put my hand on Laya's forehead. "And you're burning up again. Rest. I'm going to go talk to your loverboy who thinks he can feed you with kisses alone," I say as I shake my head. *I will never love anyone if this is what it will reduce me to. Maybe what I feel for Dovid is also a fever of sorts, and it will pass.* I kiss Laya's forehead. "I'll be back soon."

"Kiss him for me!"

"I will not."

"Good. Don't. He's mine."

I sigh and make my way out of the house via the kitchen.

"Where are you going?" Dovid stops me.

"Out."

"I'll come with you."

"No, no. I'm just getting some…herbs…some spices from the market to make Laya tea."

"We have spices in the cellar: chamomile and thyme, rosemary and lavender…come," Dovid says, taking my hand in his. "I'll show you." There is a wicked look in his eye and his hand is warm in mine, but I can't follow him. *I have to go meet Fedir.*

"I'll only be a few minutes. It's something unusual I need. I'm positive you don't have it in your cellar."

He grins at me with a glint in his eye. "Why don't we go check and see?"

I close my eyes and shake my head. "I can't."

"Come on, Liba…"

"In your house? With your mother here, and your brothers and father?"

"The cellar is dark…"

"And you're being silly. I have to go."

I duck out the door before he has a chance to follow.

I meet Fedir at the back of a tavern. He leads me into an alleyway.

He looks both ways and cocks his head as if he's listening for something.

"What's wrong?" I ask.

"Nothing," he whispers. "Just making sure that we're alone and no one's listening."

"Well, are we?"

"Yes, so it seems. For now."

"Are you expecting someone?"

"There's always someone listening."

"My mother says that."

"Smart woman."

I'm getting frustrated with this conversation already. What does my sister see in him?

"You asked me to meet you here," I say. "Are you going to tell me how you can help heal my sister? Because if not, I have more important things to do."

"I'm the only one who can heal her," he says in a way that's almost sincere, and that gives me pause.

Still, I roll my eyes at him. "That's what she says too. Now, can you give me a practical cure? How can you heal her? With what herbs or tinctures?"

He shakes his head. "I mean it. I hold the only cure."

"Because you're the one who made her sick to begin with?" I raise a disbelieving eyebrow at him.

"Something like that."

"What did you do to her?"

"It's complicated."

"Love always is. Explain it to me." I'm not letting him weasel his way out of this.

"I can't."

"So I'll report you to the authorities."

He smiles. "And they will find nothing. You think they will believe you over me?"

"Yes, actually I do. What about what you did to Jennike? I know you had something to do with that."

"No. You suspect. There is no proof." He cocks his head at me and smiles again, slyly.

"Are you saying you did it?"

"Did what?"

"Got her sick? Kidnapped her…or worse?"

"Do you want your sister to get better or not?" I can see he's losing his patience.

I take a deep breath. "How do I know you won't make her sicker?"

"You're just going to have to trust me." Fedir grins, his green eyes holding worlds of malice.

"I don't trust you at all."

"Well, you'll just have to take your chances."

"I have one question for you." I put my hands on my hips and take a step forward. "Do you love her?"

Fedir blanches.

"It's not a difficult question: yes or no?"

"I care for your sister very much."

"That's not a yes. I bet you care for all the girls you trick and woo, right before you break their hearts. Do you know that my parents will never approve? If she ends up with you, they will sit *shiva*; they will disown her. It will break their hearts, but that is what they'll do because it's our tradition. And they'll regret it for the rest of their lives. I've seen the heartbreak that such a thing causes, and it's not pretty."

"It's not like that...Laya is..."

"Laya is fragile. Laya is trusting. Laya is not meant for you."

"Laya *is* meant for me." Fedir's voice suddenly has a hard edge.

"So tell me you love her, because if you're going to take my sister away from her family, you need to understand what it means. You need to understand that she will be cast out. If she ends up with you, there is no going back. She will be dead to us." The words make my teeth ache.

He curses under his breath. "What is it with you Jews?"

"Do not talk to me like that."

"She's different from you. She looks different; she acts different." He sniffs the air around me. "You are not the same at all."

I frown and back away. *How does he know? How can he tell?*

"I love your sister," he says as if he's admitting it to himself. "I didn't expect to. You're right that my brothers and I enjoy the game. We like to jump from town to town, from girl to girl. We spread cheer in every village we visit. We give people what they want—delicious produce and the truth about the cancer that lives among them. But I feel for Laya what I have felt for no creature. If her family does not love her and will cast her out, it's clear to me what I must do. You really are a despicable people if this is how you treat the ones you love."

I recoil. He thinks his words are true, but he doesn't understand what it means to be a Jew, the way we protect ourselves and each other, how we ensure Jewish continuity by marrying within our faith. He doesn't know we honor the memory of the many Jews who died *al kiddush Hashem*—sanctifying God's name—in order to preserve our traditions. He doesn't know that Jews always come out battered, bruised, but still triumphant. Because we believe in God, in community, in compassion, and in the power of our people to endure. His words hurt, but they don't scratch the surface of what I am, what we are.

"Thank you for your time, but I don't think we need your help anymore," I say. "I will take care of my sister. Please…just stay away from her. She doesn't understand that she is going to lose everything…"

"No." He shakes his head. "It's too late for that. Laya will be mine. And if you get in the way, if you get in *my* way…strange things have been known to happen to girls in the woods."

My hands start to shake and I make fists to stop the claws I know will come.

"No human remedy will heal her," he calls out as he walks away.

Something in his voice gives me pause. "Wait!"

Fedir keeps walking—or more like slinking—along the alleyway with a grace that actually doesn't look human at all.

"Fedir! Wait. Come back. Explain!" I chase after him and put a hand on his back to stop him.

He turns around and stares at my hand on his shoulder.

"You lost your chance." He sniffs my hand, then licks it.

I snatch my hand away.

"Hmm…" he says, licking his lips. "Maybe not so human after all."

"What…what are you even talking about?" *He doesn't know what I am—does he?*

Fedir turns around and with impossible speed he pushes me hard up against the brick of the narrow alley. "I think you know exactly what I'm talking about."

I close my eyes as I feel the bricks dig into my back. I clench my teeth just as I feel them get sharper. I gasp for breath and close my eyes. *No. Not here.* I grasp at the air for calm.

He shoves me harder and I feel myself start to lose control. My fingertips are tingling, every pore of my body aches.

Fedir sniffs the air and grins.

I breathe in hard, fighting for control. "Please. Can't you just undo what you did to her?"

He lets me go with a sigh. "You don't know how much I wish I could."

"What?" I'm breathing hard and trembling with fear. I rub my arms. "What does that mean?"

"I made a mistake," he spits. "I never should have touched her. I'm paying dearly for that mistake now. My brothers don't understand. But I care a great deal about her..."

I look at him and it seems as though there are tears in his eyes.

"Just bring her to me," he says. "I need to see her again."

"I don't trust you."

"If you want to save your sister, you'll have to," he says. "I need to see her—alone. If anyone else is with you, or with her, I won't come."

I let out a breath. "Fine. Just once. One chance to fix this mess. That's all I'm giving you."

"Bring her back to the cottage. I'll wait for you there."

"Wait, no! But..." And before I can respond I see Fedir's body contort. He crouches down on all fours and suddenly his skin turns into tabby fur. His head grows smaller, his body shrinks, and he transforms into a cat and jumps from the ground up to a window ledge. He looks down at me, meows playfully, then leaps up to the roof of one of the homes that line the alleyway.

My blood runs cold.

I turn and run back to the Meisels' house as fast as my legs can carry me.

58

Laya

I lie back down to rest.
I'm so tired and weak.
I close my eyes
and then I see him.
The swan from the rooftop,
from the tree,
from my dreams.
His hair is white-gold,
and his body
looks like cream.
He is young,
about my age perhaps.
No, older.

Pro shcho vy? I whisper.
My hand
goes to my mouth.
What language
am I speaking?

His eyes are black orbs,
soft and kind.
Like mirrors.
Reflected back at me,
I see a swan, elegant
in white and gold,
with an orange beak
and soft black eyes.
And I know
that it is me
reflected in his eyes.
Atop the head
of the swan
there is a crown—
it looks like it's made
of dew and diamonds.
I blink, and the image
is gone. He nods
and tips his chin
in my direction
as if to say,
That is you.
That is your future.
That is what
you are destined
to become.
Koroleva, he calls me.

59

Liba

When I get back to the Meisels' home, Dovid is in the shop with his father. He sees me walk past and rushes out from behind the counter to open the door. "Liba! Wait!" He follows me from the shop into the house. "Did you get what you were looking for?"

"I need to take Laya back home," I say.

"What? Why?" His face falls. "We can take care of you here. Both of you."

I close my eyes. "I have to take care of my sister. Her needs come before mine."

I feel Dovid's hand on my face. "Look at me."

I shake my head. I can't help the tears that fall.

"Liba, please. Tell me what's really going on."

"I can't."

"I'm not letting you go. I've never felt this way about anyone before."

"Dovid, I have to. She won't get well unless she's home, in her own bed."

"She won't get well without a doctor and some real food and a properly heated home," he replies sharply.

"You don't understand."

"You're right. I don't. You keep putting yourself in danger for a sister who keeps making bad decisions. Why? When will you decide to put your own needs first?"

"Please! You're not making this any easier. I made a promise to my mother—it's not a choice, Dovid. I'm responsible for her. She's my sister. Wouldn't you do anything for your brothers?" *The emotions are too much. I know what I want, but I can't have it. Laya always comes first. And besides, I'm as "other" as Fedir. Perhaps that's what he sees in Laya. A kindred spirit.*

Dovid is not right for me. He can't be right for me. We are as different as the sun is from the moon.

"Liba, there is definitely something in those woods. A bear, perhaps, or a pack of them. You said that strange men followed you. What if they took you? What if something happened to you? I'd never forgive myself." He shuts his eyes.

"I'm so sorry, Dovid. I know that what I'm asking makes no sense. But if I want Laya to get better, I need to go back home." I don't know how else to explain—what am I supposed to say? *My sister is a swan and she's afraid she will sprout wings in your living room? She fancies herself in love with a cat-man who says that only he can heal her—but he won't help us if we stay here. And yes there are strange men out there, and maybe a bear, but I'm really supposed to protect her from a flock of swans, though lately they are seeming like more and more of a good option.* It's certainly a tale out of a children's book—except it's not—it's frighteningly real.

"Why can't you just accept that someone cares about you?" He raises his voice in frustration.

He leans in close and I think he's going to kiss me, but he puts his arms around me in a tight hug. I hesitate for a minute. He says, "I'm here for you, Liba—we'll get through this together." And I reach my arms up and put them around him, all the muscles in my body suddenly losing their tension.

All the worries—all the fears of what will become of Laya, and

of who I am and what I want and what I might become—fall away.
For one brief blissful moment I don't think about my sister, or the
swans or the bears, or about Fedir and his brothers. I don't think
about my teeth or my nails or the fur that threatens to burst out of
my body and consume me. I don't think about the strange men in
the woods, or Jennike, the Glazers who disappeared, my parents
who could be dead, injured, or lost. I only feel his strong arms holding me, and I don't care what happens as long as he never lets go.

I feel his breath on my neck and I think, *We breathe the same
air. We are not as different as we seem…we believe in the same god,
practice the same religion, like the same food, laugh at the same jokes.
I want this—a normal family and a home where I don't need to fear
the woods around me.*

He looks up and his eyes lock with mine. In a tone of voice
that tells me it takes everything he has, he says, "I trust you. I'll
wait for you. How can I help?"

I see that saying it costs him something. That maybe trust is
the most powerful gift that anyone can give you.

I swallow, and think about what it might cost for me to trust
him. I wonder if what I feel for him is love, because I do feel
drunk when I'm with him—lightheaded, my whole body buzzing, like the time I drank more than a *bissl* of Tati's schnapps and
felt it burn through my body from my head down to my toes.

I lean forward and kiss him, lightly at first, but then my hands are
in his hair and it's like nothing else can quench my thirst like his lips.
Perhaps I'm not so different from my sister after all. We kiss until he
pulls away and shoves his whole body back against the wall behind
him, breathless, eyes dark now, like marbles dipped in chocolate.

He clenches his eyes closed. "You drive me wild."

I laugh. Because I am wild. I am a beast. And maybe, just
maybe, Dovid could be okay with that.

"Let's get the wagon ready," he says, his voice coming back
to him. "I'll take you home."

"You're changing the topic," I tease.

"Yes, for the benefit of both of us. Because if I kiss you again I will not be able to control myself, and embarrassing things might happen in this hallway."

"I don't have a problem with that," I say.

"But my mother might," he says.

We burst into laughter. I peck him on the cheek and sigh. "Okay. The wagon it is."

He smirks at me. "Indeed. Might be a little bumpy."

I put my hand over my mouth. "That is not what I meant at all..."

"Heh." He grins. "But I did. God, Liba, you drive me crazy. I just want to..." He shakes his head. "I...think we should pack up the wagon."

I smile to myself, but my face is on fire. "Me too."

"I'll go break the news to my mother. Wish me luck, I'm going to need it."

I laugh again, then I pause and put my hand on his arm. "I... I promise to explain more on the way, okay?"

He nods. "It better be good."

"It is." *My mind races already.* I grab his sleeve in my fist. "Thank you. I owe you everything."

He shakes his head. "You owe me nothing."

"No...I do. And one day I'll make it up to you. I promise."

"Don't promise. Just take care of yourself and your sister. Everything else can wait...even if I don't want to."

I walk towards the living room where Laya is resting.

Dovid calls out after me. "No matter what, I'm not leaving you alone! You can't get rid of me! And that's a promise!"

I look over my shoulder and smile at him. But in my head I know that he can make no such promise. My parents and the Glazers have shown me that anyone can leave at any point in time for any reason. Promises can be broken.

60

Laya

The wagon sways
　　as I watch the sky.
There is an alphabet up there
of twigs and branches,
leaves and wings;
bird feet write histories
against the sky.
Do I want to be a swan?
When will I grow wings?
I try to decipher
what it all means.

I see a large white shape
against the gray of sky.
It looks like a swan.
Is it him?
Following me.
Following us.
I don't even know his name.
My eyes trace its figure
from its golden beak,

to its tucked-in feet,
the arc of its neck
suspended in sky
and its wings,
graceful and arched.

My heart fills with yearning
and my eyes follow the swan
all the way home.

61

Liba

Laya is cocooned in a bed of blankets in the back of the wagon amid baskets of supplies: meats, cheeses, home-baked breads and dried fruits, sacks of vegetables and herbs.

"It's too much, Dovid," I say. "We can't possibly take this all from your family. You promise you'll take some back to them?"

"My mother would wallop me if I did."

"I'd like to see that."

"I'll bet you would," he grins.

I blush and we look at each other, the moment charged with electricity.

I put my hand in his and we hold the reins together, fingers entwined. I can't believe myself. Was it only a week ago that Mami and Tati left and I was a timid obedient daughter? How quickly people change…but somehow between the quiet of the forest, the crispness in the air, and the shock of my hand twisted in his, this just feels right.

"Liba." Dovid clears his throat. "I care about you so much that I feel like I'm willing to follow you to the ends of the earth. Which is the only reason I agreed to this. My mother and father think that you and I have both lost our minds. So can you please, please explain why I am taking you back to your house when there is danger lurking in the forest, and you could have been safe with us in town?"

I take a deep breath and look up at the sky. "Not all people are what they seem." My heart beats fast in my chest. *Is this really where I tell him?*

I don't want to lose him—I don't want to lose what we have, and being with him is the only thing that feels right lately. I take a deep breath. "I think that Fedir might have poisoned my sister. I know that sounds crazy, but...there's something wrong with that fruit. I have no explanation for it. It doesn't make sense, but he did something to her. I know that I should keep her far, far away from him, but I went to see him this morning in the marketplace—I lied to you. I wasn't going to get an herb; I was seeking another remedy. He says that he can heal her. I shouldn't trust him—but the doctor doesn't seem to have a cure. What if he can? What if it's as simple as that? I have to try. I fear for her life, Dovid. What if the fruit is poisoned?"

Dovid laughs. "Then wouldn't the other men and women in this town be sick too? I don't think it's poison."

I turn my face away. *I knew he wouldn't believe me. I shouldn't have said anything at all.*

"Liba, wait, I didn't mean to laugh." He puts his hand on my arm. "It's just a lot to take in."

"It's okay, Dovid. I didn't expect you to understand. As soon as we get back, you can just leave us be and go home. I know it seems crazy, but it's what I have to do."

"No, that's not what I mean. Liba, please. Look at me."

I shake my head. *I should never have trusted you*, I want to say. But I also understand how far-fetched it all seems. Suddenly it dawns on me: maybe this is why Tati said I should never marry someone from the village—nobody here could possibly understand. And that thought saddens me most of all, because if Tati was right all along, I've just been deluding myself.

"Liba, please!" He stops the horses and drops the reins, turning to face me. He reaches his hand up and strokes the side of my face. "Look at me, Liba. Talk to me. I'm listening; I'm trying to understand. What if I stay with you the whole time? I don't care what my parents think—what anyone thinks. I'll sleep over and...I'll meet Fedir with you so that he won't trick you or hurt you or Laya. I believe you, okay? It doesn't make any sense, but...let me stay and help. You don't need to be up against this alone."

I turn to look at him. I'm fighting the tears that threaten my eyes. "He said he'll only meet Laya alone. He won't come if anyone else is there."

"You realize how suspicious that sounds, right?"

"I know. But it's what I have to do."

"I don't like it. I don't like any of this. I'll stay in the woods when he comes—I won't be far away. But I'm not going to walk off like an idiot and let something bad happen to you."

Dovid picks up the reins and snaps them, urging the horses back into a trot.

I lean over and peck a kiss on his cheek.

When we pull up to the cottage, he says, "I'll carry her. Go open the door."

I take the traveling blankets off my legs and jump off the wagon. I go to open the door to the cottage, but the door swings open. I smell something off.

"Someone was here."

"What? Where?"

I sniff the air. "No. Not here anymore."

"Stay with Laya—I'll check the house." He leans down and takes a pistol out from a satchel in the back of the wagon and walks into the house.

I go around to the back of the wagon and climb up. "Laya?" I say.

"Hmmph?"

"Someone was in our cottage."

"What?" Her eyes open lazily. "Who?" she says as she stretches.

"I don't know. The door was unlocked. Something smells off. I can't place it."

"The door was unlocked another time too…"

"When?"

"When the bear was inside. You and your nose."

When it dawns on me, my hand flies to my mouth. "Laya, I know exactly who smells like that. But what were they doing in our house?"

"What?"

"Ruven…and maybe Alter. Damn them. What do they want now?"

"It's not safe."

"Oh, Laya," I laugh. "Of course it's not safe. It stopped being safe in Dubossary a long time ago…but Fedir is coming by later and he said he'd only meet us here."

"Fedir?" Her eyes light up.

"Yes. Your *meshugge* boyfriend who says that only he can cure you."

"All clear!" Dovid calls as he hops up onto the back of the wagon. "Let's get you settled."

When we walk inside he asks, "Shall I carry her up the ladder?"

"No, it's okay—you can put her on the bed downstairs."

As I fix the sheets and blankets for Laya. I smell the intruder stronger than ever.

"Liba, you're uh…sniffing that bed really strangely," Dovid says.

"Sorry. I…you can put Laya down. It's just…I have a really good sense of smell. Mami was always teaching me about herbs and teas…"

"You smelled tea in the bed?"

"No, silly." I smack his arm.

I turn to look at Laya and see that she's crying. "I'm sorry," she says. "I failed you. I failed everyone. I didn't realize what they were. I'm so sorry. They came, Liba. They came for you and I didn't notice the signs until it was too late."

I exchange glances with Dovid.

"Laya...*husht!* Lie down. It's been a long day. Try to sleep." I don't understand what she's saying. "Maybe her fever has spiked again," I say. *I'm determined to get to the bottom of this illness once and for all—whatever it takes.*

Laya shakes her head. No and no and no again, working herself into a frenzy that makes me dizzy just looking at her.

"Laya-bell, we'll figure it out in the morning. For now, just rest."

"No...I've ruined everything, everything, don't you understand?"

Dovid looks at me. "Shall I go get the doctor?"

"No. Can you...just stay here with us for a bit please? Do you mind standing guard at the door? That would make me feel better." *Dovid can keep Ruven and Alter away from us. And in the meantime, we can wait for Fedir.* "I want to get her changed."

"Your wish is my command." He says it with such tenderness that it nearly breaks my heart. Just before he opens the door, he turns and says, "Have I ever told you how beautiful you are?"

"Stop," I say.

"Why?"

"Because you don't need to say that."

"You're right. I don't *need* to—I want to."

I shake my head. "I'm not beautiful."

"Why would you say that, Liba? Who in your life made you think that about yourself?"

I look down at the floor. *I'm a beast!* I want to scream at him. *Just go away…If you knew the truth of what I am, you wouldn't be here.*

"Beautiful is not what is beautiful, but what one likes," he says.

Tears fill my eyes.

"I have to take care of Laya," I say.

"And I have to take care of you. Look at me, Liba."

I shake my head.

"Why are you crying? I'm here. I'm going to watch over both of you."

This will end badly. This will end in pain.

Laya coughs from the bed.

"I'll be just outside the door if you need anything," Dovid says with a sigh as he walks out.

Laya is trembling as if she's having a fit.

I hold her in my arms. "Just a little more time and Fedir will be here. I promise."

But she can't stop shaking and I can't stop the tears that fall.

62

Laya

I let Mami down down down.
They've come for her.
It's Ruven and Alter.
They're the bears.
I was so busy with Fedir
I wasn't paying attention.
I need to speak to Liba.
I need to tell her everything.
But what can I tell her?
That bear-men are here
to take her away?
What would Mami
want me to do?

I search my mind
for fragments of memories.
What else have I forgotten?
What else am I
supposed to know?
I hear the sounds
of bird feet on the roof.

It makes my chest hurt
and my back ache.
I shiver and wrap
Mami's blanket
around me.

I want to go out
onto the roof
and see who is up there.
But I can't.
I am too weak.
I've lost control
of everything
that matters.

63

Liba

Dovid knocks on the door and calls out, "Can I come in?"
"Yes!" I walk over and open the door.

"I didn't know if I was interrupting anything…I heard voices nearby in the woods. I think it's the search party. I think they found something…"

"You should go see…"

"No. I won't leave you alone."

"Please. I want to know what happened."

"What if something or someone comes while I'm gone? Maybe they're just waiting for me to leave you."

Maybe they are or maybe, just maybe, Fedir is waiting for Dovid to go.

"I won't leave you," Dovid says firmly.

Think, Liba, think.

"Then I'll go. You stay with Laya."

"No! You're not going out there alone! Are you crazy? I won't let you go."

"You don't get to tell me what to do!" I rage at him and make a move for the door. "I'm afraid sometimes, yes, but that doesn't make me weak and it doesn't stop me from seeking out the truth. I am my father's daughter, and I'm proud of that." And as I say the words, I actually start believing them. "I'm not afraid of danger. I'm only afraid of losing everyone I love."

Dovid rubs his hand over his face. "Liba, I care for you very much, don't you get that? Why don't you understand that maybe I'm scared too, huh? Maybe I don't want anything to happen to you because...I'm in love with you..."

I can't believe his words. "You barely know me..." I say.

I can't do this now. I don't know what I think. So many conflicting thoughts and emotions swirl in my mind. I don't have time for this. *Where is Fedir?*

"I know it's not the place or time," Dovid says, "but... do you feel the same way about me? Does this...do we have a chance?"

I don't know what to say to him. He doesn't know the truth about me. And none of this can be real until he does. I swallow. "I will think about it if you go out there and see what happened."

"Why are you doing this?"

I look away from him. "Please."

He shakes his head and sighs. "Fine. Lock yourself inside. Barricade the door. You understand me? I won't be gone long."

"Thank you." My eyes shine with gratitude and relief.

"But, Liba?"

"Yes?"

"Don't make me wait forever."

64

Laya

We wait
and wait
and wait.
No one comes.
Not the bears.
Not Fedir.

I will die of thirst
and pain
and heart-
break—
where is he?
Why didn't
he come
for me?
why
why
why

65

Liba

As we wait, I put the kettle on and take out a volume of Talmud. The stories in it will calm me. They always do. Someone knocks at the door.

Laya looks up from the bed. My eyes meet hers across the room and I rush to open the door.

It's Dovid. He looks terrible—like he's seen a ghost.

"What happened? You're back so soon!"

He shakes his head. "They found another body. Mikhail Sirko."

"What? No...!" My hand goes to my mouth. "How? He wasn't even missing—was he?"

"Since last night apparently. In Yankl Feldman's orchard down by the river—again. His body—" His voice cracks. "—was drained of blood. Just like Jennike's. But there's more. Apparently, after the news about Jennike, there was a pogrom—in Kishinev. Forty-nine Jews were killed, women were raped, hundreds were injured, Jewish homes and businesses destroyed..."

"What?" My heart starts to pound so fast that I have trouble breathing. "Why?"

"There were articles about Jennike, that she was found in the Feldmans' orchard drained of blood. They blamed the Jews. And

the Bishop in Kishinev called for action. And now Mikhail..."
His face pales. "Liba, I fear for Dubossary. For all of us."

Drained of blood? What does that mean?

I think about the Hovlins and their big rumor-spreading
mouths—the anti-Semitic slurs I heard from them in the marketplace. I wonder if they told the newspapers, if they're responsible.
None of this happened in our town until they showed up. And
now another *goy* was found dead in a Jewish man's orchard?
Perhaps they are the ones that have something to hide.

Dovid looks as haunted as I feel. Nothing good will come of
this. He knows it too.

"Come, sit down," I say. "I was making tea."

He sits and stares down at his hands. "It wasn't gruesome,
not if you didn't look closely. But there were gouge marks at his
wrists, ankles, and neck. A ring of thorns, as though he'd been
chained or bitten. And his lips...they were red and raw, nearly an
open sore where his mouth used to be. The men said that Jennike
looked the same when they found her. Who could do something
so horrible?"

I swallow hard so as not to vomit and I place my hand on his
arm. "What is everyone saying?"

"The *kahal* thinks it was a bear. But I'm not so sure. It didn't
look like a bear did that. All they're saying is that it doesn't look
good that Jews found him, just like we found Jennike. The police
are looking for someone—or something—to blame. And there
are already riots happening—all because of something that happened in Dubossary! Can you believe? Most of the *kahal* cleared
out and went home. There's a meeting tonight at the Heimov-
itzes'. The *kahal* plus all the men who searched. Those men you
told me about were there too, searching with us in the woods
when we found Mikhail."

"They were?"

"They seemed really suspicious to me. But they said they

would come to the meeting tonight. There is talk of sorting out a proper self-defense organization. Not just patrols. Arming us all with weapons. If they come for us, we'll be ready. My father says that he'll be damned if he'll let a massacre happen here. If we all go out to hunt for the bear we can put a stop to this before the rumors spread and show the *goyim* we had nothing to do with this."

I can barely breathe. "How is Esther Feldman taking it? She must be a wreck."

"She's beside herself. The Feldmans fear for their lives—they are going to go stay in town now with the Kassins."

"But...what happens if you find a bear and kill it, but the murders don't stop?"

"There is no other explanation that makes sense," Dovid says. "We have to do something. We'd all better hope it's a bear. Tonight we'll hunt. Tonight and tomorrow and the night after that, until we find the beast and kill it once and for all. Either that, or someone must find out what really happened to Jennike and Mikhail before the villagers here all point their fingers in our direction."

66

Laya

Jennike is dead.
  Mikhail is dead.
Gone gone gone.
And Dovid,
the one my sister loves,
says that they will hunt
tonight
for a bear,
a beast.
My sister is a bear.
And there are bears here
who have come
for her.

Somehow,
I must
protect her.

I feel myself
wasting away.
I will die

if Fedir does not
return to me.

My head spins.
I am in orbit.
I see stars;
they surround me.
I look for his lips,
the only constellation
I know.

Everything aches.
Your love,
I want to say to him,
was better than wine.
I am parched for it.
Come back to me, Fedir,
please come back.
Kiss me.
My lips are dry
but my eyes
are wet.

67

Liba

The villagers gather in the cemetery. Frost coats every tomb-
stone in an icy sheen and our breaths ome out like puffs of
cloud. Jennike's mother, Galina, sobs and mewls, sounding like
an injured kitten. Her father, Ivan, is stoic and trying to look
brave, but I can see that he is broken. Today the town will bury
Jennike. Tomorrow, Mikhail.

Dovid stayed back with Laya so that I could be here.

I've never been to a Christian funeral. I can't believe I'm even
standing in the Christian cemetery. Yet I can't stay away. Something did this to Jennike, someone killed Mikhail, and it wasn't
a bear. There are journalists in town; they've already written
articles blaming it on the Jews. If only I could prove what I know
in my heart—it was the Hovlins, it has to be. As much as I don't
like Ruven and Alter, the way that Miron and Fedir threatened
me shines the guilt in their direction. And Laya is the only proof,
the only one who might know the truth, but she won't say anything. I pull the hood of my cloak down so that it covers as much
of my face as possible.

I'm trying to nurse Laya back to health. I've tried everything
I can. Every sapling and plant I find, boiling leaves, drying and
crushing them into powder, feeding them to Laya like a broth.

I've gone to Krakover's drugstore and tried everything that Velvel the Druggist suggested. Nothing works. And still Fedir does not come.

I twist the stems of the daisies I hold in my hands as the villagers shovel rich dark soil onto the coffin below. As the last few clumps of earth fall, the pastor speaks.

"We are gathered here today to celebrate the life and to honor the memory of Jennike Belenko. It is the untimely and brutal death of this daughter of the town of Dubossary which has brought us together but it is her life that we wish to remember. Jennike was a bright spark. She brought love and life to her parents. We are drawn here by our common love, our common respect and our common grief. We are thankful that Jennike lived among us, even for a short time. God is great. God gives and God takes. God will revenge the slain as he sees fit and we will root out the evil from our midst."

Amen.

"A person's days have been described like the grass of the field in their brevity, but they also represent a flowering of creative potential, of beauty. And that's what Jennike was—a flower cut off in her prime. Just as the trees of the great Kodari forest shelter us, so may we find shelter in the boughs of kinship, family, and community as we mourn this loss. Blessed be the name of the Lord."

Amen.

The villagers begin to disperse and follow Jennike's parents back to their home.

I linger, wanting to put my hands on the warm earth that I know will soon turn cold, wanting answers that perhaps only Jennike can give me. I close my eyes in a long blink and I think of her, all alone down there under all that earth. I think of the bride and groom in the Jewish cemetery, how at least in their death they had each other. Who does Jennike have now? When

I open my eyes there are tears on my cheeks. I bend down and put daisies on her grave. I look around for a rock.

But as I do so I hear someone shouting. "Murderer! Murderer!"

What? Who? Did they find the culprit? I stand up and look around and see that Borys Tomakin, owner of the town's tobacco factory, is pointing a finger in my direction. I look behind me, and my stomach falls. He is pointing at me.

68

Laya

I dream of a lazy
sleeping vine
twined around a tree,
inching its way slowly
upwards to the sky.
It wants to reach the sun,
but the forest and the branches
keep getting in its way.

My hands twist and turn
like leaves fluttering;
my heartbeat
says the same thing
over and over again:
he didn't come for me
he didn't come for me
he didn't come for me

My heart is a pearl
hidden inside me;
he held it, shiny and warm

in his palm.
But now it hurts.
Why does it
hurt so much?
I must go find him.

Fedir didn't kill Jennike.
I know what happened.
I saw her fall.
I must find a way to prove it.

I must fix this.
I must fix everything.

69

Liba

I run all the way back to the cottage. I can't breathe—it's like I have one long heartbeat. I am shaking from head to toe. I must get back to Dovid and Laya. I must protect her. Dovid has a gun. Maybe he'll know what to do.

I make it back home and bang on the door as loud and fast as my shaking hands will let me.

The door opens and I duck inside, slamming it behind me and bolting it closed. "Dovid! Dovid! They think I did it," I scream. "They're coming for me."

"What?" He looks out the window. "What are you talking about? What happened?"

"They saw me—" I can't breathe. "—putting flowers on her grave...Borys Tomakin..." I sink down to the floor. "He called out, 'Murderer!' " I gasp for air in big gulps. "I ran, Dovid, I just ran..." I start to sob. "I didn't know what else to do..."

"Did they come after you?"

"I don't know..." I can't catch my breath. "I heard crashing in the trees...Yes. Maybe. I don't know. What should I do?"

"Stay here. Stay inside. I will go speak with them." He takes out his pistol from a satchel in the corner and I can see that his hands are shaking too.

"You need to go tell the *kahal*..."

Everything in me hurts.

"Don't worry. Stay here. I will handle them."

"Dovid! Wait!"

"What?"

Tears tumble down my face. "I don't want anything to happen to you..."

I see his eyes shining. "Don't worry, Liba. I'll figure it out. Just stay inside, stay down, and hide. I will take care of this. I promise."

He goes outside and I bolt the door behind him.

I crawl over to the bed on all fours and climb under the covers. I cover my face with the blankets and wrap my arms around Laya, trying to stop my shaking.

It feels as if an age goes by.

"Liba?" Laya whispers. "What's wrong?"

"They're coming for me..."

Laya sits up in bed. I can see it takes all of her strength. "Who?"

"Get down!" I whisper. "Stay quiet!"

Thankfully, she listens to me.

"What happened?"

"It doesn't matter...It's all over for us."

"Is it the bears?"

My stomach drops. "What?"

"Those men, who came for Tati...the bears?"

I don't know how she knows what they are. I pull the blankets over both of our heads and I whisper, "Tell me what you know, Laya..."

When there's a knock at the door, I cringe. Will they shoot me in the square? Will they take me to jail? Will I even get a trial?

"Liba, open the door! It's me!" I hear Dovid's voice.

I crawl to the door and open it, staying as low as possible. Dovid is there with his father and Shmulik the Knife.

"What happened?" I ask.

"We caught up with them on their way here," Mr. Meisels says. "We convinced them to go talk to the Chief of Police. To blame you is clearly ridiculous."

"What are we going to do?" I say.

Laya turns over in bed and says hoarsely, "We're going to fight."

Everyone looks at her. "What?" I say.

"That's what Tati would do," she whispers. "He would fight them. We need to prove that you didn't do it. And we need to let them know that the Jews of Dubossary will not be blamed for this. We will not go down without a fight. Jennike wasn't murdered," she says.

"What?" I look at Dovid and the men behind him. "Come inside," I say.

They lock the door behind them.

"Laya, what are you saying?"

"She fell on the ice; I saw it happen. So did Mikhail. He and his uncle, Bohdan, took her back to his house. That was the last time I saw her."

"But I thought you said you saw her with the Hovlins? Why didn't you tell me this before?" I say.

"I thought I saw her one night, but there were a lot of people there. I could have been mistaken. What I do know is that I saw her fall—there was blood on the ice."

The men all look at each other. Dovid's father says, "Someone needs to go to Bohdan Sirko's house."

"We have to let the police know," Shmulik says.

"But will they believe us? With Laya as the only witness?" I ask.

"We have to prepare for a fight either way," Dovid says. "There are enough of us. We can't let a pogrom happen here. We can station ourselves all over the town, at the river and the docks, in front of every home. We can prevent it from happening here, or at least go down fighting."

"Have you lost your mind?" Shmulik says to Dovid. "We just have to tell the truth, and this will all get sorted out."

Mr. Meisels shakes his head. "No. Dovid's right. Forty-nine Jews lost their lives in Kishinev. Over what? A rumor that started here—twenty-five miles away? What makes you think that anyone will listen to reason now."

"We have to try," Shmulik says.

"Sure. We can try. But we must organize ourselves in the meantime, and if we're smart about it, we can outnumber them. Liba, stay here with your sister. Dovid and Shmulik will guard the door, and I will send others back here too. Shmulik—you talk to them when they get here. Tell them what Laya said. I will organize the *kahal*. Some will station themselves at the river; others will help Dovid guard the house. I will go knock on doors. There will be no pogrom in Dubossary tonight."

Dovid and Shmulik go outside to guard the door. I open the chest under my parents' bed, hoping they've left some weapons behind. Sure enough there are knives there: sharp black claw-like blades which must be my father's, and a pistol. I tuck a knife into each of my boots and the pistol into my skirt. Then go outside.

"What are you doing? Why are you out here?" Dovid says.

I tug the pistol out of my waistband. "Joining you."

"Liba! Put that down. Go back inside! Do you even know how to shoot that thing? What if they come here and see you! They could shoot you on sight!"

I shake my head. "No. This is my fight too. Maybe it's even my fault. I shouldn't have gone to the funeral. I will stand here beside you and defend Dubossary."

"Liba, this is madness. You'll be killed."

"Then leave. Go back and protect your own home. I can do this by myself."

"You've both lost your minds," Shmulik says. "Get inside, both of you. I'll watch the door."

Dovid and I go back inside.

"What don't you understand, Liba?" Dovid says. "They killed Jews in Kishinev who had nothing to do with any of this—just because they were Jews. Do you have a death wish?"

I am stronger than you know, I want to say. *I can protect you.* I open my mouth to say something, to try to explain, because it's about time that I finally tell him the truth.

But then we hear rustling on the roof. I look up, my heart racing, expecting swans—but it's Laya I see.

"Laya! What are you doing?"

She has the skylight open. She sways on her feet and grabs the open window for support, then rights herself, and climbs the rest of the way out onto the roof.

70

Laya

I know what
I have to do.
This is
my only chance.
I have to fly.
Maybe the swan
is out there;
maybe he can
show me how.

Liba follows me—
she is up
on the roof
now too.
Laya, this is crazy.
Come back down,
she says.

What? I can't
get dressed?
I can't

get up?
I can't climb
up onto the roof
if I want?
I'm sick
of being sick,
I say.
And you can't
keep me here
anymore
with promises
that never
come true!

I know
my words hurt,
but that is
my intention.
I must save
my sister.
And this is
the only way.

You're barely steady
on your feet! Liba says.
This is dangerous.
Please…come back inside!

No! I say.
You've held me
captive.
You fed me
poison,

to make me weak,
to make me dizzy,
to make me sleep.
Fedir told me.
I'm leaving.
I'm going
to the one place
where I feel safe
and happy.
The one place
where I feel good
and warm
and well fed
and sated.

Laya, my sister says,
you aren't talking sense.

Sense? I laugh.
Funny you should talk
about sense
when you lied to me.
You said
he'd come for me.
I thought
maybe he was
held up,
maybe he couldn't
make it.
I would never doubt
my sister Liba,
my sister

who always does
everything right.

I feel weak.
My skin prickles
with sweat,
a sheen of moisture,
everywhere.
My back aches;
my legs feel weak.
I thrust my arms up high,
reaching for sky.
My arms arc up
and down again.
I feel nauseous.

I crouch down
gasping for breath;
every bone
in my body
feels like
it's going to crack.

Dovid? I hear Liba say,
but she is far
far away.
Did she drink
something? she asks him.
Did she eat something?

Nothing I saw…
he says.

Ha! I cackle.
He lies too!
You are made
for each other.
Liars! Both of you.
I will get
out of your way
so you can have
this house
all to yourselves.
That's what
you wanted
all along—
to get rid
of me,
to poison me
with all those teas
that you prepared.

The pain is too much.
Everything hurts.
I start to cry.
I need him,
I say to them,
Don't deny me
the happiness
that you've found.
I will die
if I don't see Fedir
again.
I don't care
anymore
what Mami

and Tati
will think.

Liba reaches out
and tries
to take me
in her arms.
But I don't want her
touching me.
I shriek, but it comes out
more like a honk.
I try to pry
her arms off mine.
I flap and flail
and lash out
at her, but my hands
are not hands
anymore;
my fingers
don't work
like they should.
Liba lets go
and I lunge
for the edge.

You are not
my sister
anymore,
I spit out.
I take a step
off the roof
and jump.

I start to fall,
but the air catches me
and in one last
rack of pain
my arms become wings,
my nose a beak,
my feet webbed,
already tucked
beneath me
ready for flight.
I flap my white arms—
my wings!
And take off
through the woods.

I bare my long neck
for the branches
that arc above me
sometimes crashing
into trees,
sometimes soaring
high above them.
I didn't know
that I could move
like this
but the air
guides me.

I am a sacrifice,
I tell the moonlight,
and the sky.
I will save Liba.
Her life for mine.

No matter
what it takes.

In the closing
eye of night,
I'm finally free.
I imagine myself
strobe-lit; the stars
are lanterns held aloft.
The forest beats for me;
I feel connected to it
even as I rise
above the trees.
My blood runs in
its veins. The sap
runs in my veins.
The trees call for my blood
and I answer their call.
I will save
our town.

I've had dreams
of trees like living things,
my arms like branches,
my fingers turned to vines,
my back growing leaves
like feathers, forming
verdant wings.

I will become one with this forest
and Fedir will guide me,
his lips my compass.
He will quench my thirst;

he will hold me in his arms.
If I go to him,
perhaps they will leave
Dubossary alone.

The swan didn't come.
Only Fedir can help me now.
I will find out
who killed Jennike
and Mikhail.
I will clear his name
and Liba's too.
It is the only way.

I have brought this on us all.
Because I didn't
tell the truth
of what I saw.
It is the last thing
I can do.
The only thing.

71

Liba

Seven paces wide and nine paces long.

I trace the width and length of the living room again and again.

Twelve paces make a circle.

I feel like a caged beast.

I thought that Dovid saw her turn, that I would need to tell him everything, but he just saw her fall. He ran around to the back of the house, thinking he'd find her broken on the ground, but she was gone. I said that she landed on her feet and ran off. If he saw the swan flying above us, he didn't make the connection. Why should he? It makes no sense. None of what I am, what we are, makes any sense at all.

And so I pace. Alone with my thoughts. *Should I go after her? Should I stay here? Should I wait outside with Dovid for the men I know will come, hungry for my blood? Should I prepare her bed for when she comes back again, still heartsick and cold, hungry and wild, and without him.*

How can you trust a man—any man? I wonder. This one just keeps disappointing her. She pines for him endlessly, but he leaves her unsated, thirsty, a shadow of herself.

And yet Dovid is here for me. Dovid doesn't leave my side.

Dovid watches me pace, concern in his eyes. He gets me to drink. He makes me food to eat. He holds me and lets me cry on his shoulder as he strokes my long black hair. He tries to get me to sit, to stop, to breathe, to calm myself, to stop this frenzy of fretting, to soothe my agitation.

Perhaps there are different breeds of men. What separates one from the other?

I feel the cold trail of one tear, and another. And in an instant, Dovid is beside me again. His warm arms surround me. "Hush, love, don't cry again. There's nothing you can do. She made her choice. We all make choices."

"My parents will be devastated," I say. "This will break their hearts…"

"I know," he says. "But there really is nothing you can do…"

Then it hits me. *The swans, Liba. The swans. You can call them.* There *is* something I can do. And it's better than staying here like a caged beast with an endless cramping in my gut.

I owe her this.

72

Laya

I cross the pine glade
into the clearing.
It has taken
everything I have
to keep flying.
I am weak and covered
in scratches and scrapes.
I see the clearing
up ahead
but I don't know
how to land.
I crash to the ground
with a thud.
Everything hurts.
I'm bruised
and broken.
But my body
is human again.

I hear something.
I flit my eyes open

and look up.
Fedir...
He takes me
in his arms.

He kisses me
and I feel alive again.
Revived.
I latch on
to his lips
and start to suck
hungrily.
I bite down
and taste blood
and it is so good
and sweet.
Everything buzzes
and tingles.
I feel better
instantly.
And I know
that I did
the right thing.
He will take me
to the lodge
and I will find
some answers.

I'm so glad you came,
he whispers.

I waited for you, I say.
Why didn't you come?

There were others there…
He shakes his head.
Others? I say.
I don't understand.

I wanted you alone
with no interruptions, he says.

I thought
that you'd forgotten, I say.
I could never forget you.
His eyes shine.
But now you're here!
Now we can
be together forever.
Yes! I say. *Yes,*
that's what I want too!

He takes me
through the clearing
and to the fire circle
before the Hovlin lodge.
You come willingly? he asks.
I do. It was only Liba
that held me back, I answer.
You wish to be mine? he says.
Forever. Only you, you you, I say.
I smash my lips against his.
I feel his brothers gathering
around us.

Fedir breaks the kiss.
He puts me down.

He takes my hand
and turns
to all his brothers.
Behold! With all of you
as witnesses,
I hereby pledge to wed Laya
in three days' time.

What? I say.
Everything happens so fast
I'm not sure I understand.
I think I just agreed
to be his wife?

You will be my Queen,
he says.

I start to laugh—
it's absurd.
Queen?
Queen of what?
The forest?
The air?
The orchard?
Fedir leads me away.
I can't stop laughing.
Hush, Laya, hush, he says
but everything is funny.

He leads me to a cabin—
a small one—
it smells like home.
The bed is soft;

I sink into it.
He lies beside me.
I press my lips
to his again.
He touches me
and I feel
more alive
than I've felt
in days.
My toes tingle
so much I laugh.
It tickles,
this feeling of him
and me
alone in bed—
oh my, alone
alone
alone

I turn to wrap
my arms around him,
but he is by the door.
He whispers, *Rest, my love,*
just rest. I will be
back for you.
Stay here.
Do not leave
the cabin.
I have things
that I must do.

But wait! I say.
Where are you going?

But he is gone.
When I get up
to go after him,
to find the evidence
my sister needs
to prove her innocence,
the door is locked.

I've exchanged
one cage
for another.

73

Liba

I put my coat on, and my boots, and take my father's weapons with me—both blades, the gun—and the blood-stained feather Mami gave me. I must call the swans.

"Liba, this is madness—you can't go out there. They're looking for you," Dovid says.

I hear what he's saying to me, what he continues to say, but it's not something I can hear right now. "There's something I have to do."

"I can't let you go out there."

"If it was one of your brothers, and you knew that you could save them, would you go?"

"Yes, in a normal situation, but not if people were out there looking for me, accusing me of murder!"

"She's the only family I have left. I promised my parents I'd take care of her!"

"She made her choice. There's only so much you can do..." He shakes his head. "How do you think she would feel if they caught you on your way to find her, or help her, and you ended up in jail...or worse..."

"She's my sister. I would lay down my life for her."

"That's exactly what you're doing if you go out tonight."

"Then so be it."

"You're impossible!" Dovid says.

"I have to do this alone," I say.

"No. I'm coming with you. Wherever you go, I go."

I huff in frustration. "Okay, fine," I say, but really I have to get away from him. I need to call the swans.

We walk out of the cabin.

"We're going after Laya," I tell Shmulik.

"You're crazy, both of you," he says. He looks at Dovid. "Your father will have my head."

"I'm not letting her go alone."

He takes my hand and we set off.

We arrive at the old oak tree without encountering anyone. That alone makes me worry. Why are the woods so quiet? So still? I let go of his hand. Something feels off. The air is hazy... I rub my eyes and suddenly I see we're in an orchard. But that's not possible. The trees around us are heavy with jewel-like fruit. *Is this what Laya saw that day?*

"Dovid, do you see fruit in the trees?"

"No, why do you ask?"

"Wait for me here, and if I don't return within the hour, go for help."

"No! Liba, I'm not letting you go ahead without me."

"Please, Dovid, please! I beg you. I need to do this alone."

He lets out his breath in a sigh of frustration. "Why? I'll let you go if you tell me why."

"It's going to sound crazy."

"I'm all ears."

"I think that this part of the forest is enchanted. I think that it will only let girls through. That's how the Hovlins lured people to their lodge, and that's how nobody was able to find them."

"You're right—it sounds far-fetched. But I agree with you that something in the forest here feels wrong. Something in the air makes me want to turn back and not walk this way. Go. See if your theory is correct. Try to find their camp. I'll stay here and watch the forest. But I'm coming after you in half an hour if you're not back."

"Thank you." I turn to go. This time, as I walk I feel the trees parting for me. There are fruit trees everywhere. I look for a place to stop and call the swans, but no place feels right. Something leads me in a certain direction. I can't argue with the air and the branches that guide me.

I walk through the pine glade as if in a dream, propelled forward, and I see a clearing with a fire pit in its center. Nobody's there. There is a large lodge just across the way that suddenly appears as if it's carved out of the very trees that are still rooted there, and some small cabins that dot the surrounding forest.

How did they build all this so quickly? They've only been in our town for just over a week…

I take a deep breath and knock on the door of the first cabin I see.

Nobody answers.

I try the next cabin, and the next.

"Hello?" I hear a voice.

I think it's Laya! But she sounds odd. And it seems like the door is bolted from the outside. I unlock it and open the door.

"Thank God! You're alive! You're okay…" I crush her to me.

"Of course I'm okay." She looks at me quizzically. "What are you doing here?"

"I've come to rescue you and take you back home."

"Rescue me?"

"Yes! Let's go! It's quiet—nobody saw me come here. They must all be out at the market. If we go now, we can escape before they get back. I unbolted the door—now's your chance to escape. Let's go!" I take her hand.

"Liba! Stop!" Laya smacks my hand away. "Are you mad?"

"Shhhh! You'll alert someone."

"There's no one to alert," Laya says in a voice that doesn't sound like her own.

"I know! That's why we need to go right now!" I grab her hand again.

"No, stop, Liba, you don't understand!" Laya bats my hand away from hers again so hard it hurts.

"What?" I say.

"Look at me," Laya commands, sweeping her hands over her skirt and fluffing her hair.

I look. And I see that she is dressed in a beautiful gown the color of moss and cranberries. Her hair is clean and woven with golden leaves and branches. Her cheeks are pink and her eyes sparkle.

"Don't you see? Fedir has asked me to marry him, and I said yes."

"You said what?"

"I said yes. I meant to come tell you, but time feels like it's flying by…with so many preparations for the wedding and coronation."

"Coronation? What are you talking about?" My mouth gapes open. This is not my sister. She's not acting anything like herself. Her voice is languid, dreamy, as if she's tired…or drugged.

"Oh yes, I'm to be Queen. Did I forget to mention that? Perhaps I did. Well anyhow, I hope to see you there if you can make it. I will be wed in three days' time. Fedir was here before, but he left to make plans. There is a closet here full of beautiful clothing—all in my size! But now you must be off—I have much to do to prepare my trousseau. And I don't think they will be pleased to see you here."

"Your trousseau?" I shake my head in disbelief.

"Mami would love it so," she says. "But alas, she'll probably never see it. By the time she comes back, we may be off to the next town or village." Laya's hands flit through the air, as if painting a picture on the wind. "Fedir said he would send a messenger bird with an invitation to you, but you know how birds are." She laughs, then tsks. "So flighty. It's no wonder it never reached you."

I shake my head again as if to clear it. Something in the air is making me feel foggy and distant as well. *A messenger bird? What is she talking about? What has happened to my sister?* I blink and rub my eyes, and for an instant I see that Laya is dressed in rags. And on her head is a crown of thorns. I squint my eyes and blink them, and she's dressed in finery again. I don't understand. I can't believe any of this. *You are a swan*, I want to say. *Swans mate for life, and you have mated yourself to a monster.* But I can't get the words out.

"I invited Mami and Tati too, but I guess they can't make it, which just shows you how much they really care about me."

"Do you even hear yourself? Mami and Tati are in Kupel! Or did you forget that? And they would never come to your wedding. You're marrying a *goy*!"

"Well..." She flaps her hands and looks this way and that. "Their loss." She busies herself with inspecting a piece of her hair.

"Laya, what has come over you?"

"People change. I'm changing. And one day soon Fedir will take me far away from here. They will sell their fruit and tell their tales in the next town, and I will help them."

"You're only fifteen! I wish you'd wait a bit and think this through."

"Well, maybe Mami and Tati should have thought about that before they left us. But Kupel was more important...wasn't it? The Rebbe is more important than you or me. They made their choice, and I made mine. Just look at this house!" Laya smooths her hands over the velvet brocade of the window drapes. "And these clothes! I have taken care of myself. There are riches here beyond compare. We should take a stroll over to the lodge and I'll show you everything." She points out of her front door across the clearing.

My sister has never cared for clothes or finery. This conversation just keeps getting stranger and stranger. "Laya, you were locked in this cabin from the outside. I'm not going into that lodge with you. What if it's a trap and they lock me up too? You have a chance to run away, right now, with me. Let's go!" I grab her arm.

"No!" she screeches.

I stop and stare at her. *Who is this person and what have they done with my sister?* I let go of her arm. "Laya, they've gotten inside your head. You're going to wake up from this dream and you will regret everything. Please, please come with me now. I'll ask you one last time nicely, but if you don't agree, I may need to drag you away from here by force. I don't think you understand what you've gotten yourself into."

She takes a deep breath as though she is steadying herself. "This is what Fedir said would happen. You're jealous. Of course you are. There's something strange about the fact that I got chosen first, right, right, right? Something strange about the fact that I'm prettier and nicer and that someone came along and snatched me up and took me away to give me the life that I deserve? A life that Tati could never give us! Well, I'm not giving this up.

"You will spend the rest of your days alone in a hovel with the butcher's son and never see a town other than Dubossary. One day, this town will matter so little that it will be swallowed up whole by the Kodari. The forest will take back what belongs to it, together with everyone in the *shtetl*! You spend too much time trying to be perfect, trying to do everything right. But it's only a matter of time before Dovid learns what you really are—a beast. You're jealous, spiteful, and self-absorbed, like everyone else in this town. Get away from me! Go back to that stupid hovel and live out the rest of your miserable days. But I'm staying here. I only hope that Dovid is still there waiting for you."

I feel my face turn ashen. Maybe there is truth to her words. I won't take her from here by force if this is the way she really feels.

"Well, I guess there's nothing more to say, is there?"

Laya slams the door in my face and my eyes smart with tears.

I can't believe everything that just happened. I turn and run as fast as my legs can carry me. I tear past Dovid, who is waiting for me, and he follows. I run until I get to the river behind our house, where I sit on its banks, not caring that the hem of my dress gets wet, not caring how cold I am, or that Dovid tries to get me to go back home with him. He holds me and consoles me as I cry bitter tears into the river.

74

Laya

I lost my chance
to get away.
It might have been
my only chance.
I lost my sister too.
It's all my fault.

He locked me in.
I know that.
He said it was
to protect me.
From who?
I wanted to know
but I didn't ask.
The door is unlocked now
but I sit in darkness
and hear the sounds
of the forest around me:
chord progressions
of insect calls
and birdsong.

String instruments
concealed in trees,
and branches that sing
heartsick melodies
if you listen.
I long to add my voice
to the symphony.

My throat hurts
but not from thirst.
From silence.
I should have told people
what I knew.
What I saw.
Now I wait
and watch
and listen.

I will find a way
to clear her name.

75

Liba

I wake a few hours later all alone and hear the scratching of feet and feathers on the roof. *The swans!* I think. I bolt up in bed. *All is not lost. Maybe they can still help me.* My heart swells with hope.

I climb down the ladder and see Dovid napping down below. I don't remember much of what happened after I ran from Laya, and my insides start to hurt again when I think about the words she said. Dovid was here for me, that I know for certain. He must have brought me inside and told me to lie down.

I find the stained feather and clamber out the skylight and onto the roof.

I sit upon the thatch and close my eyes. I hold onto the feather and take a deep breath. I remember his name. *Aleksei Danilovich.* I say it like a wish: "Aleksei Danilovich," blowing his name at the feather, and again, "Aleksei Danilovich," and squeezing my eyes and exhaling to the wind as though I was wishing on the sky and the air, "Aleksei Danilovich! *Bud'laska!* Please come! Laya needs you," I say, the way Mami would have. But all is quiet and I'm still alone.

I listen and wait, but all I hear are other birds and the sound of the wind in the trees.

Oh well. I sigh. *It was worth a try. I know Mami said they'd come, but she didn't call them, I did, and I don't know if they'll honor a promise they made fifteen years ago.*

I start to slide down the roof and back to the upstairs window when all of a sudden the wind shifts and I smell moss and honey. I look up, and a swan descends. Its wingspan is nearly wider than the roof. I cower and hold onto the chimney as the great bird comes to rest upon the roof beside me.

My heart is pulsing in my chest impossibly fast. My hands itch in places that I know only claws grow. I clench my fists. *I must be brave*, I tell myself. *This is for Laya.* I take a deep breath and will the tingling in my hands away.

The largest and most beautiful swan I've ever seen comes to sit beside me.

"I need your help," I gasp.

The bird does not reply.

"My sister has been taken. Well, not exactly taken—she went of her own free will. She's locked in a cabin, though she seems to be okay with it. But she was poisoned. At least, I think she was. There was definitely something in the fruit she ate, or in the mead she drank, or on the lips of that boy she kissed. And when I was there visiting her, for a minute, everything felt like a mirage. I think that the men who took her might be responsible for two murders as well, but I have no way to prove it. My sister thinks they're innocent. I've done everything I can and I didn't know what else to do, so I called you."

Silence.

I start to laugh. *Narishkeit. What a fool I am, talking to a bird. Yes, it's a swan, and he came when I called, but he's mute or dumb or just a bird. What did I expect?* I shake my head.

"*Ne zvazhay*," I say. "I don't know why I'm out here talking to a bird. As if you could do anything. I guess that's just how desperate or crazy I've become."

A gust of wind then circles the house, a whirlpool of dust and air, and I tremble and draw my arms around my knees, and with a rush of feathers and the popping sound of bones, the bird beside me becomes a man.

A naked man.

"*Oy!*" I scream and my hand goes to my mouth. I close my eyes.

"You act like you've never seen a man before," he says in a tone that's almost like a honk.

"Not a naked one." I'm trembling. *A bear afraid of a bird—how ridiculous*, my mind says, but I can't stop my body's reaction.

"You have nothing to fear. Open your eyes."

I open them and beside me is one of the most beautiful men I've ever seen. His skin is powdery-white and covered in fine white down; his eyes are black as coal. His hair is long and blond and silky—*Almost like Laya's*, I think—and now he's covered with a cloak that looks as if it's white fur. I reach out to touch it and realize that it's made of feathers—the same kind of cloak that Mami took out of the trunk that night.

"You're beautiful," I say.

The swan-man laughs. "Dmitry Danilovich, at your service," he says, bowing his head. "You spoke my brother's name."

"I did."

"Why?"

"My mother told me before she left that if my sister ever needed anything I should hold this feather and call his name."

"She spoke true. But why should I help you?" He sniffs the air. "You are not one of us. You are..." He wrinkles his nose in disgust. "...a predator."

"A what?" My blood runs cold. "Don't be ridiculous," I say. "I'm just a girl."

"How do we know this isn't a trap? That you don't have all your kind waiting in the house or in the woods to devour us all?"

My kind?

"There's only me," I say, but I think of Ruven and Alter, though of course I don't mention them. "I didn't need to call you here," I say, indignant. "I only did because I thought you'd care. My mother is one of you, and that means that I'm actually part of you too—half swan. Swans mate for life—at least, that's what she told me. Aleksei was her mate. I thought that maybe that meant something. But I guess it doesn't. Never mind." I turn away from him and make it look like I'm heading back inside.

"It does mean something." He pauses. "It means everything. Tell me what's wrong."

I shrug my shoulders. "My sister is not well. It's like a madness is upon her. She met this boy in town, Fedir Hovlin—he sells fruit in the marketplace with his brothers, and ever since she spent time with him and ate of the fruit she hasn't been herself. Now they're engaged, but he's keeping her locked in a cabin. My mother made me promise to call you if Laya was ever in trouble, and she is. At this point, anything is preferable to who she's with."

"That does not inspire confidence."

I rub my forehead. "That's not how I meant it. You have to understand: the community we live in, it's very insular. My father will never approve of Laya's choice—not Fedir, or a swan... she's only fifteen. I want her to know that there are choices out there and I thought that maybe if she met one of you...my mother said that swans mate for life and I wondered if...does my sister have a mate? Could she meet him? It's a far shot, I know. But if she knew she had a choice. If she saw that there was another way..."

Silence.

"If you don't want to help me, fine. Just go back where you came from. I can help myself. She's to be married soon anyway, so it's probably too late."

I start to climb down off the roof in earnest.

"Wait!" Dmitry says.

"Why should I?" I sigh, defeated. *This was just a stupid idea. Like all my ideas. How could the swans possibly help me? Will she hate me for saving her? Is it possible for her to hate me more than she already does? I can't do anything right anymore.*

"Your sister is mated?" he asks.

"I don't know. Does she have a swan-mate?"

"That's not what I meant. She's 'engaged,' as you say in human terms? Has she mated with him?"

"I don't know. I hope not. She's living with him now, so something of that nature may have happened or could be about to happen. I hope he waits until marriage." I swallow. "If you could just…help get her out of there. That's all I ask. I'm not asking for a miracle—I just want my sister back."

"I must discuss this with my family. I'll be back. Here—" He plucks a feather from his cloak and hands it to me. "This is my promise." And in a rush of air and feathers, he shifts back into a swan and takes off.

I watch him go and shake my head.

There's nothing I can do now but wait.

76

Laya

I feel something at my lips.
It smells divine. Like Fedir.
I open my mouth
to kiss him,
but I sink my teeth
into flesh instead—
a peach.

My mouth moves
against the fruit.
It's so tasty!
I latch onto it
and begin to suck.
Mmmm, Fedir, I moan,
my eyes closed.
It is delicious.
But then
everything spins.

He picks me up
and carries me

out of the cabin.
My eyes flutter open
but I am tired tired tired.

Something is wrong—
the fruit tastes bitter
where it should be sweet
and the arms that hold me
are too thin; they smell
like something sour.
I try to open my eyes but
something is blinding them.
I gag; the fruit tastes bad.

He carries me down
a staircase.
Down down down,
we go, farther and farther
in a spiral
around and around.

He stops,
I feel my head loll.
My limbs are limp—
I have no control
over my body.
What is happening to me?
Mami! Tati! Liba!
Help! Help! Help!

He kicks open a door
and lays me softly on a bed.
I open my eyes and I see

Zusha Glazer,
on a bed:
what is he doing here?
My head lolls to the side,
and I see Hinda Glazer too.
They are both sleeping,
but they look pale.
Hands force
my mouth open,
and the peach
is there again.
I try to suck
at the flesh,
but my lips
are sore
and bruised,
the meat
of the peach
is nearly gone.
My teeth gnash at the pit,
my lips pucker
in search
of more juice,
anything
to keep me feeling
something
something
something.

I force my eyes open again.
Why are the Glazers here?
But I only see Miron
standing above me,

not Fedir.
He ties down my feet.
He grabs my wrists.
I try to fight him
but I have no strength.
The peach rolls
to the ground
and I feel
pain pain pain.
I try to cry out,
but I have no voice.

He punctures a vein
at one wrist
and then the other.
I turn my head and see
the first drop of my blood
drip down a vine-like tube.

This is all
you Jews
are good for,
he says. *Your blood*
is sweeter than wine.
But your souls
are filthy.
I won't allow
Fedir to crown
you Queen.
I gasp and writhe
as he clamps down
on my ankles, first one
and then the other,

deep gouges of pain
and pressure,
something sucking
at my veins.

My eyes are wide
and searching.
I feel panic;
my lips try
to form words
but they are swollen
and numb.
I can't form
coherent thoughts.
I take deep breaths,
struggling to keep
breathing.
When Jennike fell
on the ice,
Bohdan didn't know
what to do with her.
He feared he'd be blamed.
That's what Jews are for,
I told him.
But Mikhail,
that pest, was snooping
around here;
he kept trying to stick
his nose in our business.
Blood is blood,
I always say.
But Jewish blood
is cheaper.

I can't
feel my feet,
or my legs.
It is a blessing
because it doesn't hurt
but I am scared
and cold
and I feel as if
I am all alone.
I was wrong.
So wrong.
And now I will die
and Liba too.
I couldn't save her.

It feels like a drug
is pumping
through my veins,
but my veins
are pumping
into other veins.
My blood
feeding tubes
that look like vines.
I asked for this.
I came here willingly.
I should have known
that it would end
this way.
Liba was right.
I'd hoped
that it was all
a misunderstanding,

that Bohdan
had taken Jennike
and killed Mikhail.
But I was wrong.
So wrong.

Miron brings his hands
to my neck;
there is a vise-like thing
with six thorns
crafted out of wood.
It is a crown,
like the one he placed
upon my head
that first day
in the meadow.
It forms
six red punctures
at my throat.
The pain is exquisite,
and I think,
This is how it ends,
this is how I die,
everything is over.
They will blame
the Jews,
everyone in the shtetl
is going to die.
I will never
see my parents again.

He puts his lips to mine.
He tastes like ash,

like rotten garbage.
I try to purse my lips
to spit at him.
But I can't do anything.

My brother thought
he could outwit us all,
he says. *My brother thought*
that you were special.
Now he will see
that all Jews bleed
the same.
The roots are thirsty, Laya—
your blood will water them
and you will breed fruit
red and ripe
that we will feed
to all the gullible people
in all these backwater towns.
And one by one
these shtetlach
will destroy themselves
with hatred.
But we will be
long gone.
Soon, the Kodari
will cover everything again
and all you humans
will be gone,
swallowed up
by the earth,
by your own hatred
and stupidity.

I open my mouth
and let out a long,
sharp cry
just before the world
goes black.
It sounds distant,
but clear
like the crooning
of a bird,
but really,
it is the sound
of my heart
breaking.

he betrayed me
he betrayed me
he betrayed me

77

Liba

I pace the cottage again. I can't tell Dovid about the swan-man, and I don't know how long I can wait for Dmitry to come back. Time is running out. "Let's go back to the Hovlin lodge," I say. "Come back there with me. Help me take her away from them. She's being held against her will."

"Liba." Dovid shakes his head with exasperation. "There is no lodge."

"How do you know that for sure?"

"I saw nothing."

"That's because it's an enchantment."

He shakes his head again.

"Dovid, I'm not crazy!" I yell. "She was locked in. And she was not herself. I can't wait anymore. Tomorrow will be too late!"

"Liba, stop. Please. You aren't well. Think about it. You went there already and she chased you away. Listen to reason. Maybe this is the choice she made." He grabs my shoulders and I struggle against him. "You can't save someone who doesn't want to be saved."

"You don't understand," I say to him as I pull away. "How can you possibly understand when you can't even see what I'm talking about?"

"Laya, do you hear yourself? Okay, listen to this. What if your roles were reversed? What if you'd agreed to be my wife?" He blushes and wets his lips with his tongue. "And you'd come to live with me in a cabin I built just for you." He pauses, as if the words he says hold physical weight. "But I locked you in because there were creatures in the forest that I wanted to protect you from."

"You would lock me in from the outside?" My heart hurts.

"But what if Laya came to you, to our house—" He swallows. "—and demanded that you leave me? That I'd enchanted you?" He puts his arm out to touch me, but I turn away from him.

"How do you know that she's not happy?" he says. "What if she claimed that you'd lost your mind to marry me? What if she didn't approve? And your parents didn't approve? What would you do then? Would you still choose me?"

I stare at him, frozen in place, because his words ring too true. *Would I?* I don't know the answer.

He shakes his arms at the sky in frustration. "Do you even know what you really want? Because if you don't, then don't presume to think you know what she wants. Don't make a decision for someone else when you're not even brave enough to make one for yourself!" he shouts. There are tears shining in his eyes as he gets up, walks out of the house, and slams the door behind him.

I choose you, Dovid, I want to say. *I've already chosen a hundred times. If I could, I would choose you...*But I can't. What man could ever love a beast?

It's clear to me I need to end this now. The swans haven't come back. They won't help me. Dovid won't help me. Laya's life hangs in the balance. I know what I must do.

I follow him outside. "You don't understand," I say. "I'm going to go get my sister, even if I have to kidnap her and fight my way out of there. Are you with me or against me?"

"Liba! Please—see reason!" he cries.

"Then you're against me," I say. "Goodbye, Dovid." And I

walk away, tears wetting my cheeks as I set out for the Hovlin glen again.

I'll threaten Fedir and his brothers. I'll force them to confess. And if all else fails, I'll call the beast within me. I'll become the very thing I fear, once and for all. Laya is worth it. She's worth everything.

I get as far as the old oak tree and start to make my way into the pine forest when my foot snags on what feels like a root and I tumble and fall. Someone grabs my hands roughly and something else tugs at my feet. And suddenly my hands are bound. I gasp and take a breath to scream just as a rough rag is shoved into my mouth and a dark cloth goes over my head and face. The world goes black.

78

Laya

I dream that I'm
with my mother again
in the glen behind our house.

She looks at the sky
and waits, watching silently.
What are you doing, Mami?

Wait here, she says.
I wait wait wait,
and squint at the setting sun.

I hear the flapping of wings
before I see them.
A dozen birds descend,
surrounding us.
As their webbed feet
touch the ground
they grow and shift,
turning from white
downy feathers

into pale fuzzy skin.
I cannot look away.

Mami cups her hands to my ear
and whispers:
Terpinnya, dochka!
she says.
Listen to them.

The swans raise their arms
up to the sky and feathers
fall like rain.

Nmaye! Mami cries.
Twelve sets of swan eyes
look upon her.
Tears fall from her eyes.
My heart beats so fast fast fast
I think it will grow wings
and fly away.

The time has come
for her to know,
Mami says.

Laya, look upon them, Mami says.
This is the brother
of Aleksei Danilovich,
who was your father.
His name is Dmitry.

What is Mother doing?
Who are these people?
I close my eyes.

A cold hand
touches me. I gasp
and lurch back,
but there's
another hand,
and another,
the hands
pull me forward.

They turn me around.
I bring my hands up
to cover my face, but someone
takes them, holds them;
there are cold fingers
in mine.

Ne biytesya,
the voice croons.
Open your eyes.
I shake my head.
Tears fall.
Shhh…do not cry.
Open your eyes;
look straight into mine.
I open my eyes a slit,
enough to see that it is
the youngest of the swans
who holds my hands.
I shiver as his feathers
brush my skin.
Just like I shivered
the first time
I touched him.

This is Sasha,
my cousin's son, Dmitry says.
He sees things that others
cannot see.
He is your mate.
You are family, sim'ya,
he says to me,
and this swan
will be your King—
vash lebid—
when the first sign of wings
begin to bud on your back.

Mami is crying,
but they are tears
of joy.
Aleksei would choose you still,
dorohyy, Dmitry says to Mami
and dries her tears
with his thumbs.
Come with us.

Mami shakes her head.
It's too late, she says.
He puts his fingers
beneath her chin
and tilts her face up.
He kisses her cheek.
Mami shakes her head again
and says, *It cannot be.*
Take care of her? she says,
and looks at me.

Dmitry puts his hand out
and touches my forehead.
Sasha takes my hand in his
and squeezes it.
I feel my eyes close.
One day you will be Queen,
daughter of my brother;
one day you will rule in my place,
and people will worship you
as they worship all of us,
the swans of the cross,
the children of Saint Anna.
My head is spinning.
You will rule in the way
that your father
would have wanted
you to rule.
I feel myself falling.
But you will not make
the same foolish choices.

79

Liba

I groan as I come to, head throbbing. I try to open my eyes, expecting darkness. Instead I find myself bound to a tree, with nothing on my face. I see that I'm in a clearing; by my feet are two bedrolls, a smoldering fire, and a makeshift campsite.

"The *prietzteh* awakens."

I look around. *Where did the voice come from? A princess? Me? Was I wrong about the Hovlin men? Are these the men who killed Jennike and Mikhail? Is their fate to be mine?*

Two men come out of the woods. Ruven and Alter. Breath leaves my lungs.

"Why did you do this to me? Who are you?" I scream. I feel my temper flare, a rumbling ball of fire in the pit of my stomach.

The men walk over and stand in front of me.

"I demand to know who you really are!" I try to claw at the tree and the ropes that bind me.

Alter elbows Ruven. "The *zaftige moid* is getting *heldish*."

"Shut up, idiot," Ruven says.

I shout again in what sounds almost like a roar. "I'm going to scream until you let me go."

"Did you hear that, Ruven? Only fools rely on miracles," Alter tsks.

"Give me some answers or I'll scream again and the whole village will come running," I say.

"She has a point, Altisch," Ruven says. I hate the look on his face, the smirk. I hate every hair on his head.

"Don't call me that," Alter says through his teeth.

"Let's spare ourselves the agony and get right to it, eh?" Ruven says. "Where is your father?"

"I told you I don't know!"

"But he left. Where did he go?" Ruven's eyes are cold steel.

I close my eyes and grit my teeth. "I told you. They went back home. To Kupel, to the Rebbe."

"But that's not possible!" Alter says.

"What? Why?" My heart drops into my stomach.

"Because the Rebbe went to his *oylam*. He passed away. And we didn't see your parents on the road," Alter says calmly. "So tell us the truth now."

"The Rebbe's dead? *Baruch dayan ha'emet*. Why didn't you say so the first time we saw you? Does that mean that my parents never made it to Kupel?"

"Maybe they walked a different way," Ruven suggests. "Perhaps we crossed paths in the woods."

"Or maybe something happened to them…" I whisper. I feel my skin go cold.

"We came to get your father," Alter says, "because your father is the Rebbe now."

"But Yankl came here a few weeks ago to tell us. Why did you have to come too? And why the secrecy?" *Nothing makes sense.*

Ruven and Alter exchange a look. "There are politics at work that you don't understand," Ruven says.

"And perhaps your father should have been a bit more forthcoming with you," Alter adds.

"Do you really think it's possible that she knows nothing?" Ruven asks him.

"Can you please talk to me? I'm right here. What am I supposed to know? Why have you tied me up like this? What does
any of this have to do with me?" I am cold with fear. "Are you
going to kill me? Did you kill Jennike and Mikhail?"

"What? No!" Ruven barks.

"Then what do you want from me?"

"Your father comes from a long line of Chassidim, Rebbes
who are considered almost like royalty by their followers. It is
no small thing that the Rebbe died, and if your father is named
his successor—as he should be—that means that you and your
family are part of that dynasty."

"But there are others who seek to discredit your father,"
Alter says. "Who think that because of your mother, he is not
worthy to lead us. And one of the considerations is...he has no
heir. Only...you. You have no brother, and if you know anything about what you are, then you know that it is vital to us,
to the Berre Chassidim, that what we are and what we can do is
carried on."

"Do you know what you are?" Ruven asks.

"Why should I tell you anything? You've shown me nothing
but cruelty," I say.

"Look. We can help you save your sister," Alter says gruffly.

"What?"

"You heard him," Ruven says.

"And you had to tie me up to tell me this?"

"No," Alter says. "We will help you save your sister, but you
have to tell us what we want to know."

"We're on your side, Liba," Ruven says.

"How do you even know where Laya is?" I ask.

"The forest has ears," Alter says.

"Okay. Fine." I shrug. "Be cryptic. But if you want to help
me, why did you kidnap me?"

"Because everything has a price, *prietzteh*." Alter rasps in a gravelly voice.

"*Ich hob dir!* I'm no princess." I spit at them.

Ruven shakes his head and laughs. "You know nothing. Alter, let's go."

"What's that supposed to mean?" I snarl.

"I'm sure those Hovlin men would like to make you into a *malka*, just like they've done to your sister who was as beautiful as the seven worlds, but that didn't help her, did it?" Ruven taunts.

"Maybe she's happy there." I try to act nonchalant. "Who says I want to save her?"

"Because she will become their captive slave." Alter's voice runs cold as a knife blade. "A blood prisoner. A queen in name only. They will water their orchards with her lifeblood until she is nothing but a shell, a husk of herself. Just like they did to the Glazers and to Jennike and Mikhail. The blood that is being spilled in these woods, in towns all over Bessarabia, makes fruits that are as unnatural as the men who grow them. They have one goal and one goal only—to bring back the Kodari forest, their ancestral home. And they think that the fastest way to do that is to sow fear and hatred into people's breasts. If people hate each other, they will blame each other, and eventually they will kill each other. And what better group of people to start with than the Jews?

"They kill a non-Jew—like Jennike—or anyone who gets in their way—like Mikhail. They spread rumors on the wind and poison people with their bloody fruit and their lies. They bring about a pogrom, but by the time it starts, they're gone. Disappeared. Already setting up their lodge and their fruit stands in the next town. If your sister survives, she may become their Goblin Queen. But she will forever be shackled to their service—her human blood is the only precious thing about her. And if she dies first, they will simply find another victim.

"We thought we'd find your father and take him back with us, and we weren't sure about you—if you were his daughter through and through. Because if you are, you are priceless. There are many men who would give anything to make the daughter of the new Rebbe their bride. You have *yichus*—pedigree—sure, but what we want to know is: do you have the holy blood?"

"Holy blood?"

"Can you shift, Liba? Can you change? Are you a bear? Or are you just a girl?" Alter says.

I swallow hard.

"But now that we're here and we see what's happening, in Kishinev," Ruven adds, "and maybe in Dubossary next. We think we must try to stay and fight, to rid the woods of the goblins for good. Before Kupel is next."

"Did you say goblins?" I whisper. *Anything is possible, Liba, anything.* I hear Mami's words: *know that people are not always what they seem.*

"How can I trust you? I don't even know you," I bluff. "It sounds like a fairy tale."

"He's not *meshugge*, Liba. It's true," Ruven says.

"Tsk. Tsk. Tsk. So many questions. You think that only in dreams the carrots are as big as bears?" Alter scoffs and ticks his head from side to side.

"Okay. Fine. Don't answer me. Look, perhaps the fruit is enchanted, I admit that. And their last name is Hovlin. But they aren't goblins. That's the most absurd thing I've ever heard."

"With a fairy tale and with a lie you can lull only children to sleep, don't be naive, *prietzteh*," Alter huffs at me. "Just like swans can't turn into humans and bears can't turn into men?" Alter scoffs and dismisses me with his hand. He starts to walk away.

"Wait!" I growl.

Ruven comes close to me and sniffs the air just like I've seen Tati do a thousand times. He looks at Alter. "Do you think it possible?"

"*Oyfen himmel a yarid*, in my opinion," Alter says. "I don't have time for this."

"What are you talking about?" I wail as I feel tears begin to smart in my eyes.

"Okay, okay. Calm down. If we untie you, do you promise not to run?" Ruven asks.

"Waste of time, Ruvy. *Aroisgevorfen*," Alter sings from across the way. He is packing up their things.

"I don't promise anything," I spit at him again.

"Fine," Ruven sighs. "Have it your way." He starts to walk away. "Come on, Alter, let's go. Maybe a night alone in the forest will get her to change her mind."

"Untie me immediately! *A broch tzu dir!*" I scream into the forest.

Alter runs over and shoves a piece of cloth in my mouth, gagging me again. He gets up close to my ear and says, "You can't change the world with curses or with laughter, *yenta*. You need to shut up now." His breath stinks of alcohol. I cringe. He walks back towards Ruven and they disappear into the trees.

I fume and chafe at the ropes that bind me. *They sound so much like Tati that it hurts. Is Tati really the Rebbe now? I don't want to go back to Kupel with them. I don't want to marry a bear. And what are these stories they tell about goblins? They know about the swans…but why does this feel like a trap? If only I could get to my knives. If they're even still on me…and what about my pistol—did they take that?* I try to sense it at the small of my back, but feel nothing there. I feel myself getting angry again, but instead of trying to calm down I close my eyes and let the rage fill me. *If I get mad enough maybe I can cause my claws to grow, and I can rip these ropes to shreds.*

I harness the ball of energy that I feel building inside of me. I wrap it in cold black fury that feels as thunderous as a waterfall. I let that energy churn within me. Then I find hunger—it isn't hard to find; it's ever-present. I realize now that I expend energy always trying to calm it, to deny it. There's no denying anything anymore. I don't want to be tied to this tree. I don't want any part of these men, or these enchanted woods. I don't want to be tied to those Hovlin boys who took my sister. I don't even want to be tied to Dovid anymore. I just want to be free.

I let it all roil inside me and I spread it through my body, from limb to limb, channeling it especially to my hands, trying with all my might to turn my anger into strength.

I am powerful in my own way, and I do know my own mind. I got so lost in trying to take care of everyone else that I forgot to take care of myself. It's my turn now. And I'm going to be the beast I've spent so much time denying.

I feel my fingers tingling. It feels like pins and needles, but sharper. I squeeze my eyes shut tight and banish all negative thoughts. *Concentrate, Liba, concentrate. What was it that Tati used to say? Necessity breaks iron. And suddenly I realize—that was how Mami freed him! You can become anything you need to be when the time is right...*

The pain in my fingers is exquisite. It feels good. It feels like freedom. And just when I think that my fingers are about to burst into flames or fall off or lose sensation forever, I feel them open up. I feel my flesh melting away and nails burst forth. Yes! I gasp out in pain as I feel the sharp teeth in my mouth tearing through the fabric of the gag. I spit it out of my mouth, and then I roar. I twitch and slash at the bark behind me...the ropes come free and I drop to the ground, face first.

My feet are still bound to the tree. I reach a sharp-tipped hand down to my feet to slash at the ropes too, but then stop halfway. My hands feel different. *I* feel different. I bring my hand up to my eyes and scream in terror. Where my fingernails once were, there are now claws, black and sleek, like finely honed obsidian, and on the back of my hands and on my palms, thick sleek black-brown fur has grown in.

I hear the crunch of boots by my head.

"Well, well," I hear Ruven say. He crouches down beside me. He strokes my hair and moves it out of my eyes. I realize that while my hands have turned, the rest of me feels normal.

"Don't touch me!" I roar.

He takes my grotesque hand in his and just as I am about to slash at him, I watch as with perfect control, his hand grows claws and fur to match my own.

I shriek again, this time in fear.

"Shhh," he whispers. "Calm down, Liba. It's okay." He looks to Alter. "Untie her feet. It's okay—I got her."

I feel the ropes at my feet go slack and I jump up with every intention to run.

"Oh no, you don't," Ruven says, catching me in his arms and holding me tight. "You're not going anywhere like that."

I struggle against him, but he doesn't move. He's bigger and stronger and he holds me in a vise so tight that I can barely breathe. Still I struggle, but he doesn't budge an inch. *Maybe if he thinks that I'm stopping the fight he'll let go enough for me to bolt.* I let myself relax in his arms.

He starts to ease the pressure, and I use all my strength to try to kick and claw at him to get away again. But he catches me and holds me harder than before. I know his arms will leave bruises. I can't help it. I can't control myself. I hate him. I hate everything and everyone—the Hovlins who have taken my sister from me. My parents who left us. Dovid who says he loves me but won't love me when he finds out about this hideous beast inside me. And I hate myself, because I can't save Laya. I can barely save myself.

"Shhh, Liba, shhhh. It's okay," Ruven says into my ear. I don't want to listen to his words—I hate them, I hate him, but

I'm suddenly too tired to fight. "Come. Let's sit down by the fire now," he says. "Alter, can you pour her something strong to drink?"

Alter grunts.

I shake my head. I feel broken.

Ruven lets me go and I slump to the ground. I try to wipe my tears away but I realize that my hands are still claws. Which makes me cry more.

"Here." Ruven produces a handkerchief and dries my eyes. His hands are normal again.

"Help me," I whimper. "Teach me how to turn them back," I say, pointing at his smooth hands.

Alter clears his throat and looks at Ruven. "We can do that," he says, "but first, you must make us a promise."

"Why should I promise you anything?" I spit, suddenly angry again, but I can hear my voice is shaky.

"*Genug iz genug!*" I hear Alter say. "Can you complete the change, or can't you? That's what we need to know."

80

Laya

Still I dream.
I wake up
in my own bed,
covered in Mami's
feather blanket.
I have one, soft,
cream-colored feather
clutched in my fist.

Mami is
by my side.
She picks
small feathers
from my hair.
There will come a day
when you will need
to remember
what you are,
she says.
Why? I ask.
I cannot explain.

The day will come.
You will know
when it comes.
You must follow
your heart.
My heart?
I shake my head.

You will understand
when the time comes,
she says.
Why, Mami? I ask.
Shhh…let me
brush your hair.
You are as different
as the sun
is to the moon.
Both my daughters—
one day you will both
shine bright.
One day
you will learn
that love
does strange things
to everyone.
And that is when
you will have to
make a choice.

I toss and turn
as I dream.
What did she mean?
Have I already made

my choice?
Is it too late?
Is this love?
Or something else entirely?
I don't know.
I don't know.
I don't know.

What if I shifted
back into a swan?
Could I fly
away from here?
I struggle,
but the vines
hold me tight.
They run deep
in my skin,
and my blood
flows strong.

81

Liba

I close my eyes and hear my father's voice: *better to die upright than to live on your knees*. I take a deep breath. I don't owe these men anything.

But suddenly I know that there is only one answer. I know it in my bones the same way I crave meat and dream of cold dark rivers. I will show them what I am. How dare they doubt me and play these games. The rage fills my blood and my bones. The pain is both glorious and excruciating. I have power that courses through me that nobody can claim.

I start to change before their eyes. I am crouched down on all fours, panting, as I shift into the same bear form that I saw my father once take. I have the same fur—almost black, the same blue eyes—and I turn to roar at Alter, but suddenly he is a bear too. I bare my teeth and try to run, but he is faster, bigger, stronger. He catches me and blocks my way, and that's when I hear another roar. It doesn't come from me or him. I feel the rumble of it in my bones. I turn my head and see that Ruven too has shifted. And as much as I want to deny it, he is magnificent.

But that's when we hear footsteps in the woods—all three of us turn and see men in the clearing.

"No!" I call, but it comes out only as a roar. It's Dovid and his father and one of his brothers. They hold guns, and Dovid's is trained on me.

I feel my eyes smart with tears and everything comes crashing down around me. This is the self-defense organization out on patrol. They are out hunting for the bear they think mauled Jennike and Mikhail. I know who did it, but I couldn't find the proof in time. And now I am both predator and prey.

Alter jumps in front of Ruven and me. He roars and starts to charge at them. I don't want to see anyone get injured, but I can't let Dovid shoot me. I whimper, and soon I feel a paw on my back. It's Ruven. He nudges me with his nose; I have no other choice but to follow him into the woods.

Once we are deep enough in the forest, Ruven shifts back into human form. He is naked, and I cannot help but look at him, even though I shouldn't. But I can't think about him—I must think about Dovid, and my bear body fills with heat.

"I'll be right back," he says. "Please just stay here and hide." It's only then that I realize I have no idea how to turn back into myself again.

Ruven goes off. I'm scared. I try to turn myself into the smallest bear-shaped rock I can conjure. *What if Dovid comes this way?*

Soon I hear rustling in the trees. I brave a look up out of my rock-cocoon and see that Ruven is back and dressed. He holds a rucksack and I see him stuffing his bear-fur back into it.

"Alter must be trying to lose them or to chase them off. I just hope the old fool doesn't get himself shot."

I whimper again.

"Oh, *deigeh nisht*! He can take care of himself. You, on the other hand, cannot."

I bare my teeth at him.

"Oh shush. How long have you known you could do this?"

I growl in response. *This is the first time I've shifted, but I saw my father do it once...*

He nods.

Wait, what? Can Ruven understand me? Nothing makes sense—there is so much that I don't know. All I can see are Dovid's hard, cold eyes looking at me across the barrel of his gun.

I close my own eyes.

How do I turn back? I ask Ruven in a bark.

"Still your body with calm. Fill yourself with a long stretch of river. Picture skin and hair, not fur and claws. Desire your old form but not with passion—with something like disinterest. With cold, calculated calm. Envision the fur washing off of you in water..."

As he speaks, I feel my bones and skin start to obey. I wish for cold air on my skin, for the peace of the river, for the days before I knew that I could do this. I beg the wind for the softness of my skin and the satin of my hair. It is less painful to turn back into the form I've always known.

I shed my brand-new coat as though I have come in from the cold. I look at my hand and see pink nails and flawless skin. Never have I been as happy to see my own body. I look up at Ruven and grin, only to realize that he is looking at me and that I'm naked. I cry out and try to cover myself, then see a bearskin at my feet. Not father's, not Ruven's—mine! I bend down to pick it up, but Ruven throws me a tunic.

I look up and he winks at me. There is hunger in his eyes, but not for food. I shiver. *No, Ruven, I am not meant for you. I have made my choice...*

"Put this on," he says. "It'll make it easier for you to stay human."

My face is red and flushed. I turn and slip the tunic over my head. I pick the bearskin up and inspect it.

Ruven is beside me. "It's beautiful," he says. He looks at me. "You're beautiful."

I shake my head. "You don't get to say that to me."

"It's true," he says.

"In general, I find that when you want to get to know a girl, it's best not to kidnap her first." I look back in the direction that we came from. "I can't believe that was Dovid."

"He is a hunter, *yingele*, or did you not know that? All men are beasts inside. Some just show it differently than others."

I feel nauseous. I am officially a bear, my sister is gone, and the boy I love just tried to kill me. He looked at me as a predator looks at prey, with fear and hatred in his eyes.

"Don't get all *farklempt*—it's time you know who and what you are. Your Tati probably warned you to stay away from the boys in the village," he says. "There was a reason for that."

Ruven tosses me a package; I catch it on instinct and open it. Inside is smoked meat. I look up at him, and he tosses me a flask as well. "Sit down and eat. The change takes a lot out of us. We always need fuel after we shift—that is, unless we hunt." His eyes sparkle wickedly and I swallow hard. "There are lots of different kinds of hunters in this world," he says. "It's what you hunt, and why, that makes the difference."

I sit down on the grass and start to chew on the meat.

"You realize you will need to choose a husband from the tribe. Your blood must live on for future generations. And you'd be wise to choose someone who can carry on in your father's place."

A chill runs through me; all the hairs on my body stand on end. I stop chewing. "And let me guess, this person is supposed to be you."

He comes to sit beside me. "I'm sorry that it had to come to this. Up until a few weeks ago, we didn't know that you existed. We knew that Berman Leib had a daughter…but not that you'd carried on the trait."

I shrug. "The way my mother tells it, you all cast him off for marrying her. Even though she converted."

"The Rebbe regretted it every day of his life."

"How do you know? What are you to the Rebbe?" I open the flask he tossed me and sniff it.

When I look up, Ruven is chuckling. "It's just river water," he says.

I take a few long swigs. "How do I know that you don't want to kill my father? Or kill me?"

He shakes his head. "Being the Rebbe is not a burden to be taken lightly. There is nobody like your father. I barely remember him—I was just a boy when he was taken prisoner, and then when he came back with your mother and was cast out…but I've heard the stories. It is…an honor to meet you, daughter of Reb Berman Leib. You must be a very special girl."

I shake my head sadly.

"Liba…I'll always regret that we drew the shift out of you in the way that we did. It…well…it usually happens quite differently. Will you forgive me?"

"I will never forgive you for what you did to me," I spit at him. I take another sip of water. "How does it usually happen?"

Ruven's neck turns red. "Well, sometimes it's with your first kiss. Other times it doesn't happen until…your first, erm…*shtup?*"

My skin goes cold. *This means that Dovid was at risk every time I kissed him…No! I didn't know…How could I have known? Why didn't Mami tell me?*

"So the choice was to kiss me or threaten me? Good choice." I cock an eyebrow at him. "I always knew that I wasn't as good-looking as my sister, but this seems extreme."

"No! Liba…please don't think that. If your father hadn't left the village, had I known about you, it might have happened in a different way. But these are dangerous times. A sword is dangling over the heads of all the Jews in Bessarabia right now. And the goblins aren't the only ones spreading rumors. Sometimes all it takes is a fight over a herring barrel…When we saw that Berman was gone, we had to know if you were his daughter, if you could shift…We had to be sure. And I knew that you had already given your heart to another. We saw…"

"So you were spying on me? I thought so, but I wasn't sure. Why on earth would I want anything to do with you if this is how you treat people? The people of Dubossary may not be Chassidim, but they treat each other with dignity. And right now that's more than I can say about you."

"Fair enough," he says. "You can think what you want. But I've been dreaming about a black-haired girl for as long as I can remember. I just didn't know that it was you."

I shake my head and walk away from him. I hate how cocky he is, how sure of himself. I am nothing like him and I never will be. Even if I am a bear.

Soon, Alter comes limping back.

He grunts out a roar of greeting. Ruven tosses him the rucksack and he goes off into the woods to shift.

A minute later, he comes back and sits down.

"Are you injured?" I ask, wondering why I care…except, he put himself in harm's way to protect me; he was willing to take a bullet for me, and that is worth something. It's worth a lot, actually.

"No." He shakes his head and rummages in the satchel for a parcel of meat and a flask. "It's an old injury—it acts up when I run too fast."

He looks from Ruven to me and back again. "What happened between the two of you?"

Ruven shrugs. "We talked. Are they gone?"

"I lost them," Alter answers. "Sent them in a different direction. They'll be giving up the hunt soon, and if they find their way back here, all they'll find is two men having a bite to eat with a lovely young *maydele*, eh?" He raises a toast to me with his flask. I can smell that his is not filled with river water.

I look away.

"Well, cut to the chase, Ruvy—what have you told her?"

"Not much. I was waiting to see if you'd come back at all,"
Ruven says.

"Funny, very funny. It'll take a lot more than three hunters to
catch this *alter kocker*." He grins and takes another swig. "Well,
what are you waiting for? More hunters?"

Ruven shrugs and looks off into the distance.

Alter grunts, "Fine, I'll just get on with it. You see, this man
here—" He slaps Ruven on the shoulder. "He's a distant cousin
of yours. And I brought him here with me to find your father, and
you. The time has come for us to claim you, Liba. Because unless
your father reappears, we need a Rebbe, and if Ruvy marries you,
he'll be next in line."

I stare at Alter open-mouthed. "What? That makes no sense.
What about my father's brother, Yankl?"

Ruven shakes his head. "He can't...he doesn't shift. We don't
know why."

"How dare you!" I growl at Alter. "Am I just a pawn to you
to use as you see fit for political gain? Who says I want to marry
Ruven? Or anyone else for that matter?"

The grin drops from Alter's face. "What did I say?"

I turn and look at Ruven. He twiddles with a blade of grass
by his leg.

"This is a joke, right?" I start to laugh. "Why aren't you more
upset?" I glare at Ruven. "He tricked you too. He brought you
here to find my father when really he wanted you to meet me—'*if
I even existed*'—which I clearly do, and I think Alter knew that.
I don't know what you're playing at. You really thought that
you could stalk me and threaten me and kidnap me and tie me
up, and that that was the way to my heart?" I look back and
forth between the two of them. They don't look at me, or
say anything.

"That's not how you treat a woman." I raise my voice. "That's not how you treat anyone. You don't get to decide my future. You don't get to decide when I shift. I don't care whose daughter I am. My father doesn't get to decide my future either. Only I can make that decision. You thought you'd come here and find me, introduce me to Ruven, we'd fall instantly in love, and you'd go back to Kupel with everything sorted? Or maybe you thought, *Oh hey, Ruven, we'll just knock her over the head and take her back with us—it'll all work out.* Well, I have something to tell you— there's no way in hell that I'm going to marry you, Ruven. I'm already promised to another."

Ruven and Alter look at each other.

"Surely you're joking," Ruven laughs. "Dovid tried to kill you. You saw! How could you possibly still want to be with him?"

"Because I love him. And he had no idea the bear was me."

The men look at me and shake their heads.

"Liba," Ruven says. "I don't think you understand what you are…"

"I understand very well. And I've already made my choice." *I know my heart and I'm not afraid to say it—the way I feel about Dovid is the truest thing I've ever known.*

"Love and hunger don't dwell together," Alter says.

Ruven clears his throat. "Listen, I had no desire to come on this expedition. I knew nothing about you. I didn't know we were looking for you when we set out. I only thought that we were looking for Berman.

"I love someone in our village. Her name is Tirza, and even though my parents were against the match, I had every intention of marrying her. But now that I've met you…" He sighs and rubs his face. "You belong with the members of your pack. All we're asking…" He pauses and looks into my eyes. "All I'm asking is that if we help you get your sister back, will you consider coming back home with us to our village, just to see what life is like there? To see where you come from, and who you really are?"

"I won't do anything until I speak to my father," I say. "And I owe it to Dovid to tell him the truth. After that...well, I'll have to see if there is an after. However, I would like your help in getting my sister back. Clearly you know that she's not my father's daughter, but she was raised in his house and he considers her his flesh and blood. Any protection that you are willing to offer me, I would like you to extend to her."

"*A broch tzu dir...*" Alter mumbles.

Ruven puts out a hand to silence Alter and tilts his head at me. "What do we get out of it?"

"What? You won't even help another Jew? A girl who your new Rebbe considers his flesh and blood?"

"But she isn't, is she?" Alter smirks.

"I'm done with this. I'm done with you." I cross my arms over my chest and look away.

"Liba," Ruven starts, "if you want our help, you're going to have to do better than that..."

My mind races. I want nothing to do with these men, but I'll do anything to get Laya back. "Fine. I'll offer you a compromise," I say, thinking quickly.

"Okay." Ruven nods. "Let's hear it."

Alter rolls his eyes and mutters a curse.

"You need my help to get into the Hovlin lodge. The woods there are enchanted. I think that's why the search parties never found anything. I could see the lodge and the orchards, but Dovid couldn't. The *kahal* of the village has formed a self-defense organization. And I have an idea..."

"Go on," Ruven says.

Alter mutters to himself, but I'm not deterred.

"My mother once told me that my great-grandfather became a bear because of great need, and her great-grandmother became a swan that way too. We can all become what we need to be in a time of danger—maybe that's what all the men in this *shtetl* need, a little confidence, some fur on their backs.

"The *kahal* is meeting tonight. If we can convince Laybel the Furrier to give all the men in the self-defense brigade some furs to wear when they go out tonight—furs with big bear heads still attached like the ones the villagers wear when they dance to welcome in the new year, we'll give anyone seeking to do us harm the fright of their lives. They'll be expecting Jews, not animals. And maybe—if we surround the town, armed and in costume—maybe, just maybe, tonight, in this great time of need, the *Aybishter* will see fit to make a miracle happen here."

Alter shakes his head. "It won't happen."

"Why not? Who says it won't?" I say.

"Because your great-grandfather was a very special man. Not just anyone can transform…Even Yankl couldn't," Alter argues. "I don't think you realize how precious you are."

"He's right," Ruven concurs.

"We'll never know until we try," I say. "Give them a chance. Maybe they will surprise you. The Jews of Dubossary are fierce. Let's give them hope. Let's help them believe that being a Jew means always changing—staying true to what you are, but adapting to your surroundings. That's what our people have always done. Let's give them something worth fighting for.

"And while the men organize themselves and everyone's busy here, the three of us can sneak away and go rescue Laya. I'll go back to the clearing and talk to the Hovlin boys. I'll ask them to sell me some fruit. If I get my sister out of there, I will need some fruit to keep her sustained until we figure out how to cure her. You can wait for me in the woods nearby. I'll play their games and get them to take me into their lodge. We'll come up with a call, some kind of sign that I will send you. We know you can't get through the enchantment in human form—maybe you'll be

able to get through in bear form—and you can provide a distraction while I get my sister out of there. Right now, I think that's
our best shot."

"What do we get out of it?" Ruven asks.

"In return for your assistance, I agree to go back with you
willingly to your village to meet others of my kind and learn
more about your way of life. That doesn't mean that I agree to be
your wife. Not now, not ever. But I will go back with you—with
an open mind."

Ruven gives me a boyish grin and a wink. "Done." He sticks
his hand out for mine.

I take it.

"I think it's a good plan," he says. "Eh, Altisch?"

Alter grunts and shakes his head in disapproval.

Ruven shakes my hand, but he doesn't let go. His eyes meet
mine and I shiver.

What did I just agree to do?

82

Laya

I hear the door open.
Someone is touching me.
My feet.
My wrists.
Pressure at my neck.
And pain.
Sharp and wild.
Something is ripping
at my wrists,
at my feet,
at my neck.
Air! Air! Air!
I can breathe.

There is softness
wrapped around
my wrists
and ankles
and neck—
they feel
a little better.

I try to move and feel
that I am not bound
to the bed anymore.

My face is wet
but not from my tears.
Something wet falls
on my face.
I try to open my eyes.
It is hard to see.

The roots stop sucking
at my veins;
there is blood everywhere.
The vines flail
in all directions,
seeking another source
of nourishment.

My eyes flutter open
and I see him.
Fedir. Cat-like eyes
stare down into mine
and I watch
as he plunges the thorns
into his own flesh
without care.
There is something
twisted
in his eyes.
It is love
and anger
and pain.

He bends down to kiss me.
I love you enough, he says,
to let you go.

The vines suck hungrily
at his flesh.
But they shrivel up,
as though his blood
is salt and ash,
not flesh and blood.
The rot spreads,
starting at the roots
of the plants
that bound me
and spreading
up up up into his arms.
He gasps in agony
and I see him transform.
Not into a cat
or a rat
or a parrot
or a weasel,
not a dove
or a wombat
or a snail,
but a goblin,
hideous and strange.
Hook-nosed and ugly.
He rips the roots
out of his flesh
and gathers me
in his brown
and shriveled arms.

He picks me up,
swaying on his feet,
he stops and starts.
He kicks open the door
and creeps along the corridors
until we are free free free.

But when we get outside
Miron is waiting for us.
He is grotesque.
A goblin too.
How did I not know?
How did I not see?
I close my eyes.
It's surely over now.
I made my choice—
the wrong one.

83

Liba

The *kahal* is meeting at the home of Donniel Heimovitz. When I knock, two men come to the door with pistols ready. They see me, wrapped in my bear cloak so that no one will recognize me, and their eyes grow wide. I let the hood drop for a second and they usher me in.

When we go inside, I let my hood down fully.

Dovid gasps. "Liba! What are you doing here?"

"I'm here to present the members of this worthy *kahal* with a plan."

The men erupt in laughter.

Dovid comes to my side. "What are you doing?" he whispers. Every eye in the room is on us.

"Trust me," I say, and I look into his eyes. His eyes hold mine and he nods.

"Permission to speak?" I say to everyone in the room.

They murmur among themselves, but I take a deep breath and raise my voice. "These men are from my father's *shtetl*. They are here to help. They came here to find my father because my Tati is now the new Rebbe of Berre. They claim that the Hovlins are responsible for what happened to Jennike and Mikhail." A hush goes over the crowd.

"My father set off to Kupel a few weeks ago. He was hoping to arrive there before the Rebbe died. He didn't know that the Rebbe was already dead, and that these men—" I motion to Ruven and Alter. "—were out looking for him."

I swallow and steel myself—I feel as if I'm shedding a layer of skin. "If something happened to my father on his way there, or if for some reason he does not return, I am next in line to succeed him and the man I marry will be the next Berre Rebbe."

Dovid takes in a sharp breath. I can see out of the sides of my eyes that he looks very pale, but I can't stop to think about that now. I must keep going.

"We spoke to Laybel the Furrier earlier today and came up with a plan…"

We leave the Heimovitz home as the men are all donning fur cloaks. Dovid's eyes meet mine as I turn to go, and I know that he and I need to talk but I can't stop now.

I spend the night in the woods with Ruven and Alter. We tell the men that we will patrol the area around the Hovlin glen. I think that Alter sleeps because I can hear his snores, but I don't sleep. Everything buzzes in my head: the way shifting felt. The way that Ruven looked at me when I was naked. The fact that my father is the Rebbe now, and I am his daughter, heir to a kind of throne. But more than anything I think of Dovid. What his eyes looked like when he heard what I said. How pale his face was when he realized what it might mean for him…and me. He stared at me as I spoke, but I couldn't tell what he was thinking.

I love him. I love the way he treats me, the way he looks at me—not with hunger, but with tenderness. I had already made my decision in my heart. But when he stared at me over the barrel of a gun, it made me wonder. Could he love me if he knew the truth—that I am a beast he tried to kill? That I will always be a beast? That marrying me means becoming a part of my family—even the next Berre Rebbe? Is he up to the task? Is it fair of me to ask that of him? What if he doesn't want that kind of life? What if I don't?

Inside I am a river, always flowing, always changing. I know now that I am powerful, but still I feel powerless to control my fate. I look up at the stars in the sky. I can't count them. I let my eyes flit to the forest that's always surrounded me. Strength can also feel like fear. Tears wet my eyes when my mind drifts back to Dovid: his eyes cold and pointed at me behind the barrel of a gun, then when he looked at me as though I was the most precious star in all the heavens. Black and white and black again.

I force myself to think of something else. Is Laya in Fedir's bed tonight? Does that mean that she will become a swan when she lies with him? What will he do if that happens?

What would it have been like to transform with Dovid in my arms? My body warms just thinking about it, but then I shiver. Because I could have killed him. And—more than ever—I don't know what the future holds for me.

At midnight, we set out for the Hovlin glen. Ruven and Alter follow me. If I am to be a beast, then I will act like one. I will go in there, get what I need, and fight my way out. And I must do it alone. Right now, I am the only one in town who can get through the enchantment. I will not be afraid. I will draw on my strength to save us all.

"Wait for me here," I say to Ruven and Alter when we're nearly at the glen. "I'll talk to them and get the fruit. I'll find her and then I'll call for you. In the meantime, watch the river and the forest. Keep it safe for all of us."

"You can't just go in there alone," Alter says.

"But that's what we agreed upon," Ruven counters.

"Only if we couldn't get in," Alter huffs.

"Can you both stop telling me what I can and can't do?" I shout.

"*Husht*," Alter says and cocks his ears at the trees around us.

"Sorry," I whisper. "If you come with me, something in the enchantment may shift—we can't take that chance. One of us needs to get in there and I must get some fruit, so we need to go with what we know works. Me first, you follow, and if I need your help, I will call for you."

"I don't like it, Liba." Ruven frowns.

"You don't have to like it. But this is what we're going to do," I say. I turn my back on them and walk through the woods until I get a glimpse of the clearing. The fire is out and I don't smell smoke. As I slowly step out of the woods and into the clearing, I see Viktor. His eyes meet mine and he goes still. Had I not been watching I wouldn't have seen it—a slight wince, a hesitation—but then he smiles, wide and open.

Why did he hesitate? The pores of my skin prickle and I shiver to shake it off. *Not here. Not now. Not yet*, I tell my body. *I'll let you know when I need you.*

"Is Fedir here?" I ask. "I'd like to speak to him."

"Not at the moment," he answers, and I see his eyes shift. "What can I tempt you with, pretty? Have you come for fruit?"

I swallow and nod. "I have. I cannot keep myself away anymore."

Viktor grins. I can tell that he doesn't quite trust what is happening, but he opens his arms wide. "I'm so glad you came by…" His smile is mischievous. "Why don't you follow me inside the lodge? That's where we keep our stores of apples, russet and dun, cherries, peaches, citrons and dates, grapes for the asking, pears red with basking…"

The way he chants I can tell that I'm supposed to be entranced. My mouth wants to water, but I won't let it. I realize that I am stronger than this enchantment because I know what I am, because I'm more than I used to be, and I've embraced it—my otherness.

"Plums on their twigs," he continues, "pomegranates and figs..." He takes me by the hand and leads me after him into the lodge. His hand doesn't make mine tingle. I feel it there, like an itch, but it doesn't travel up my arm.

Five of the brothers look up as I walk into the lodge.

I don't remember all their names.

"Brothers, look who came by?" Viktor sings. "She wishes to sample some fruit. What a fortuitous day. You know that your sister is to be married today?"

"I do," I say. "I came to give my blessing."

"You have blessed us with your presence." One of the brothers steps forward. "I am Marten—it is a pleasure to meet you." He bows to me. "Your sister is still sleeping—that is all she seems to do," he says. "But you know that—you're her sister."

I plaster a smile on my face because no, he is wrong: that is not Laya at all. But I can't let on. I must continue. If I am to break my sister out of here, I must buy fruit from these men. I must not close my ears to them.

A different brother extends his hand. "I am Helix—pleased to meet you," he whispers. "Won't you take a seat? Have a drink?" He leads me to a chair and places a golden cup of mead before me.

"Why, thank you," I say. "You are so kind, but I am not thirsty. I merely want to buy some fruit and take it home." I don't sit down.

Viktor raises his voice, "Dear brothers, why don't you bring up some trays and baskets, let's put out a spread?"

Two of the brothers scurry off. Helix and Marten stay; they are so close to me that I can smell them: it is not a good smell. There is a vague odor of rot under the cleanliness of their clothes and their skin. I wrinkle my nose. *Did Laya not smell it on them? Or am I different now—more beast than girl, more predator than prey?*

From across the clearing, one of the brothers arrives in a rush. It is Miron, the dark-haired one. "What's happening here?

Where...?" he says loudly, and stops when he sees me. I recall the first time we saw him in the forest: he was the one who made Laya a crown. His chin is pointed. He smiles when he sees me; his teeth are small and sharp-looking. *I don't remember his teeth looking like that before.*

"What have we here?" he says.

"A visitor. She wishes to bestow her blessing on her sister on this special day, and buy some fruit in celebration," Viktor says.

"Fruit? How lovely. Will she sample some too? You must know that we are...quite busy with all the preparations, but we always have room...I mean, time...for a guest. Unfortunately your sister is not feeling well. We do not wish to wake her. She must gather her strength for the day ahead."

Is she still in that cabin? I wonder.

"I didn't come here to see Laya. She and I have had...a falling out."

"Oh, how unfortunate," Miron croons.

"I came to bestow my good wishes. I'm sure you'll pass them on for me. Is Fedir here? Perhaps he can receive my blessing on my sister's behalf."

"Oh..." Miron says and something in his face twitches. "What a shame, what a shame—Fedir is not here right now. He is off, you know..." Miron's fingers tremble. "Last-minute preparations for the ceremony. I will be glad to convey your sentiments to the happy couple."

I don't know how I know, but he is hiding something.

"Thank you," I say. "I will celebrate for her alone, and toast to her health with some mead and some fruit."

The two other brothers come back with trays of fruit. They place them on the table before me.

"Oh, wonderful! I will fill my skirt with fruit and then be off." I toss a silver coin onto the table and hold out my apron.

"An apricot, my lady?" Viktor picks one off a tray and extends it to me. "They're your sister's favorite."

I shake my head. "No. I did not come to taste or try. Just to buy."

"Some strawberries?" Miron is beside me. He holds them up to my mouth. "Come sit with us. Let us toast to your sister's good health. The feast has not begun and night is a long way off. Break your fast with us."

I press my lips together and shake my head. *Where are they holding her?*

"It's a shame to take the fruits from here," Miron sings. "Their bloom will die, their dew will dry, their flavor will just pass you by. This is the place, not just to buy, to taste and feast and eat of all good things. Be our welcome guest. Stay with us, rest here." He points to a chair.

"Melon, ripe and sweet?" Helix gently places one in my hands. I smile and place it back down on the table.

"I must go. Someone waits for me in the forest," I say, hoping to let them know that I am not alone. "Perhaps I will just give my sister one last kiss upon her brow. Where is her room?"

Miron's eyes narrow. He licks his lips. "She cannot be bothered right now."

I shiver and rub my arms. "If you won't sell me fruit, please give me back my coin."

"Raspberries?" Marten places them in my palms. They stain my fingers red. I shake my head. "Try one for me—do not be proud." He grins and brings my hand up to my face. I drop the berries and take my hand from his.

"Now look what you've done!" he says and bends to pick them up.

I step back. "I only wish to purchase some," I say. "I already paid."

A tall and thin brother is suddenly beside me, stroking my hair. "You can pay in coin or kind. I'm Artur." He extends his hand and I reach out to shake it but suddenly it's overflowing with pomegranate seeds. He places them in my palm. "Perhaps you like them tart," he says. "I like the tart ones."

Everything in me tells me to run, to flee, but I must take fruit with me and figure out where my sister is being held. I bring them to my mouth and crush them up against my lips. I let the brothers think that I've sampled of their fruit. I feel the pomegranate juice stain my chin. I feel the tart-bitter taste outside my mouth. I hide my closed lips behind my hand and pretend to savor and chew.

"Here, have more," Artur says and extends another handful. As soon as I remove my hand, he shoves them at my face. I gasp, but quickly shut my mouth tight. The seeds burst against my skin as I shake my head. I will not taste them, no matter what they do to me. But then I realize that I can't open my mouth to scream. *How will I send a signal to Ruven and Alter?* I moan and smile and mime enjoyment of the delicate seeds. *Think, Liba, think. There must be a way.*

The last of the brothers comes up to me. "I don't think she tasted anything, dear brothers. Look, her mouth is stained, her cheeks and chin, but not one drop has been consumed. Perhaps a peach will tempt you? I'm Kliment." He holds a peach up and I smile sweetly.

Suddenly Miron pins me to the table. "What are you playing at?" he growls. His hands are full of grapes when I see him change. He is not a man, he is a beast—a goblin. His arms and legs shrink; his face twists and changes. A bulbous nose grows and a hooked chin gives way to hideous gums and razor-sharp teeth. I want to open my mouth to growl, to will the change to come and tear all of these beasts apart, but I can't. Not yet. I have to find my sister. I struggle against the arms that pin me down.

I will not cave. Nothing they do will get me to open my mouth for their poisoned fruit.

"She is too proud," one brother barks.

"What's good enough for one sister is not good enough for the other?" another hisses.

"'I only came to buy some fruit,'" another mocks.

They are all goblins now, hideous and strange. The enchantment is completely gone. I feel the absence of it in the air, like something palpable. *Maybe Ruven and Alter will feel it too? Even if I can't open my mouth to call, perhaps they will still come.*

I decide that I will be still and silent. I will fight these goblin men in my own way. The beast inside me rages, but I won't let it out. They will not break me. I feel claws dig into my skin, fruit pressed to my arms, my legs; everything is sticky; they mash fruit to my mouth, so much fruit, I cannot breathe. They squeeze juice onto my face—I close my eyes. They tear at my clothing—I press my legs together. They grasp for flesh—I hold my arms tight at my sides. My socks are wet with juice; my toes curl from the cold. One brother grabs my hair and pulls my head back, holding me down. I press my lips together as hard as I can while another brother tries to prise my mouth open with his hard and bony fingers. They hold my hands and shove fruit in them.

I know now what my body can do, but I choose not to shift. Deep inside myself, I find stillness. The river is there and it flows strong. If I am a beast then I am no better than they are. I am not a creature of the forest. I am the Rebbe's daughter now, a real *bat melech*—the daughter of a king. I am better than all of them. The one thing we Jews know how to do best is survive. My lips are smothered in fruit flesh, but I will beat them at their own game. I am stronger than they are—not just in body, but in mind too. I have strength of spirit, and I will get what I came here for.

I think of Mami, of her golden hair and her skin, lily-white like mine. I think of all the things she told me, the faith she had in me that I could protect my sister. But I've learned that sometimes protecting someone also means letting them go. Maybe that's what Mami meant all along. I am the beacon that my sister will find her way home to.

I let the golden fire of rage fill me, but I do not shift. I can be like a tree, covered in blossoms. I can be whatever I want to be. These goblins are just wasps and bees who try to sting me, but they cannot penetrate my bark. I erect a golden dome around me, complete with a tall spire. I am a ship at sail. I fly my flag, and they cannot take my standard down.

I feel their pinches like stings, but they do not hurt me. I feel the beat of their legs against mine, but I do not mind their kicks. I feel their claws dig in to maul me, but I too have claws—I am just choosing not to use them. I hear their laughter, but my body quakes with cold. I feel my pulse shudder against my neck, but there is nothing on earth they can do which will cause me to open my lips. I get to choose what kind of strong I want to be. I will be strong for Laya, and this time it means being silent and still.

Soon I hear them slowing, as they grow tired of this game. Though they've ripped my dress to shreds, soiled my stockings with juice, bloodied my arms with their claws, bruised my body with their fists and feet, I will not give in.

I feel the coin I gave them hit my skin. "Take your stupid coin," they say. "You are not worth ten of your sister. She is gone anyway. She escaped on the back of a golden-white swan. But you are bitter where she was sweet, and even the trees do not want your blood." Miron spits at me.

She escaped? With a swan? I keep my mouth shut and climb off the table. I am shaking, but more from adrenaline than fear. I may be a bear, but that is not what makes me stronger than all these men.

I fill a basket with fruit and limp my way from the lodge. They do not stop me. I drag one foot, and then another. Everything hurts and my skin tingles. Step by aching step I cross the clearing, leaving the glen, and I feel the enchantment breaking behind me. The trees are withering; the ground quakes. I start to run. I feel the silver coin in my pocket and it gives me courage. They may have broken my body but I defeated them. I got the fruit I came for. I see Ruven and Alter, but I run past them.

I run through the ache and the pain. I only need my sister. She is all that matters. And now I can feel it in my blood, in my untainted veins. I can smell it in the air: she is home. She found her way back. She is waiting for me.

84

Laya

When the wind shifted
I opened my eyes
and a swan landed
in the glen. Sasha.
He stopped in front of Fedir
and spread his wings.
Miron lunged for the bird
but Fedir knew
what he had to do.

He put me on Sasha's back
and said,
*To love means to sacrifice
everything that you are.*
I saw him fall down,
weak and drained of blood.
Miron ran to him;
he held him in his arms
like a brother would,
but Fedir was cold and still.

Sasha lifted off
and took to the sky
with me on his back
and brought me home.

I see it all
over and over again
playing in my head
like a broken memory.
Was there anything
I could have done
differently?

Laya! Laya!
I hear a voice.
My eyes flutter open
but they are
heavy heavy heavy.
Everything hurts.

Did you miss me?
Hug me, Laya-bell.
I tried to get you fruit;
I am the fruit now.

I open my eyes
and see my sister—
she is battered and bruised.

Please, Laya, she says,
take this fruit
from my flesh;
no one else can.

My hands reach up to my hair.
I want to tear it out at the root.
What have you done? I rasp.
Have you tasted of the fruit?

Liba shakes her head.
I did not taste, though they
beat and bound me;
they pinned me down
and shoved fruit on me.
But I resisted.
They are gone now, Laya.
Kiss my skin, she says.
Lick it off me—
I can heal you.

There is so much
we need to say, I think,
and shake my head,
No, no, no.
My throat still hurts.
I do not want
your light hidden, I say,
your spark destroyed.
I do not want you undone
in my undoing, ruined
in my ruin ruin ruin.

Let me save you, Liba says.
Only I can.
She lies beside me;
my arms reach for her.
I taste her skin.

I lick the fruit
from her arms,
and her face.
I rid her
of the poison
that I brought
upon us all.

But my lips burn.
They scorch.
The juice
is wormwood
on my tongue.
Something is wrong
wrong wrong.

I start to writhe and twist.
I rip at the dress
that binds me.
I beat my breast,
and bare it.
Like a torch, my hair
lights up the room.
It is a mane,
it is a crown.
I reach my arms
to the sun.
I am a caged thing
freed freed freed.

85

Liba

There are many types of love. But there is nothing like a sister. Mine is a golden swan. She is long and lithe and her wingspan fills the room. She is glorious. She is free. I watch her flit and fly.

The door bursts open. Ruven sees me on the bed, my dress torn, my skin bruised. I am covered in what looks like blood to him and there is a swan flying above me. He growls in rage, gets down on all fours, pawing at the ground, shifting, ready to pounce on Laya.

I open my mouth to scream, but there's a knock at the door. "Liba!" a voice says. "Liba! Are you in there?"

Ruven lets out an unearthly roar and the door swings open.

Dovid is there, rifle ready, wearing a fur cloak. But he sees Ruven first, a real bear, and he thinks he knows the difference. He fires a shot.

Laya flies around the room in a frenzy, golden and white feathers rain down.

My hand goes to my mouth but it is too late. I am about to scream but it comes out as a growl that turns into a roar. I can smell Ruven's blood and the way it wets his fur. *This was not supposed to happen. Not like this.* My bones pop; the aches and bruises fade into hurt of a different sort. But I close my eyes and force the shift away. *Not here, not now, not in front of Dovid.*

Dovid is a beast for acting without thinking, but what was he supposed to do? He saw a bear, and in his eyes it was the bear that has been stalking our woods all this time—the bear that was in our house, the bear that may have mauled and killed Jennike and Mikhail. I didn't want to go to Kupel with Ruven and Alter, not really, but I don't want Ruven to die. I want to get to know him, just a little bit. If what he says is true, the death of a real Berre Chassid when there are so few of us left may be more of a tragedy than I realize. No matter which way of life I choose in the end, it is clear to me now. There are many different kinds of beasts in this world.

Dovid's hand trembles and his eyes go wide as Ruven shifts back from a bear into a man, naked and covered in blood.

He cries out in horror.

"What have you done?" I roar at him and rip the gun from his hands. I close my eyes, but I can't hold it back anymore. I get down, panting on the floor.

"Liba…What's wrong? Did I hurt you? How? I…I don't understand. Oh God, what is he? What's wrong with you? What's going on?" He looks terrified, as though he wants to flee. "There's a mob of men with torches on the river!" he says. "I came from there. Oh God, what have I done?"

I reach my hands to him, but then I see what he sees. Hands that are claws, and brown fur. And suddenly I am too tired to control anything. I let the change come. He will see everything. Girl and beast and girl again.

Panic-stricken he looks from me to Ruven and back again, but it is too late. There are no more secrets.

86

Laya

There is blood on the floor
and a man who is a bear.
My sister is a bear too.
She is beautiful and strong.
I am a thing of feathers.
I want to cry
but I don't know how.

Where I felt free
I now feel trapped.
A man lies bleeding
and my sister hurts;
the pogrom has come;
we will all die
and there is nothing
I can do about it.

I don't know
how to become
a girl again.
I am just a swan now.

A bird.
A thing of feathers and air.
What can I possibly do?
Sasha came,
and then he left.
He said
he'd come back
with all the swans.
Everyone makes promises.
My sister is the only one
who keeps them.

I know what I must do.
I fly up out of the house
onto the roof.
I open my beak
and I let out a cry.

87

Liba

Ruven's head is cradled in my lap. He's still breathing, but he struggles.

The door bursts open, and there before me are my parents.

"Mami? Tati?" My hand is over my mouth and I don't know if I should cry or scream. I look from one of them to the other and back again. They look pale, haggard, and haunted.

Alter is behind them. "I went to find them. A swan showed me the way," he says.

"Ruven!" Tati says. "*Ribbono shel Oylam*, what happened?" He rushes to my side. "Who did this?"

Alter goes down on one knee, hand over his mouth; he looks as if he's seen a ghost.

"He was shot, Tati," I say. "It was an accident. It was Dovid Meisels, but he didn't know. He thought it was a bear attacking me."

My father prods Ruven's wound. "Did this happen when he was in bear form?" he asks.

"Yes," I say.

"Should I go get the doctor?" Dovid asks.

Alter gets up. "Oh, no you don't. Not if you shot the gun that killed him."

"I didn't know," Dovid says, meeting his eyes. "I came into the cottage and saw a bear, a swan, and Liba. What was I supposed to do?"

I don't know what to think. I can't meet the eyes of the boy I love, the boy who said he loved me. "I'll go," I say.

"You can't go out looking like that," Alter says.

I look down at myself, covered in what looks like blood but is mostly fruit, and I shake my head. "It doesn't matter. Ruven matters—I won't let him die."

"Please—let me go," Dovid begs, closing his eyes. "It's my fault. I don't want Ruven to die. I was supposed to raise the alarm. I was on my way to tell the people of the *shtetl* that there are men with torches and guns on the river. The pogrom is here. Let me go get the doctor, and I can alert everyone on the way. Please let me go."

"How do I know that you won't flee?" Alter asks.

My eyes meet Dovid's. I see only pain. "He won't," I say.

Alter lets him go. "It's on your head, *prietzteh*, if he disappears."

I swallow and nod. "Dovid, listen. What you saw here tonight…Know that people aren't always what they seem." I hear Mami's voice in my head again. "You are stronger than you know."

His eyes meet mine and I see a hint of understanding. There is fierceness there, I know there is.

He swallows hard, turns, opens the door of the cottage, and sets off at a run.

I try to keep Ruven comfortable and breathing.

"Can you stay with him, Alter? I need to speak to my parents."

Alter grunts and switches places with me.

I launch myself into my father's arms. He catches me, and I feel his body convulse against mine. He is crying. *Why is my father crying?*

"They're gone, Liba. Everyone's gone...There's nothing left."

"What?" I don't understand.

"Kupel. First the Rebbe, he was *niftar* when we got there, but after Kishinev, they came to Kupel. They put everyone into the *shul*..." He shakes his head. "It's all gone, Liba. Burnt to the ground. Everyone...Six hundred Jews..."

I don't know what to say.

I look over at Mami and I see that she is crying too. I hug her to me.

"Tati, listen: the *kahal* organized the Jews of Dubossary to fight back tonight. But is there anything you can do to save Ruven?" I ask, looking up into my father's eyes which are so very like my own.

He shakes his head. "Even the shift cannot heal a gunshot wound, and he is too weak to try it."

"Okay, so we wait for the doctor," I say. "Is there anything I can do?" I look from my father to Alter. "Some kind of tea I can brew? A bandage? A salve?"

"Sage, oregano, and lavender," Mami calls out. She is climbing the ladder.

Laya! I forgot about her! Is she on the roof? But Mami is here now—she can help her better than I can.

I go to the kitchen to start brewing hot water and crush the herbs. And I hear the call. It's Mami. And I know then that I've heard the sound before. I just never knew what it was.

She trumpets out a sound like the honk of an instrument. It is so loud I think that all the village must hear her. She sounds it again and again and I know that she is calling them home.

Alter stiffens. "What is she doing?"

I can't help the grin that spreads across my face. "She's calling the swans," I say.

"The swans?" Alter grunts. "Ruven is bleeding out on the floor and she calls swans? Swans were what got us into this mess."

"No. A swan helped you find my parents. And these aren't just any swans. One of them is my sister," I say. "She needs help too. She is not well. She needs her family."

Tati shakes his head. "What happened to her? Why is she ill?"

"It's a long story…" I say.

"They are not her family," Tati mumbles.

"She needs them right now. It's been a long time without you, and much has happened."

Tati takes a look at me. "You don't look so good yourself." He turns to Alter. "Altisch. *Oy*, Altisch. When I got there…" He shakes his head. "Everything was gone…everyone…Nothing's left. Everyone…everything is ash…" Father starts to sob again and bites his thumb. "You and Ruven are all that's left."

Alter looks shocked. He is white now too. I feel as though all the ghosts of Kupel are spinning around our cottage, all the memories, specters of all the Jews who went up in the sky with the smoke.

Alter embraces my father. They cry onto each other's shoulders. It is not something I have ever seen my father do. Not even at a funeral. My stomach hurts like I've been punched. There is too much sadness here. Too much sorrow. I go back to the kitchen to brew the tea because I don't know what else to do.

Is that what will happen to Dubossary tonight? Is fire to be our fate? I set more water up to boil, then bring a cup of tea and sit beside Ruven. I place a tea-soaked rag at his lips. "Try to drink from this," I say. I take a second rag and dip it in the brew, then place it on his wound. He winces and his whole body arches up in pain.

"I'm sorry," I say. "So sorry." His eyes flutter open and he sees me. I don't want him to die. That's all I can think. I don't know what will be with Dovid, but I do want a chance to get to know Ruven. He and Alter and Tati are all that's left of Kupel, of my father's people. We are all that remains of the Berre Chassidim. We must live. We must find a way to survive.

There's a knock at the door. "The doctor!" I say.

"I came as fast as I could," Dr. Polnikovsky says, breathless. He has his daughter with him. Dovid is just behind them.

Alter nods his head at Dovid and Dovid returns the gesture. "I have to go back," he says. "The men have gathered by the river; they're preparing for a battle." He looks to Alter for permission.

"Go," Alter says. "*Chas ve'shalom* this should become another Kupel." He catches his breath and can say no more.

Dovid looks at me. I know there is so much he wants to say, but he turns and runs back out the door and to the river.

"I boiled water," I tell the doctor, "and this is tea I brewed with sage, oregano, and lavender."

"I need you all to clear out so that I can work on him in peace," the doctor says. "My daughter will assist me."

"If you need anything, we will be just outside the door," I say.

As soon as we get outside, we hear the flapping of wings. First a dozen swans land upon our roof, then another dozen come, then a hundred, and more. The sky above us darkens. We run down to the river bank and we see them: fifty men making their way down on a barge, holding torches, wielding pistols, but they are all looking at the sky—as awestruck as we are.

I see the Jews of Dubossary lining the banks of the river, dressed in furs, each one primed and ready for a fight. I think of Mami's stories about Saint Anna of the Swans.

For a moment, it seems like anything is possible. I blink, and suddenly the men of our town each take on a shape, a form: Isser the Cobbler's son is a fox; Heshke the Cooper is a wolf; Reb Motel the Silent is a bison; Shmulik the Knife is a nighthawk; Pinny Galonitzer is an elk; and Dovid, my Dovid, is a bear.

My heart soars.

I blink and they're men again, just men, but I feel as if I've seen into their souls and I know—and I know that they know—that we will survive, because being a Jew is worth fighting for.

The swans dip towards the barge, surrounding it in a sea of white feathers. The men cross themselves and drop their torches into the river. They are crying and trembling with fear. The boat starts to turn around.

88

Laya

The swans surround me
like in my dream.
But there are more of them now.
More than ever.
They fill the sky—
it is glorious.
Mami speaks to them.
She asks why they
did not come sooner.
Why were they
not watching over me?
They were! I honk,
and everyone looks at me.
I want to put my hand
over my mouth.
But I don't have a hand
only wings.
I can't believe the sounds
that come from me.
But they seem
to understand.

When I was held captive
by the Hovlins, I say,
a swan took me away from there
and brought me home.

Why was no one here
to witness her transformation?
Or is this not the first time
you have changed? Mami asks me.

It's not the first time, I say.

So much happened
while we were away,
dochka, Mami says.

Dmitry comes forward.
She was inside a cottage
full of bears, he says.
We were not going
to enter.

Do you betray your own kind?
Mami is fierce in her anger.

A different swan
steps forward. Sasha.
I was watching, he says.
I've been watching her for years.
My name is Sasha.
She was not in danger,
and I have not forgotten, he says.
I never will.

Well, when did you plan
on showing up? Mami says.

A war between the bears
and the swans at this point
is not advisable,
Dmitry says.

My daughter is not a pawn.
Mami's voice has an edge to it,
sharp sharp sharp like a knife.

Enough! I scream
and it comes out
like a trumpet shriek.
Can someone please
help me become
myself again?

They all look at me.

I do not know
how to change back,
I whisper.

89

Liba

We stand in wonder at the river bank and watch the boat retreat. The men of Dubossary raise their voices in a cheer. I look at my father, but his face is streaked with tears.

"It's not over," he whispers. "They will come back."

"But Dubossary is saved!" I say, and I clutch his hand in mine.

"Only for now, *zeiskeit*, only for now," he sighs.

We walk back to the cottage.

Alter looks at me. "They're gone, you know. The Hovlins."

"Gone?" I say.

"When you ran from there, Ruven and I tried to attack them—we ran into the glen, but they were gone. Whatever you did broke the enchantment. The lodge disappeared."

I shake my head in disbelief.

"No fruit falls from withered trees," he says. "But they will be back. It isn't over. We didn't kill them. We might have weakened them for a while. They will move on to the next village. It is not safe for the Jews in Bessarabia anymore."

"It is not safe for Jews anywhere," Tati says.

"I wanted to chase their scent, but Ruvy was having none of it—he followed you," Alter says.

"Do I even want to know who you're referring to?" Tati says.

"It's a very long story," I reply.

Alter concurs. "Very long indeed."

We are back at the cottage and I see Dovid coming through the woods in our direction.

As much as I want to tell my father everything, there is also something that I need to do.

"Will you excuse me for a moment?" I say to Alter and Tati. "I need to speak to Dovid privately."

Alter gives me a look that says *how dare you consort with a murderer* but I ignore him.

There are things I need to say.

I walk up to him. "Dovid...can we talk?"

He shakes his head. "I didn't know, Liba. I thought you were in danger."

"I know. I'm sorry," I say.

"Why are you apologizing?"

"Because I should have told you. I was too scared to tell you the truth. And maybe had you known...you would have thought before you fired."

His eyes are wide and scared. "I shot a man."

I smile sadly. "But you didn't know, Dovid. It's not your fault. And anyway, Ruven's not the only one you pointed a gun at today."

He winces. "Was that you in the woods? Oh my God..." His hand goes to his mouth and it looks like he's going to be sick. He pitches forward. "Liba...oh God...I'm a murderer."

"Dovid," I say softly. "It's okay. You didn't know. If anything, it's my fault for not telling you."

"No." He shakes his head yet again. "It's not okay. It will never be okay. I am a beast."

I can't help it. I start to laugh.

He looks up at me, brow furrowed in confusion, tears in his eyes. "Why are you laughing at me?"

I take a deep breath. "Because I'm the beast, Dovid. That's what I always said about myself. I was so afraid of telling you the truth that I lied to you. I thought if I told you what I really was..." I sigh. "...you would never want to be with me. I'm a bear. You've seen it now with your own eyes. And apparently I'm the Berre Rebbe's daughter too. I'm not a normal girl that you can settle down with. I only wanted to feel normal...to feel sought after and loved. Thank you for giving that to me. I will always remember that you made me feel like I was precious, like I was someone worth wanting."

"Liba," Dovid says, tears in his eyes. "I could never think any less of you. You are precious to me—to everyone here in Dubossary. You saved us all tonight. When we were down by the river...did you see what happened? The swans filled the sky, but something else happened too..."

I want to see what he says, to make sure that I didn't imagine it, that it wasn't all a mirage. I shake my head.

"It was like the air was charged with electricity, with magic, with potential. I looked up at the sky and then looked at the men on the riverbank all around me, and for a minute my whole body tingled and I felt like I could be anything I wanted to be, anything I needed to be...and all I wanted was to be a bear so that I could be worthy of you. When the swans descended and the men turned away, I couldn't see it anymore, but I felt it, just like you said. I know it sounds crazy, but I believe it. Anything is possible." Dovid swallows. "How could you believe that I would think less of you? Yes, it was a shock. But it's a part of you and I love you. I still do." He looks down and covers his mouth with his hand, stifling a silent sob. "But I guess that future will never be."

He looks so broken that I don't know what to do with myself.

"Dovid, I…"

"No, I know that everything's changed now," he croaks out, tears running down his cheeks. "But I want you to know that it wouldn't have mattered to me at all. If anything, it makes you more beautiful. Because you are strong and powerful, and it makes me believe that maybe one day I can be whatever it is I need to be too."

"Dovid, please, look at me."

He shakes his head.

I put my hand on his cheek and tilt his chin up so his eyes meet mine. "I love you. It took me a while to figure out what it was that I was feeling, but I don't have any more doubt. I'm brave enough to stand up for what I believe in—and I believe in you, in the possibility of our love, and a life together. It will be a long road because we must see if Ruven lives; we must see what will be with Tati, what will become of him and us now that he is the Rebbe of a town and a group of Chassidim that doesn't exist anymore. And I am the last of his line—now more than ever.

"I don't know if he will rebuild his *kehilla* out of the ashes, or if we are the last of *Chassidei Berre*, and Kupel will not rise again. And I don't know what that means for me and you."

"Liba…do you really mean it?"

I nod my head. "I do."

He puts his hand over his mouth to stifle a yelp of joy and takes me in his arms and holds me tight. "I'll do anything, Liba. Anything to be with you. I'll even be a bear."

I close my eyes and smile. What I feel for Dovid is the one thing that I know for sure. I don't know if my love for him is enough to overcome everything that stands in our way, but I know that I'm willing to try.

"Dovid," I say. He looks up at me.

"Thank you for everything. For believing me. Without you, I don't know if I could have managed to change. I don't know if I would have had the courage to save Laya. You taught me that I was worthy of love, of your love, and I wouldn't be the same person I am today without that."

He shakes his head and looks away, tears falling down his cheeks.

"My father always says a friend is not someone who wipes your tears—he's someone who doesn't make you cry. And, Dovid, you never made me cry."

I lean over and kiss him.

90

Laya

Sasha turns away from me.
I see his body shake
and shimmer shimmer shimmer.
In a rush of feathers
he is just a boy,
a naked boy.
He puts on
the feather cloak
that falls to his feet
and turns to me.

You need to think
of earth and soil, he says.
Not of clouds and
wind and air.
Think of feet
touching the ground,
of arms, not wings,
of falling, not flying.
Imagine a thud
to the ground

and roots
which bind you.

I shudder.
I feel nauseous suddenly.
I never want to think
of roots that bind me
ever again, I say,
and hide my beak
under my wing.

He puts his arm out—
I'm sorry, Laya.
I didn't mean
to cause you pain.
Think of the things
you loved to do
when you were human.
Think of things
that ground you.
Things that bring you joy.

I think of my sister.
Of what it was like
to laugh with her,
to cry with her,
to sing with her,
to make her tea
and watch her bake.
To take forest walks,
and sleep beside her.
How she always
protected me,
and cared for me.

I think of shoes.
I think of soil
between my toes
and how much
I would like
to hold a mug
of tea again,
between my fingers.
I wish for fingers fingers fingers.

Then I feel it:
an inward sensation.
It's the reverse of
pins and needles
because all the pins
and all the needles
want to be
absorbed by me.

My wings shrink into arms,
my webbed feet lengthen
and separate into toes.
I feel taller and slimmer
surrounded by feathers
and air air air.
I'm me again.
I've never been so happy
to see my naked skin.
I look down
and see a cloak
just like the one
my mother left behind.
But this one's mine.

It's gold and white.
It's everything that's beautiful
in this world.

I look up:
they have all shifted.
They are swan-men
and women, with hair
and eyes and skin
like mine. Their eyes
are all on me
but his
most of all.

My eyes meet Sasha's.
I blush, and expect to see
him looking at me
with hunger in them
the way that Fedir did,
the way that all men do.
But I don't.
I see tears.
As if he's waited
his whole life
for this moment.
And he can't
believe his eyes.

I bend down
and grasp the cloak
and bring it up
to cover me,
but all the time

my eyes stay
trained on his.

I am something
between human
and beast.
Ever-changing.
I will always
be changing;
I understand this now.
And these swans
are part of my family.
But they are not
my only family.

My father might be a bear
but he will always be
my Tati. And my Mami
will always be
something other—*acher*—
different from everyone
around her.
And that's okay.
I am a part
of all of these people,
bears and swans,
and they are a part of me,
and my sister.

Liba Liba Liba
I need my sister.

91

Liba

Dr. Polnikovsky emerges from the house. "I got the bullet out and dressed the wound. He was lucky: it missed his vital organs. All that Ruven must do now is rest and heal. He should pull through, but you must watch him closely for infection. I will come back and check on him and change his bandages."

Tati, Alter, and Dovid thank him and shake his hand. He leaves and we all go into the cabin, even Dovid, though Alter still gives him dirty looks that say, *I plan to kill you later.*

Ruven is sleeping on the bed.

Alter checks on him, then turns to Tati and me. "Liba agreed to come back with us to Kupel. But now...I don't know where we should go."

Tati looks to me with eyebrows raised.

I swallow and nod. "I did agree, Tati. But...you and I should talk."

Tati opens his mouth, but Alter speaks again. "We have an opportunity here, one that may never come our way again. Liba is both swan and bear. The swans will do her bidding—she can bring them under her rule."

"What?" I say, teeth and claws halfway to being bared. "How

dare you! I will do no such thing. No group of people should be ruled by another!"

Tati's arms surround me. "Calm yourself, Liba."

I shrug him off and take a deep breath, but when I say, "I will not!" it comes out as a roar. I close my eyes and call the river, and let it wash over me.

I open my eyes and say, "Never would I agree to subjugate anyone, or anything. Laya is my sister. The swans are her people. The bears are mine. Perhaps there is swan in me too. But none of that matters. Before that and before everything we were sisters. We will always be sisters. No one has the right to control anyone. It doesn't matter what they believe or what type of creature they are. More than anyone you should know that right now. People are being burned in synagogues because of what they believe. You do not protect people by ruling over them, by telling them what to do. Laya is mine and I am hers because we love each other; we protect each other because we care. The swans saved all of us today, or did you not see that? They filled the sky. Sometimes protecting someone means letting them go, letting them live their own lives. Respecting their beliefs. I used to think differently, but my sister has shown me that there is another way. That is what love is. It is trust. Being strong enough to let someone you love live free…"

My voice cracks and suddenly Laya is beside me. She takes my hand in hers and I feel stronger.

"I don't care what Laya looks like and I don't care what people she belongs to. I love her." I look over at her and smile. "And that is why I will always protect her, but only in the way that she needs to be protected."

A feather drifts down and lands on my nose. I turn and see that all the swans are sitting in the loft. I see them nod their heads at me and it feels like something big. Something important.

Mami climbs down the ladder and takes me in her arms. "I

have something to say." She turns to face everyone. "*Dochka*, I am so proud of you. You have given me courage. I have learned more from you in these short hours than I've ever learned from anyone. I must make something right."

She meets my father's eyes across the room. She looks at him and says, "Sixteen years ago, you came into this cottage and found me in bed with a man."

There are murmurs and whispers throughout the room.

"Hush!" she commands. The room goes silent. "You thought that I was being forced, that the man in bed attacked me. You did what you thought was right as my husband, my protector. You killed the man. And I was too scared to tell you the truth. But I must tell the truth now, before the eyes and ears of everyone in this room. I went into the arms of that man willingly."

My father's eyes grow hard.

Nobody breathes.

"He was my mate. His name was Aleksei Danilovich. And even though I was happily married to you, when he came to see me, I could not deny him. I betrayed you. And all of this—" She gestures to the swans up above and the bears in the kitchen. "—is my fault. The rivalry between all of you, which in itself contains the roots of hatred. I should have told the truth then. But I was a coward. I did not know that it is possible to hold more than one kind of love inside you. But I was wrong all those years ago, because I loved Aleksei and I was too scared to tell you how I felt. I am learning now from my daughters what love really is. Laya was born from love, and Liba was born from love too—our love."

Her eyes soften. "I love you," she says to my father. "I always will. But I have lived my life in guilt and pain over Aleksei's passing. He lives inside me still, and he lives in Laya—every time I look at her I see him. But I will not let my daughters live a legacy of pain and rage. I will not let my daughters suffer for the lie I lived. If I had told the truth then—that I went into Aleksei's arms willingly, that I loved you both—I might have lost you. I might have lost Aleksei too, but perhaps had I been brave enough, I could have saved us all."

She looks to the largest of the swan-men up above in the loft. "Dmitry, there is something I must do. For Aleksei. For his memory."

Dmitry closes his eyes and clenches his jaw. The pain of having lost Aleksei is etched on his face as though it happened yesterday—not sixteen years ago. Sasha picks up Mami's cloak and hands it to her.

She goes to the edge of the cottage and bashes in a floorboard with her fist. She lifts out a jar, hugs it tight, and transforms into a swan. She is majestic: White and grey and delicate even though her wings are large and strong. She flies up out of the skylight and opens the jar. Ashes scatter over the roof of the house and the garden and the forest that surrounds us. When she comes back inside and turns back into a woman, her face is streaked with ash and tears.

She kneels on the ground before Tati and bows her head. "I have been a swan for the last time."

The room is silent. Everyone waits for the axe of Tati's words to fall.

"Rise, Adel," he says. His voice is hard, but there is tenderness in it. "I would never lift a hand to harm you. I loved you then and I love you now. It may take me some time to forgive you, but I believe that your words are truth. I know that one can love two things at once, for I loved being a Berre Chassid, but I loved you too. And I was willing to give up everything I was to be with you. But I have caused much of this mess myself. I wanted to protect you so much that I did not see anything other than my rage. If I have learned anything these past years with you, it is that I can control the beast within me far more than I ever thought possible. I know now that I can be what I need to be, what I am, anywhere that I am, in any skin. It is enough for me to be *your* husband, your Rebbe, your lover and protector. But I also love you enough to let you go if that is what you choose. Please don't give up your wings."

Mami leaps into his arms. She kisses him fiercely and I can do nothing else but grin from ear to ear. I am proud of my parents. Of who they are and what I know they can become—for us and for each other. I am proud of my sister, a glorious swan who may have saved us all, who did what she needed to do most in our time of great need—she brought the swans. And I am proud of Dubossary, of the fierce Jews that surround me. My heart feels like it will burst.

When Tati puts Mami down, I see that there are tears on his cheeks too.

He looks at me and at Laya. He puts his hands out for us. They are giant hands, great big bear hands. I place my hand in his and when I look up, I see the Rebbe in him for the first time. Here, in this room, he is brave and wise, a king among men, and I am filled with pride.

"I claim you both as my daughters," he says, even as he hears the rustling of feathers from above. "It does not matter who else claims you." He shoots a look up at the loft. "You come from royal lines, holy lines, and you both have the power and the privilege to lead us all. I trust that as my daughters you will make me proud. You already have." He goes down on one knee and bows his head to us.

Dmitry comes down the ladder. Tears streak his face. He picks the feather cloak up from the ground and places it around Mami's shoulders. "Adel, please keep this. You do my brother honor; you do us all honor. Please accept my apology on behalf of all of us." He bows his head to her. "Ever shall you fly with the sun on your neck, and your face lifted to the sky. The swans will always come when you call."

Laya looks up to the loft and her eyes meet Sasha's. He comes down the ladder.

"Tati, Mami, I have something to tell you," she says.

Sasha stands by her side and Laya takes his hand. She looks at him and he smiles back at her. They look right together, like Laya finally belongs somewhere.

"Sasha has flown to America. He says that it is a wide open land. There are cities there where Jews can live freely. All kinds of Jews. He says that he can take me there. And when I get there, I can send for you." She looks around the room at Alter, Ruven, and Dovid. "All of you."

Sasha speaks, his voice is clear and strong: "I have always loved Laya. I have dreamt of her since the day I was born. And I've been watching her. She and I have met now a few times." He smiles at Laya and she nods back. "But Laya had some things that she needed to do before she could find herself. I know that you don't know me, but some things are destined by the stars. I will take care of your daughter. I will protect her. And she speaks true—we will fly far away from here, but then we will bring you all home."

Tati's eyes sparkle with tears. He sighs. "Laya, you don't need me to tell you that this was not the match that I would have chosen for you. But nothing that happened in the past few weeks is what I would have chosen. How can I condemn you to a life of fear, a life of suffering, especially when I see how quickly every-thing you know can be taken from you in a puff of smoke and ash. Go, *dochka*, my *shayna maydele*. Go to the *goldene medina*. We will join you there if the *Aybishter* wills it. There is nothing left for the Jews here in Dubossary."

Laya looks at me. I look back at her, and we smile.

Tati gives us a great big bear hug, one like only the Berre Rebbe can give. Tears sparkle on his beard, and I know that if I tasted them, they would taste bittersweet, like goblin fruit.

I look over and see that Ruven is awake, his head is off his pillow, and he is watching everything unfold. He smiles too.

The world feels big and wide and full of possibility.

I take Laya's hand and squeeze it, and she squeezes back.

Author's Note

On March 20, 1903, the body of a young Christian Ukrainian boy named Mikhail Rybachenko was found drained of blood in the garden of a Jewish man named Yossl Filler in the *shtetl* of Dubossary, on the border between the Ukraine and Moldova. As the London *Jewish Chronicle* said then, the boy was found "there in a fruit garden close to the river." A similar story also happened in a nearby Jewish hospital: a young non-Jewish girl was found poisoned (by suicide) there and the Jews were blamed. This quickly turned into a blood libel (a false accusation that the Jews used the blood of non-Jews to bake Passover *matza*) and the non-Jewish anti-Semitic newspapers of the day called for a pogrom (a violent riot with intent to massacre a certain ethnic or religious group) against the Jews. The Jews of Dubossary organized themselves into a self-defense corps and they fought back and prevented a pogrom from happening in the town.

But Jews in the nearby *shtetls* in the Kishinev area suffered: about fifty were killed, a hundred were severely wounded and five hundred were slightly injured, seven hundred houses were destroyed, and six hundred stores were pillaged. And from then on, the pogroms continued in many other towns. Between 1881 and 1920, there were over 1,300 pogroms in the Ukraine.

As a result of the pogrom in Dubossary, my great-uncle, Abraham Krovetz, made his way to America via Ellis Island in 1905. From there he was able to bring almost his entire family over to America to join him, including my grandfather, his brother, Joseph Krovetz. My family also made their way from the nearby town of Kupel to the USA at around the same time.

On September 3, 1940 the Nazis came to Dubossary. Again the Jews of Dubossary tried to fight back. This time, they were not successful. The Nazis rounded up six hundred Jews and put them in the main synagogue in the town and then burnt it to the ground. They led the remaining 6,000 Jews of the town to the nearby woods where they shot them all and buried them in a mass grave. Every family member of mine who did not make it to America from 1903 to 1912 was slaughtered by the Nazis in 1940, together with the rest of the Jews of the town. Only 100 to 150 Jews from Dubossary survived.

Dubossary was really the first attempt at a pogrom in 1903 from what I can tell, but the stories I drew upon—of the herring barrel, and people going missing, people being killed in the town of Gomel—these were all things that happened. According to the annals of history, they happened in 1903, but mostly after what happened in the town of Dubossary. Any inconsistencies and fallacies are my mistakes, and though much of the story of the town of Dubossary and the people in it is based on stories I heard and read, I took great license with the truth and made it my own. This is a work of fiction and any resemblance of any of my characters to anyone living or dead is non-intentional.

The original idea for this story came to me because I wanted to write a retelling of Christina Rossetti's *Goblin Market*. I loved that it was a tale of sisterly love, and that both sisters, in their own ways, try to save each other. As I started to tell the tale, I did research into my own heritage, into the Chassidic stories that I was raised on and into some Ukrainian, Moldavian, Russian, and Romanian folktales.

The *"Shpoler Zeiyde"* tale is a well-known one. His last name was Leib and he was from the town of Shpole in the Ukraine. He was a Chassid and a follower of the Rabbi known as the Baal Shem Tov. As the tale goes, he danced in a bearskin to save another Jew. Many Jews, including one of my grandfather's relatives, used the name "Dov" which means bear, or "Dov-Ber."

The bear is also the national symbol of Russia and there are many Russian folktales about bear-men and bear-women—the tale of Morozko, the Slavic God Veles (Volos) who is Lord of the Forest and his animal form is a bear—all of these influences shaped my creation of Berman Leib and his clan.

Russian and Ukrainian folklore is full of swan-maiden and swan-prince myths and I drew inspiration from them, as well as from perhaps the most iconic swan myth—Leda and the Swan. One fairy tale, "The Tale of Tsar Saltan," was an inspiration for my book. Many of these swan tales are written as part of *byliny*—Russian epic ballads loosely based on historical fact and greatly embellished with fantasy. I also drew upon a few more *byliny*, but most notably the story of "Danilo the Luckless" and the character Sadko (which is actually a Jewish name—Zadok) in the Novgorod Cycle. *Sadko* is also an opera written by Nikolai Rimsky-Korsakov. "Danilo the Luckless" (the inspiration for the name Danilovich in my tale) was written by Aleksandr Nikolaevich Afanas'ev, who is often referred to as the Russian Brothers Grimm. Danilo's wife is a swan bestowed upon Danilo by a water monster. This swan-maiden can make magical things happen with the flutter of her wings and the shake of her head. The first serious collection of *byliny* was collected in mid 1700s by Kirsha Danilov (another inspiration for Danilovich).

Mikhailo Potyk is another example of a *bylina* that features a swan-woman, and in this tale a swan-maiden makes a wedding agreement with her husband that they will be buried together. This connected me back to the Dubossary cemetery and the well-known grave of the bride and groom there.

"Leda and the Swan" is a tale from Greek mythology in which Zeus, in the form of a swan, seduces and/or rapes Leda who then bears Helen and Polydeuces. She also gives birth to Castor and Clytemnestra (children of her husband Tundareus)—and her daughter Clytemnestra is traumatized by what the swan did to her mother.

I was also very much inspired by Terri Windling's fairy tale series: I remember the books being published in the 1990s when I was a teen and I eagerly awaited every installment. I must mention Patricia C. Wrede's *Snow White and Rose Red*, the tale of two sisters in the woods who are kind to a bear that eventually turns into a prince, and Jane Yolen's Holocaust retelling of Briar Rose. I must also give a nod to Jonathan Safran Foer's *Everything Is Illuminated* for his richly nuanced depiction of *shtetl* life and for telling the tale of what it was like to go back and look for his family's town (like so many towns in the Ukraine)—of which nothing remains. Margo Lanagan's *The Brides of Rollrock Island* was also an inspiration—it is a tale of sea-brides/selkies who get trapped in human form by their husbands who steal their seal cloaks/skins. Katherine Catmull's *Summer and Bird* features a mother who leaves her swan cloak behind and two sisters who set out to find their parents, and I was also inspired by her book. After my story was already written, Naomi Novik's *Uprooted* came out and when I read it I said, "Oh...so this is part of my story too."

I was inspired by the sensuality of these tales and also the sensuality of *Goblin Market*, and was determined to write something that contained this element. As a great lover of fantasy and history, I have also always been seeking a way to combine the two and to delve more into my own Russian/Romanian/Moldavian/ Ukrainian heritage. I grew up hearing my grandparents speak Yiddish, but especially my grandmother, Nettie Bunder. As I looked for words to use to bring Yiddish back to life in my tale, I started to hear my grandmother's voice and many of the words I wanted to use popped into my head before the internet completed its search for the terms. Though my parents and grandparents were all born in America, I feel these bloody roots of my past in my bones and I know that the reason that I am here today has only to do with the decisions made by a handful of brave relatives of mine over a hundred years ago to leave Dubossary and Kupel and Kiev and Riga and Bender and to make their way to America.

Glossary

Note on pronunciation

A lot of the Hebrew words that were used in this time period would have been pronounced with a Yiddish accent as opposed to the proper Hebrew pronunciation. That type of pronunciation, though, is still quite popular even among non-Yiddish speakers, especially in Orthodox Ashkenazi circles in the USA, Israel, and around the world.

In terms of the Yiddish turns of phrase and pronunciation, I followed the way I remember my grandmother speaking it, with her intonation. Her family was from Romania, but she was born in the USA, so her Yiddish may either be what she learned from her parents, or a mix of both Yiddish from her parents and the Yiddish she likely heard around her growing up. Because many Hebrew words are also used in Yiddish, one could arguably dispute that some of the Hebrew words also belong in the Yiddish words list (and vice versa). I tried to be as comprehensive as possible.

Note that the sound represented by "ch" in the Hebrew and Yiddish phrases is pronounced as a throaty "h," such as that found in "loch."

Hebrew words

acher—other

am segula—the cherished/chosen people

Am Yisroel—the People of Israel

asur—forbidden

ayshes chayil—"a woman of valor"; also a song sung on the sabbath

baruch atah Adonai eloheinu melech haolam—blessed are you, Lord our God, king of the universe

baruch dayan ha'emet—blessed is the true judge

bat kol—echo

bat melech—daughter of a king; good girl

be'ezras Hashem—with God's help

brocha—blessing

challah(s)—traditional bread for the sabbath and high holy days

chas v'shalom—God forbid

chassid(im)—a sect of Jewish mystics, founded in Poland in the 1700s

cheder—religious school that starts at age three

Chovevei Zion—an organization founded in response to the pogroms to promote Jewish immigration to Palestine

chuppah—canopy under which a Jewish couple is wed

daled amos—a measurement used in the Talmud (about seven feet)

Eloykim—God

Eretz Yisroel—the Land of Israel

Hashem—God

Hashem yishmor—God preserve us

havdallah—"separation" a ceremony that marks the end of the
  sabbath and holidays

kaddish—mourner's prayer

kahal—community

kehilla—congregation

kiddush—sanctification/blessing over wine

malka—queen

mamzer—bastard

matza—unleavened flatbread eaten on Passover

Midrash—Biblical commentary on the Bible (at times, folkloric
  in nature)

melaveh malka—escorting the sabbath queen; a Saturday night
  festive meal

meshugge—crazy

meshuggene—crazy person

mezuzah—parchment contained in a decorative case,
  traditionally hung on a doorpost

minyan—quorum of ten men for prayers

motzei shabbes—Saturday night

motzi—the blessing made over bread

niftar—passed away

niggunim—melodies

oylam—world

oymen—amen

Ribbono Shel Oylam—God (master of the universe)

sakanas nefashos—life-threatening

sforim—holy books

shabbes—the sabbath

shalom aleichem—peace be unto you, or hello; also a song sung on the sabbath

shalos seudos—the third meal on the sabbath

shekhted—slaughtered

Shema/Shema Yisroel—the "Hear O Israel" prayer said before bed

shidduch—arranged marriage

shiva—seven; the seven days of Jewish mourning

shomrim—guards

shtuss—nonsense

Talmud—a central text of rabbinic Judaism

Torah—the bible

tsuris—troubles

tzitzes—fringes that religious men wear

ye'varech'echa Adonai ve'yish'merecha—may God bless you and keep you

ze seudas Dovid malka meshicha—this is the feast of David, King Messiah

zichrono livracha—may his/her memory be for a blessing

zmiros—songs

Yiddish words, phrases and sayings

a bi gezunt—as long as you're well (don't worry so much)

a broch tzu dir!—a curse on you!

a dank—thank you

a ritch in kop—crazy in the head
a shaynem dank!—thank you very much!
alter kocker—old man
arein!—come in!
aroisgevorfen—a waste
Aybishter—God

babka—yeast dough pastry, usually made with chocolate
    or cinnamon
bahalterlekh—hide and seek
bekishe—black coat
beshert—destiny or soulmate
bissl—a little bit
blech—hotplate
borsht—beet soup
bubbemeisses—old wives tales; foolishness

chap nit!—don't grab/not so fast!
cholent—meat stew left overnight on a low flame to be eaten on
    Saturday afternoon because of the prohibition against
    cooking on the sabbath

danken Got—thank God
davens—prays
deigeh nisht!—don't worry!
der emess iz der bester lign—truth is the safest lie

es iz nit dayn gesheft—none of your business
es tut mir bahng—I'm sorry (it sorrows me)
ess gezunt—eat in good health
essen—eat
eyn, tsvei, drei, lozer lokser-lay—a counting game with
    nonsensical rhymes

fantazyor—fantasizer, dreamer
farklempt—emotional, choked up
farschnickered—drunk
fluden—layered pastry

gelibteh—beloved
genug iz genug!—enough is enough!
goldene medina—the golden country, America
Gott in himmel!—God in heaven
goy(im)—non-Jew(s)
goyishe—non-Jewish
gribenes—crisp chicken or goose skin cracklings with fried onions
gut morgen—good morning
gut shabbes—good sabbath

heldish—brave
husht!—shush!

ich hob dir!—drop dead!
ich hob dir lieb—I love you

kapelye—ensemble, group of klezmer musicians
kashrus—kosher standards
ketzele—kitten
klezmer—traditional Eastern European (Ashkenazic) Jewish folk music
kneidlach—dumplings made from matzo (matzo balls)
kugel—baked pudding or casserole, generally made from noodles or potatoes
kuppel—skullcap

lekach—Jewish honey cake
lokshen—noodles

mamaloshen—mother tongue (Yiddish)

mandelbrot—Eastern European Jewish cookie baked in a loaf, then sliced thin and baked again

mandlen—soup nuts/flour dumplings

maydele—sweetheart/little girl

mensches—decent people

nafkeh—whore

narishkeit—nonsense

nebbishers—simpletons, losers

nishtgedeiget—don't worry

nu?—so? and? well?

oy—oh; oh no!

oy vey iz mir—woe is me! oh no!

oyfen himmel a yarid—much ado about nothing (in heaven there's a big fair)

oyfvakn—wake up!

prietzteh—princess/prima donna

rugelach—an Eastern European Jewish pastry made in the shape of a crescent by rolling up a triangle of dough around a filling

schmaltz—chicken fat

schnecken—cinnamon/sticky buns

shabbesdik—shabbes-like; appropriate for the sabbath

shaygetzim—non-Jewish men

shayna meidel—beautiful girl

schnozzle—nose

shikseh—non-Jewish woman

shkotzim—non-Jewish men

shlofkepele—sleepyhead

shoyn—enough

shul—synagogue

shunda—shame; tragedy

shtetl(ach)—village(s)

shtieble/shtieblach—a small room(s) or space(s) used for communal prayer

shtup—have sex; fuck

tichel—scarf/head covering

trayf—non-kosher food

tsatskeh—plaything; sexy woman

tze gezunt—you're welcome

umbeshrein—God forbid!

varenikes—Eastern European dumplings usually filled with mashed potato or cheese

vechter—watchman

vos iz mit dir—what's wrong with you?

yenta—a blabbermouth

yingele—young one

zaftig(e)—attractive and plump

zaftige moid—plump/sexy/attractive girl

zay gezunt—be well/goodbye

zeiskeit—sweetheart (term of endearment)

Yiddish sayings

A friend is not someone who wipes your tears—he's someone who doesn't make you cry—*A khave iz nit dafke der vos visht dir op di trern nor der vos brengt dikh bekhlal nit tsi trern*

Beautiful as the seven worlds—*Shain vi di ʒibben velten*

Beautiful is not what is beautiful, but what one likes—*Nit dos iʒ sheyn, vos iʒ sheyn, nor dos, vos es gefelt*

Better caution than tears—*Besser frieher bewohrent, eider sh peter beweint*

Better to die upright than to live on your knees—*Besser tsu shtarben shtai'endik eider tsu leben oif di kni*

Every heart has its secrets—*Yedeh harts hot soides*

I need it like I need a hole in the head!—*Ich darf es vi a loch in kop!*

Let a goose loose in the oats and she will starve to death— *Aʒ me ʒetst arein a gandʒ in hober, shtarbt ʒi fun hunger*

Love and hunger don't dwell together—*Libeh un hunger voinen nit in ainem*

Necessity breaks iron—*Noit brecht eiʒen*

No choice is also a choice—*Kain braireh iʒ oich a braireh*

No fruit falls from withered trees—*Fun fartrikenteh baimer kumen kain paires nit arois*

With a fairy tale and with a lie you can lull only children to sleep—*Mit a meisseh un mit a ligen ken men nor kinder farvigen*

You can't change the world with curses or with laughter— *Nit mit shelten un nit mit lachen ken men di velt ibermachen*

You think that only in dreams the carrots are as big as bears—
Nor in cholem ʒeinen meren vi beren

Ukrainian words and phrases

bud'laska—please

dochka—daughter
dorohyy—darling
dubroho ranku—good morning

koroleva—queen

malyshka—little one

ne biytesya—don't be afraid
ne ʒvaʒhay—never mind
nmaye!—no!

pro shcho vy?—what are you?

sim'ya—family

vash lebid—your swan

ʒhyd(ovka)—male/female derogatory term for a Jew

Acknowledgments

First and foremost a massive thank you to agent-extraordinaire, Brent Taylor, who believed in me and my work when I had almost stopped believing. Thank you for your endless insight, advice, ideas, and gut instinct—more than anything, I feel lucky to call you a friend. To Uwe Stender for running such a stellar agency and hand-picking a team of literary agents who know exactly what to do to make dreams come true, and for being excited about the pitch for this book together with Brent, which gave me the courage to keep writing it.

Thank you to the entire Orbit/Redhook team for making my lifelong dream a reality. To my editor Nivia Evans—your passion, sensitivity, and insight were invaluable—all of this book's shine I owe to you. To Anna Jackson and Joanna Kramer at Orbit UK—I feel very honored to have been able to work so closely with both of you. To Anne Clarke and Tim Holman for believing in me and this book. To Ellen Wright, publicist extraordinaire—thanks for making everything possible. To Lindsey Hall for falling in love first and for taking a chance on me and this book—I am forever grateful. To Rebecca Yanovskaya for interpreting my book into one of the most stunning covers

I've ever seen. To Tomer Rottenberg, rockstar photographer, for taking the perfect photos every time.

I know that people like to say "it takes a village" but I think in my case it's more accurate to say that it takes a lifetime of encouragement—my journey began with my parents, who always supported me as a reader first and foremost, feeding the voracious need of a daughter who read books well beyond her years, and then as a writer. To my dad who said "writers write, always" even though there were days I wanted to burn "Throw Momma From the Train" with fire for giving my father that ammunition to use against me. (Newsflash: it worked.) And to my mother, who fought for me as a gifted kid who was miserable in school, who listened to me, who continues to listen to me every day, and who helped me create the opportunities that formed me into the person and the writer I am today.

Thank you to my teachers—Arlene Fishbein and Marlene Mitchell—who recognized the writer in me in elementary school and cultivated that talent, not just by encouraging and believing in me, but also by entering my work into contests that showed me that I had what it takes. To the correspondence course writing tutors that Johns Hopkins University's CTY/IAAY program provided me with. To Erica Rauzin who took me under her wings and taught me how to spread mine. You always took me seriously, and you not only kept up with my frantic reading pace, but you taught me how to be a real writer. There were many other teachers along the way—who taught me Torah, Halacha, Tanya, Likutei Moharan, History, AP English—and who introduced me to the Rabbis and authors who inspired this book—sometimes against their better judgment. You formed me into the reader, writer, and agent I am today.

Thank you to Johns Hopkins University's Writing Seminars program—not only for accepting me Early Decision, Early Admission and getting me the hell out of high school, but also for giving me a place to thrive, to encounter both your incredible teachers and other upstart writers like me. To Greg Williamson for teaching me to be the poet I am today. And to Chaim Potok z"l—I was so lucky to have met you, but even luckier still to be able to call you my teacher.

Thank you to my beta readers (and friends!)—Gili Bar-Hillel, you are so much more than just a beta reader—thank you for being a listening ear and for loving *Goblin Market* as much as I do. To Jill Schafer Boehme for being a shoulder to cry on but also for the endless support—so excited to celebrate this amazing year together with you! Helen Maryles Shankman, Holly Bodger, Stacey Filak, Adam Heine, Stephanie Feldman, Kaitlyn Sage Patterson—this book would not be what it is today without your insight.

Thank you to my friends, of which I am so lucky to be able to say that there are many. I consider myself forever blessed to have you all in my life. Thank you for understanding why I sometimes disappear for weeks on end. (I truly don't prefer the comfort of my computer screen and my imaginary friends more than I enjoy spending time with you—it just seems that way.) Thank you for giving me a place on your couch, for endless culinary and other kinds of support, for bottomless cups of coffee and sympathy, for reading both trash and treasure with me. You know who you are.

Thank you to Deborah Harris—for changing my life by taking me in to the Deborah Harris Agency family. To George Eltman, Efrat Lev, Ilana Kurshan, Hadar Makov, Ran Kaisar, Geula Geurts, and Shira Ben-Choreen Schneck for being there for me day in day out, listening to both my frustrations and my triumphs. I could ask for no better gift than to work by your sides and to love my job with all of my heart.

Thank you to my kids—Nachliel Yishayahu, Avtalyon Yitzchak, Lehava Aderet, Shaanan Shalom and Nehorai Ahallel. Thank you for understanding (though I'm not always sure that you do) why I spend so much time in front of my computer. I only hope that I've instilled within all of you a love for reading and writing, but more than anything, I hope that you will always let your imagination soar and take you to all the places in your dreams.

And last, but never least, thank you to my husband Jonathan, for loving me, believing in me, and supporting me through it all, even though I know that there were many times when it wasn't easy. You stuck with me through thick and thin. I think it most apt to end on the pasuk that your grandfather taught you, that you inscribed on one of the first gifts you ever gave me: "Hazo-rim Be'dimah Be'Rena Yiktzoru—those who sow with tears, will reap with joy."

About the Author

Rena Rossner lives in Israel, where she works as a literary agent. She is a graduate of Johns Hopkins University's Writing Seminars program and McGill University, where she studied history. All eight of her great-grandparents immigrated to America to escape the pogroms from towns like Dubossary, Kupel, Riga, and Bender. It is their story, together with her love of Jewish mythology and fantasy, that inspired her to write *The Sisters of the Winter Wood*.